Defying Gravity

Defying Gravity

The Sixth Collection of Fiction by
D.C. Area Women

Edited by Richard Peabody

ISBN-10: 0-931181-40-2
ISBN-13: 978-0-931181-40-5
First Edition
Published in the USA

Some of these stories have previously appeared: Eena Ruffini's story appeared online in anderbo.com. Julia Dubner's story might have been published in a short-run lit mag twenty years ago, but we can find no record of it.

Book design by Nita Congress.
Cover by Sheep Jones, © 2013, "Practice."
Printed by Main Street Rag Publishing, Charlotte, NC.

Paycock Press
3819 North 13th Street
Arlington, VA 22201

www.gargoylemagazine.com

In Memory of
Elisabeth Sullam and Eleanor Ross Taylor

"Listening to language, feeling stories unfold and poems arrive, being present to the page—I do not think of it as a career, I think of it as a devotion."

—Naomi Shihab Nye

S pecial thanks to: Hildie S. Block, Laura Bolt, Michelle Brafman, Steve Caporaletti, Kathy Carlon, Lia E. Carroll-Hackett, Susan Coll, Caitlin Cushman, Lora Engdahl, Barbara Esstman, Kristy Feltenberger, Nan Fry, Sid Gold, James Grady, Donna Moss, Theresa Burns Murphy, Marci Nadler, Leslie Pietrzyk, Rick Rofihe (anderbo.com), Gregg Shapiro, Julie Wakeman-Linn, and Paula Whyman. Plus special thank yous to Art Taylor for gigs at Fall for the Book at George Mason U.; to Jud Ashman, Robin Ferrier, and everybody at the Gaithersburg Book Festival; to everybody at One More Page Books in Arlington; to Eileen McGervey, Terry Nebeker, Lelia Nebeker, Lisa Chavez, Jill Beres, and Sally McConnell, and also everybody at Politics and Prose Bookstore; to Bradley Graham, Lissa Muscatine, Susan Coll (redux), Sarah Baline, Mark L., and Hannah.

Contents

Introduction

*O*kay, here we go again.

As we go to press with this sixth volume of the *Grace and Gravity* series, I already have enough authors lined up for a possible seventh volume sometime down the road. I'm still having as much fun gathering the stories, corresponding with the writers, and assembling these collections as when we did the first one back in 2004.

The count is now at six volumes of writing by 249 local women, adding up to 2,500 pages. Impossible numbers. Who knew there were so many talented women fiction writers in the D.C. area? No way there were that many women fiction writers in the area back in 1976 when I began *Gargoyle Magazine*. I don't know whether it's due to the creative writing program boom or the economic bust of the past decade, but more and more people seem to be valuing art once again. Some of the women in this book are natives, and others have landed here because of school or jobs or relationships. Others, like our blurbers, have left the area.

Each of the six volumes has had a slightly different bent, and this one could be themed "Things Are Not What They Seem." Lots of peculiar goings-on. While this volume gathers more mother-daughter stories than other volumes in the series, there are also a lot of ghost stories, pseudo-ghost stories, and ghostly trappings. I have never required stories to be set in the area, and this volume is the most geographically diverse—ranging from the D.C. area and Baltimore to locales far and wide—Antigua, Belize, Boston, Canada, India, Kansas, Liberia, New Orleans, New York, Oklahoma, and Serbia.

This collection features the "beautiful forgotten," to share a line from p. m. korkinsky's hallucinatory vision, with a primary focus on every type of loss—elder care, accidents, broken bones, death, dementia, adultery, war, funerals, widows, prodigal fathers, alcoholics, prodigal daughters, fires and other disasters, rape, prodigal nuns, and husbands who are always missing when you need them the most.

But that's not all. A brief description of the work in these pages would include snakes, urban legends, pregnancy, alternative families, a lawsuit as seduction, crazy roommates, tattoos, helicopter parents, "mother says" parental warnings, the Riverfolk, blood, juju masks, nail polish, Down syndrome, Nico impressions, boy fights, stories within stories, sex, girl fights, macaws, dogs, vomit, Grandma's stories, a magic cigar shop, masturbation, a survival bubble featuring only lawyers called "LawyerSphere" (which just has to be a TV show someday), serial killers, victims, survivors, rape, the devil and his family, and erotic dreams about Rosie O'Donnell.

Who are these awe-inspiring women writers? Teachers, students, journalists, lawyers, editors, playwrights, directors, producers, script writers, former lawyers, massage therapists, bloggers, arts administrators, translators, and retirees.

Some are known to me—I'm pleased to present work by established writers: Solveig Eggerz, Katie Pickard Fawcett, Arin Greenwood, Melanie S. Hatter, Brooke Kenny, Anne Levy-Lavigne, Veronica Li, Mary Claire Mahaney, Allison Nichol, Valerie O. Patterson, Anne Sheldon, and Suzanne Stroh have short story collections or novels out. Malve S. Burns, Julia Dubner, Allison Nichol, Bethanne Patrick, and Julie Shields have published nonfiction books or edited anthologies. Jacqueline Jules is a critically acclaimed children's writer, and p. m. korkinsky and Marija Stajic have published poetry collections.

We also offer first published fictions by Cathy Hostetler, Stephanie Joyce, Maggie Nye, and Bethanne Patrick.

Some had to be steered my way—Malve S. Burns, Diana Friedman, Arin Greenwood, Shelagh Powers Johnson, Anne Levy-Lavigne, Kathryn Murphy, Lisa Nanni-Messegee, Judith O'Neill, Maggie Nye, Anne Sheldon, and Suzanne Stroh. Others found me—Julia Elliott, Trasi Johnson, Barbara Moore, and Marija Stajic. Still others had to be tracked down—Kate Lu, Jocelyn McCarthy, Eena Ruffini, and Krista Waple.

Why do I keep doing these books? Because it still needs doing. Because somebody has to see this work through to publication. Because all of these writers need support, validation, promotion, and an audience. Maybe something will come of this exposure down the road? Maybe not?

Meanwhile, I'm glad you're along for the ride.

—Richard Peabody
December 2013

Malve S. Burns

A Hot Munich Afternoon

MALVE S. BURNS has published an illustrated history of *Washington's Second Blair House* and is finishing a memoir of growing up in Germany after the Nazis, "Flying Blind." Before finally daring to write full time, she taught German literature at University of California–Irvine and the University of Southern California, and worked in university development and international programs at several schools, including Johns Hopkins University and George Washington University.

The young man was sitting on a step of the stone arcade, cradling his mandolin, not even looking at the girl above him. He played his instrument with such tender passion, as if the mandolin were the center of attention instead of the girl whose song had lured us toward the pair. The girl, a delicate porcelain figure with brown hair and brown eyes, hovered above him like a saint. Her throat was thrust forward as she poured her voice into "O mio Bambino caro." Her eyes and face showed no emotion; all feeling had rushed to her voice.

Her song carried us skyward. We soared until a near-imperceptible something pulled us back down. I looked around me, unsure what had happened, when I heard it again—the shadow of an undertone that broke the aria's spell. The smile on my friend's lips froze; a frown formed on the forehead of the woman next to me. The mandolin player dropped his face so low that his eyes disappeared from view, while the girl's voice, released from the high register, resumed with melodious grace.

Instantly we forgot about the disturbance, the rising heat, and the traffic din. Once again, we listened with one heart and one receptive ear until the discordant note returned. I couldn't bear it and broke away, leaving my friend, the crowd, and the girl behind just as her voice regained its regular mode.

At Marienplatz, I bumped into a thick crowd of people. I listened but couldn't hear a sound. After I slipped between bodies to the front, I saw a man push a sword down his throat. The bovine breath of the crowd, their soaked shirts, and the drops of sweat on the lip of the swordsman made me gag. I shoved my way back out.

The sky appeared drained of blue, sucked dry by the heat. I watched in amazement how doves could still rise above us, carried by brittle air. Following their lead, I ended up at the arcade right next to the hat set out for collection by the performing pair. I dropped a coin into the hat just as the girl's voice began to break. The player's face fell, the belt round the singer's waist drew in. My friend grabbed my hand and pulled me back to the hotel.

"Let's go to the Hofgarten," he said, as dusk fell. "I'll get us cool drinks and we'll chill out in its wooded spot. Tomorrow, the Oktoberfest schedule kicks in."

Balancing our drinks in tall plastic mugs we settled on a bench in the shade to the sound of fading applause from somewhere across the lawn. We watched older couples stroll by welded together by time and younger ones perking with expectation. We listened to the click-click tapped out by the paws of the dachshunds. We eyed women and girls in dirndls, with ample bosoms on show. We took a long draft from our cup and leaned into the evening breeze.

Then, suddenly, they appeared: the mandolin player and his charge heading for a line of shrubs. Just before they dissolved into darkness, I saw him lift her, lower her against his body, and snap her in two as if breaking a branch. He grabbed both halves, placed them on his shoulder and walked on. I could not see clearly because of the falling night, but I could have sworn he stopped again, just for an instant, and kissed the mandolin that hung from his neck.

Tracy Alig Dowling

Accident

TRACY ALIG DOWLING has published articles, reviews, poetry, and fiction in a variety of journals and periodicals, including the *Washington Post*, *America Magazine*, and *Potomac Review*. She has won numerous awards for both poetry and fiction, most recently the Betty Gabehart Prize for Short Fiction and the F. Scott Fitzgerald Short Story Award, both in 2011.

My mother is standing at the zinc-coated Maytag, pulling diapers through the wringer. It is April 1950, one of the first really beautiful days. She has pushed the machine outdoors and the whir of its small engine and the rhythm of its rotation were the earliest form of music I knew.

I see that day, although I do not yet have eyes, for I am still only a clump of cells. Having formed myself the night before, I am deciding whether or not to attach myself or proceed merrily along and not make anything of myself at all.

Thus was I conceived in April, and my own children were born in April, events my brother Liam sees as significant; numerological thinking being an attribute of his fearful and mystical outlook. Does the body anticipate major events with the recall of stale memory? I will replace my mother's damaged child with a fresh new one and present it to her one day next winter, my genes, chromosomes, DNA all say to one another while patiently waiting for the appropriate partners to link with, making decisions the brain sees no necessity for, but Life, with its own decrees and determinations, knows a debt must be paid and exacts its own restitution.

All I know is that I remember vividly April 20, 1950, with its nascent green carpet of grass beginning to cover the backyard, the paisley print of my mother's apron, the smells of lye, bleach, and freshly turned earth. Lilies of the valley were sprouting on the side of the house, and Liam, my brother, played in the sand pile under the kitchen window.

My mother was happy that day, contented, grateful, fulfilled, until she saw my brother's mangled body and the blood on the pavement of the driveway next door. Although my cells had happily attached by that particular moment and were ready to draw deeply from the nourishment of my first and ultimately only home, when her blood ran cold, so did mine, new as I was. Her terror was my terror, her pain and guilt mine.

"YOU WILL GRIEVE FOR THIS child at every stage of his life," I hear the doctor saying to my mother. Liam and I play on the floor of the waiting room, and he is beginning to weary. I know that he is tired and unhappy when he begins to torment me, for I am his punching bag, his willing victim. He does not hear the doctor, he never hears anything about himself, but lives in a world of his own. But I hear everything, once again the pain of my mother overtakes my body. I feel it in the pit of my small stomach, on the surface of my eyes, and I gladly let him climb on top of me and start beating me, let him tickle my three-year-old body until I start to wet my pants.

My hysterical laughter distracts my mother and she steps out from the doctor's inner office to give me a shake. "Stop it," she says. "Stop it right now." I am glad to let her shake me instead of Liam, for Liam is owed a debt, a debt I can help my mother pay. I understand that, somehow she knows I understand that. "Don't tickle your sister, Liam," she says mildly. The ruckus has distracted her from her tears, and the doctor graciously sends the three of us off. Liam limps at her side with his uncoordinated gait, his lopsided face grinning slightly.

LIAM IS ALWAYS GRINNING, SEEMING to laugh at something far below the surface of things, some eternal joke that the rest of us know nothing about. He brings me a book to read to him, a book about animals, Reddy Fox, Bowser the Hound, Paddy the Beaver. Although he can read, it tires him, for he reads slowly. Today, however, the story is only of passing interest.

"Do you know that in two weeks Santa Claus will come?" He slurs his words and drools slightly. I try to talk just like him, but Mums corrects me. "Don't talk like that," she says sharply.

"Liam talks like that," I say.

"I said, don't talk like that." She means it and I realize once again what is OK for Liam is not OK for me. I also know that Santa does not really come, but I'm not supposed to tell.

I AM STUNNED WHEN HE tells me he likes a girl, has a girlfriend. We have sworn to one another we would never have a girlfriend or boyfriend, never marry. Only sissies do that. Liam is terrified of being thought a sissy. I am not going to be a sissy either, and out of respect for him, out of my love for him, I refuse to wear a dress, refuse the patent leather shoes my mother tries to force upon me, insist on my jeans, tennis shoes, and his old sweaters and plaid shirts.

When he talks about Nancy I notice that his Bugs Bunny grin is actually a shy smile, and I see the beginnings of grief in his face. It is a face that will eventually become rutted with anguish, and an irrevocable sense of failure.

The girlfriend is his dream I decide. I listen to him talk and he even shows me a picture.

"WHY AM I SO DIFFERENT?" he asks my mother. "Is there something wrong with me?"

"You aren't anymore different than anybody else," she snorts. Or "No, there's nothing wrong with you."

I look up from my book. It is reassuring to hear my mother say it. If she can say it, I can say it.

No, there's nothing wrong with my brother. No, he wasn't damaged in the accident. My mother said so, that is the truth. I don't doubt her, I am sure it is true. But I no longer let him hit me, no longer believe his outrageous stories. I hate him. He is different, and that makes me different. How can I tell my mother that?

Finally I am free to hate Liam and what he has done to my family because I realize my mother hates him too. The anger she has restrained for so long has taken its toll. I see it in the lines in her face, in the limping movements of her arthritis-wracked body, hear it in the one-on-one outbursts she has with Liam, those brief stifled explosions in the violence she struggles daily to keep at bay.

TODAY I AM LEAVING HOME, leaving for good, although I can see that my mother is telling herself that this is temporary.

"I should have gone to college instead of you," she sniffs. "Or Liam. He's the older, he's the boy. That would have been fair."

I stare at her incredulously. We both know, don't we, that Liam is incapable of college, barely got through high school? I realize that she has convinced herself again that a normal life is denied him not because he isn't normal, but because of the caprice and spite of circumstances, a force that is against her and her son, a force she sees me escaping.

Not that I ever will.

SHE IS HAPPY, I CAN see she is happy. My babies make her happy—my three-year-old Bobby she worships, regarding him as the responsible one, the one you can count on. But it is Myra she coos to, bounces on her lap, embraces with a tenderness I haven't seen since early childhood.

"You will never guess who this child is like," she beams. "Guess."

I can't guess, her enthusiasm baffles me.

"Liam," she says. "Myra is like Liam."

I talk with Liam on this trip home, the first time we have really talked for years. He lives on the family farm now, in the old house with half a dozen cats. He wants me to walk with him to the creek, where he has set up some makeshift trout lines.

It is June, my sensibilities have been citified after these many years away, and I am not prepared for the insects that are buzzing around the slightly stagnant water. It is becoming a very hot day.

The lines around his eyes are now deep creases. What was once merely an expression has become the mask of tragedy, and when he tries to smile, he is fighting not only a spirit of hardened desperation within himself, he is having to work against muscles in his face that haven't moved in the direction of happiness for decades.

I smile back, and he comments on my chipped front tooth.

"I feel bad every time I see that tooth," and he reminds me of how it broke—he was throwing rocks at me, small pieces of gravel from the limestone driveway. I can feel the click against my teeth, remember my mother's chagrin.

"How did that happen?"

"Kids were throwing rocks at me," I tell her. "I don't know their names."
She looks at me sharply…does she know what I know?

I realize, these thirty years later, of course she did.

"Liam," I say, "I never even think of this tooth, and nobody notices it
except you. Forget it."

But he will never forget it, I know that. Liam forgets nothing, he is the
recorder of conflicts great and small within the circle of Mums, himself,
and me. He is the conscience of the family, the pool wherein we look to
find our not-too-pretty selves, the reminder that original sin is a reality, still
doing its damage.

IT IS ANOTHER JUNE, a cool day this time. I am home to help Mums
clean up the old bungalow, get it ready to put on the market. The piano,
does she want me to sell the piano? Who gets the silverware? I spend a day
just going through old photographs, realizing as I sort, the importance of
writing something—anything—if nothing more than a date—on the back
of snapshots and photos.

There is a beautiful cardboard photograph of a picnic—women in white
waists, men in straw hats—taken when? where? of whom? My mother
doesn't know. The photos progress through the century that has been her
life, and I find pictures of myself, Liam, cousins, birthday parties.

The pictures of myself are unordered, random—individual portraits
from the annual school package, a graduation picture, photos of Christmas
mornings and piano recitals.

But Liam's life has been ordered by his birthday, and there are snapshots of Liam holding a cake, candles lit; pictures of Liam surrounded
by neighborhood children he barely knew; small black and white glossies
punctuating the sentence of pain that is his life. Birthday parties had been
important to Liam—important for him to have, important for Mums to
give. The neighborhood children would come, eat their cake and ice cream,
and just as quickly go.

I stare at one picture after another, attempting to remember the names
of the neighborhood children.

"What are you looking at?"

"Pictures, Mums. Remember all those birthday parties?"

"Birthday parties?" She looks blank. Can't she remember? She is sitting in her recliner and I take the album over to her, put it on her lap. She stares at the pictures in disbelief.

"It was my fault," she suddenly says. She lifts herself slowly from the chair, lets the photo album and the photographs spill on the floor. "Will you pick these up for me?" she pleads. She hobbles toward the kitchen, her four-pronged cane leading the way.

"I was irresponsible, it was my fault."

It is the first time I have ever heard her say it.

Julia Dubner

We Meant F Only

JULIA DUBNER lives in Rockville, Maryland, with her husband and two children. It has been over twenty years since she wrote "We Meant F Only"—it is gratifying to have it included in this anthology.

*A*ugusta's twenty-seventh birthday, and the jig was up. We'd been sharing the house—the kitchen, the bathroom—going on eight months. She rented the two upstairs bedrooms and I slept in the basement. I didn't mind, really; I had my water bed and a space heater that hummed like the lover I'd never had.

So Augusta'd been getting checks every month from her father in Indiana, him thinking she's seeing a therapist once a week. But for her twenty-seventh birthday (Augusta's older than me, but no wiser, I argue), Dad sent a Hallmark card, roses on the front and a puppy inside, and beneath the preprinted birthday message he'd written: "Augie dear, I'm afraid I can no longer finance your self-discovery. Enclosed is a token for your birthday. Buy something nice for yourself."

She pulled a check from the envelope and waved it toward me. "Twenty-five dollars. Not even a buck for each year."

"Sorry."

"No more living in luxury," she said. "I can only afford the bedroom now." She'd been using the money from Indiana to rent the second room (an extra room is better than therapy, she said), which she called her studio, but she also grew plants in there—herbs and wildflowers in shallow wooden boxes. Her art, I mean I was no expert, but it mostly looked like glitter anthills to me. Lots of glue, lots of moons. Once I asked her why she picked that particular medium (I didn't know what to call it). "First it was to see how ugly I could make it," she said.

"Why do you want to do ugly art?"

"Well, you know, fantasy busting. In school we learn that glitter is the closest thing to magic. Put it on a card or painting and all of a sudden you've transcended kindergarten mediocrity. But then I got into pushing it, as a material. Add some sawdust, see what it can do. Now I'm hooked."

At the time she was working on a big tableau, with tall peaks and molded forms like buttes. She'd let the glue blobs dry and then cut off the tops with a jackknife. I liked that piece, actually, if you can like something so abstract. It made me think of the moon's surface, how you dream about standing there and touching all the stars, picking them out of the sky and plopping them right in your hand. She gave the piece to me as a gift, which kind of took me by surprise.

As you might guess, the glitter got into every corner of the house. Augusta would sweep and try to keep it in studio confines, but without much success. I never said anything, though. It was her room; she paid the rent. Or used to. After the birthday card she moved all her extra stuff to the basement, next to the washer and dryer, and we had to find a third person.

I put an ad in the *Post*. "M/F wanted for 1 b/r in 3 b/r, 1 ba house with 2 F's. Good location." It's my house—my mom made the down payment on it for me after I graduated from Maryland. Not big or anything, just a galley kitchen, two bedrooms upstairs, and one bathroom (believe me, that's the killer), but it's mine. That's what Mom said: "Kate, you have this to hold onto, not like when your father left, and we didn't have a pot to piss in." So I needed to take care of things, get some rent coming in to pay the mortgage.

Augusta saw the ad in the paper and went absolutely nonlinear. "You put 'M/F'? How could you?" She was tying bunches of herbs to hang from the kitchen ceiling to dry. I'd bought a box of empty baby food jars at a garage sale once, and then an actual spice rack from Murphy's, but she refused to convert her jungle.

"I don't care. As long as they pay the rent."

"Women are cleaner," she said, dropping crinkles of oregano leaves all over the floor. "We keep to ourselves. Men are all over the place, just all over the place."

"So we set up a cleaning schedule and we throw whoever it is out on their butt if they don't keep to it." But it wasn't just cleaning. I remembered when Augusta was moving in eight months before, how she'd asked me first thing when she came to see the place if I had a boyfriend and if he'd be spending the nights. I told her she didn't have a thing to worry about with me, which is the truth because I haven't had a date since my sophomore year in college, with the guy who checks your bags when you're leaving the library to make sure you haven't stolen any books, but that's another story. She went on and said she didn't like men in the house, didn't like the mess or the smell or them leaving the seat up. "I lived with my father for ten years. I've had enough living with men for ten lifetimes." She tied the last of her knots, dragged a chair into the kitchen, and started hanging her bouquets from an exposed water pipe.

"You can't say you don't like men, though." Augusta slept away about three nights a week. It was a continual source of wonder for me. She never told me a word about them, just left a clean slip of notepaper on the dining room table, with a first name and a phone number in case I needed to reach her. The latest names were Will and Lars.

"They have their good points. But I never bring them home, do I? A man's place is not in my home."

"I wouldn't know much about their 'good points.'"

She looked down at me from the chair, hand on her hip. "Cut the sexual frustration act, Kate," she said. "You could get out of the house once in a while. Just don't make this housemate search into a dating game, OK?"

Augusta was always trying to push me, giving me names of guys she knew from the community garden down on Tilden Street. The truth is, I've had a taste of the love thing and it's not for me. That book checker started sending me roses and calling me every day and the whole thing just snowballed into a mess of unnecessary entanglements. It ended up he was so upset, I couldn't go into McKeldin if he was working, and who wants to think about when they can and can't go into the library? I mean, the squishy feeling you get in your stomach at first is nice and all, a good ride, but I guess I just don't like having to answer to anybody. My mom answered to my dad for twelve years and look what it got her—child support till I was eighteen and a chip on her shoulder the size of Delaware. I think she gave me the house as a bulwark against sexual tragedy, but I wasn't taking any chances.

I looked up at Augusta fastening her herbs—I had to admit I liked the scent of basil wafting through the house, like a clean push of mint to cover up the lived-in smell that houses get after a while—and she seemed all-knowing, towering over me on the chair, twisting and tying, twisting and tying. "If you really want me to, I'll call and change the ad," I said.

"Good," she said. "I knew you'd come around."

Giving in to Augusta was nothing new. The past eight months had been peaceful mostly because I was so good at it. I generally stayed out of her way, and Augusta had plenty she thought she could teach me. Not that I agreed to everything. Her gardener friends, for one, and she was always telling me I ate badly and should go macrobiotic. She steamed her vegetables, flavored them with a handful of dried leaves, put it all next to a scoop of brown rice, and thought she could tempt me. Her side of the refrigerator did *look* nice—a rainbow of peppers and onions and twisted ginger roots. She never let any of her groceries touch my American cheese or grape juice. About the only food we had in common was carrots, but she ate hers organic, and I ate mine dipped in peanut butter.

So the calls poured in the Wednesday the first ad came out, because three hundred and fifty dollars is pretty cheap for a room in Glover Park, right near American University. We turned the men away on the phone, told them the *Post* had got it wrong, we meant "F only," not "M/F," and I had the ad changed for the rest of the week. All the rich AU students (who was I to talk, getting a townhouse as a graduation gift, even if it was a fixer-upper?) who were studying international relations called and asked if there was a driveway in the back for their car, and I had to explain that the yard was pretty much taken up by Augusta's compost heap. That turned about seventy-five percent of the girls away. Tell the truth, I wasn't looking for a student. Probably should have put "professional F only" in the ad, even though to look at us you'd hardly think Augusta and I were professionals. But I wore a suit every day (people like to see a woman in a suit at Macy's Personnel Office, don't ask me why), and Augusta put on stockings when she went into the hat shop to do the bookkeeping. That was only part time, though, so she was mostly at home in sweats or some purple gauzy thing that looked like it was left over from the disco backlash.

On Saturday a man came to the door. At first I didn't hear anything; I was in the kitchen stirring chicken noodle soup for lunch and happy to be done with five interviews. Not that any of them were going to move in. Augusta had scared most of the prospectives away with her questions about boyfriends and bathroom habits. One woman, Eleanor, seemed perfectly nice, but as soon as she mentioned she had a rowing machine and could she put it in the basement, Augusta gave me the signal, which we'd devised at the beginning of the whole business. Augusta would get up from wherever she was sitting and ask the person if she wanted coffee; that meant they were a goner.

Most of them said no to the coffee anyway, as if they knew what was going on.

So Augusta answered the door and I heard her say, "You're not an F. Didn't you *read* the new *ad*?"

At this point I was about willing to lift the ban on males, because each day that went by was that much less rent money. "What's up?" I swirled the soup with a metal spoon and felt the heat creep up to my fingers.

"It's a guy who can't read coming to see the place."

"How'd he get the address?" I took the soup off the burner, resigning myself to a postponed lunch.

"I *can* read," he said. "I had a friend of mine call. Monica. Remember talking to her? I wouldn't do this if I weren't desperate. Have you looked at these ads? They all say 'Female only.'"

"For good reason." Augusta stood there, her body wedged between the door and the frame, not about to budge. I could only see the guy because he was exceptionally tall. His clothes were pure Land's End, but nothing too fancy on account of the rain, probably. His jacket was dripping and he held a rolled newspaper, soaked through to a dark gray, tucked under his arm. He had on a white turtleneck under a turquoise and purple striped rugby shirt. Sometimes I wondered about guys who wore colors I couldn't ever have pulled off, guys with paisley ties and flowered suspenders, you'd think they'd forgotten they only worked at Macy's so who were they trying to impress, but on this guy the colors seemed like concession more than habit, a reluctant nod to fashion. I heard his story about Monica—I did remember talking to her, she had a nasal voice and sounded like she was on the verge of crying. If I were sensible, I'd have helped Augusta close the door on him, but the truth was I admired his initiative. He'd actually snuck around to get here, which maybe should have made me cautious, but I've always liked a good sneak. It's an aspect of my personality not too many people know about.

"Why don't you come in out of the rain? I'm Kate, this is Augusta." I wiped my hands on my jeans and pulled the door from her, revealing the rest of the visitor.

"Thanks, I'm Oliver." He ducked as he walked in. His sleeves were too long, so he'd rolled the cuffs up a couple times, exposing the nubby lining, but still they hung to the middle of his palms, and his fingers curled softly around the edges, as if he needed to hold onto himself to keep from falling over. He wore jeans that were faded but in a uniform way, as if he wasn't accustomed to them but didn't want anyone to know that, and peeking out from the bottom were ragg socks, red and white flecks of cotton and wool. The ankles bulged like deflated balloons over the rims of his Nikes. He shook off his raincoat and dropped it over the big armchair near the door.

That was the chair I used to watch TV; it reclined and was just about molded to the shape of my body, but Oliver sat on the seat's edge, leaning forward as if to let himself drip more efficiently onto the floor. None of this bothered me much, the furniture and floors were shot to begin with (Mom said she'd help pay for refinishing and painting, but I felt bad asking her to shell out any more money), but Augusta decided to get twisted up about it. She looked at the coat on the chair, then looked at me, then back at the chair, waiting for me to say something to Oliver, tell him to move. She had her hand on her hip, and she was tapping her right clog against the floor.

"No places want men," he said, which struck me as profoundly funny, but he didn't laugh. "It's a real problem."

"We were looking for a woman," I said, sitting on the couch and leaning forward toward Oliver. I went to this seminar once where a big H.R. expert told how when you want to give people good vibes in an interview you imitate their gestures, so if they lean forward, you lean forward; they cross their legs, you do the same. And the opposite holds true: if they lean forward and you lean back, it's curtains for them. The expert said you didn't really even have to think about all this, that it was an instinctive response. So I guess I was sending a good message to Oliver, whether or not he knew it, whether or not it was just to get at Augusta.

"*Are* looking for a woman," she said. "We've been getting calls all week. Off the hook." She stood behind the couch, making me turn around and interrupt my monkey-see, monkey-do conversation to answer her.

"I think we can keep our options open, don't you?" I said, sweet as pie, which for a second I forgot Augusta didn't eat.

"We've got plenty of options. I don't know why you asked him in."

Oliver reached behind him and started shaking out his jacket again, standing up. "I'm sorry to bother you. I was hoping you might be convinced." He looked down at his feet, pretending to check for mud, which there was plenty of in the treads of his Nikes. A damp forelock of hair pointed down toward the floor, a perfect black shark's tooth that used to rest on his forehead but now, with his head down, floated on air, on nothing. I'd like to see that hair dry sometime, I thought, wondering if it was just the rain that made it fall over his eye like that, or if he had cowlicks.

"Please stay," I said. "We're just a little tired. Stay for an interview."

"Are you sure? You won't be sorry," he said, like a salesman. "I'm neat and I'm in touch with my feminine side."

"Charming." Augusta had one foot on the stairs now, tapping her clog, loud as a woodpecker against a windowpane. Clogs took a certain person to carry them off—I for one could never have done it, announcing myself like that. She wore them at all hours of the day, too, Sunday mornings not excepted. I wanted to throw one of her loose clogs that was lying under the coffee table at her. Standing there like *she* owned the place.

"Sit down, Oliver. You want some tea? It's pretty wet out there."

He hung his raincoat over the back of the armchair again. Augusta looked at me, as if this one gesture could damn both Oliver and me for all time, the same as if we'd taken a knife to Bambi or eaten Big Macs. "Thanks," he said, "that'd be great."

Augusta clopped upstairs as I made him the tea, which didn't take long since we'd been keeping the water hot for potential coffee losers, and when I came back with some decaf Earl Grey, Oliver was leaning back in the chair, wet hair fanned out against his yellow slicker. He scanned the living room from his perch, taking in the scattered newspapers and thumbtacked Monet prints. Ours was an unmistakably female house, I realized, though I couldn't say why. We didn't leave bottles of nail polish on the mantlepiece or Diet Coke empties on the coffee table. Maybe it was the basil smell, mixed with cinnamon and soap, or the doilies under the lamps. I'd never thought about the house like that before, but Oliver's immediate ease surprised me, and seemed unlikely though not exactly wrong. I didn't usually care how men were fitting in, most everything revolved around them anyway and I'd taught myself to stop paying attention for survival's sake, but when a man is just there, in your own house, he's hard to ignore.

Floating inside all his big clothes and sitting in the big armchair, Oliver looked fragile. His tallness kind of sank into the folds. Except for the tips of his fingers (which were still grabbing onto his nubby cuffs) and his face, clothing covered every inch of him. Even his face had a bit of a Fred Flintstone shadow to it, but maybe that was because of how dark the living room got when it rained. I felt like I'd been staring a long time, but when I cleared my throat and said, "Here you go," big curls of steam were still floating up from the mug.

"Great," he said, straightening. He took the mug from my hand directly, not waiting for me to put it on an end table, as if he were purposely going for contact. But I always read too much into these things, so I forgot about it and concentrated on how cold his hands were. Then he said, "Will Augusta be joining us?" and gave me this smile. His teeth stood up fine against his white turtleneck (my mother's advice to me since I was twelve: never wear anything whiter than your teeth, especially for pictures and interviews), and he smiled like we were in on some secret together and nothing could stop us, not even mad roommates in clogs.

"Good question," I said, and yelled up the stairs, "Augusta, you coming or what?" Oliver's presence seemed to steel me against Augusta, and I wasn't sure I liked the feeling. I mean, there was Augusta, and then there were her trappings, the things you had to take as part of the whole package—her clogs (which she justified by saying they were percussion instruments), her spirulina powder, her baskets of basil and parsley and open bags of potting soil. She didn't answer my call and suddenly a little dart of guilt hit me, guilt about bringing Oliver onto the scene, making him tea, leaning back and forth in sync with him. "Can you wait another minute?" I asked him. "I'm sorry to keep holding you up."

"I'll just drink my tea and look around down here."

Augusta was sitting in her room, her only room now, cross-legged on her bed, starting a new art piece. She held the Elmer's bottle about a foot above the wood and made tiny circles in the air with the orange tip. A thin string of glue collapsed onto the wood, a crazy curlicue. Her other hand sprinkled sawdust mixed with glitter onto the wet glue. She looked so cramped, her knees up to her chin, the bed bouncing slightly as she waved her arms.

"You coming down?"

"How long have you been dreaming of tall men?" She didn't look at me, just glued and sprinkled, glued and sprinkled.

"Augusta, what are you talking about?"

"I want to know. I gave you that dream journal, so you have no excuse to act dumb about it. How long?"

She'd presented me with the journal, a bound notebook with marbleized covers, for my twenty-third birthday. It was sitting by my bed, its covers faded from purple and turquoise to brown and gray, its pages blank. "I never dream."

"You shouldn't live with your dream boys."

"Who's a dream boy, Augusta?"

"You've let him in the house." Glue and sprinkle, glue and sprinkle, faster now, big blobs on the wood.

"You let men in the house," I said. "The gas guy comes in the house."

"Not to live."

"If you came down you could help me interview him. We could decide together." I picked up the corner of her bedspread and rubbed the crinkly gauze between my fingers. Maybe I should've put my hand on her shoulder or her hair or something, but I've never been good at tender moments. When she looked up at me, there were tears rimming her eyes.

"You don't want my help," she said, blinking, holding back. "You've made your decision. You just want to fuck him. Right there on the recliner, on his wet, stinky raincoat."

"You're imagining things, Augusta."

"He's an M. An M, M, M. What is there not to imagine?"

"I need the money. I have a mortgage. If it's not coming from your Dad, it's got to come from somewhere."

"Don't mention him, he's the one." She waved her fingers, covered in glue and glitter, above her head. "My father needed the whole house as his humping ground. I heard him call it frolicking to one of his women. Like a playpen. So he'd buy me a Pooh Bear or a Barbie and I'd know to stay in my room." She laughed, but the tears were still coming. "I just want to keep this place safe."

"Why didn't you ever worry about me bringing someone home?"

"I knew you wouldn't."

Augusta always claimed she could predict the future. I didn't believe it, didn't even care, until now, when she started pointing her magic wand at me.

"Just be careful what you wish for, Kate." She mushed one of her hills between her fingers, glue oozing out in slow trickles around her thumb. She used to peel off huge pieces of dried glue from her hands and, if the sheaths survived fingers intact, hang them up in her studio, like phantoms of herself. If I walked past her room at night, and the light was on and there was a breeze through the window, I'd see these feathery shells of Augusta's hands swaying against the wall. Usually they only lasted a few days, then dried up and fell to the floor and floated around the house like dead leaves.

"You can come down, Augusta. Nothing's decided." I looked into the room that used to be her studio. The only trace Augusta had left was a tiny glitter outline of a butterfly, breathing flames toward the light switch. She made the butterfly soon after she moved in; I guess my homeowner instincts had been pretty dull then, not that they were so razor sharp now, but I hadn't said anything about her spreading Elmer's on the wall. The room seemed so small, would Oliver even fit? Would his head graze the ceiling, his feet stick out the door if he lay down? I stared for a minute more, filling the room up in my head with bookshelves and a dresser and a bed, maybe a nail in the wall if he needed to hang ties. He was a salesman for sure, and salesmen needed ties. The butterfly kept looking at me, though, knowing it was there to stay.

When I got downstairs, Oliver was hunched over the stove, stirring my pot of chicken noodle soup. He filled up the kitchen, not only with his body—he was thin as well as tall—but also with his shadow, and the implied hypotenuse between the two. With his nonstirring hand, he batted away the bunches of dried herbs that knocked into his forehead, occasionally twisting off pinches and sprinkling them into the soup.

"You always take over the kitchen the first time you come into a house?" Augusta stood behind me. She must have followed me down the stairs, tiptoe on her clogs, because I was surprised to hear her voice.

"Well, I had to save this soup. The oil slick on top, ugh, an environmental hazard."

"You get a chance to look around?" I asked. Augusta opened the refrigerator, probably checking to make sure he hadn't helped himself to anything else.

"Oh, yeah. Plenty of cabinet space. You got any Tabasco?"

Augusta stepped between me and Oliver. "Excuse me, but I don't think it's any of your business what we have and don't have here."

"Well, Tabasco just makes the soup taste better. I was only asking." He kept stirring. "How about plain old black pepper? Herbs are fine"—he swatted at the bunch of tarragon swinging in front of him; a few leaves fell to the floor—"but this stuff needs a little spice."

I opened the cabinet next to his head and brought out the pepper grinder. "Here. You cook a lot?"

He ground a solid stream of pepper into the pot for a few seconds. "Oh, I love to cook. Big fat gourmet meals. The kind that keep you digesting for days." He stirred and ladled out a bowlful of soup. "Try this. I think the pepper just hit the spot."

"I'm a vegetarian," Augusta said, "and Kate won't eat anything retouched out of the can. Believe me, I've tried."

Augusta was really jazzed on knowing all about me today. I decided to get down to brass tacks. "Before I taste this, Oliver, you got a steady job? You'd be able to pay the rent, if we offer you the room?"

"I can give you first and last today, in cash." He passed me the bowl, balancing it on his palm. All he needed was one of those silver plate covers like they have in the movies, to unveil his masterpiece.

My spoonful was hot and tasty and went down easy. "Delicious," I said. Augusta stood with her hand on her hip, but her shoulders were pulled close together and her fingertips sparkled and her eyes were still red. The three of us didn't exactly fit comfortably in the little kitchen, but I knew I had made up my mind about Oliver, and that nothing, no one, would turn out simple anymore.

Solveig Eggerz
Fear of Snakes

SOLVEIG EGGERZ, a native of Iceland, is the author of the award-winning novel *Seal Woman*, published in 2008 by Ghost Road Press. Solveig holds a PhD in comparative literature from Catholic University of America. She lives in Alexandria, Virginia, and teaches writing workshops in the Washington, D.C., area, including the Writer's Center in Bethesda, Maryland.

Bird builds houses. He used to take me to construction sites. I guess he really wanted a boy, but I was the only thing available. So he did boy stuff with me, pretending I was his boy. An incident changed my life.

We were at an abandoned house. Bird ripped up some floorboards with a crowbar. A tangle of black snakes looked up at us. Writhing in and out of the pile, they stared at us with cold, loveless eyes. They were confused or maybe ashamed as if we'd discovered them naked. I couldn't stop looking at them. I didn't know then that snakes only seem to stare because they don't have eyelids and that they flick out their tongues for information.

After that I started sneaking snakes into the house. I liked to look at them. The way they moved fascinated me. Sort of like throwing your heart over the bar and your body will follow. Part of their skeletal framework moved forward. The rest of the body filled in the spaces later.

But I was repelled by how they ate. Or was I just afraid? Did I have a phobia? I got the idea that the reason I was so into snakes is because I was scared to death of them. And I had to overcome that. My hero was not Justin Bieber but Brian, a snake handler in Australia who catches the most venomous snake in the world, the island taipan.

Mamma screamed when she found the boxes containing slithery bodies under my bed. For my thirteenth birthday, I got breasts and celebrated with a snake tattoo over the left one. A friend of a friend gave me the tattoo. He didn't care about my age. The kangaroo on my butt came later. Now that I'm twenty-one, it jumps when I squeeze the left cheek. I'm saving it for the grand finale in a strip poker game.

High school put me at the misfit end of the spectrum. I drank and not only experimented with sex but perfected it, with the kind of guys who wouldn't know your name next day. I inhaled whatever was going around. Rolling my eyes and passing out were my form of exercise. Bird's car wound up in a ditch with me at the wheel. After that, different kids, all of them wasted, drove me home.

One night I crept in at three a.m. Bird sat on the edge of the sofa with his fists down, ready to push up and into confrontation with me, his loser kid. He pretended to hug me, but I heard him sniffing my breath.

"Would you like to go to boarding school. Might be a nice break for you."

"Out of my way, asshole."

"Now, honey—"

That's all he said. Why didn't he call me an ungrateful little bitch? Tell me to shape up or he'd smash my head in? Why didn't he take off his belt and beat me bloody? I stormed off to my room, in a dark cloud of patricide. He never would've let me curse him if he loved me. I kept forcing my parents to reject me, slap my face, throw me against the wall, make me feel like I was theirs.

In my room, I reached into my underwear drawer, took out the Wild Turkey and chugged it. Lying in the darkness, I thought what a little shit I was. Underneath my bed, my corn snake stirred. His scales glided against the sides of the box. I took him out and let him crawl up my arm. When his dry scales touched my skin, I felt the usual chill of fear. I had to face up to it. I could do it.

I felt the weight of the snake as he moved across my hands and up my arms. Still holding his coiling body, I pushed open the door of my room and walked past the living room. Bird never looked up. Shifting the snake's body to my left arm, I opened the front door. The grass was wet under my bare feet. I walked to the place where our grass ended, and the cluster of trees began. I set the snake down. I couldn't see him, but I heard his body make its way through the grass toward the trees.

Letting that snake go made me feel better about cursing Bird.

❧

MAMMA AND BIRD SENT ME to summer school to make up flunked classes. A guy named Stone was my lab partner in science class. He was big on religion. As time went on, and I got more into the strange evolutionary history of snakes, I sensed how the Book of Genesis and Charles Darwin slugged it out inside Stone. Sometimes I thought he'd explode from the clash.

Stone introduced me to his uncle Borso, a snake breeder and handler. He bred ball pythons, morphing them into a range of autumn colors to match a woman's wardrobe. His small house was filled with kids who ran barefoot on a burgundy colored shag rug and spilled stuff out of sippy cups. Borso's basement smelled of chlorine. The floor was tile with a drain in the center. On the walls were photos of a blonde wearing different color bikinis. At her neck she held a ball python that matched the fabric.

"That's Tina from the Netherlands," Borso said. "You need a job?"

I nodded.

"Good. I'll pay ya in snakes."

I was wearing a denim miniskirt and a denim jacket. Borso leaned over me and walked his fingers up my thigh. "Snakes are always looking for a dark place to hide."

Next day after school, I reported for work in long pants tucked into hiking boots and a long-sleeved blouse. On my head I wore my chocolate-colored Fort Western Star 2X wool hat. Bird had bought it for me because the wide brim keeps ticks out of your hair when you're squirrel hunting.

Borso taught me how to pick up snakes and to support the body. He kept mostly nonvenomous snakes, such as garter snakes, pine snakes, and milk snakes, but he also had a couple of eastern diamondback rattlesnakes. On my second day of work, he showed me how to extract their venom.

His fingers looked huge as they gripped each side of the rattler's head.

"Hold his butt," he said. I picked up the writhing back part of the snake.

With his other hand he reached for a jar that was covered with something that resembled plastic. He forced the snake's gaping jaws down onto the plastic so that its fangs pierced it. His thick fingers massaged the venom glands to either side of the snake's head. Then he stroked the top of its head.

"Makes him a little angry, so he'll give more."

The venom pearled from the snake's fangs, forming a golden stream that oozed down the side of the jar.

"Thanks buddy," Borso said, still gripping the rattler's head. I followed him to the box, carrying my part of the snake.

"Is this for your private use?" I asked as he put a lid on the jar of venom and labeled it.

"I send it to the lab. They'll get anti-venom out of it. Or maybe some anti-wrinkle cream. Aging divas in Hollywood love it, better than Botox."

I touched my face. Mamma might like a jar of the stuff for her sixtieth birthday.

"Time for a break," Borso said and removed his shirt. He took a couple of ball pythons from their cages and lay down on a bath mat on the tile floor. "Get me a beer," he said. When I returned with an open bottle, the eight-inch-long snakes were crawling through his chest hairs. He raised his head slightly and sipped from the bottle.

Amani Elkassabany

A Planting Season

AMANI ELKASSABANY'S short fiction has appeared in *Shattering the Stereotypes: Muslim Women Speak Out* (Interlink Books, 2005), *Women's Lives* (McGraw Hill, 2007), and *Mizna* and *Callaloo*. Amani teaches English literature and writing at Thomas S. Wootton High School in Rockville, Maryland. She feels most alive when she's dancing, most present when she's writing, and most happy when she can do both, though not simultaneously. She lives in Bethesda, Maryland, and is currently at work on a novel.

*O*n a cool morning in April, I dressed for work as I usually did: a cotton T-shirt, faded overalls, and leather work boots—the kind of clothes Mama thought only a man should wear. If she had her way, I'd be wearing skirts that fell below my knee and loose-fitting blouses with high necklines. I pulled my curly hair back into a ponytail and looked at myself in the bathroom mirror. No makeup. Even though Mama thought I was finally old enough for makeup, I never wore any.

Every morning, I pressed my finger into the soil covering the roots of the African violet that sat on my dresser. With just the right amount of sunlight and water, I had managed to keep it blooming since last August, and I was proud of this. The sight of those delicate purple flowers soothed me, and I silently delighted in the knowledge that I had a small part in bringing those blooms into being.

I passed Mama's closed bedroom door on the way to the kitchen. I was glad she was still asleep. I knew what she would say if she saw me in my work clothes. *If you're going to work, find a job that women do—a nurse, a teacher, even a secretary. It's no wonder you're still not married. How do you expect to find a husband when you dress like that?* My clothes, my job. These were the small ways I disappointed Mama. Not being married. Not wanting to be married. These were faults Mama couldn't forgive.

But Mama's forgiveness was something I stopped expecting a long time ago.

I stood in our kitchen making coffee, which amounted to breakfast for me on most days. I filled my cup and added neither cream nor sugar. I drank only half of what I poured, but that didn't stop me from emptying the entire contents of the pot into my cup. I liked the smell of brewed coffee perfuming the air of the kitchen that Mama and I shared. Baba had been gone for a while, and now that Amir had married Manal and moved out last summer, it was just Mama and me.

My morning breakfast routine—like all the routines in my life—was familiar, comforting, a small series of tasks that allowed me to forget that it was only the two of us now in the house on Maverick Lane. Besides, my routines made me feel safe. They were something I could count on, something to focus on so that my mind wouldn't wander, and my imagination wouldn't see things that weren't there.

I touched the soil in the small pot of mint that I kept on the kitchen windowsill. Still moist. The window faced south, so I moved the pot onto the countertop to keep it out of the morning's direct sunlight. Even though it was hard to be with Mama, I looked forward to coming home for the small pleasures it afforded me: pinching a few mint leaves from their stalk and letting them steep in a cup of hot tea. Exactly the way Baba used to make it.

I washed my coffee cup and noticed my fingernails as I held my hands under the running water. I always clipped them close to the tips of my fingers to keep any soil from getting underneath. In the corner of my thumbnail there were just a few traces of earth, which I pried loose with my forefinger, then brushed into the sink, watching the tiny flakes disappear into the rush of water from the tap. When I wiped my hands on a kitchen towel, I paused for a moment and studied the shape of my fingernails. The long nail beds with delicate half-moon shapes at their base reminded me of the hands of a woman who modeled wedding rings on a billboard I had seen in downtown Lawrence. She had only clear polish on her nails, but they were attractive, and made her hands look elegant and sophisticated. I imagined how my nails might look painted a pale shade of pink and turned the word *beautiful* over in my mind. When I was little, I used to hide my polished nails from Mama. I banished the word—along with the image of my painted fingernails—from my head.

I dried the coffee cup, placed it back in the cupboard, and wiped down the sink. I checked the faucet for spots and rubbed one out so that the chrome gleamed. In some ways, I was very much my mother's daughter.

I walked out the kitchen door and circled around to the front of the house, and walked down the steps to the driveway. I fished through my purse for my car keys but couldn't find them. When I went back in the house, I saw Mama sitting at the kitchen table. In front of her was a tin pie plate holding a mound of raw rice, her eyes fixed on the grains. Her fingers sifted through them, isolating any cracked or discolored ones, removing any grain that had even the slightest defect in it. Once, when I was younger, Mama asked me to help her with the rice. I picked out the stones and the grains that were brown all over, but Mama wasn't satisfied. She went back and found twice as many grains to throw away as I did, ones that seemed just fine to me. After that, she always picked over the rice herself.

When Mama looked up at me that morning as I stood in the doorway wearing my T-shirt and overalls, my hair pulled back into a ponytail, I saw a look of disappointment in her eyes so deep that I felt as small and discolored as the flawed grain of rice she held between her fingertips, waiting to be discarded. I often felt as though Mama might be happier if only she were rid of me.

"Is that all you ever wear anymore?" She asked in Arabic.

"These are my work clothes, Ma." I answered in English.

"I don't know why you work that job. It's not a job for girls."

I was twenty-five years old.

Mama began poking at the mound of rice again.

"I'll see you tonight," I said, taking the keys from the hook near the kitchen door frame.

"I invited Amir and Manal for dinner."

When Mama complained to Amir about my job, my clothes, and mostly about my unwillingness to consider any of the men she thought were suitable husbands for me, he sided with Mama and held me responsible for Mama's distress. I thought I could count on Manal as my ally, but ever since she had the baby, she was preoccupied with feedings and diaper changes; maybe she just didn't have the energy to come to my defense as she used to.

"Amir is bringing a friend."

I felt a dull ache in my stomach. "A friend? Which friend?" I knew Mama could hear the anxiety in my voice, but she continued to stare at the mound of rice, her fingers turning the grains over and over.

"Kareem." Mama's voice was flat. "You remember him."

I didn't.

"He came to Amir's wedding," Mama continued. "A nice young man."

I had no memory of ever meeting him.

"I still can't believe my son got married before his older sister."

Kareem was the third man in as many months Mama invited to the house on Maverick Lane with the intention of making him my husband. When the two suitors before him had showed up at our house, I barely spoke two words to them before going to my room. Later, Mama had told me it wasn't polite to ignore these visitors. She had tried to convince me that since they were friends of Amir's, it would look bad if I didn't at least say hello. *Do you want to embarrass your brother? People talk, Mama had said. What will they say when they know you aren't even interested in getting married? What will they think of you? Of our family? Isn't it bad enough that Baba is gone and you have no father to protect your reputation? Amir has tried so hard to do what's best for you, and you are being selfish and ungrateful.*

"Not again, Mama."

"It's for your own good, Nadya. If you were back home, you would have been married a long time ago."

Mama talked about being back "home," even though we had left Egypt eighteen years ago.

"What if I don't want to get married?"

"Aeib aleyki," answered Mama. "Shame on you. A girl your age, still single, still living with her mother. It's not normal."

It was useless to tell Mama how I really felt.

"You know what Baba believed. The same thing my father used to tell me before I was married: 'A girl is a trust that hangs around her father's neck.'"

Years ago, when I talked about missing Baba, Mama had always told me it was best not to think about certain things. Now, it was she who was talking about him, reminding me often that I would surely be a disappointment to him if he were still alive.

"Do you want to dishonor your father's memory?" Her voice was heavy with accusation.

I was no longer the adult Nadya on her way to work; I was the helpless, wounded girl who missed her father. Not only did Mama's words make me painfully aware that Baba wasn't here, but when Mama tried to bring him back, she turned him into a man I didn't know.

I shook my head. "No, Mama, I don't." I had to bite the inside of my mouth to keep the tears collecting at the bottom of my eyes from spilling over my lashes.

I DROVE DOWN MAVERICK LANE and out of Prairie Hills. The rays of the rising sun turned the fields of wheat on either side of the road a pale orange. I rolled down my window and let in the morning air. I smelled the dampness of dew on grass, the sweetness of buds on tree branches. I savored the quiet of this moment. It felt good to be alone in my car, away from Mama. *Maybe I don't have to go back.* I had thought this before, but never considered it as a serious possibility. Mama had made it clear that the only right way to move out of her house would be to move into the house of man who would be my husband.

I could not imagine being married to any of the men Amir had brought home for me to meet. I could not see myself living with Mama forever either.

While I waited for a traffic light to turn from red to green, I searched through a stack of cassette tapes, not looking for anything in particular, simply deciding which one I was in the mood for this morning. When I bought my green Chevy three years ago from the used car lot on Haskell Avenue, I made sure it had a cassette tape player. I wanted to be able to play the songs that Baba listened to. The day he died, I gathered all his cassette tapes into a shoebox and put them under my bed.

I pushed *A Story of Love* into the tape deck. The voice of Oum Kulsoum filled the car. Baba always called her *El Sitt*. The Lady. He told me she was the grand lady of song not only in Egypt but throughout the Arab world. If he had known the word diva, that was the word he would have used to describe her. Baba used to translate her songs for me as I sat in his lap. It was then that I learned that there were two kinds of Arabic: the classical Arabic used in poetry and the Qur'anic verses I learned in Islamic Sunday school, and the informal Arabic my parents spoke to Amir and me in everyday conversation. Oum Kulsoum sang in both styles. *A Story of Love* was in the dialect I had heard spoken at home:

> I have tired of love
> And the story of love
> And of all those who say they are in love

I mouthed the words in Arabic as she sang them.

Charlie and Penelope Foster were already at the nursery when I got there. Charlie, the owner, wore an olive T-shirt and khaki shorts. His fair skin was weathered from outdoor work, and the brown had all but gone from his beard, which was nearly as gray as his hair, cut close above his ears. He wore metal-rimmed glasses on a brown cord around his neck and perched them on the tip of his nose when he read the balance sheets. He started this nursery from a greenhouse and built it into Foster's Flora, not the biggest nursery in Douglas County, but one that attracted customers who appreciated the fact that Charlie and Penelope listened to them.

Charlie's wife, Penelope, designed the nursery and built up its client base, starting with her neighbors and friends, who spread the word to their friends. Penelope parted her brown hair down the middle and plaited it into a single braid that swung over her shoulder. She wore jade earrings that dangled from her delicate earlobes. When she smiled, wrinkles appeared around her eyes. But the blueness of her eyes lit up her face and even her wrinkles seemed to glow.

Charlie studied this morning's delivery order. The skin on Charlie's forearms was tanned, but I could still see the scratches from the work of lifting and planting heavy shrubs and young trees.

"Morning, Dee." He had given me this nickname a few weeks after he hired me.

"Hey, boss. Hey, Penelope."

"I've got some blueberry muffins in the back. Help yourself, sweetie," said Penelope.

"Three big jobs today. Better get started," said Charlie.

"No job is so pressing it's going to come between Nadya and one of my homemade muffins," said Penelope, glancing sideways at her husband.

"I'll take it to go," I said.

Charlie hauled bags of mulch and topsoil into the truck. I placed trays of annuals onto a tiered metal cart—yellow and red variegated marigolds, white begonias, purple pansies, crimson salvia—before I loaded them into the truck in front of the blossoming forsythia bushes and fragrant Leland cypress trees. The routine was comforting: load the truck after sunrise, dig and plant in the morning, work the cash register after lunch.

I had only been working for Charlie a month when he asked me to close up the nursery. That meant that Charlie and Penelope could go home early. Sometimes, when they didn't know I was listening, they talked about what they did at home: quiet dinners, long walks with their dogs, occasional visits from their grandchildren. Once I heard Charlie tell Penelope that life after fifty was good, and I wondered if that might be true for me. Maybe in twenty-five years, my life might become something I could describe as good. Though I doubted it.

As I loaded the last of the plants into Charlie's truck, Penelope came out and touched my shoulder. "Telephone, Nadya. I think it's your mother."

"I'll be in the truck," said Charlie.

I picked the receiver up from the counter. "Mama?"

"I need you stop at the store before you come home."

Mama spoke in Arabic, but I answered in English, as usual. "Can we talk later?" It was hard for me to say no to Mama. "I'm just about to go out on a job."

"That job isn't for you, Nadya."

I felt myself grow impatient. "Mama, I need to go."

"I don't even know what to tell Amir to say to Kareem about your job. It's not respectable."

The thought of meeting Kareem was bad enough, but now Mama had made it worse. Mama's disapproval of my job, her conferring with Amir about how to explain what I did to Kareem. It was all too much. I felt my heart race and I couldn't catch my breath.

"Nadya? Are you listening?" Mama's voice seemed to spill out of the receiver into my ear.

I turned around and saw Charlie in the driver's seat of the truck. The engine was running. I took a deep breath and managed a feeble reply. "Mama, Charlie's waiting."

"I don't like you riding alone in the car with that man."

"He's my boss."

"In Arabic, Nadya. They'll hear you."

"I can't talk now." I switched to Arabic, even though Charlie and Penelope were both out of earshot.

"Manal's not coming over tonight. The baby's sick. I don't have time to make dessert."

Reluctantly, I promised Mama I'd stop at the store on the way home.

"Everything OK?" asked Penelope as I hung up the phone.

"Fine," I lied. Everything had not been OK in years.

"You sure? Your face is as pinched as a pruned rosebush."

"My mother gets a little worried sometimes."

"Must be lonely now that your brother has moved out."

I nodded.

"Good thing you're still at home."

AS CHARLIE AND I DROVE down Thornton Street, I looked for the bulbs we planted last November outside the entrance of my old elementary school, long gone to make way for the Douglas County Counseling and Mental Health Services building. I always welcomed spring, but fall was a planting season I had come to cherish more. I saw the fruit that had come from last fall's labor: daffodils, tulips, and irises. I remembered laying bulbs into the cool ground, buried treasures that lay dormant until the sun's rays warmed them enough to drink the moisture thawing in the deepest layers of the soil. Their roots found it and soaked it up, channeled it through to bulb, and stalk, to petal and stamen. Even though I knew where they were, I was always surprised to see these small gifts that spring from the soil, bursting forth in strange and wonderful shapes, in bright yellows and flame reds that warm the April landscape. Deep, vibrant colors that defied death, a glorious reminder that all sleeping things awaken eventually.

Charlie and I drove to a quiet neighborhood just outside the campus of Kansas University and pull up to a small brick house in a cul-de-sac. The sky was sunny and clear and the morning air smelled clean. "Beds on each side of the front porch, Dee."

Charlie laid out the garden hose along the ground and curved it in the shape of the flower bed while I took the tools out of the truck. Just as I positioned the spade inside the hose, Charlie handed me a pair of gloves. "Don't forget these."

I held the handle of the spade in my gloved hands and bore down with all my weight on the spade, feeling it sink deep into the soil. The scrape of metal slicing through earth was the only sound on that still morning, and I settled into the rhythm of that repeating sound as I continued pushing the spade into the soil, creating an edge where none existed before. When that was done, Charlie, who had been doing the same work on the other side of the porch, gave me a nod.

We unloaded bags of topsoil, limestone, and mulch next, and Charlie knelt near the pile of bags.

"Hand me the box-cutters, Dee." I knew that Charlie always kept a pair of orange box-cutters in the caddy of garden tools we took out on jobs. But when I looked, it wasn't there. I turned to Charlie and shook my head.

"Must've left 'em at the store."

He reached into his jacket and pulled out a pocketknife. I watched Charlie take off his garden gloves so that he could grip the knife with his bare fingers and pull the blade from its housing. He curled his fingers around the handle of the knife, his thumb and forefinger at the base of the blade. I felt a pain in my side, and realized I had been holding my breath. I saw the exposed blade catch the gleam of the sun and wanted to turn away from the sight of the sun dancing across the metal, but all I could do was stare at the pocketknife. My breath was shallow, and the pain in my side had gotten worse.

As Charlie sliced through the top of one bag after another, I felt the damp chill of sweat in my armpits. Sheets of plastic, which had moments ago securely contained pounds of shredded bark, came undone from one swipe of the blade. Seeing the exposed mounds of mulch frothing from those open bags made me think of a wounded animal, its skin flayed by some kind of predator. Everything inside me turned cold.

Charlie folded the pocketknife and put it back in his pocket.

I stood frozen, my legs heavy, my chest tight.

"Nadya? You all right? You look pale as a ghost."

I took one long breath and blinked for the first time in what seemed like minutes.

"Fine. I'm fine," I replied. I didn't want to lie to Charlie, but how could I tell him that the sight of those bags splitting open made me shiver?

I shook my head and let out a small sigh. "Just a little hungry, I guess. I'm going to get the rest of that muffin from the truck." I hoped I sounded convincing.

A few minutes later, I was filling beds with limestone and topsoil and digging holes for the marigolds and salvia. I inverted the plastic containers into my gloved hands before I placed the plants in their nests. The dark brown mulch warmed the flowers' stems. A robin landed on the edge of our flower bed, his red crest full with spring, and I began to feel warm again.

WHEN I GOT HOME FROM work, I saw Amir's car parked in front of the house. The last time he came over, he had also brought a man to meet me. Now, my little brother was acting like my father again.

I felt my stomach tighten and sat in the car thinking about what to do next. I could turn around and drive—back to work, over to Manal's, through downtown Lawrence, anywhere to avoid going into the house. But I knew that if I left, Mama and Amir would only continue to pressure me—she with sharp-tongued comments about all the ways I had disappointed her, he with a list of reasons why marriage was the right thing to do. I was terrified of going into the house, but I was also tired from work, and I didn't want to show up at Manal's without telling her I was coming. What worried me more was not going in, what Mama would say to me about dishonoring Baba's memory.

I had also forgotten to stop at the grocery store on the way home. Maybe I could forget that Kareem was coming over, too. Just decide not to meet with him, tell Mama I was too tired, and go straight to my room.

But how long could I hide there? Since Amir had moved out, Mama paid more attention to me than she ever had. She seemed more ready to point out my faults to me and more determined to convince me I would improve only by getting married.

Before he died, Baba used to tell me that God had made us caretakers of everything. He said this often, as we walked through Prairie Park or drove past the wheat fields on our way to Kansas City or watched snowflakes fall and land on the bare branches of the dogwood tree in our backyard. "*Subhan Allah*," Baba often said. When I asked him what this meant, he said "God created so much beauty, and it's our duty to take care of it."

I thought about the African violet on my dresser, its brilliant purple flowers delicately perched in the center of a whorl of dark green leaves. I loved to run my fingertip over the soft fuzz on the pale pink underside of one of the oval-shaped leaves.

I was comforted again by the fact that I could act in this capacity—as a caretaker of all beautiful things. When I planted flowers and pruned rosebushes and helped roots take hold in the earth, I felt connected to Baba in a way that I didn't feel doing anything else. It was a small and humble connection, but it opened a widow, and I let myself bathe in the sunshine pouring through. Whenever I thought of Baba, the protective armor I wore tight around my body begin to loosen, if only for a moment.

Even though Mama and I had been together since Baba died, I had often felt alone in her company. Wedding myself to a man wasn't going to change that. Staying with Mama definitely wasn't going to change that. I sat with my memory of Baba. Though he had been gone for years, it was these moments of silent remembrance that gave me the tiniest glimmer of hope when feelings of loneliness enveloped me.

Mama, Amir, and a man I had never met before were waiting inside. I gripped the steering wheel to keep my hands from shaking. I closed my eyes and saw myself living in a place where there would be no more visits from suitors, no more nagging from Mama, and where Amir would have to call first if he wanted to come over.

Julia Elliott

Monitor Magic

JULIA ELLIOTT produces documentary films and videos for nonprofits. She lives in Washington, D.C., with her husband and two daughters. Her first published fiction won *Boulevard* magazine's Short Fiction Contest for Emerging Writers.

One couple we knew lived in an apartment building that had a bar in the basement called the Magic Hat. It was the kind of place frequented by college kids: sticky floors, dim lighting, couches that smelled of beer and sweat. The couple had never been inside—just wheeled their stroller around the smokers knotting up the sidewalk outside the entrance—but for many nights they had joked about taking the baby monitor down and getting a drink. They were tired of drinking beer in front of the TV while their children slept, but bemoaned the cost of a babysitter.

Then one night, they just did it. It was a Tuesday in January, so not so busy that they couldn't find seats at the end of the bar. They put the monitor, squat soldier of child safety, between their drinks. The husband sipped his beer and retold a story from work. The wife traced the rim of her sauvignon blanc and mentioned the book she was reading. Every now and then, she held the monitor to her ear, relieved to hear only the gentle oceanic fuzz.

By the second drink, they were talking about how cute it was when Emma, the four-year-old, talked about the "armadildo" in *Good Night, Gorilla*. How advanced it was that the one-year-old, Sasha, could fit Cheerios onto her snaps. The husband's knee brushed against the wife's thigh. She laughed and shook her ponytail down her back.

It changed their entire week. They had more patience with the kids. The wife didn't mind cooking three separate dinners, and the husband volunteered for the two-hour bath and bedtime routine. They made love three nights in a row.

They went to the Magic Hat several times that winter. The wife held the monitor on her lap, but mostly they forgot about it. Once, it slid onto the floor and the battery rolled beneath the bar.

Then one night, the wife looked down and saw the bar of lights screaming orange, the color of fire, ambulances, and traffic cones. A flash of terror shot up her spine and she snatched the monitor up. *What is it?* the husband hissed, leaning in close to listen with her.

Hi, Mama, a sweet little voice said through the static. The wife grabbed her purse and sprinted up the stairs. The husband paid the bill, hands shaking. When he reached the apartment, the wife met him at the door, her head cocked in that puzzled way. *Fast asleep,* she said. They went into the bedroom and stood over their daughters, listened to the blissful rhythm of their breathing, inhaled the powdery smell of plastic baby dolls and clean diapers. Back in the living room, they both agreed that what had sounded like Emma must have been someone else's baby, a moment of monitor cross frequency. *But let's not do that anymore,* the wife said.

Within a few weeks, though, the apartment had closed back in on them. They were testy with each other and short with the kids, so they broke down and snuck out, monitor in hand. They were halfway through their drinks, had begun to relax and talk with shiny amazement about Emma's skill on the monkey bars, Sasha's adorable habit of wearing Emma's underwear on her head, when the husband noticed the lights. He seized the monitor and they both leaned in close. *I love you, Mama, Daddy.* It was clearly Emma's voice, Sasha's gurgles and squeals.

This time, the husband ran upstairs and the wife paid, knees jiggling as the bartender ran her credit card. When she reached the apartment, heart ready to stop, her husband stood in the doorway, baffled. Both children were asleep.

They went back and forth on it for a few days, and when they decided to go back to the Magic Hat, it was in part to test if what they thought had happened might really have happened. They had two drinks. They flirted halfheartedly with each other. Mostly they watched the monitor, tucked between the beer bottle and wineglass. When the orange lights glowed, they had a quick tug-of-war. They could hear the baby babbling, but for much longer, more insistently than ever before. The wife won, the husband leaned over, and Emma's voice came over the static. *Sasha says she cries when you drop her off for daycare because she wants you to pack the blue sippy cup. She hates the pink one.* They looked at each other, astonished, and then sprinted up the stairs.

It became a ritual. They still enjoyed the drinks, the time away from the apartment, the adrenaline rush from doing something so reckless. But they both knew that they really went for the secrets.

When you guys fight about who is doing pickup, it makes Sasha chew her fingers and I can't eat my lunch.

Daddy, that shiny shoe you were looking for the morning of your big meeting? The "fucking" shoe? It's in the dress-up box.

Mommy, sorry I had that temper tantrum in the middle of Target today but I really hate it when I'm telling you a story about baby unicorns and you keep texting. And you should know that when I'm telling you a story about baby unicorns what I'm really telling you is that Jason sometimes touches me during naptime when Miss Marcie isn't looking and that is why I bit him.

If you tell Sasha "good job!" one more time, she's going to throw up.

Every night, one of them rushed home while the other paid anxiously. Every night, the girls were sleeping peacefully. The terror started to subside. They came to expect the little sleepy sighs, the powdery smells, the peace only occasionally rippled by a shout from a drunk smoker on the street below. They teetered in a fragile place between knowing it couldn't be real and praying that it was.

The last night they went to the Magic Hat, Sasha had a cough and the husband had to convince the wife it would be OK to leave the house. The bar was crowded for a Tuesday, and the husband changed his mind and wanted to bag it, but the wife said as long as they were there, they might as well stand against the wall and have one drink. So the monitor was in her purse, and when they finally thought to check it, the lights had been orange for god knows how long. *Emma?* the wife hissed into the little speaker, blushing, knowing Emma could not hear her.

Mommy, Daddy, listen, Sasha is going to be a computer programmer when she grows up. And marry a rich man. I'm trying to decide between circus performer and vet. I'll be OK, though. Don't worry. I know you love me. Sasha knows it, too. You did the best you could. Good job.

They left without paying. Sprinted up the stairs so fast their ribs hurt. The husband nearly broke the key in the lock. And what they found, of course, was their worst nightmare realized: the crib empty, the covers thrown back on the toddler bed, the children gone. The police found no sign of forced entry, no note, no foul play. It all came out—the bar, the monitor, the drinks, the children left behind. It even made the news, prompting a brief national discussion on parental negligence among semi-successful urban Gen X-ers.

They never found the children, and that couple moved away from here. How could you stay, after such a loss? We wagged our heads, expressed our horror. But in our hearts we wondered: what secrets would be revealed if we had the balls to leave our children and get a drink at a bar?

Katie Pickard Fawcett

Noma

KATIE PICKARD FAWCETT grew up in eastern Kentucky and has lived in the Washington, D.C., area since the 1970s. Her first novel, *To Come and Go Like Magic*, was published by Knopf in 2010 and was selected as a Parents' Choice Recommended Book, listed by the Bank Street Children's Book Committee as one of the Best Children's Books of the Year, and won the Evelyn Thurman Award for Best Young Readers Book. She was a social worker in Appalachia, worked for the World Bank's publishing department, and currently tutors students in writing. Visit her on the web: katiepickardfawcett.wordpress.com.

*Y*ears later Noma would remember "one giant leap for mankind" in connection to the Watusi, the Monkey, and the Swim—small steps she'd taken on the dance floor when she was eighteen. Two men would be inextricably laced together in her mind—Neil Armstrong and Mingo Nash. An astronaut and a hippie. Both had lives completely foreign to her own.

She and Mingo had kissed beneath the moon when Neil Armstrong was taking his first step on it. Neil and Noma had both made giant leaps into a strange new world. That's how she liked to remember it. Now, in her late fifties and newly divorced, Noma is recalling that time long ago and wondering what happened to the boy in bell-bottom jeans and Bob Dylan T-shirt she'd kissed that night.

Back then she figured Mingo looked like everybody else where he came from, but he didn't look like anybody in Sweetwater, Kentucky. The long hair automatically made him a dirty hippie who was probably on LSD. But Mingo was neither dirty nor on drugs of any sort, at least not to Noma's knowledge. She knew everything about him that one could know about another human being and still feel like a stranger.

Oh, my goodness—those eyes! She could never fully describe them. Alternately they were black or deep brown with a flurry of little flecks that turned to gold in the sun. How could a human being have such strange, beautiful eyes? She wondered now if they were still that pretty or if they'd gone watery and lifeless like the eyes of some of the men she knew. Most of all she wondered what they'd seen.

Mingo Nash had dreamt of seeing the world. That's why they split up those many years ago. Noma could not see herself, a puny little girl from a muddy Kentucky hollow, traipsing down the streets of Paris, France, or riding a boat through some South American jungle. Mingo had wanted to see it all—the beautiful and the broken. In the end, she couldn't muster up the courage to go with him. How could she leave everything she'd ever known for some almost-stranger?

Last evening Noma's daughter Lynetta and her husband Paul had come for supper. Lynetta is her youngest. She's a third grade teacher, but doesn't have any kids of her own yet. Noma's other two, a girl and a boy, have children. She has been blessed with three healthy grandkids. She feels lucky. And old. Several times a week she babysits, cooks, or cleans for one of the families. Noma is willing, accommodating, and dependable.

As she sits this spring morning drinking coffee on the front porch with the old cat Rosie purring contentedly on her lap, she considers her good qualities. After the divorce came through, she had two sessions with a social worker who had encouraged her to make a list of her best qualities and to concentrate on those when she felt low. She'd never gotten around to the list. Now, she thinks, in addition to the aforementioned traits, she is also a good mother and grandma, a trusted friend, an adequate cook and housekeeper, and well read. This last is evidenced by the assorted cases and stacks of books in her living room and bedroom and on the extra shelves Raleigh built in the laundry room. Over the last few weeks, she has come to accept the fact that she has spent the better part of her life living in books, living in someone else's stories.

Noma has garnered two points of wisdom from this realization. Being well read has been something of an albatross in her relations with her neighbors and friends in Sweetwater. In the middle of an everyday conversation at the Piggly Wiggly, Noma will be struck with an idea, an observation, or a theory that fits the situation. But she's learned not to mention these things for fear of being laughed at or alienated completely. What she wouldn't give to have someone to talk to about books, ideas, theories…and possibilities.

The other point she's learned is that, as much as she enjoys living in someone else's stories, she dreams of having the courage to tackle one of her own.

This morning, as she's sitting on the front porch drinking coffee, she hears a car coming down the lane. It's Lynetta's red convertible. She's got the top down and her long brown hair is blowing in the wind. What a sight!

Noma's girls are pretty. As much as she hates to admit it, she knows they got those good looks from Raleigh. She feels like spitting out his name, but she's got a mouthful of coffee.

Lynetta gets out of the car and retrieves a box from the backseat. Now, what on earth could that be? Noma thinks.

"Hey Mama." Lynetta waves with one hand and holds onto the box with the other. "I got you something."

Noma follows her daughter into the house, and Lynetta plops the box on the dining room table and starts peeling away the packing tape. It is only now that Noma notices the picture of Raleigh. She thought she'd gotten rid of them all, but this one is sitting on the little corner shelf behind a red vase with only half the photo visible, the half that has the string of fish Raleigh is holding. It was taken last year at a Tennessee lake where Raleigh was supposed to be spending the weekend with his fishing buddies, a group of men he'd made friends with over in Tennessee. It turned out, of course, that there'd never been a group of fishing buddies in Tennessee. The "buddy" taking the photograph was Margaret Williams, who had been Raleigh's secretary for many years and, apparently, his girlfriend as well. Noma discovered the affair when Margaret's biological clock started running out and she had a showdown with Raleigh in front of everybody in the office. Sometimes Noma wishes she could have been there; sometimes it just makes her sad.

While Lynetta fiddles around with the box, Noma opens the glass doors of the corner cabinet and takes down the photo frame and slips out the picture.

"What's that, Mama?" Lynetta asks.

"Nothing," says Noma. "Just something I forgot to throw in the trash."

Noma goes to the kitchen, rips the picture into the tiniest shreds, and tosses the pieces among last night's spaghetti sauce. She looks at the glossy bits of paper getting smeared in red sauce and thinks about blood, about how in the movies they use ketchup to make bloody-looking scenes. She gets sick to her stomach when she watches violent scenes even though she knows it's ketchup. Life's like that, she thinks. It's hard to separate the fake and the real and sometimes one hurts just as bad as the other.

She takes a butter knife from the sink and stirs up the garbage so the little pieces of Raleigh and his fish disappear, and she wonders when his love for her turned from real to fake or if it was fake all along. The frightening thing is that she's not even sure of her own. Did she ever truly love Raleigh Malone? That's the sort of thing one ought to know without a doubt.

"Voila!" Lynetta folds open the box top as her mom walks back into the room.

"What is it?" Noma peers at the flat black object in the box. It's obviously some kind of machine.

"It's a laptop, Mama." Lynetta pulls out the machine and flips up the top. "Haven't you ever seen a computer?"

"I've seen them in the stores," Noma says. "But what are you doing with this here?"

"It's yours," says Lynetta. "You need to get online." She tells Noma how she can make friends, look up stuff, and connect with the rest of the world. "You can order your books," Lynetta says. "You can get cheap used books from Amazon."

Lately, Noma has had to be very selective with her book buying and mostly uses the library. She doesn't get much money from Raleigh and it's hard to pay the mortgage much less anything else.

"I can't afford a machine like this," Noma says. "Besides, I don't have a clue as to how to use it."

"It's a present," Lynetta says. "And I'll teach you how to use it."

Over the next few days, it's obvious that Lynetta has second thoughts about this more times than she can count. Noma is not a fast nor cooperative learner when it comes to mechanical things. She can't see herself "entering the twenty-first century" as Lynetta puts it. Noma had been happy once, or she thought she'd been happy once, or she thought that she should have been happy once. A lot of feelings get all tangled up together and concentrated on this new need to learn how to operate a machine in order to "connect" with the rest of the world. She'd always had Raleigh and the kids and didn't think she needed any other connections, though sometimes she'd wake up in the middle of the night feeling like something had gone missing. She could never identify it. Is it possible that it was something she'd never even had?

"Just think, Mama. You'll be able to talk to other people who like books," Lynetta said. "You'll find people who share your interests. You know you're not going to find that around here unless you stick to reading romance and detective stories, and I know you don't like that."

No, Noma did not like romance and detective stories. She did not like blood and gore or sex on paper. One romance story she'd started reading on the advice of her neighbor Millie Reese spent the first five pages describing a man's sexual apparatus. She quickly lost interest. And she wondered why all these church-going women had allowed themselves to get dragged down in that mush. A good love story was one thing, and the best she'd read didn't need to describe a man's apparatus. They respected the fact that intelligent readers could picture it in their own minds. If you've seen one, you've seen them all.

Once Noma struggled through the basics of operating a computer, she got on a roll. Things started coming easier. She bought five books from Amazon for less than two dollars each. She learned how to listen to music. Irish Celtic, Spanish guitar, Hungarian dances. Nothing was beyond her reach. She journeyed back to the sixties on YouTube, watching the old bands play again like it was yesterday. And the music brought with it a barrage of memories. Sometimes she could almost touch, again, in her heart the young girl who had loved the boy with long hair and bell-bottomed jeans. The one she'd been afraid to follow. He was stuck in her mind like corn in a chicken's craw.

Lynetta dropped by a couple of times a week to see how Noma was doing, to have coffee and chat, or to watch one of their favorite television programs. But Noma was always on the computer with Rosie the cat curled up on her lap. It would be entirely understandable if Lynetta had become irritated with her mother, but she didn't. She was all smiles and encouragement.

The others, however, were beside themselves. Noma was never available to make supper or babysit or run errands. Ginny, the oldest daughter, had two kids and another on the way. She had depended on Noma to make supper most nights after school. Instead, Noma made vegetable soup and sent it in plastic cartons—three times in one week! And she had forgotten to pick up Billy and Zelda's laundry, which she was accustomed to doing every week to wash with her own. Her son and his wife worked long hours at the insurance company. Noma felt guilty. She spent one whole day doing two weeks' worth of laundry with her laptop sitting on the washer. That day Zelda's favorite white silk blouse was shrunk to doll size.

❧

ON A FRIDAY NIGHT A few weeks after Noma got the computer, Lynetta calls to ask her to go to the movies. Lynetta's husband Paul has to work late and she wants to see this new movie that came out last fall and has finally made it to the theater in Carson. Everybody's talking about it, she says. Noma doesn't want to go. She's joined a book-blogging group that gets together every Friday night to discuss what they've read that week. Noma is amazed that with a few keystrokes she can talk to Miranda in California and Dolly in Oklahoma and a girl who goes by "Pink Mouse" in Australia. There are at least ten others, but these are the ones she likes the best.

"It's earlier in Oklahoma and California," Lynetta says, "and it's the middle of the day in Sydney. You can talk later."

Finally, Noma gives in to Lynetta. She sends emails. Regrets. She's going to the movies with her daughter. She'll be back by eleven o'clock, however, if they're still online.

The movie, *The Social Network*, changes Noma's life. She doesn't approve of the crazy goings-on in the movie, but the young man at the center of it all is as smart as a whip. Noma walks out of the theater into the cool night air, feeling as if she has turned a page from the prologue to the real story.

Back home, she walks in the door, flips on the lamp, and watches Lynetta's car lights head out of the lane and onto the highway. She hurries upstairs and turns on the laptop, waiting impatiently while the clicks and hums of the computer go through the various stages of booting up. Booting up! Noma even likes this new language she's learning.

She signs up for Facebook. Searches for Madison Nash. Surely he wouldn't go by Mingo at this age. There are twenty-five people with the name Madison Nash. She looks through the photographs. Nothing is familiar. Half the photos are of young people in their teens, twenties, thirties. Of course, that's how she remembers Mingo. But he's not in his teens now.

Noma scours the older faces. Would he already have gray hair? She doesn't have gray hair. He wouldn't be overweight. He was a skinny boy. Could he be the man in the nice white shirt? Probably not. The one carrying a surfboard? Maybe. But that pot belly and hairy chest? She didn't think so. She looked at the states when listed—Vermont, California, Colorado, Ohio. Mingo had been from Pennsylvania. She thought it unusual, even peculiar, that no two people with the name Madison Nash lived in the same state. She looked at the birthdates, but didn't find one for July third, Mingo's birthday. The dates either didn't match or were not listed. It was no use. Even if Mingo were among this bunch of men she could not identify him.

Several days pass and Noma vacillates between giving up on the search and obsessing about it. Finally, she has narrowed down the Madisons to three possibilities. Two have pictures taken at a distance so it's impossible to see the details of either man's face. If only the pictures showed the eyes. Those eyes! They were burned into her memory. One man didn't have a picture, but the information about his musical interests showed that he liked all the same bands her Mingo had liked.

Noma is poring over the computer screen in the wee morning hours, thinking about composing a message to send each man. She does not want to offend the man or his family. She wonders how other people handle this sort of thing. Surely others have tracked down old friends and family. What on earth could be wrong with that? But is there some sort of protocol?

Noma walked the floor, made herb tea, lit a candle, and set it on the windowsill. She listened to flamenco music, her latest passion. What was she doing? What if these men had wives who read their Facebook messages? What if one of them was a murderer? What if he tracked her down?

She decided against sending any messages to anyone. It had been a crazy idea from the start.

At three a.m., the telephone rings.

"Yes?" Noma whispers as if she might awaken someone in the empty house. "Mama, what on earth are you doing up this late?" Lynetta's voice is full of concern on the other end.

"How'd you know I was up? You got me out of bed." Noma is not used to lying.

"We just drove by your house and saw the lights on," Lynetta says. "We went to the late show in Carson."

"Oh, I'm sorry," Noma says. "Was it a good movie?"

"*The Social Network*," Lynetta says. "I wanted Paul to see it."

"Good," Noma says. She's still walking the floor, carrying the phone, and eyeing the computer screen.

"So?" Lynetta says. "What are you doing up this late? Are you feeling bad?"

"Oh no," says Noma. "I'm getting ready to go to bed now."

"But…"

"Good night now," says Noma. She hangs up.

Noma goes into the bathroom and washes her face, applies cream, spreads double cream into the wrinkles around her eyes. She wonders if Margaret Williams has wrinkles that you can see up close. Margaret is just thirty-eight. She's young enough to have Raleigh a whole new family. That's the sad fact that women have to face, she thinks. A man never gets too old to have a family. Well, maybe some do, but not Raleigh. She imagines him being as spry as he's ever been.

When she comes out of the bathroom, Noma turns off the lights. The last thing she wants is another one of her kids to drive by and get worried and come barreling down the lane. She sits back down at the computer, touches a key, and it comes to life, the screen glowing in the dark like something from outer space.

My name is Noma… she begins. She tells only a little about herself, figuring her name alone will ring a bell—or it won't. She describes Mingo. She mentions Neil Armstrong taking his giant leap for mankind. She cuts and pastes and clicks on the "message" button three different times. It is four a.m. when Noma turns off the computer and crawls into bed. She cannot recall another time when she was so bold, when she was able to muster up this much courage. She's still shaking inside when she finally falls asleep.

During the next few days she gets messages from the two men with pictures saying they have no memory of her and they've never been called Mingo. One of them, from Charlotte, North Carolina, tells her he has a family and is happily married and doesn't want to "friend" her. Well. What's that all about? She didn't ask to be friends. The third one, the one with no picture, doesn't even write back. Not a word.

The days fly by even as they get longer. Sunrise melts into sunset. Noma chats with her book friends on Fridays, does the laundry for Billy and Zelda, and offers to come by after school on various days to make supper at Ginny's house. She leaves the computer off until night time. She adds new friends to Facebook, mostly now friends of other friends. Some people she does not even know, like the woman in China who is over there teaching English and feeling lonely.

Laura Wilson, the San Diego woman in China, asks Noma about Sweetwater. At first Noma says there's not much to tell, but then she writes about the dogwood and redbud blooming in the mountains, the day she spotted a goldfinch in the snowball bush, the first butterflies of the season. Laura Wilson likes hearing about Sweetwater and Noma likes hearing about China. She cannot imagine life again without her "connections." With every new picture Laura posts on her Facebook page, Noma feels like she's right there with her, walking along the Great Wall or the streets of Beijing or sitting in a McDonald's where everyone else is Chinese. The neighborhood kids gather at this McDonald's to do their homework every day. It's like daycare over there, Laura says. Noma laughs. Noma laughs a lot these days. She remembers that Raleigh never wanted to go anywhere except fishing and never had much of a sense of humor. He rarely laughed in their house. Could Raleigh have been unhappy all along—like she was? There, it was out. Unhappiness. She'd never attached that word to their life together, but now it seems like the one thing they'd had in common.

Three weeks to the day after Noma sent her messages to the men named Madison Nash, she opens Facebook one evening and sees that she has a message. It's from the man without a picture.

Dearest Noma. That's how it starts! Noma cannot recall ever having been called "dearest" by anyone. What a nice gentleman, she thinks. Very polite. The message goes on to say that this Madison Nash has been away for several weeks in a place where he did not have access to the Internet. Noma cannot imagine such a place in this day and time. If Sweetwater, Kentucky, has the Internet, even WiFi, the whole world must have it.

She reads on. He does not tell about the place with no Internet or say what he was doing there, but he does mention that he would like to tell her about his experience in person. Noma feels the blood drain from her face, her arms go limp at the keyboard. What if this man is a criminal? What if he's just trying to arrange a meeting? How many times has she heard or read about those warnings? How foolish of her, a mature woman, getting caught up in this craziness like a young kid.

She scrolls down the message, afraid of what she might find. Then it leaps out to her—a sentence about the blue skirt and yellow sweater she wore on their first date, how her father had told him politely that he needed to cut his hair because no one could see his eyes. *But* you *saw my eyes*, he wrote. *You called them gemstones.*

"Yes, yes I did." Noma says this out loud as if the man is right there in the room. At the same time she feels her face flush with embarrassment. Gemstones. Only an eighteen-year-old would say something like that or perhaps the heroine of one of Millie Reese's romance stories.

She takes a deep breath, like filling up her lungs will make her insides settle down, but no amount of breathing makes any difference whatsoever.

Noma gets up, walks into the bathroom, looks out the window, and sees a bunch of robins pecking at the mulch in the garden. She needs to get her planting done. The sun crossed the equator weeks ago. The tomato plants ought to be in the ground. The peppers…and lettuce…and spring onions. Everything will be late. Take hold of reality, Noma says to herself. This is real. This is my life. I am not a teenager anymore.

She was eighteen years old when Mingo came to Sweetwater on a volunteer summer program from a northern university. He ended up transferring to the local college in nearby Jellico Springs and stayed two years. Two years in a teenaged life is nothing, not enough to make a difference. That's what they all said back then. *You'll forget about him in no time. He's a hippie; he'll never amount to anything. You take off with him and he'll leave you alone in some foreign place.* Mingo had his heart set on India, of all places. They had leprosy in India! What was she thinking?

A year later she had married Raleigh. She quit school because Raleigh didn't want a college wife. He loved her so much, he said, that he didn't want to think about her being around those fast-talking, northern college boys who would promise her the world just to take her away from Sweetwater. Raleigh worked for his daddy at the sawmill. Some day he would be taking over and she would never need to work, he said. It was a dream-come-true life for any girl in her right mind, but it broke Noma's heart. Raleigh had made all the choices along the way.

Noma's nerves settled a bit as she followed her usual routine. She walked around the house, looking out the windows. She went to the kitchen and brewed a cup of tea. She lit a jasmine-scented candle and placed it on the table, then sat back down at the computer.

Madison Nash told about his travels. He'd seen the world. Gone to India, China, Russia, Europe. Some work. Some play. That's how he put it.

I never stopped loving you.

The words danced in front of her eyes as if they had taken on a life of their own. In what had to be the next breath he'd written that he'd been married twice and had three kids. Ha! Noma laughed to herself. He was just a man of fancy words, after all. Obviously, he had not spent all those years pining away for her. Still…

She read on. He'd been divorced for five years, he said. His kids were out of college and on their own. Next month he was headed back to a place he loved in the mountains of Mexico to teach English at a university. He described a town draped in bougainvillea and blue skies with rainbow-colored houses and dazzling light. The air was filled with the sound of church bells and music and laughter, and the markets brimmed with exotic fruits and flowers. It was an ancient town, he said, with cobblestone streets four hundred years old. But it was also a place that overflowed with new life, where it was possible to be anyone you wanted to be.

Come with me.

Noma knocked over her tea cup. The hot tea was burning a streak down her leg, but she jumped up quickly and ran for paper towels to mop it up before it reached the computer. What if it seeped into the new laptop and she lost this message? She moved the computer to a chair and dried up every speck of moisture, rubbing the desk like she was removing the varnish. When she was done, she flopped down in a chair and laughed until she cried.

Come with me.

The words stared at her like an unblinking neon sign. They danced in her mind, coursed through her veins, and stuck in her heart. She could almost hear his voice. Noma's life paraded across her mind's eye, a life filled with freedom from choice, with someone else making the decisions. Funny thing, she thought, when you don't do the choosing, you don't have to take the responsibility or the blame. Noma had spent a relatively blameless life. She was respected by everyone and had enjoyed the support of the whole town when Raleigh left her for his floozie. They'd had to go all the way up to Louisville to get married because no preacher in Sweetwater would marry the two of them.

How could a person like Noma give up this kind of status? It was all she had left. A woman with such a sterling reputation could not allow herself to go love crazy in her senior years and mess up the image she'd sacrificed so much to sustain.

Tears ran down Noma's cheeks when she sat back down in front of the computer. She would have to answer, to write one last message. She looked away from the screen, ignoring those last three words. It was simply too late for a place that overflowed with new life, where it was possible to be anyone you wanted to be.

The keyboard felt warm to her touch. For some odd reason it reminded her of the white cat Rosie that had always curled up on her lap when she watched the news with Raleigh on winter nights. It struck her that Rosie had for years generated the only warmth in that room.

She typed OK and hit "reply."

Diana Friedman

Disintegration

DIANA FRIEDMAN'S fiction and essays have appeared in many journals and magazines, including *Newsweek*, the *Baltimore Sun*, *Flyway: Journal of Writing and Environment*, the *Huffington Post*, *Sport Literate*, *Bethesda Magazine*, and *Whole Earth Review*. Her work has received multiple awards, including the Alexander Patterson Cappon Fiction Prize, and has been shortlisted by *Glimmer Train*, *Hunger Mountain*, and Red Hen Press. This chapter is excerpted from her novel-in-progress, "All That You Can Leave Behind," a contemporary story of desire, dislocation, and U2 infatuation. Friedman lives in Maryland with her family. Her work is available online at www.dianafriedmanwriter.com.

S outhbound 270 from Germantown is still heavy, and toward the lane divide, the crash is to the far left. Yet Jake continues driving alarmingly fast, somehow oblivious when a truck sideswipes them, causing the car to swerve onto the shoulder, tip onto two wheels, and then pitch onto its side, smashing the door inward and trapping Jonah in the backseat. Jeannie climbs out her window, waving frantically for help as smoke pours from the hood. This must be Washington, D.C., because no one will pull over to help and she cannot get cell coverage, her voice hollow as she descends into hysteria until, pushed by the shrillness of her own voice, she is thrust into the morning.

Jeannie shuts off the clock radio, the remnants of the traffic report still mingling with the dream. It's been like this nonstop the last few weeks, the intensity of her dreams increasing exponentially, sleep scarcer than ever. On top of that, the second short story has taken on a life of its own, waking her up at all hours with full-steam dialogue. Of course, she's not helping matters by staying up past midnight to answer its call, nor does the fact that a few days ago, a third one hatched, this trio the beginning of something good, something cohesive—a collection of stories or, dare she even think it, the middle chapters of a novel.

In the early morning silence, torrents of embryonic phrases filter through her semi-consciousness as she reaches for her notebook. It's only five minutes, but five minutes it is, because aside from locking herself in the bathroom and the fifteen-minute Metro commute, there is no other time to steal, except at night, but that sleep deficit is growing dangerous. Last Wednesday, at Shoppers Food Warehouse, she'd almost hit a woman in the parking lot. It was dark, raining hard, and she had been driving Jake's car, bigger and slower than hers, so it wasn't totally due to exhaustion. Then again, she'd been driving his car because, two days earlier, she'd gotten halfway to CVS not realizing she'd left the emergency brake on, until she pressed hard to slow the car and it didn't respond. She'd pulled over, her hands trembling around the wheel. The Honda now awaits a new brake drum to the tune of three hundred dollars. Jake would be considerably irked if he knew why.

There is one other matter too, small but not insignificant, contributing to the distractibility. Five days after she sent the story, Killian emailed to say he had received it and looked forward to reading it. It's been over a month, though, and nothing. How long does it take to read a short story?

She uncaps the pen, but no more than three lines have made it to the paper when Megan appears at her bedside, as if she has beamed directly into the room.

"Mom! What time is it?" Her eyebrows press together so hard they almost meet at the top of her nose.

"Seven fifteen. We're fine."

"But Jonah's not up. And you haven't made my lunch. What are you still doing in bed?"

Jeannie drops the notebook on the night table, hoping to pick it up as soon as Megan is out of sight, but downstairs, Megan shadows her every move. Jeannie smears peanut butter onto the bread and tops the sandwiches with jam, wedging them into Baggies as Megan sighs loudly.

"Mom. You forgot to cut off the crusts."

Jeannie slices off the edges and throws the sandwiches into the lunch boxes.

"Mom." Megan jerks her hand forward. "You put mine in Jonah's lunchbox and his in mine. And where's Jonah? We're going to be late."

Upstairs, Jeannie finds him sitting calmly in his Superman underwear, maneuvering a stack of Legos between his legs.

"Why aren't you dressed? It's seven thirty."

He clicks a dark blue triangle onto the top of his castle. "You didn't give me my third warning."

"This is it. Put your clothes on."

But when he appears in the dining room in an orange monkey shirt and Nike gym shorts, Jeannie slaps her cheeks. "No, no, no. It's March. Pants. Long-sleeve shirt."

"Mom. It's 7:43." Megan rises into the first octave of despair while Jonah chews slowly, spooning his Cheerios around the bowl. They are only five minutes late out the door, but as soon as they reach the path along the creek, Megan sprints ahead.

"Mom. Do you know who the world's third richest man is?" Jonah lumbers behind, Megan already out of sight.

"Mom. Do you?"

"Do I what?"

"Do you know who the world's third richest man is?"

"No."

As they turn the corner, Megan comes back into view.

"Carlos Slim Helu. He has thirty billion dollars. Do you know how he made his money?"

"No."

Megan stops suddenly, spinning around. "Mom, I forgot to tell you. Yesterday in art class we started a project using animal designs from Indonesia. Isn't that cool?'

Jonah tugs on Jeannie's arm. "She interrupted me. I was talking."

Megan glares at him. "That's because you never shut up."

"Mom. She just told me to shut up."

"No, I didn't. I said you never shut up. No one wants to listen."

"Mom, she just told me to shut up again."

Jeannie flattens her hands over her ears. Jonah is indeed a walking Wikipedia, but Megan is no verbal small fry either. Last week, the two of them launched into physical combat over who got to walk on Jeannie's right side. She pulled them apart and explained she had two hands, plenty to go around. That battle now exhausted, they've moved into new squabbling territory—verbal space.

When they reach the school, she is more than happy to deposit them both, working off the leftover tension with a quick run before meeting Lila at Kerry's Kitchen. The tables are packed so closely, the couple next to her can probably hear her breathing. Lila arrives a few minutes later, and when she takes off her coat, Jeannie can't stop grinning.

"Have people started patting your stomach without asking?"

Lila grabs the menu. "Only Dave. But he's allowed."

"Can I?"

"Sure, but let's order first. I'm famished." Lila has clearly completed her first trimester, because the luster has returned to her face, and when the food arrives, she digs into her fish as if she's starved herself for weeks and suddenly rediscovered food.

"I can't believe how good everything tastes. I couldn't eat for months, now I can't stop."

Jeannie bites into the salmon, surprised to find it a little dry. Even Lila's trout looks cakey, but she seems unbothered by it.

"Are you back to the painting?"

Lila nods. "With acrylics. And I got a call from Mountain West. The pieces sold out before the show even opened. When Sam found out, he FedExed me the contract."

"So you signed?"

"I did. They're excellent with PR. That's the main thing. I know it's a sellout, but I've had enough of marketing myself. It truly is a pain in the ass."

"That's fantastic about the sale. Which ones were they?"

"I don't think you've seen them, a triptych of garden settings, but abstract. You know," adds Lila, her mouth full again, "I had this revelation the other day, after I heard the pieces sold. It's not that I don't think I'm good, but to create something that has intimate meaning to me— how can it say so much to someone else that they're willing to pay that kind of money for it? It's not like literature where there's an actual story you can follow, or music, where your ears literally tell you something. Anyway, with the triptych, I think I was ovulating when I did it, I was worried with the pregnancy, but my hormones are so fucking out of whack, it's fine. Oh, and I got a call from the *Washingtonian*. They want to profile me."

"Jesus, Lila. And you're still having lunch with me."

She smiles. "If I like the writer, should I pass your name along?"

"Thanks, but I don't have time to be messing around with anything freelance."

"Speaking of which, did you ever post up the rejection letters, do an installation piece?"

"No. But I pulled an old story and finished it. And I've got two more percolating."

"I knew it." Lila shakes her finger at Jeannie. "Did you submit it?"

"Not yet. I gave it to someone to look at first."

"Oh," says Lila, mopping up her sauce with a piece of bread. "Anyone I know?"

"Not really. That guy."

Lila frowns. "Who?"

"You know, the guy in Ireland, the one who sent me his story."

Lila leans back, rubbing her stomach. "I'm always starved, but then I feel like I've eaten too much. Why did you give it to him?"

"I don't know. He sent me his."

"You guys are still emailing?"

"A little. He's interesting. Different."

"Just so long as he doesn't ask for a picture," says Lila, laughing.

Jeannie rolls her eyes. "Actually, he did."

Lila laughs again. "Please tell me you didn't send one."

Jeannie picks at a loose thread hanging from her sleeve, fiddling with it until it breaks loose. "Well, we had this email exchange about it, and it did seem kind of unfair, since I'd seen his."

"That's hardly the same thing." Lila squints across the table. "He had his on his website. Anyway, I assume he knows you're married, so it doesn't even matter."

"You know," responds Jeannie, "that hasn't even come up. It's just two people communicating about writing."

Lila smirks. "Then what does he need a picture for?"

"Trust me, Lila, it's not like that. Besides, I sent it almost a month ago with the story and I haven't heard a peep. I'm pretty sure he's not jerking off over it."

Lila signals the waiter for water, grinning widely now. "Well, here I thought you'd finished with Bono, but all you've done is trade in your obsession with one unattainable Irish guy for another."

"Are you kidding? Who says I want to attain him?"

"Do you?"

Jeannie sips her wine slowly. How can she possibly answer that? He is sort of cute, in that one picture anyway, but she's never smelled him, never stood next to him, never heard his voice. She cannot begin to imagine how he might feel to her touch.

"Honestly, Jeannie, what does he need a picture for? Did you read Dave's series? After the pictures, it's a short hop from emailing to efucking."

"Jesus, Lila, we've never even talked."

"OK. But keep in mind, you are married. To one of the nicest men on the face of the planet."

"Easy for you to say. We've barely spoken the last three weeks and the only thing we can agree on is a trip to Spain—he finally caved on that." She shoves her plate to the middle of the table. "I don't mean to be harping on this, but I feel like I've barely seen him in months. And the lack of sex? I am talking complete climate change—out of nowhere. If a woman did that, don't think for a second the husband wouldn't be complaining or running out to find someone else." She leans back, drumming her fingers on the table. "I know, it seems completely impossible, but I don't know what to think."

Lila nods. "It doesn't sound like Jake. Have you found any odd credit card receipts, anything like that?"

"No, but he's smart enough, he'd use cash."

"True. But I don't see it. Not Jake."

"Can men even physically go that long? Don't they have that weird biology where they have to discharge it every so often?"

"Have you checked for a man stash, you know, Victoria's Secret catalogues, lubricants, a pile of magazines?"

Jeannie drops her head in her hands. "No. And I don't want to."

Lila grins. "Maybe our next outing should be a field trip to Sugar's Toy Shop in Baltimore."

Jeannie rolls her eyes. "For me or for him?"

"Look," says Lila, her expression serious now. "I know you're worried about Jake. But it's better to work that out than be messing around under the guise of an artistic friendship. That's just asking for trouble."

Heading home on the Metro, Jeannie does not pull out her story; her eyes instead are glued to the carpet. Lila may be her best friend, but how can someone who has always had her pick of men—the sexy English painter they met in London, her professor at Pratt, the lead singer from Damascus Blast, the hottest indie band in Baltimore, then finally settling down with the love of her life—even begin to understand how this works? Has Lila forgotten about that awful night in Amsterdam when they went to the Paradiso Club, both of them stoned out of their minds on hash cakes? Lila sought out the lead guitarist of one of the bands and they'd all gone drinking, none of the musicians paying attention to Jeannie until everyone paired off and she wound up with the drummer, ugly as a skunk. He pushed his tongue so hard into her ear, it sounded like a bomb. She had not wanted to go to bed with him, but they'd all gone back to the houseboat and it had been expected, so she did it, once again in Lila's shadow, sleeping with unappealing men to slake her hunger for affection. No, when you've lived as Lila has, men dripping with desire and falling at your feet, this is not something you understand.

And honestly, this time, there was nothing to get; the flirtation, if it could be called that, was mild, the whole interaction nothing more than a simple engagement with someone who shared a passion. How is that asking for trouble? He lives three thousand miles away; she's never met him and, from the looks of it when she opens her email later that afternoon and sees no response, knows she never will.

Why the complete silence? Maybe the story was awful and he was so embarrassed he couldn't bring himself to email her. Jeannie reaches for the story, and fingers through the pages. No. She's written enough over the years to know when something's good. The answer is right in front of her, and completely disheartening even if not at all surprising. In college she'd dated a nice guy, Brad, who was not all that attractive—a large nose and fish eyes—but he was quite funny, even a bit charming. Jeannie had appreciated his patience, assuming he wanted to be sure before taking things to the next level. The day after they started fooling around, he broke it off, saying he'd been hoping for a skinny girlfriend on his next round, the skin lifting off her arms at the memory of that one.

OK, fine, she found Killian attractive, yes, but where was the crime in that? Nowhere, really, just in her own stupidity. As usual, Lila is absolutely right. He got what he wanted for his story and the rest was some stupid flirtation for him, his primitive male mind imagining her one way. He didn't even ask for a picture, that last email nothing more than a silly joke, and then she sent three. Probably scared him all the way to Slovenia.

So what might he have done with the photos? Maybe he had a betting pool with his groovy tattooed record store coworkers and he, having imagined her a Dallas cheerleader, lost, and then, embarrassed, tossed the whole package.

Really, sometimes her own foolishness amazes her, as if nothing is clear until after the fact. The following Monday morning is no exception when she is thrust awake by a sharp buzzing, smack in the middle of a dream that is both terrifying and glorious, as if something hard has been cracked open from deep inside. But when she sits up, she can't figure out where the sound is coming from. It's not the alarm, the radio, the phone, and not until she jumps out of bed does she realize it's Jake's cell. By the time she finds it, buried under some papers on his night table, the caller has hung up. It's only six forty-five, but Jake's car is already gone, and now, slightly more awake, she remembers him saying something about an early meeting. She flips the phone open, but no name is attached to the number.

With spring a few weeks off, the light filters softly into the room, and she reaches for her pen; just a few seconds to jot down the dream. When she checks the time a few minutes later, though, it's seven twenty! Megan will be apoplectic.

Which she is. Today there will be no shower; her boss, Allen, is at an all-day conference and who cares if she stinks on the Metro? But when she enters the alcove to leave her notes by the computer, a connector erupts between the last two stories. This is how she's going to build them into a novel. Right there. Jeannie grabs a pen. Three minutes, that's all she needs.

Except now Megan is screaming at Jonah so loudly that Jeannie returns to the hallway to investigate, dodging as Sir Stripes, a little brown tiger, comes flying out of Megan's room straight at Jonah.

"What's going on?"

"Jonah ate my science project."

"What?"

"Mom. It's not funny."

"I know, honey. I'm sorry." But the image of Jonah chewing on Megan's papers like a goat is indeed humorous and Jeannie has to force her lips out of a smile.

"I got Mike and Ikes and Fruit Roll-Ups to build a cell and I needed them for the Golgi bodies and the mitochondria and he ate a Fruit Roll-Up."

"Daddy said I could have one."

"Aren't there ten in a pack?"

"Yes, but I need all of them."

"How can you need so many? How many cells are you making?"

"He shouldn't have eaten it. It was mine."

"Daddy said I could," repeats Jonah.

"You're such a liar."

"Stop," says Jeannie. "I want you both dressed in five minutes, and Megan, you can get your own breakfast this morning."

She retreats into her bedroom, trying to recall the connector. But Jonah stands just outside Megan's doorway taunting her. Jeannie drags him across the hall and deposits him in his room.

"Do not move from there until you are dressed and ready to come downstairs."

In the kitchen, she fixes the lunches quickly, then reaches again for her pen just as the screaming resumes, this time both of them. What could Jonah have possibly done now? One more sentence and then she'll go.

Jeannie has just lowered the pen when she hears a screechy terror scream from upstairs that sends her stomach straight into her throat. She's had nightmares about this, forced herself to close her mind to the possibility of it, but now that she's actually hearing the sound and suspects what it is before she turns the corner, it still seems impossible. But there it is: Jonah, flying off the top step, head first. His body is angled as if entering a back dive, but there is no water to cushion his fragile body below, just hard, hard wood, his head slamming into the banister, the force sending him ricocheting like a rag doll across the stairway, where he lands straight on his neck, and then rolls into a series of backward somersaults. He doesn't even know how to do a backward somersault; surely his neck has broken, because no one can survive a flip at that angle, and indeed, when he lands at the bottom of the steps, it is into a crumpled heap, his body motionless. Megan stands at the top of the stairs, mouth frozen open, hands still outstretched from where she pushed him out of her room and he tripped over her backpack in the hallway.

That's it. Five seconds, a lifetime erased. Game over.

Jeannie crumples to her knees and pulls him onto her lap. "Jonah. Jonah. Are you OK? Jonah!"

He remains absolutely still, his eyes frozen open, no air moving in or out of his chest.

"Megan," she yells. "Bring me the phone. Now."

Megan screams as she stumbles down the stairs, heading straight for Jeannie. She squeezes Jonah to her chest, desperately trying to recall CPR, but what if he's punctured a lung? Would that make it worse? She pushes on his chest anyway, trying to will the air back into his lungs, but if he has broken his neck then it's all futile, his respiratory system's completely down. She hugs him to her chest, praying now, for lack of any other recourse. Miraculously then, Megan somehow hands her the phone, and Jeannie punches in 911.

As soon as she connects, the dispatcher says, "I'm sorry, ma'am, I can't hear you."

"Megan, please," cries Jeannie. "I need you to be quiet."

Megan's mouth is closed, though, just little sobs escaping, and it is, thank God of all Gods, Jonah screeching. You need air to scream, so he must be breathing. And his eyes are flickering around the room now too, so he is conscious. But his screech is like a banshee's, the pitch higher than anything she's ever heard from either of her children in their combined sixteen years of existence. And after hanging up, she sees why: a white and pointy shard pushes through the skin midway down his left arm.

Jonah's breaths are uneven between his shrieks, but the air is going in and out without complications, it seems, and then, he sits up, neck intact, head straight, legs moving, no blood anywhere. Jeannie draws in what must be her first breath in minutes now, while Megan, panting hard, tries to burrow into the other side of her lap.

"Mommy, I can't breathe. Mommy, I think I'm going to die."

"You're OK honey, count to ten."

"Mommy, did I kill him? Oh my God."

"No, honey, Jonah's OK, he's going to be OK."

Megan collapses into her shoulder, as with one finger Jeannie manages to call her neighbor Peggy, who arrives two minutes later and helps Megan calm herself; by the time the paramedics arrive, the only noises filling the room are Jonah's intermittent high-pitched shrieks.

"All right, what do we have here?" says the head paramedic, a burly Hispanic man with a full head of dark hair and neatly clipped goatee. He motions for his companions to get the stretcher as he sets a large black box on the floor and then kneels down next to Jonah. "What happened?"

"He fell down the stairs."

The man looks up to the second floor. "That's quite a tumble." He reaches gently for Jonah's arm. "All right, champ, I know this is going to hurt, but can you wiggle your fingers for me? Yeah, that's good, now let me see you do that on your other hand, the left one, yeah, just like that, great. Here, can you tell what finger I'm squeezing?"

He stands as the other two men deposit the stretcher. "Let's get the arm first and then we'll load him up."

He turns to Jeannie. "Did he hit his head?"

She nods.

"Lose consciousness?"

"I don't know. I don't think so."

"Hey, champ. Do you know where you are?"

Jonah, suddenly aware he is surrounded by three strange men, starts wailing loudly again, and when they gently lift his arm to immobilize it with a makeshift splint, he lets out another shriek, sending Jeannie's heart straight back up her throat. He is dressed only in his T-shirt and underwear and she covers the bottom half of his body protectively.

"Megan, please go get his socks and pants."

But Megan remains paralyzed by the couch. Peggy nods toward the stairs. "Which room?"

In the ambulance, Jeannie dials Jake's number as one of the other medics climbs in across from her and radios to the hospital. "I've got a compound fracture, possible radius ulna with displacement, good distal pulse and grip, after a fall down fifteen steps. Patient is alert and oriented times three, acting age appropriate, we're about fifteen minutes out, would like orders for morphine, patient's approximately..." He lifts the blanket. "Twenty kilos."

Jeannie shuts the phone. "Morphine? You're giving him morphine?"

"What's morphine? Is it going to hurt me? I don't want morphine." Jonah's lower lip quivers furiously.

"OK, Jonah," says the paramedic, squeezing his good arm gently. "I have to put this in, you're gonna feel a little pinch, so just hang on."

"Do I get a say in this? Do you have to give him morphine? He's only six."

"It's just a little, until they can set that bone properly and talk to you about other options for pain management." As the man slips the needle into Jonah's arm, he screeches again, and Jeannie grabs his hand.

"Here, honey, squeeze me hard."

"Ow, ow, ow, Mommy, ow that really hurts." Jonah's hair is matted to his forehead as if he has been stranded in a downpour for hours.

"I know that didn't feel good," says the medic, "but very shortly you're both going to thank me."

Jeannie squeezes his hand hard as she lowers her head, unable to look at the fat needle penetrating Jonah's tiny arm.

But the medic is right; less than a minute later, Jonah's eyes roll back up into his head, and then, after surveying all of the equipment around him, he rolls his head away from Jeannie toward to the man and says, "You know, I didn't fall. I really didn't." His words emerge slurred, as if he's half asleep.

"No?" says the man, winking. "How'd you wind up like this, then? Did you jump?"

"She pushed me."

The man closes the medical box slowly. "You were pushed?"

"Yeah, I didn't fall, her, my, I ate her science project even though my dad said I could, it was a Fruit Roll-Up, so she pushed me."

The medic glances at Jeannie briefly, and then averts his eyes, reaching for the chart.

"His sister. They were fighting and she pushed him into the hallway and he tripped."

He nods, making a few notes in the chart just as they reach the emergency turn-about, where the hospital staff pull Jonah onto a gurney and straight into the ER.

"We're going to need a CT scan and an X-ray. Possible concussion, he looks pretty confused to me," says the attending doctor, a lightly built man who seems barely old enough to shave.

"He's doped up on morphine, for God's sake," says Jeannie.

"Oh." The doctor opens the chart. "We will need to get that arm set ASAP. Don't want it going septic. When did he eat last?"

"I'm not sure," says Jeannie. "Jonah, did you have breakfast?"

"I ate Megan's science project."

"No, I mean this morning."

"I ate her science project and that's why she pushed me. But Dad said I could. Mom, am I going to be late to school?"

Jeannie turns to the doctor. "I don't know, I don't think he had breakfast, but he may have had some candy."

"OK, let's start with the pictures." Jeannie follows alongside as they wheel him to X-ray. As she waits outside, another doctor—the surgeon—introduces himself. His voice is cold and curt, but his hands are firm and steady, and unlike the youthful residents circling the hallways, his temples are gray, a reassuring sign.

"So, we don't know if he's eaten?" He gives her a reproachful look.

Jeannie shakes her head. She must be the only mother in the world who doesn't keep track of every morsel of food going into her children's mouths.

"I'd like to give him anesthesia, but I can't take a chance if he's got anything in his stomach. We'll give him a block and up the morphine. I'll be back as soon as we have the pictures."

Jeannie tries Jake again on his cell, and then his direct line, but his work voicemail seems to be down, redirecting her to another box, and just as they wheel Jonah from the X-ray room back into the hallway, another man, plump and short, taps Jeannie on the shoulder.

"Sorry to bother you. I'm the social worker. I just need to ask you a few things. Can you tell me what happened?"

"He fell."

The man scans the chart over the top of his glasses. "It says he was pushed."

Jeannie feels her hand clench around the cell phone in her pocket. "He and his sister had a fight—he was taunting her from the hallway because her door was off its hinges. It was a complete accident. She pushed him out of her room and he tripped over her backpack and fell down the stairs."

"Why was her door off the hinges?"

"Because she slams it too much."

"Do they fight a lot?"

"Yes."

"Have they ever hurt each other before?"

"No."

"Actually, Mom." Jonah's eyes circle the room slowly. "She does kick me a lot when you're not looking, and one time she hit me really hard on the back."

The social worker scribbles a note. "Has he ever been seriously injured before?"

"No."

"Actually, Mom, one time I got hit by a soccer ball and my nose bled. And another time I slammed my hand in the car door."

"Where were you when it happened?"

"Home."

"Did you see it?"

"No, I was in the kitchen. Making breakfast."

"And what about the father, where is he?"

"I have no idea. At work, probably doing the same thing as you, because he's not picking up his cell phone and the county voicemail seems to be down."

"He works for the county?"

"For the schools, he's a school counselor and I don't know, maybe he's in a meeting today, I don't know, I was asleep when he left."

"So you were asleep when this happened?"

Just then, her cell buzzes. Finally. That must be Jake. Relieved for the opportunity to excuse herself, Jeannie flips it open. But it's Peggy, inquiring about Jonah and calling to let her know that when she dropped Megan at school the tears were again flowing. As soon as Jonah's eyes close, Jeannie calls the school. Sure enough, Megan is in the front office, crying that she wants to come home.

"I know honey, I'll be there as soon as I can. I can't come now. I'm at the hospital."

"Mommy, is Jonah going to die?"

"No, sweetie, he's going to be fine."

Megan sniffles loudly into the phone. "Mommy, why can't Daddy pick me up?"

"I'm trying to find him, OK?" She calls Jake, but again, no answer, and this time she is blocked from his voicemail entirely. She tries Lila, too, and then hangs up, remembering she and Dave are in West Virginia for a long weekend.

The surgery seems to drag on for hours, but at least the interrogations have ceased, and while Jonah is having his arm set in the cast, she calls Jake again. Not until they're heading home in the taxi, Jonah heavily sedated beside her, does she remember that Jake's cell is at home. She calls his school directly, but the secretary doesn't know where he is either, and puts Jeannie through to his voicemail, which again bounces her into another message box.

At home, Jonah falls into a profound sleep in his bed, and Jeannie jumps in the car and races the ten blocks to get Megan. She is uncharacteristically silent and as they open the door, she says, in a very small voice: "Mommy, are you going to punish me?"

"Megan, honey. No." Jeannie pulls her onto her lap, folding her arms around her tightly.

"Mommy." Megan rubs her eyes. "Did Jonah almost die? Could he have died? Because I really don't want him to die."

"I know, sweetie. And no, he didn't almost die. Accidents happen. And we were all lucky today it wasn't worse. But the stairs are dangerous. You two need to be more careful. OK?"

Megan nods as Jake pushes open the front door. His shoulders are already raised in a query, the annoyance in his voice impossible to miss as he drops his briefcase by the front door.

"Why didn't you call me? I went all the way to the school and they told me you'd picked them up."

"Where were you? I've been trying to find you all day." Jeannie does not intend to fire this as an accusation, but after the weight of the day, it is impossible to release gently.

"I had to go to court," says Jake, his tone shifting into defensive mode. "The social worker was out and the assistant principal asked me to handle a case last minute. It took all day, I had to file a petition for educational neglect, the kid is out of control, the mother..."

Jake continues speaking, but his words float like air bubbles above his head, no substance to them at all. Their child came within millimeters of dying and Jake is going on about the tribulations of some other kid. And yet, in this bizarre universe she seems to have rocketed into, layered on top of all of the stress of the day is the undeniable fact of how handsome he looks today, his hair curled roughly around his face, his skin set off nicely against a crisp white Oxford shirt she's never seen before.

Jeannie looks up. "Is that why you left early? To go to court?"

"No, I just told you, they asked me to go last minute. This morning I had to meet a parent before school—"

Jeannie interrupts. "That's why no one could find you."

He sits down across from her, the awareness slowly seeping in that something is off kilter. "Everyone OK?"

Megan buries her head against Jeannie's shoulder, sniffling again.

Jake glances around the room, his voice deepening with worry. "Where's Jonah?"

"Upstairs. Sleeping."

"Is he all right?"

Megan wipes her nose, and shuffles off to the kitchen.

"More or less." Jeannie presses her fingers into her cheekbones, hoping to staunch the imminent flood, at least momentarily.

"What do you mean? What's wrong?"

She shakes her head, closing her eyes. If she looks at Jake now, she really will lose it.

"Megan pushed him and he tripped over her backpack and fell down the stairs. His head hit the banister, he had the wind knocked out of him, almost broke his neck. They don't think he has a concussion but we have to check on him every four hours for the next two days, and he did break his arm—his bone pushed through his skin, so we spent the day at Children's Hospital where they doped him up on morphine, and then took him into a three-hour surgery for a radius ulna fracture. They're worried it might get infected so he's on a heavy dose of antibiotics. He's also still got morphine in his system, our six-year-old, doped up on morphine."

"Jesus." Jake blinks rapidly. "Should I check on him?"

"I just did."

"Unreal. The one day I was in court, I never go to court. And there's no way to reach me there. On top of it, I just happened to leave my cell home to charge."

Megan reappears holding a plate with a smiley face of apples, raisins, and Goldfish.

"I made Jonah a snack. Do you think he'll like it?"

"Yes, sweetie, that's very nice of you. But please don't wake him, OK?"

"Jesus," repeats Jake, as Megan heads upstairs. "Did you see it?"

"You have no idea. I watched him come within a fraction of losing his life and I was unable to do a thing." The tears burst full strength now with the vision of Jonah's head smashing into the banister, his neck bending at that terrifying angle.

Jake squeezes her hand gently. "Hang on. I'll be right back."

From the couch, Jeannie can hear Jake and Megan moving around Jonah's room, and when Jake returns a few moments later he slides in next to Jeannie, folding his arms around her. "I'm sorry you couldn't find me. Literally, it's the one day I was unreachable."

"You can't imagine. He was in surgery for three hours, awake, without me, I can't even…the ambulance guy, the hospital social worker, all of them interrogating me. I'm surprised they didn't lock me up."

"Don't take that personally," says Jake. "It's just their job, but my God, what a nightmare."

His heart beats fast against her arm. "I probably should have put the door back on the hinges, huh?" And then suddenly, he lowers his head onto her shoulder. "Jeannie, I really don't know what to say. I'm sorry."

"It's OK." She wipes her face with the back of her hand. "There's nothing you could have done."

Jake pushes his glasses to the top of his head and begins tugging on his fingers, as if trying to loosen them from their sockets.

"No, I'm sorry. I feel like we live on the edge and one more thing will push us over and I don't know what to do. I feel pressure from all sides. I can't seem to do anything right. I can't make enough money to keep our heads above water, I can't make you happy. I feel like a complete failure. And now this. Because I left the door off the hinges."

She shakes her head. "Jake, you're not a failure, not in the least."

He stands abruptly, crossing to the other side of the room. "It's never enough, not at work, and then I come home and it's the same thing. It's relentless. I'm sorry, I really am. For everything."

Jake leans into the window, pushing his fingers into his eyes as if to staunch his own impending flood. That's a lot of apologies for anyone; for Jake, a monumental quantity. They did emerge sincere, yet it's hard not to wonder if all that contrition was rooted in repentance, or if there was some guilt woven in there as well.

Jake slips his glasses back on then, and motions toward the stairs.

"I'm going to check on Megan. I'm assuming she didn't take this very well?"

Jeannie nods. He returns with Megan under his arm a few moments later and motions toward the door. "It's been a rough day all around, for everyone, so we're going to pick up some burritos and cupcake mix and come home and do some baking. A little bit of comfort food would do us all well this afternoon."

He kisses Jeannie on the mouth, his hands gripping her arms as if he's back from a six-month tour of duty overseas. But as he slips his coat on, she can't stop staring.

"What?"

"I like that shirt. Is it new?"

Jake nods.

"It looks good on you."

"Thanks." He motions to Megan. "Come on, let's go before the lines get bad."

Upstairs, Jonah dozes lightly, the snack plate tipped over on his bed. She picks up the Goldfish crumbs, just as her cell buzzes in the other room. But when she goes to answer it, she realizes it is Jake's, not hers, signaling missed calls. More parents, at this hour? She opens it, relieved to see the notification is from her missed calls today. But when she scrolls down, there are seven from that same number that called this morning, as if someone else had been desperate to find him.

Well, why not? If he had a meeting, why wouldn't the parent call?

As Jeannie scrolls up to delete her calls, she accidently hits call return on the number from the morning, and disconnects quickly. But a few seconds later, the caller phones right back, and Jeannie answers to apologize. There is silence on the other end, though, even when she repeats hello four times.

She squeezes Jake's phone hard. Even if she did call back, what would she say? *Who are you? Are you screwing my husband?* As if someone would even respond to that. And surely, if there was something going on, there would be something to find.

But where to start? She yanks opens Jake's bottom drawer, but it is stuffed with clothing, same as the others, jammed with his sweaters, T-shirts, bottom to top, as expected.

Until she reaches the top drawer. It's filled with socks and underwear, but the clothing is pushed forward as if something's taking up space in the back. And sure enough, tucked into the rear corner, is a tightly closed white paper bag.

Christ. How does Lila know this stuff? She's like a fucking psychic. Jeannie sits on the bed, holding the bag quietly. She needs this today like a hole in the head. Honestly, wouldn't ignorance be better? She peels back the edges, anyway, her teeth gritted.

Inside, there are no lotions, creams, porno magazines, or expensive jewelry. None of that.

Just underwear.

Jake has never bought himself underwear. Ever. But inside this bag are six packages of brand-new Jockey shorts.

She returns the bag to the back of the drawer and sits down on the bed.

What exactly do you do with information like that?

From across the hall, Jonah lets out a cry and Jeannie rushes to his room, cooling his forehead with a wet towel as he whimpers back into sleep.

When he finally stills, his breathing regular, she tiptoes into the alcove, her butcher block storyboards still papering the walls and bookshelves. How exactly, then, is this done?

In all of her years, her own mother Annie never looked back. But here, in suburban D.C., years away from the bright lights of New York, one story done, a second blossoming, a third incubating, clearly this writing life she's tried to reclaim is not meant to be. Because the very space of germination and incubation into which she has allowed herself to descend requires a complete retreat. How do you manage a family amid the mental chaos required to cultivate a story?

You don't. Obviously. Could she have been handed any more of a wake-up call than today?

She tugs the large sheets down from the bookshelves, Jake's collection emerging first. It would have left her father salivating, and it would not have been an impossible sight—the two of them enjoying his compilation as peers. Melville, Joyce, Updike, Faulkner. On the other shelves sit Jeannie's books—her father would have approved of these too. Except he can't see them, see her, will never know her children, will never be there to answer a call about Megan's anxiety or Jonah's accident, or help her navigate this troubled spot in her marriage that seems to be growing each day.

She tucks the sheets under her desk, the books exposed now. All this literature, it's supposed to inspire, move others to greatness, but really, all these books do is traverse the same themes of love, loss, abandonment, desire. And so many of them—written not because the world needs them, but because there are so many people who need to write. Sadly, for some, even that isn't enough; Anne Sexton and Sylvia Plath, both spilling their personal anguish, receiving acclaim, their inner lives validated, and yet both still walked out, leaving behind small children to forever deal with the ultimate rejection.

Certainly, that's not an option, but maybe she too could swallow a magic pill, same as Annie and the rest of America, find contentment in a legal and socially acceptable drug-induced stupor.

Because, really, Jake didn't have to even say it, the first sign was there weeks ago: missing Megan's class presentation. Forget the lack of time. No, the real issue is how to sit with an inner vision while staying present in the maternal moment. Not even present, but active. Attentive. Unfaltering. Vigilant. She may not be locking her children out like Annie did to her, but this morning one of them almost died.

Jeannie presses her palms hard into the edge of the desk.

So why on earth did she even try?

Because there is nothing like the bliss of letting stories explode and take you where they will.

And unlike others, she didn't keep that story under lock and key; rather, she hurled it into the world. Of course, she hurled it to the wrong person, although that's another matter. Before sending it, she confessed she felt naked debuting the story, but that's not quite right. It's bad enough the pictures turned him off—really, that was pure juvenile stupidity on her part—but to be dismissed as a writer—that feels more akin to having her skin torn off.

Honestly though, why should she even care what that stupid man thinks? Just because her child lies sedated with an ulna fracture in the next room and her husband is buying underwear for the first time while receiving calls from someone who hangs up when his wife answers? No, that's absurd. These two universes are completely discrete. All right, maybe Lila had a point, maybe she did turn him into a fantasy man, just a little. That's done now.

But the story? It's bad form to hang onto someone's work with no word. Sure, it was an email relationship, and without voice and vision, all rules of accountability vanish. Humiliating as it is, she will send him an email, because she wants that story back. Even if it's just assurance that he tossed it. She does not want it marooned out there—it was a good story and it deserves a home.

After that? There are a lot of things you need to make this work, and as much as she didn't want to hear it when Jake said it, they have made their choices. After today, there should be no remaining doubt: same way she ran out of room on the floor a few weeks ago when storyboarding her work, there's no room for this either.

Jeannie jerks the remaining sheets down from the dormers, the alcove returned to its original sterility. She reaches for the drudge pile, spreading a Scholastic order, termite inspection contract, and 1040 booklet across her desk, making sure there is no empty space, no temptation, no room for anything else. Same as she should be working harder on her marriage, because clearly something has fallen to pieces. Maybe she does press too hard and needs to cut Jake more slack. Maybe she's pushing him away in some way she can't even see.

With the last sheet down, her desk surface once again covered, the alcove looks exactly as it did before she let herself get swept up this useless endeavor. And then, just to be sure, Jeannie reshuffles the rest of the household papers, spreading them out across her desk so it is once again a patchwork of other people's needs, precisely the way they set everything up—precisely the way everything is supposed to be.

Arin Greenwood

The Lottery Winners

ARIN GREENWOOD is a former lawyer, now a writer and editor with the *Huffington Post*, where her favorite story involves a Virginia cat who ran a shockingly competitive campaign for a U.S. Senate seat. Arin's first novel, *Tropical Depression*, was put out by teeny indie publisher Back Porch Books in 2011, and was loosely based on her five-odd—sometimes very odd—years working as a lawyer on the Pacific island of Saipan. Her second novel, a young adult thriller called *Save the Enemy*, was published by Soho Teen in November 2013—and, given the exciting and scary subject matter, luckily isn't autobiographical at all.

Nick and I were having lunch in Baltimore when my brother Kenny called to say he was pretty sure our parents had won the lottery.

His evidence was scant but compelling: The winning ticket had been sold at the Cumberland Farms in Providence where our mother always picked up her weekly ticket, and no one had yet come forward to claim the prize—convenient, since our parents had just left that morning for a cruise in Russia and couldn't be reached.

Kenny thought this could only add up to one thing. That we, as a family, had suddenly become extraordinarily rich. Rich beyond student loan repayments. Rich like no more temping. Rich like living on a cruise ship.

"Huh," I said to Nick, after clicking off my phone. Nick was methodically cutting french fries with a knife and fork, looking purposeful as always as he consumed each bite. "I'm sure my brother's wrong. But what if he's not?"

I slipped into my daydream mode, imagining what I would do if suddenly I had sufficient resources.

For one, I would not be eating a bleachy-tasting salad in Baltimore.

Baltimore's a fine city if you like murders. Nick liked being near the political action of D.C. but disapproved of living in Washington itself. He thought people there were too full of themselves; he was convinced the people our age all wore sneakers costing several hundred dollars a pair. He said that Baltimore's taxes were better and we could afford three bedrooms rather than just one there.

When we first moved in a few years ago, just after law school when we were very young and unduly optimistic, I imagined we'd use the third bedroom just for really dirty sexual acts. We didn't. It's where we kept unused exercise equipment. Sometimes one of our mothers would inflate an air mattress in there and stay the weekend.

No, I said to Nick. If I suddenly had money we'd be somewhere exotic. Warm. Where the lettuce didn't taste like disinfectant. Maybe in Kenya seeing giant cats, or in the Philippines seeing little monkeys. Or maybe we'd start with Gibraltar. Why not Gibraltar? There's such a big rock there. We could start there and then drift down to Africa or east to Asia. Asia was east, right?

Or we could just start in India—I love the food, and Hinduism seems like such a forgiving religion. Yes, India! Of course India. We'd join a free-love ashram, though we'd stay monogamous while we were there. Get all flexible and enlightened. Tend to lepers, maybe. I could see myself in a saffron robe, playing a tambourine on the beach. Nick would be cutting up samosas with a knife and fork.

"I could buy you some new pants," I said. Nick didn't believe in new clothes. He thought they constituted putting on airs. His pants were all made of durable materials.

"You wouldn't still come to the LawyerSphere?" Nick said. "But we already committed to it. There's that clause in the contract we signed saying that we'll be liable for treble damages if we don't fulfill our obligations."

"Oh, fuck the LawyerSphere," I said, breezily, not wanting Nick to know I hadn't read the contract.

About a month earlier, Nick and I had agreed to spend the coming year inside of a repurposed biodome out in the desert. We were scheduled to start there in two weeks. The dome was going to be populated only with lawyers. There would be no predetermined rules and no contact with the outside world.

Some anthropologists and possibly also some television producers were studying how long it would take for the lawyers to develop a system of justice, and what our policies on polygamy would be, and where the death penalty would fit in, if anywhere.

We'd been promised that no executions would actually be completed. There would be a small stipend upon completion plus some student loan forgiveness, and there was also the possibility of LawyerSphere being televised, which could lead to some more lucrative opportunities in the long run, maybe.

Boy was I tired of doing temp work.

"If I had lottery money I'd still do LawyerSphere. I believe that commitments count. Then I'd go travel for, maybe, two weeks. Visit an island, perhaps. Then I'd start a business, I think," Nick said. "Something green, because I love the environment. Buy a house."

"A house?" I said. "Where would you even want the house?"

"We're not kids anymore. It would be appropriate to have a home," Nick said. He was slipping so deep into his own daydream he stopped cutting up his fries. "And I always thought I'd marry an Asian girl."

I'm not Asian. I wondered what I should say to these disclosures. They could mark the end of my relationship with Nick, which could make LawyerSphere very awkward.

We had dinner plans for that evening, with my brother and his wife, back in D.C. They lived there. Their sneakers cost a normal amount. It would be awkward, again, to have to tell them that we weren't coming to dinner because Mom and Dad winning the lottery had suddenly made Nick want to marry an Asian girl.

So we went to dinner where Kenny, my brother, told us that someone else had come forward to claim the prize. Our parents had not in fact won the lottery. Kenny and his wife joked about their thwarted fantasies—something about a small alpaca farm cum B&B in Rhode Island—but the whole dinner had a rather funereal air to it.

"Why not just buy the alpaca farm?" I asked them.

"Alpacas are expensive," Kenny said.

"Everything is," Nick said. "Everything."

"Alpacas hum when they're happy," Kenny's wife Betty said. "It's the nicest sound in the world."

My brother rubbed her shoulder.

"They spit when they're unhappy," said Nick. "I think I saw that on the Internet." He spilled some wine on his pants. It wiped right off.

Two weeks later, instead of going with Nick to the biodome, I maxed out my credit card and went alone to India. I wasn't worried about breaking the LawyerSphere contract; I figured treble damages or not, you can't get blood from a stone.

After getting blood from my foot when I cut it on broken glass while appreciating a sunset, alone on a dirty beach, I joined an ashram led by a man going by the name Swami Sammi. His name was Frank back in Baltimore, where he was from and intended to go back one day. I just called him "Hey" and took care of the ashram's goats. It turned out I hated yoga.

Using the free Internet at the ashram I saw LawyerSphere was becoming a big hit. It was being broadcast on some big website. The lawyers in the sphere were stars. Their hair was getting more well-styled by the day.

Nick, I saw, had quickly found himself a Harvard lawyer of Thai extraction. Nick and Phan eventually led a coup against the self-appointed leaders of the LawyerSphere parliament. So much for no executions. Non-monogamy was outlawed. This proscription turned out to be hard to enforce. Nick was wearing more attractive pants. He and Phan became spokespersons for a line of food-grade organic hair care products before the LawyerSphere year was even up.

Kenny and his wife said in an email not that long ago that Nick's products don't only work on humans—they also make alpaca fur just as smooth and soft as can be.

"Hey. I don't know where they got the money to find that out," I said to Swami Sammi one night, stroking his rough curly beard. "I honestly don't. Alpacas are expensive."

He played with a tambourine—there really was always a tambourine around—smacking it on his thigh. Swami Sammi's pants looked like pajamas. He said "Om, om, om. Don't they spit?"

"Hum," I said. "I think they hum."

Elizabeth Word Gutting

Sage in Belize

ELIZABETH WORD GUTTING lives and writes in Washington, D.C. Her fiction and book reviews have appeared in the *Rumpus*, the *Washington Post*, the *Quotable*, and *Treehouse*, among others. She was born and raised in St. Louis, Missouri.

The scariest thing that had happened so far during their seven months in Belize was his sister Petra's accident, when she and a friend visiting from Winnipeg got thrown from a pickup truck because their driver sped too fast up the road to Mountain Pine Ridge. Though both girls were miraculously unhurt—they were thrown into the leafy overgrowth on the side of the road instead of off the cliff—Sage often thinks about the alternative fate his sister may have met. Today, they are returning from town after grocery shopping and picking up weed and Petra is again sitting in the back of the pickup truck. She insists on sitting in the bed because she says she likes the breeze. Evan, their mother's boyfriend, drives, while Sage sits in the passenger seat with his seat belt buckled. From time to time he glances back to see his sister with her arm flung over the side of the truck, her curly hair blowing all around her serene face. She is nineteen and has no sense of danger.

At least Evan drives slowly. In Canada, Evan is not supposed to drive. Though he's thirty years old, he only has his learner's permit. But in Belize it does not matter, and he drives them everywhere. Today he drives even slower than usual, and the world they pass seems still. Sage stares out the window. The earth flattens out like a postcard before them, with a brown road cutting the scene in half. Both sides mirror each other with bright bushes and banana trees and rundown houses with families that have lived here in San Ignacio their whole lives, that can't imagine a home in another place, even though the homes they live in lack plumbing and often have no electricity and are prone to flooding in the rainy season.

Evan slows to less than ten miles per hour and says, "Whoa," as he maneuvers around a pothole. Sage is only fourteen but imagines that he would be a better driver than Evan. He doesn't complain, though, as Evan continues down the dusty dirt road that leads to their bungalow, picking up a bit more speed after the pothole. For one thing, Evan is stoned. There's no use talking to him now. He sings along with the reggae on the tape deck and taps his thumbs on the wheel. After he bought the weed that afternoon, he rolled a joint sitting in the truck and then stepped to the side of the road with Petra to smoke it. Sage sat in the truck by himself, certain they would call him moody or lame, but when they returned neither of them said anything, which made him think they had just been talking behind his back.

Evan turns off Bullet Tree Road, onto the gravel stretch that leads to their bungalow, and the pickup bumps up and down along the white rocks. As they pull onto the grass and park, Sage can see his mother Laney underneath the thatched roof of the central bungalow, which has no walls and is supported by tall wooden beams. She leans down and appears to be hacking with a pair of scissors, though he can't see what she's cutting. Inside, two hammocks are stretched from the beams, and Petra hops out of the truck and heads straight for the one with rainbow stripes. Evan carries the grocery bags to the long wooden counter.

"How was town, you guys?" Laney asks. She holds an old foam mattress, now cut in two. Her dark blonde hair is swept into a messy ponytail, and short pieces of hair stick with sweat to her forehead. She wears an old pair of cutoff cargo shorts and a brown tank top and her breasts hang loose and separate.

"We got groceries," Sage says, "and we bought a star fruit." He goes to stand next to her and looks down at the mattress she cuts.

"Oh, wow, that sounds killer."

Sage nods. "What are you doing?"

"I...am...building...a..." she draws out her answer as she rips a piece of the spongy fat material in two, "massage bed."

"Oh, cool."

The smell of beans cooking drifts through the open bungalow, a sweet thick smell that hangs in the jungle air.

"Evan, that smells so great," Laney says.

"You're making a massage bed, babe?"

"Yeah, got my first client. She's staying next door at Theo's."

Evan simply nods and stirs the pot of beans and Sage wishes that he would at least give some sort of encouragement, because neither he nor his sister can force themselves to comment on their mother's odd jobs. There is nothing to say, though, so Sage asks, "Where's she from?"

"The States, I think."

Sage is fascinated by the people who stay at the lodge down the road, which is owned by a woman named Theo who has intense blue eyes— prophet eyes, sharp and scary. The first time she looked at him he thought he could tell what she was thinking: "Poor lost boy." But then she never treated him like a poor lost boy, instead letting him hang out at the lodge and talk to travelers, sometimes offering him yogurt or freshly cut mango but never acting like he needed mothering. Only once did she ask about his schooling. And then when he had responded that he was home schooling himself, he had found her bluntness refreshing. "So you're unschooled at the moment," she had said, and he nodded.

"So how did you meet your client?" Sage asks. He says *client* in a forced way, though he wants to sound natural. He always, above all else, wants to sound natural.

"Oh, Theo is sending her to me," Laney says. "I haven't met her yet. I guess she was complaining about her feet and back hurting after doing some hikes, and Theo told her about how we live down the road and named a price and so here I am, making a bed."

"What price did Theo get for you, babe?" Evan asks. He is pulling his blond dreadlocks into a stumpy ponytail and watching the pot of beans simmer, his wire-rim glasses fogging up.

"Thirty U.S."

"Nice!" Evan says. "With the gig tomorrow night we'll be rich."

"Everything down here makes me feel rich," Laney says. She exhales dramatically. "Don't you love it, Petra? You're so quiet over there."

"Mm, I'm hungry," Petra says. She lies with her eyes closed and rests her hands over her stomach in the hammock.

"Well, let's eat," Evan says.

They sit together in a circle on the dusty floor, scooping beans and rice into their mouths, and it is then that the woman with the massage appointment appears, coming up the road, walking slowly through the high grass. Sage sees her first, but watches without announcing her. She has long brown hair that falls over her face as she walks with her head down, watching where she steps. She wears a knee-length skirt and a white T-shirt through which Sage can see the faint outline of her pink bra, or maybe it's the top piece of her bikini.

"Hello?" she calls, and they all turn to her.

She stands by a tall wooden beam. Sage will never forget the way she looks in this moment, her hand resting on the beam as she hesitates to cross over into their space, her arm lean as a branch. She has a strange poise, but it's not grace; something in her manner is marked with an unexpected awkwardness. And she is beautiful. No, she is gorgeous.

"Hi," Laney says, still chewing. "Come on in. You're Kate?"

"I am," she says. "You must be Laney." She walks slowly forward.

"Have a seat," Laney says, patting the floor, and Sage's face burns because they don't even have chairs. She eases onto the floor across from him, though, and doesn't seem bothered, taking off her flip-flops and then crossing her legs.

"This is such a cool place," she says, looking around with arched eyebrows and then straight up at the roof.

"I know, isn't it just awesome?" Laney says.

"Completely. I'm in awe."

"That thatched roof is something else, let me tell you. We've been here seven months now and I haven't seen a thatch like that in any of the places we've lived."

Kate nods and Sage feels immense relief when she doesn't ask how many places they've lived in—four, and not one of them has truly been theirs.

"Where are you from?" Petra says. She looks at Kate placidly, and Sage can see that her high has worn off into a languid exhaustion that will keep her acting dreamy all afternoon. He also suspects that his sister will try to befriend Kate for a few days, offering to get her high or go tubing down the river with her. There are not many kids their age in San Ignacio, and the lodge is often their best bet for meeting people, even though travelers never stay long.

"San Francisco," Kate says. "But originally I'm from outside Sacramento."

"Oh, wicked," Petra says. "I've always wanted to go to San Francisco." She wipes her mouth and says, "I'm Petra, by the way. Are you hungry? Do you want some food?"

"Oh, no, I'm fine," Kate says.

Sage clears his throat and says, "Do you like star fruit?"

"I don't know," Kate says and looks right at him for the first time. Her irises are gray-blue and watery. "I've never tried it before."

"Oh, you've got to try it," Laney says. "Ev, why don't you cut some up?"

"Right on," Evan says. He stands and saunters to the counter.

"There's just so much delicious fruit down here," Laney says. "We haven't even tried it all."

"Where are you guys from?"

"Winnipeg," Petra says.

"The coldest city on the planet," Laney adds, and laughs, deep and throaty. Sage stares at the cement floor.

"And you came here seven months ago?"

"Yep, packed up and moved on out. Took a plane to Cancun, and then a bus across the border, each of us with just one bag each."

"Wow," Kate says. "That's amazing. What made you choose Belize?"

"Cheap tickets," Petra says.

Laney laughs. "Come on, Petra, that's not all," she says. "That's not even the half of it." She turns to Kate, straightening her back like she does when she practices yoga in the morning. Sage knows she's trying to seem responsible and composed. "We needed a change. I was cleaning houses and we were broke all the time and one of the families I cleaned for needed a house sitter down here for a couple months and so we didn't think too hard about it—we just decided to go. And now we've got the same house-sitting deal with this place—just watching it for a different family from Canada."

Evan returns with the star fruit and places it in the middle of their circle. The slices are green with a glossy skin and their cut-up shapes look just like stars. Sage puts a slice in his mouth and chews; it tastes sweet, and the texture is firm, but the inside is juicy, sort of like a grape. He watches Kate eat a slice, inserting a small corner of the star into her mouth. He cannot stop looking at her lips while she chews, perfect as origami flowers. He sits cross-legged, and feels pressure pushing against the soft denim of his long cutoff jean shorts. He shifts his legs and puts his elbows on his knees and leans forward. He looks outside, past the wooden beams, over to the small house on stilts where they all sleep.

"I didn't get your name," Kate says, looking at him. Sage feels his cheeks turning red—she must have noticed how he'd stared at her.

"Sage," he says.

"That's a cool name," she says. "Like a wise man. Or I guess it could be the herb, though I thought of the wise man first." She smiles and he smiles back, unsure of how else to respond, though he is certain he will greedily savor the compliment later, when he can be alone.

"Hey, you ready to go?" Laney says. She stands and grabs a flowered sheet to throw over the makeshift massage bed, which she has positioned outside the bungalow, on the edge of the jungle.

"Sure," Kate says. She gives Sage and Kate a little wave. Evan is already up and washing dishes, as usual, totally unaware.

There are what sounds like twenty different birds chirping in the trees and bushes, and Kate says, "Wow—wow!" at the open-air setting of Laney's massage space. Laney puts on some low, trancelike music, using the battery-operated speakers, because they do not have electricity. Playing music is something Laney has rationed—batteries are expensive, even here—and Sage feels relief that she splurges now. Suddenly, he half wants her to become a successful masseuse for the tourists staying next door.

He rises and, without a word to his sister or Evan, goes to climb the stairs to the bungalow where they all sleep. Inside it is dark and cooler. Their sleeping bags are rolled out along the wooden slats of the floor and the headlamps they use at night are in a pile in one corner. He makes sure the door is firmly shut.

From the window, he can see clear across to where his mother is working on Kate. She lies on her stomach and her back is bare, long, and white. She wears only black cotton underwear. He stands frozen because he is afraid that if he moves something will change. Then he unzips his pants with his forehead pressed against the wall. For a brief minute he thinks of nothing but the warm clasp of his hand, but it's not his hand, it could be hers, or it could be inside of her. He is not far from Winnipeg, he is not anywhere particular, but he *is* far from Belize, and his heavy breaths drone out the strange sounds of exotic birds and rustling jungle leaves outside the window. When he comes, it is sudden and hot. He gasps. Immediately, he looks to the door. It remains closed. He looks outside. No one has moved. His mother kneads Kate's back, her elbow pressed between butterflied shoulder blades. He pulls his hand up and presses his eyes closed.

For an hour, then, he sleeps, flat on his back on top of his sleeping bag. When he wakes, Kate has gone.

∽

THE NEXT NIGHT IS FRIDAY and Evan is DJing at Cabana del Sol. The air is warm and a light breeze keeps going through the bar. Blinking string lights hang inside and outside, wound around fences and along the shelves lined with liquor. The floor is sand. Ex-pats and travelers order drinks from a short Guatemalan man, the lone bartender. Sage and Petra stand together against a wall that faces out to the street, where stray dogs pace back and forth, looking for scraps. Right outside the bar, a Belizean woman and man have set up a jewelry stand that lures tourists in a predictable way.

Evan hasn't started playing yet, but stands at the DJ table with Laney, and they pass a pair of headphones back and forth and occasionally Evan says, "Check, check," into the microphone. The bar plays pop songs from the States, and Petra can't help but bob her head though she generally pretends to hate fads in music.

"I'm going to start studying Mayan horoscopes," she says, breaking their people-watching silence.

"Why?"

"Mom found a cool book on it. And besides, I want to. It interests me."

"Since when have you cared about Mayan horoscopes?"

"I don't know, Sage," she says and looks away from him. "Since now? Since moving here? I think it's important to get to know the culture in Belize." They are quiet. Sage watches a tourist kick a rock towards a stray dog, scaring it off. "Maybe you should try for once," Petra says.

"What subject would 'Mayan horoscopes' fall under in school?" He wants this to be funny, but his sister isn't amused, responding with a blank look.

"Science," she says. "Or anthropology. Or philosophy." Then she adds, "Give it a break. I can study whatever I want."

Since moving, Sage has noticed they often fight like this—it's not really a fight, and they'll probably never speak of Mayan horoscopes again. There's a strained necessity to their relationship that didn't exist in Canada, even when they were so poor they hardly ate anything besides peanut butter sandwiches. Sometimes he wants to remind Petra that she's old enough to get out of here—that fact alone eats him up inside with jealousy—but the necessity keeps him quiet and leaves him feeling alternately clingy and resentful.

"Look," Petra says, "there's Kate, from yesterday."

Sage snaps to attention. "Where?"

"Over there, by the jewelry."

Kate wears her hair in a slack bun near the top of her head, and loose pieces fall down to her shoulders. She stands so straight and slim she could slip between the slats of a fence. Around her waist, she has tied a gauzy linen skirt, and Sage can see the smooth outline of her hips, the rise and fall of her small butt.

"Let's go talk to her," Petra says and heads towards Kate, who holds up a pair of shell earrings. Sage follows.

"Hey," Petra says, and Kate turns to them, and for a moment looks confused. But Petra doesn't skip a beat and leans in to hug Kate—she hugs everyone, always in the same familiar way, draping her spaghetti arms around her shoulders.

"Oh hi guys," Kate says, "you must be here because of Evan, huh? How great that you can both get into a bar, right?"

Petra nods. "Yeah, it's pretty wicked."

"So, did you come for Evan?" Sage says.

"Yeah, your mom told me about the gig yesterday. I figured…why not. It's my last night here."

Sage feels something shoot through his chest. He must be with her tonight. His only chance. He must. He stares at the back of her neck, which is the most beautiful neck he has ever seen. She asks Petra what she thinks of the earrings she's picked out, and in the background Sage can hear Evan starting up his set with a Flaming Lips song. He clears his throat and says, "You guys want to go inside?"

Kate is paying the woman behind the table for the earrings and then she turns to Sage. "Sure. Let's go."

Petra waves to a group of people and drifts away, folding into the crowd. Sage hesitates, waiting to see if Kate will want to join, but she turns to go to the bar.

"Want to stand with me while I wait in that hideous line for a beer? I'll buy you a Coke," she says.

His mouth is dry, and he feels he cannot speak, so he nods. They stand together at the bar, and though everyone pushes together, he notices only his proximity to Kate. He feels thankful that it is dark, and that people surround them. He tries to think of something to say, but she speaks first.

"It's so funny here," she says, a bit loudly and right in his ear, and he thinks he can almost feel her soft petal lips, though they do not touch him. "I love that all you have to say at a bar is 'beer' or 'stout' and they hand you a Belikin or a Guinness. Which do you want?"

"Will you get me a stout, actually? Sometimes I drink them with my dad, back in Canada, and so it's OK if I have one here, I just…" he stops.

"Sure," she says. "I started drinking when I was younger than you. I'm not judging. Oh, and I have a question for you after we get our beers, too."

He does not want Petra to see him drinking, and so moves to the front of the crowd once Kate hands him the cold bottle. It sweats in his hand. They stand next to each other near the wall, not speaking. "There's your mom," Kate says at one point, and they watch Laney dancing by herself, her arms over her head as she twists her hips and turns in a circle. Evan leans over the turntables. "She's So Cold" by the Rolling Stones—Sage has heard it at least a thousand times on the tape deck in the truck. He marvels at how each minute seeks a height more vertiginous than the last, and he depends on the music—music that Evan, of all people, gives to the night—to stabilize the space between him and Kate, to shrink it and bring them closer.

"So, wait, what was your question?" he says. "From before?"

"Oh, nothing major."

He waits.

"Just, I was wondering if you knew where I could get some bud."

"Oh yeah," Sage says. "Of course. Yeah, we have some, uh, Evan's got some in the truck out back."

"Excellent. Let's finish our beers."

She drinks quickly, and he does the same, the coldness of the beer making his eyes burn. He is thin, like his mother and sister, and already he can feel a buzz. He has only had Guinness once, the time with his father, right before he left with his mother, sister, and Evan for Belize. That night he and his father sat side by side on his father's porch, not speaking, engaging in a ritual of men—that's what his father had called drinking beers together—and Sage had sat completely still, despite the urge to squirm in his rocking chair. Now he wonders, in a distant and cool way, if he will ever see his father again. It seems wholly possible that he will not, and he feels strengthened to realize in this moment that he doesn't care about that.

"One for the road?" Kate says, and before he responds she's at the bar with two fingers up. Sage looks around quickly for his sister—he does not see her in the crowd. He worries that she will be with the throng of people outside, smoking a joint, and it will ruin everything. But as Kate walks back to him with the beers, he realizes how foolish a thought it is—what will be ruined? Checked by shame, he can hardly thank her when she hands him another bottle, this one warmer than the last.

"You OK?" she says.

"Yeah, totally."

Outside, he spots Petra standing with a group of ex-pats they know vaguely, including a couple from Florida who came to Belize on vacation a year ago and then wound up buying a house and coming back to stay. Sage doesn't understand these people, doesn't comprehend their unquestioning contentment, though he wishes he could talk with them as easily as his sister does.

He grabs Kate's wrist, just for a second, and pulls her in the other direction, away from them. "This way," he says. He doesn't know if his sister sees them leave.

The music grows distant as they wind behind Cabana del Sol to the gravel parking lot in back, where the pickup truck is parked with its windows down. Sage can just barely make out the tinny chords of "No Woman No Cry," but he can hear the loud crunch of their feet on the rocks.

Without a word, he opens the passenger side door and reaches into the glove compartment. He can't see well by the overhead light, but he can feel that there are several plastic bags with remnants of dried, old marijuana. It takes him a minute to find one with a good amount of pot, but when he does, he sees that there is a half-smoked joint lodged in the corner of the bag, and he pulls it out.

"Do you have a lighter?" he says.

"Oh…" Kate says. "Let me see." She digs in her purse. His heart races forward as he holds the joint between his thumb and forefinger. He imagines having to search for a lighter or matches in the dimly lit truck. He won't find them. They will have to go back to the bar, and he will go back to being himself.

"I have matches," Kate says, and he realizes he has been holding his breath and breathes deeply out and passes her the joint, careful not to touch her hands with his, embarrassingly damp with sweat. They fall still and stand apart by the side of the truck. She flicks on the lighter and for a brief moment her face lights up, the crescent of her lips and nose in profile, and then she inhales and all he can see is the burning orange tip of the joint.

"Wow," she says, "you're a lifesaver." She passes it to him.

He considers telling her about last fall, during the flood right after they first moved, when he smoked weed for the first and last time; he had hated the way it felt to be high, like being jumpy and nervous with a thick fog obscuring everything around him. But instead he says nothing, not wanting to be a downer, a lame-o as Evan would say, and he inhales so suddenly that the smoke burns in his lungs. He coughs hard, and to his surprise she doesn't comment and merely smacks him on the back.

"Thanks," he says.

"It's kind of harsh," she says, "but I'm not complaining."

"Can we sit down?" Sage says. The dark edges of the parking lot are closing in around him and he feels he might lose his balance.

"Why not," she says. She climbs over the back of the pickup, and he throws a leg over after her. They sit side by side in the bed of the truck with their knees up. His eyes adjust and he sees her face now. There is something animal about it; a terrifying non-humanness warps her features. Her eyes looked ghoulish, and are set deeper in her face than he realized. Her knee grazes against his.

"I can't believe you guys live here."

"Me neither."

"Do you like it?"

"Not really."

"Ha!" she says, "that's what I thought."

"Why?" he says. He hears himself, and recoils at his own defensiveness. "I mean, how can you tell?" he says, nearly a whisper.

"A lot shows on your face," she says. She raises her eyebrows, and he wonders if it's too dark for her to see how his cheeks burn. "It's OK," she says. "I'm the same way. I let every little emotion show."

"How old are you?"

"Twenty-two," she says.

"How long have you been traveling for?"

"My, you have a lot of questions," she says.

He sits quietly. He knows one thing—he is good at waiting. Then she says, "I've been gone just two weeks." She sucks on the joint again and holds her breath. As she exhales, she says in a tight voice, "I decided to travel because my boyfriend broke up with me a little over a month ago." She continues without any response, speaking as though he's not even there. "Or, really, I broke up with him after I found out he'd slept with one of our mutual friends. 'Just once,'" she says, holding up her hands, mocking the boyfriend. "Whatever. It was such a fucked-up situation. I had to get out of town. And you know, I'm really glad I did."

"That really sucks," Sage says. He feels stupid, inadequate, like the child that he is saying this. He knows nothing about love affairs or heartbreak and he sounds laughable in his attempt at empathy.

But Kate does not notice. "Yeah, it *really* fucking sucked. But let me tell you this cool thing I've realized. Keep this in mind for when you get your heart broken—if you're lucky enough to, and I say lucky because man, at least I feel like I'm alive." She pauses and takes a sip of her beer. "Heartbroken people get a free pass. I'm allowed to go on a random vacation, I'm allowed to spend lots of money on French classes or yoga retreats or new shoes..." she starts to laugh. "And I'm allowed to fuck whoever I want, because there's really no better way to get over someone. I could fuck my ex's best friend if I wanted to. In fact, I think he'd like that."

She turns to Sage and half her face is cast in shadow.

"That sounds..." his mind scrambles for something to say. Nothing. But then he decides to be as natural as possible. "That sounds sort of fun."

She laughs—hard. And he feels a rush of joy at making her laugh. And he laughs too and then when they both stop laughing he kisses her. He mashes his lips against hers, and then retreats but she kisses him back. Immediately, he thrusts his tongue into her mouth, and his hands are shaking but he brings them to her breasts. They are small and pliable in his hands. She pushes away and laughs.

"I'm stoned," she says. But she kisses him again, and then again. He's not sure he's doing it right. He pushes her against the bed of the truck and she guides him on top of her and lifts up her skirt like it's the most natural thing in the world. His head swirls and he reaches for the beer, just for something to drink, his mouth is so parched. His knees ache against the hard metal of the pickup. She scratches at his back and pulls on his shorts, and he thinks of dogs. Two strays in an alley. He has no idea what he's doing but an instinct drives every one of his movements. Suddenly, he yelps, and realizes too late that he's coming. He bangs his forehead on the bed of the truck as his body falls against hers. His cotton shirt is soaked with sweat. She pats his back, twice. He rolls onto his side, away from her, breathing heavily. A reggae-rap remix blares in the bar and the music seems closer than he remembers—everyone he knows is right behind them.

Next to him, Kate lies silently. They stay like that for an hour, or ten minutes, or it could be thirty seconds. He has no idea.

"Kate," he says.

She doesn't respond for several seconds. "Yeah?" she says. Her voice sounds different than before. He wants to peel back the night like a fruit and examine it with her from a distance. But he has nothing to say. A rigid silence forms, like droplets of water hardening into icicles. He turns on his back and stares at the dome of night sky, punctuated with dark purple clouds. She puts a hand up his shirt and grazes the smooth hairless skin on his stomach, and then takes her hand away as if reconsidering and they don't touch at all.

Maybe he'll stay in Belize his whole life. It might stop seeming so strange and temporary and just become life. Or no, he will go back to Canada. He and his sister will leave on a bus, the way they came.

Kate rises, but she isn't leaving the truck, not yet. He wonders if she's reading his thoughts again, if it's obvious to her what will become of him now. But if she knows she doesn't let on. She just tilts the bottle of beer into her mouth and gulps twice, finishing it. Sage stares at the ridges of her shoulders, like two mountain peaks, a foreign land. She turns. "We should go back now," she says.

Shelby Settles Harper

Pow Wow Girls

SHELBY SETTLES HARPER holds a juris doctor from the University of
Colorado, is a candidate for a master of arts in writing from Johns Hopkins
University, and is a citizen of the Caddo Nation of Oklahoma. Her fiction
can be found in *Outside In Literary and Travel Magazine* (March 2013),
Bethesda Magazine (July/August 2013), *So to Speak: a Feminist Journal of
Language and Art* (November 2013), and *Gargoyle Magazine* #61 (forthcom-
ing). Shelby lives with her husband and three children in the Washington,
D.C., suburbs, where she writes for the parenting blog *Red Tricycle* about
family-friendly adventures in the nation's capital.

S ome of us were princesses, with beaded crowns and tribal sashes.
We talked of saving our competition money for college at the
University of New Mexico or Oklahoma or even Dartmouth, if
we were really hot stuff. Some of us were the anti-princesses, with tight
jeans and tank tops, sneaking beers at the 49, the infamous pow wow after-
parties, when all the dances were over and the grown-ups were gathered
around the fire pit talking and laughing and drinking.

Some of us were tall and skinny, with long black hair. One of us tried
to hide the small gap between the front teeth by smiling with closed lips.
Others had thick, curly hair ironed flat at night. All of us hated our acne
and wanted to be taller or shorter or skinnier or have more shape—anything
to be different, better, than how we were.

Our favorite pow wow was the week-long celebration that our tribe
hosted every August. Indians came from across the country to our small
Oklahoma town, filling our motels and campgrounds, bringing stories
from reservations so far away they might as well have been other countries.
We'd never been west of Amarillo or north of Wichita Falls, so we were
proud that our tribe's pow wow brought the world to us.

We met up with our friends at the opening day parade on Monday, entering through the south gate, where they let the Indians in for free. For the next five days and nights, we rode carnival rides and danced, laughed, snuck cigarettes, and pretended to be the grown-ups we couldn't wait to become.

We loved the teen dance in the old barn held late at night, where we danced to Chubby Checker, the Temptations, and the Four Tops. We blushed and laughed when the boys we danced with sang along to "Let's Spend the Night Together" by the Stones. One or two of us did spend the night, in the backs of trucks and on top of Pendleton blankets, the muted sounds of carnival rides and drunks mixed in with the quick panting of the boy on top of us.

After the teen dance, some of us sat with boys on the backs of trucks, eating Indian tacos and drinking Pepsis. We liked the frybread piled high with tomatoes and cheese and ground beef, or sometimes smothered in powdered sugar and honey. Three frybread stands, but only one with a long line, the one run by the auntie we called "Superdude," and we'd play rock-paper-scissors to see which Indian had to take the money collected from our pockets and buy for all.

Some of us fell in love with faraway boys and had to pay our brothers or sisters to keep their mouths shut. *Date the whites*, our mothers ordered. *Those Indian boys won't amount to anything.* We found this confusing, because we were mixed-bloods and often reminded by teachers and store clerks that we were not white. But we just rolled our eyes and leaned in close to the boy from Nisqually, captivated by his stories of fishing in the Puget Sound.

We had favorite parts of pow wow week. Some of us liked the wrestling mud men at the opening day parade. *Look at those crazy Indians, covered head to toe in mud, only their eyeballs clear!* Some of us liked the 49, where the grown-ups smoked and drank and told stories until they either hooked up or passed out. We all loved the vendors, who sold baskets and pottery and turquoise earrings that made us feel beautiful.

Some of us liked to walk around the campgrounds on the outer edges of the pow wow. Rows of teepees and tents, lined up in a U-shape, filled with Indians of all shapes and sizes telling stories of South Dakota ranches, Pueblo pottery, and fishing in the Pacific Northwest. We especially loved talking to the visitors from what seemed like real reservations, unlike our small Oklahoma town.

Some of us liked to watch the fancydancers. When the good ones danced it was effortless and loose and we were mesmerized by the dancer's head-dress, a kaleidoscope of reds, yellows, and blues, as he bobbed his head, spun and leaped, his moccasins keeping time with the drumbeat. Watching the fancydancers, we too felt the beat of the drum in our hearts.

Some of us thought the fancydancers were real show-offs. *Look at those peacocks.* We preferred the grassdancers. We saw them as the cheetahs of the pow wow: powerful, smart, and strong. We liked the long, flowing fringe and the idea of losing oneself in the music, in the drum, to become grass blowing in the wind. We weren't the ones for flash and dazzle.

Many of us danced, too. We strutted our poise and elegance in the Women's Southern Traditional competition, bending our knees in time with the beat of the drum. Some of us danced in a jingle dress made of tobacco can lids. We proudly showed off our footwork, beadwork, and beautiful plumes.

Artists abounded in our families. We knew potters, painters, weavers, and beaders. Some of us were artists too, and all of us had dreams. We didn't know why art ran through our blood but thought maybe it had something to do with being Native people and that the Creator gifted our hands for the creation of beauty, even when the art was sad and dark.

Years later, some of us would go to college and marry white men. When our Southern-born fathers-in-law refused to attend our weddings to their sons, we pretended it wasn't because we were Indian and that they would come to love us once they got to know us.

Some of us would birth blue-eyed, blond children who still met the blood requirement for membership in our tribe. We would move to other Oklahoma towns, join Junior League, and forget that we were Indian until we looked in the mirror. We didn't realize it was written on our cheeks, lips, and eyes.

Some of us would go against our mothers and marry Indians. If we were lucky, these men worked for the tribe in the cultural preservation depart-ment or ran for council and grew bellies big with age. They didn't drink, saying they felt like everyone expected them to be falling-down drunks and even though white men could behave in such a way, they had to be better.

Some of us married beautiful Indian men who wasted away from drinking rather than painting. When we moved back in with our mothers, our children carrying their few possessions, our mothers would mutter through pursed lips, *What did I tell you?*

Always we felt compassion for our mothers, though, because we knew they had been forced to attend the Indian boarding schools, where they'd learned to hate a part of themselves. In the boarding schools, our mothers had been taught to sew and cook and keep house like white women. Our languages were forbidden, so they learned to speak only in English and to pray to one white God. Five decades later, when our children, many of them light-skinned, returned and asked about the peyote ceremonies, something we had no clue about, a light would flicker in our grandparents' brown eyes. *The prayers in the teepee worked; what skipped two generations is still alive.*

Our mothers wouldn't be able to name the official United States policies of assimilation and relocation, but these experiments would shape their lives. After boarding schools, they were sent to faraway places like Los Angeles and Chicago and Denver, sent to work as maids for white women, expected to blend into white culture.

Some of our mothers would miss home and return to the reservations or to their small Indian towns. They'd feel confused and unhappy, misunderstood by their parents, who didn't speak English and didn't recognize their children after years in the white world. Others would stay in the big cities, where they would either assimilate and survive or fade into the shadows.

All of us were born decades before Congress outlawed the adoption of Indian children by non-Native families, and many of us were taken from our homes and adopted into white homes in other parts of the country. Some of us adopted children grew up with white brothers and sisters, attending Ivy League schools alongside them. We would make our way to the other Indians on campus, and later call home and ask our blue-eyed adoptive mothers: *What is all this stuff about sovereignty?*

Some of us had parents who taught us what being Indian was really about. They taught us the language and the stories and about respecting our elders. Some of us had parents who thought they knew what being an Indian was all about, and taught us those things, until we became just as hopeless and lost as they were.

Some of our sisters, girlfriends, and aunties left their babies in trucks while they drank in bars, their children growing up with the same neglect as the stray dogs wandering the streets. We had brothers, uncles, and cousins whose lives would be ravaged by alcohol. They couldn't keep a job and went on drinking binges once or twice a month, leaving our aunties, cousins, or sisters home alone with four kids and having to turn to family for help or for money. *Sister, can you spot me some money for rent? He's run off to colored town again, drinking.*

We watched as the Vietnam War claimed our brothers and boys from the neighborhood and we held our mothers tightly as they cried and said goodbye to their sons. Then we filled our cemeteries with their bodies when their remains were sent back home to us. Every Memorial Day weekend, our mothers placed flowers at the grave sites of lost sons and relatives, and now that our mothers have passed, we continue the tradition.

Diabetes took many of our elders, and some of us said goodbye to loved ones one limb at a time. We vowed to eat healthier, starting Monday, and some of us published articles in *Indian Country Today*, proclaiming *Wake up, Native people! Frybread is NOT traditional food!* But still, we loved the sizzle of the dough frying in the pan and wanted nothing more than to enjoy a big meal with our relations.

No matter how far we strayed, the pow wows tied us to our communities and the ceremonies kept our songs alive. They reminded us of the ones the elders once sang, in languages we no longer spoke, the memories of their beautiful voices warm and comforting.

We are pow wow girls and these are our songs.

Melanie S. Hatter

Something Worth Saving

MELANIE S. HATTER is the author of *The Color of My Soul*, winner of the 2011 Washington Writers' Publishing House Fiction Prize, and *Taking the Shot*, an electronic novelette published by Etopia Press. Her short stories have appeared in *The Whistling Fire* and *Diverse Voices Quarterly*, and her short story, "Obsessed with Claudia," won the First Annual Romantic Tales Writing Contest. Born and raised in Scotland, Melanie received a bachelor's degree from Hampton University and a master's in writing from Johns Hopkins University. She has a background in journalism and corporate communications.

*E*very day I hear them screaming, and the only way I can think of making it stop is by firing a bullet into my brain. How do you continue to live after witnessing the depravity of a lunatic and the suffering he inflicted, hearing the last breaths of women just like you while you wait, helpless to save them?

I sit in what feels like an interrogation room, but this is not an interrogation, more of a record-setting. He's pleading not guilty and they need my account, eventually my testimony. I won't be able to face him in court. She's talking to me softly, asking did I know my abductor? Anyone who had met this man surely didn't truly know him—how could anyone know such evil lay inside? I shake my head.

"Please, tell me how he approached you?" She puts her hand out on the table between us—long fingers with short practical nails—and tells me to take my time. She is dressed in gray, a nice suit with a crew-neck T-shirt, not one of those low-cut shirts the crime women wear on TV. She's a real detective with brown hair tied back in a short ponytail. Very practical. As she leans forward, I see her pistol at her hip and wonder if I could grab it, wonder if I could fire steadily and end everything with one shot, or be unlucky and shoot half my face away and survive to tell the horrific tale like the seventeen-year-old I once saw on a documentary. But I don't have to end my life. Not now.

I don't want to talk to her. I want the caramel-colored cop who used a penknife from his back pocket to release me from the chair, whose arms stopped me from hitting the ground, whose brown eyes widened when I pleaded for his gun. "Please, he's coming back."

"No, you're safe now," he said.

"But he's coming back. I don't want him to touch me."

I had prayed for death and this officer's handgun nestled in a shoulder holster against his rib cage offered release. My freedom was lost on me—all I knew was that my captor was coming back.

"Where's the other cop?" I ask. Detective Practical cocks her head to the side. "The black guy," I say to clarify.

"Detective Parker?" she asks.

"The one who found me first. I don't remember his name."

She raises her eyebrows. I'm not supposed to want to talk to a man after what I've been through. I'm supposed to want to spill my worst nightmare to a woman. But it's not about sex. It's about eyes with compassion, eyes that were moved by my pain, eyes that saved me. I lay my head on the table feeling the weight of my week's bondage. Detective Parker, that's who I'll talk to.

He slides into his partner's seat across from me, takes a deep breath, and lays his palms on the table between us; thick veins swell through his skin. Do they learn this in detective school—place your hands on the table to put your witness at ease? He's nervous, I think. Perhaps he is more comfortable interrogating suspects, not taking statements from tortured victims. He leans forward, telling me with those brown eyes that he cares. "It's gonna be OK," he says. "You're gonna be OK." He says the words with such conviction, with such genuine care, that I want to cry. I want to believe him.

"Take your time." He leans back and waits. The fluorescent light makes his bald head shine as if polished with oil. He wears a dark brown polo shirt that makes his eyes look black. I stammer, not sure where to begin. A pitcher of water is on the far end of the table. He pours some into a tumbler and places it before me. I take a sip, holding the glass with both hands to stop the water from splashing because I can't control my body anymore. My hands shake constantly and sometimes my joints give way or my muscles stop functioning and I'm forced to sit with my head in my hands, bent over my lap.

"Was he a customer at the bank?" he asks.

I shake my head and begin to speak, to recount the unthinkable. I had bolted the front door. Everyone had left and all was secure. I managed a small branch and locked up every night. Joey, the security guard, usually waited with me but on this evening he hadn't been around for the last hour, so I went on with my nightly ritual—I wanted to get home. As I turned to head to my car, a shadow rose before me and everything went dark. With my head throbbing, I awoke in a seated position, my arms secured with duct tape to the arms of a wooden chair, and my legs taped to the chair's legs. My mouth taped, too. Everything secure, but not safe.

On my right were two other women, bound to chairs in the same fashion, the three of us lined up like contestants on a sick reality show, trapped in a crime drama that wouldn't end. The woman nearest me had long blonde hair loose around her shoulders. I could see the sweat trickling down her temples. The air was hot and thick, the dim light coming from windows made of glass blocks, like the bottom of Coke bottles. The third woman was Asian, her black hair contrasting with her pale skin, luminous in the dark. An equal opportunity abductor—black, white, and Asian.

Time shifted in a strange way; night and day didn't exist anymore, just bursts of white light followed by shadow. After a period of time—a day, an afternoon in the dark?—the ceiling bulb crackled and flooded the room. Heavy steps came down the wooden staircase. He was a short white man with a large belly protruding over black dress pants, average looking, like someone's uncle, like the guy from accounting you say hello to but rarely strike up a conversation with. He never made eye contact with any of us that I could tell, just looked at our body parts. He surveyed the line, as if trying to decide where to start. Relieved that he chose the Asian woman and not me, I felt the guilt start to creep inside me. He ripped the tape from her arms and dragged her from the chair to the middle of the room. Her yelp struck me in my chest and I closed my eyes. His hand surprised me as it smacked my cheek. Randomly waving his arm at me and the blonde, he yelled, "You have to watch!"

No furniture other than our chairs filled the room. The floor was vinyl and where he stood, a dark stain spread out like spilled red wine. He repeatedly slammed his flat hand against the woman's head and face until she slumped to the floor, then he removed his belt and used it to smack her legs. With an unexpected agility, he dropped his pants and was on top of her. She screeched and screamed over and over and over.

I stop talking. I can't get the words out. Sour vomit erupts from my throat as the image of the monster's actions fills my head. A uniformed officer appears with a cloth and gives me a handful of tissues that I use to wipe my mouth. Parker stands helplessly. I curl over, my forehead pressed against my knees, and say nothing for several moments.

"I'm so sorry," I say, finally sitting up. Again, he tells me to take my time. He is seated again; his hand reaches across the table and lightly touches my arm. I swallow a dry lump and ask, "So, are you married?" I need a break from the teeming images in my head, a diversion, just for a moment. He is confused and shakes his head. "Girlfriend?" This time he chuckles as he shakes his head again, perhaps just as relieved for the switch.

"I have a boyfriend," I say. "At least I think I do. He won't return my calls."

We had only been seeing each other a few weeks, but he didn't worry when I hadn't called for eight days. Here I was bound to a creaky chair in some madman's basement, and my boyfriend thought we were taking a break. "I can't deal with this," he'd said, when I called him from the hospital. What an odd response—as far as I could tell, there was nothing for him to deal with. What he likely meant was that he didn't want to provide a shoulder or support, didn't want to play the role of a loving and caring boyfriend. What had he been to me anyway? A lover, who occasionally took me to dinner, who rarely spent the night but knew how to strip me naked and make my entire body explode, who made me feel desired even if it was only on his schedule. I haven't spoken to him since that call from the hospital, two, three days ago. This I don't reveal to the detective, not wanting him to think I'm completely pitiful. Funny the thoughts that travel through your head in moments of stress. Here I was worried someone would think I was pathetic—now that's pathetic!

I sip some water, the weight of the glass straining my wrist to hold it up. "Do I have to say it? Do I have to say exactly what he did?"

Detective Parker's eyes close, just longer than a blink, before he nods. "I know it's hard, but it's important to make sure he goes away for the rest of his life. You want that, don't you?"

What I want is to go back and erase everything that happened. I begin again.

The man—the monster—had a knife hidden somewhere and began cutting her clothes, her skin, peeling her like a peach. Her cries were unbearable and I sobbed with her. He raped and cut her repeatedly. The blood was—

I stop, unable to bear the memory. The air is thick like oatmeal that's been cooked too long. After several deep breaths, I continue.

He finally left her alone, leaving her whimpering for hours. We three cried, unable to do anything else, the two of us wanting to comfort her, hold her, wipe her wounds. Wanting to charge my way out, scream, get the attention of anyone who could call the police. To cut him, stab him deeply, make him hurt, make him pay. The tape tightened as I struggled. The chair was stuck, immobile with me stuck and immobilized. We listened to her death. Her breathing slowed, gurgled, and painfully petered out, leaving a scorching silence that squeezed my brain, thumping inside my head, blistering my thoughts. A day, a night, another day, I didn't know what time passed as we twisted in our bondage. Unable to control my bladder, the stench of urine surrounded me, blotting out the smell of rotting death. The monster returned and dragged the body into the corner at the far end of the room. He stared at my legs until I screamed behind my taped mouth. Then like a wolf spider, he jumped forward into my face, and placed a knife under my chin, the blade oddly warm, his breath stinking of onions and garlic. "Is it your turn?" he taunted. Shifting to the woman next to me, he teased her in the same way. "Or yours?" He moved between us several times, as if playing eeny-meeny-miney-moe. A moment of calm descended upon me, and I stared at a black smudge on the opposite wall, waiting to be chosen. All sobs and tears expended, my heart bled for the second woman as she endured the same fate as the first. In the gray shadow of endless time, I heard her last breath and struggled with knowing I was next.

"But you saved me."

All my strength gone, I close my eyes and lay my cheek on the table, listening to the screams swirling through my brain. The police say we were held captive for five days—it could have been fifty. I don't sleep anymore, just drift into dark places where the blonde woman and the Asian woman keep asking me for help. I spent three days in the hospital and one day in my apartment before I was called to give my account of what happened.

I jerk up to see Detective Parker returning—I hadn't noticed him leave. "Do you need a ride home?" he asks. I tell him I'll get a taxi even though I want to curl into his arms and be transported *Star Trek*–style to a tropical planet in the Andromeda galaxy where my mind would be swept clean of darkness and all would be bright and untainted. No fear, no pain, no death.

Jazz curls around my ears as we ride along just above the speed limit in his black sports car—he would only take "yes" as an answer. He points down a small street off Columbia Road and says that's where he lives; it's not far from my place, five bus stops maybe. He coaxes me out of the car—I explain that it took me half an hour to get to the taxi, and that was only after the driver escorted me from my door. Detective Parker's fingers delicately hold my arm as we walk up the steps to my apartment. The keys are lost at the bottom of my purse and he waits as I fumble through tissues and receipts to find them. He hands me a business card and tells me to call him if I need anything. Anything at all.

I call him several times over the next few weeks, but hang up before he can answer. Each time, he calls me back and I listen to his messages, confused by what I'm feeling. Leaving my apartment fills my chest with sharp pains, the way I imagine someone having a heart attack would feel, but the paramedics say it's anxiety, so I stay inside to keep the sensation to a minimum and force my thoughts toward Detective Parker. Sensual thoughts that weave between the monster that thunders repeatedly through my brain. I stay inside and turn my mind to the detective to avoid the inevitable slide into the dark basement where my psyche drifts when I'm not paying attention.

News reporters knock and call then fade away. I change my phone number. My neighbor retrieves my mail when the post office complains that my box is overflowing. I pay her teenage son to get my groceries. My boss calls every week asking when I'm coming back to work, but I don't know how to respond. Never, is what I want to say. My counseling sessions are conducted by phone, although I'm supposed to be making efforts to get outside. Start with the front steps and then the sidewalk, etc. I stay inside.

The buzzer wakes me from a moment's sleep. Detective Parker stands in the door frame. He steps inside, asks if I'm OK and I sputter a bland response. He has news. "Your abductor is dead, stabbed to death in his jail cell. There will be no trial." The words float around my head until I finally absorb what he's saying. I ask to see the body—I have to be sure. Defying protocol, Detective Parker takes me to the morgue—suffering my nails in his arm as I step outside for the first time in weeks. He shows me the lump of pale dimpled flesh on a metal slab, and I begin to laugh, the weeks and weeks of fear exploding in hysterical laughter, morphing into sobs.

❡

I TAKE THE BUS TO his little street and look for his car. It's the first time I've been outside by myself for several months and the only place I can think of to go is to his house, waiting, fidgeting, watching for him, planning in my head to kick and scream if anyone approaches me. I wander for much of the afternoon up and down the block looking at the front stoops and flowers bursting from the tiny gardens. The air is fresh and I wonder why I stayed cooped up for so long. Just when I realize the ridiculousness of my behavior and decide to go home, I spot his black sports car pull into an open space near a pretty brick townhouse, and I follow several moments behind him, pressing each nameless buzzer until he answers. He is confused to find me at his door and stammers before asking, "How did you find me?"

I say nothing, wondering if following him home and camping on his block could be grounds for an arrest like those stalkers seeking autographs from their idols. But this idol was my savior, tangible in a way my mother's lord and savior never had been for me. My life had never been something worth saving—a C student with an associate degree, two cats, and a job at the bank starting as a teller, rising unspectacularly to branch manager over the course of six years, an apartment with a broken toilet and a few lovers who lasted no more than a month or two. Nothing I did made a difference to the world. Except this detective thought me worth saving, had cut me loose, patiently listened to me, and supported me. His face was all that was good inside my crowded head, his image bold among the scars and screams that filled every moment, awake or asleep. A warm welcome wasn't expected, but the irritation in his expression is more than I can bear and I consider running. "You said I could call you for anything." He remains quiet, calm, assessing me. I try to sound normal: "I just wanted someone to talk to."

"Aren't you seeing a therapist?"

"Someone who doesn't charge by the hour." On the brink of tears, I turn to go, but he calls me back and opens the door wider for me to enter. His studio apartment is spacious and brighter than expected. I present a pack of beer from my backpack—isn't that what normal people do? We sit on a brown leather couch and say little at first until I flood the air with words that have been swimming around inside me for weeks.

"I don't know how to be anymore," I say looking at the wooden floor. "I don't know how to be with people, how to hold a conversation about the fluctuating weather patterns. Who gives a damn about the rain! People are dying all over the world and all we talk about is the weather. But I can't explain. No one would understand what happened to me—how do you tell someone that? 'Yes, it's unusually warm today. Did you know I was kidnapped and witnessed the torture and death of two other women?' How do you say that to someone?"

Hysteria bubbles in my throat but his voice is relaxed, his hand reaches out and presses my arm down to my side, holding it there in comfort as we sit in silence. While I take deep breaths, he drinks his beer, watching me. My breathing settles back to a regular rhythm and, without much thought, I lean into him and kiss his mouth. His skin is warm, his scent sweet and savory. Rigid, he stares at me, not shocked, perhaps curious, so I kiss him again, firmer, goading him into a reaction. When his head tilts toward me and his lips open, I know he's mine. His hand slips behind my neck and pulls my body closer. I want to be consumed by his heat, drown in his passion, erase all memory, all images, and rise anew having shed the skin of the victim, of the coward, to reveal a newly crowned queen. Could that happen to me? Could this man, good and wholesome, lift me out of this dismal muck?

As he sleeps, I slip naked out of the bed and find his handgun on the kitchen table. I undo the strap, releasing it from its holster and hold it in my palm, feeling the weight press into my skin. The safety clip is on. I sit at the table fingering the cold metal and the rubber grip, and wonder if I have the strength to stop the screams still raging in my head.

Cathy Hostetler

Through the Wrong Door

CATHY HOSTETLER has been making up and telling or writing stories
for most of her seventy years, although this is her first work to be published.
She lives in the wilds of suburban Maryland with her husband and garden.
Time with her adult children is valued and she reads anything she can get
her hands on.

She'd hesitated at first. It had been a long time since she'd been to the movies. She preferred Turner classics on TV and the DVDs from their local library. Going out cost money and was a lot more trouble than it was usually worth. But their daughter, visiting from out of town, persisted. "You two really should get out more, Mom." And the grandchildren had clamored to see a popular, new nature film. So here they stood waiting in the popcorn line of the multi-theater complex. She looked around. The place had changed since she'd last been here. There was more of everything: crowds, noise, lights, signs… It was hard to find one thing in all that confusion.

"Where's the Ladies?" she asked her husband, whose vision was better.

He pointed and she wove through the throng, hoping the more active adolescents would see her coming and avoid her, as her dodging days were long past. She went through the door, glad to see no lines, and into a stall. The lack of cleanliness disgusted her. What was this place coming to? She fastidiously wiped off the seat several times and held her slacks up to keep them from contact with the spills on the floor. How could people be so inconsiderate of others? It wasn't until she was at the sink washing her hands that she noticed two young men against the wall. And the row of urinals.

"There's a woman!" one of them exclaimed, his voice high-pitched. He was tall, thin, with multiple braids cascading out from under a striped knit hat. He fumbled with his zipper in apparent haste.

"A woman?" the other, shorter and stocky, echoed.

She only took a brief glance, more than sufficient. She stared ahead, sure her face was beet red, as she hobbled as fast as she could toward the exit. Their laughter, from the one almost a shrill giggle, followed her. As she went through the door, she looked up. The word was high on the wall above, only the little symbol on the door itself. She was sure she had looked and seen—but, no, the symbol with the skirt was on the next door.

She paused a moment, panicked at the crowd and noise. Did she even know which way to go? But there, past the multitude, she could see her husband, taller than most, his white head like a buoy indicating safe passage. That nerve-flaying giggle seemed to pursue her across the lobby. Fortunately the two stayed behind, near the far wall. She was sure she could hear them, though, through all the other noise, laughing and talking with their friends. "Can you believe…? A fucking old woman!"

She kept her back turned and stood as close as she could to her husband until they could enter their theater. She didn't need to worry about being followed there. That sort would never attend this kind of movie.

She was too embarrassed to tell her family, then or later. At odd moments, though, the memory rose to consciousness like a bubble of gas from the bottom of a swamp, ruining her enjoyment of the movie. It was not just shame that twisted her gut, but dread. This was worse than leaving her purse in a restaurant, forgetting her best friend's birthday, or buying more milk when they were out of eggs. Worse than putting in twice the flour and leaving out the sugar when making a recipe she'd known by heart over sixty years. She could not shake the feeling of being stalked by something deadly. That night she lay awake, reciting the multiplication tables to herself, and could almost feel it breathing on her.

Shelagh Powers Johnson

My Father

SHELAGH POWERS JOHNSON is a writer and Montessori teacher, originally from Brooklyn, New York, and a long-time resident of Washington,
D.C. She received her MFA in creative writing from American University,
and her work has been published in *Portland Review*, *apt*, *Avatar Review*, and
Clackamas Literary Review, among others. She can usually be found writing,
reading, and helping her kindergartners become little writers and readers.
She lives in Petworth with her awesome husband and their awesome dog.

The first time I saw my father after nearly four years, he threw a plate of eggs at me and accused me of having an affair.

"Cheating bitch," he'd shouted, and the plate had smashed against the wall behind me. I could feel the spatter of yolk on my arm as he pulled the blankets up over his bare white legs and grabbed a bottle of syrup from the tray in front of him. "Crazy French *cunt*." He hurled the bottle at me and it broke open at my feet.

He was propped up in bed—*bedridden*, Nathan had warned me when I said I was coming to visit—and his body looked frail, sunken, like the body of an old man. His graying skin hung in folds around his eyes, as if the bones of his face were shrinking away. He glared at me, squinting. "How long have you been making a fool of me?" he asked. He swept the tray from his lap and it clattered to the floor. "How long has this been going on?"

I brushed bits of egg from my shirt. "Daddy…"

"Get the hell out of my house."

I felt a hand on my arm. Nathan pulled me out into the hallway, shutting the door behind us. I slid to the floor. The egg yolk had begun to dry against my skin. Nathan ran a dish towel down my arm and the yolk lifted off in flakes, like the skin of a snake.

WHEN I WAS GROWING UP, my father refused to ever make a scene in public. He was a different person when we were out of the house. I found my public father fascinating, a stranger whom I'd watch in awe. In public he smiled a lot; he made jokes and laughed loudly; he kept a protective hand against the small of my mother's back, and sometimes I'd feel the soft weight of his palm on the crown of my head, as if he were saying to the world, "These belong to me."

Before we went out, my mother would smooth back my hair with bright satin ribbons, scrub my and Nathan's fingernails until our skin was raw and our nails were as smooth and pink as seashells. She'd put on a dress that swished and rustled as she walked, and my father would look at her as though the two of them shared some wonderful secret. The world outside our house made him into a content man, and being outside those confines made my mother different too. Around other people she was charming, alive. It seemed like she touched my father more, as if being seen as his wife reminded her that that's what she was. That he was hers and that wives touched their husbands. At home she left him alone. Even as a child I could see how fiercely she loved him, but it was a hesitant love. It was the love of someone trying not to squeeze too hard, afraid that handling the object she cared about most meant that surely it would break.

As much as I liked this public version of us, there was something about knowing my father would always keep his cool that made me fight against him, simply because it was the only time I could. I was overcome by a need to test him, to see how far I could get. I was a doctor prodding at my patient, laying pressure on different spots, pushing against sensitive organs to see what would finally make him cry out. It was exhilarating, seeing my father fail to react.

Sometimes I'd play tricks on him, watch the flush of red that crawled up his neck and into his cheeks, threatening a thunderous anger that would never erupt when we were in the safety of the outside. Once at a fancy restaurant I'd unscrewed the lid of the salt shaker under the table and then placed it casually beside him, waited for him to shake it out over his steak, tried to hold in my laughter when he'd emptied the entire contents onto his plate in one dramatic mound of white. He'd hissed something at my mother under his breath, his hand shooting into the air to alert the waiter, but that was all he could do. He never asked me if I'd opened the lid. He never yelled. My mother ordered him another steak and he stayed silent and still, his eyes fixed on something beyond our table. She pretended nothing had happened.

My mother never had it in her to discipline us. She said that she'd been taught everything the wrong way and didn't want to make the same mistakes with us. "Yelling and hitting doesn't solve anything," she'd said to me once. "It doesn't teach anything but how to yell and hit." I wondered how she had ever ended up with my father.

I WAS FOURTEEN WHEN I met my father's mistress. It was a Fourth of July party, the week after my birthday. Nathan was away at camp in Monterey and my mother said I could stay downstairs until midnight if I promised not to drink and not to brag to Nathan about the party when he got home. I wore a bikini top I'd found in my mother's closet, lavender triangles that hung loosely over my breasts and tied together with beaded string that dug hard into my skin. My mother laughed when she saw me but said the color made me look tan so I left it on, wore it down to the party with a pair of tight denim shorts and a gold locket I'd gotten for my birthday.

Margaux was sitting on a piano bench next to my father, who was playing along to a jazz record and singing under his breath, his voice gravelly, slurred with liquor. She was smiling and swaying, a cigarette pinched between her lips, her dress draped low on her shoulders so I could see the hard angles of her collarbones. She was tall and pale, with powdery skin and a thick twist of black hair pinned to the back of her neck. Her arms were thin and she had no breasts at all, her chest nearly concave beneath the sheer fabric of her shirt.

"Bonjour, Caroline," she said, but she pronounced it "Caro-leen," and her throat caught on the sounds as if she were trying them out for the first time.

"Why are you dressed like that?" my father said when he saw me. He lifted his fingers from the piano keys and slammed down the cover. "For Christ's sake, Caroline."

Margaux smiled up at me, wrapped an arm around my waist, her long fingers stretching around the curve of my hip. She held an ashtray in her hand and the glass was cold against my skin. "I think she looks lovely," Margaux said, and her accent made each word sound new. I smiled back, pulled my stomach in tight. Her eyes were level with my torso and I wanted her to notice the cinch of my waist, the new rise of my breasts.

My father's eyes flicked across my bare body and he shook his head. "You look like a hooker," he told me.

"Let her have her fun," Margaux said. She swirled the wine in her glass, lifted the glass to her lips. "While her body is young and exquisite." She smelled like ginger and cigarettes.

When I found her and my father in the den a few hours later, I didn't recognize her for a moment. My father was holding her long black hair in his fists while she leaned naked over a gold-plated mirror, her face pressed close to the smears of powder. She looked up at me and just smiled. My father was bare-chested behind her, his legs wrapped around her frail white frame.

"Get out, Caroline," he said, but I could barely hear him. Margaux was silent. Her breasts hung small and limp over the hollow of her stomach.

And then my mother was there, pulling me from the room, shutting the door noiselessly behind us. "It's past midnight," she said. Her eyes were dark, the blues and grays of her makeup smudged across her lids like the spread of new bruises. She looked down at my bathing suit; the fabric sagged around me and I felt suddenly childish. She shook her head, tugged at the strings behind my neck. "You stubborn thing, you wore it all night long."

DOWNSTAIRS, NATHAN TOLD ME THAT music was the only thing my father always seemed to remember. "Half the time he doesn't know who the hell I am, but the man could pick Charlie Parker out of a lineup." He poured me a cup of coffee and slid a bowl of sugar across the kitchen table. Above us, the sound of my father's record player pulsed through the floorboards. "Once he wakes up a little he'll be glad you're here, even if he's not sure who you are." Nathan stood at the kitchen window, his arms folded tightly across his chest, his foot tapping along to the shrill whine of saxophones. I wondered for a moment how he could stand living alone in this enormous house with a man who couldn't even remember his name.

"He called me a cunt." I poured some milk into my coffee mug and it sloshed over the edge. Nathan reached across me and smeared the spill away with the palm of his hand, and I smiled up at him, took his wet hand in mine. "Two strokes and he still knows I'm the bad one."

Nathan laughed and wiped his hand along the leg of his pants. "I'm sure that wasn't meant for you, Caroline."

My father was a month shy of his sixtieth birthday and dying of liver disease, having suffered nearly enough brain damage to wipe his memory clean. "He's only got a little while left," Nathan had told me when he called to let me know he was moving to Montauk to be with our father. "A few months at the most. You should come."

My father lived in what used to be my parents' vacation house, a huge bungalow on the tip of Long Island where he moved with Margaux when I was eighteen, a few years after he divorced my mother. The house sat right on the beach, its entire back wall built of glass so that the blond wood of the ceilings and floors framed the stretch of beach outside like a mural. When it stormed the ocean rolled up over the dunes, feet from the house, and when I was younger I imagined the waves lifting the house from its roots like a tooth pulled from its gums, carrying us off into the sound while we slept.

"Has he mentioned Mom at all?" I stirred my coffee around, lifted a sip into the bowl of my spoon.

"Not really. He talks about women all the time, but I never know who he's talking about. He's always saying he has parties to go to." Nathan shrugged and sat down beside me. "I guess they're parties that happened twenty years ago."

When I told my mother that my father was dying, she said it was because men can't survive without women. "Women can outlive their husbands by fifty years. They can live alone their whole lives," she told me. "But men without women just fade away."

When Margaux died last year, my mother said I should go to the funeral. I was living in Los Angeles, a few miles from my childhood home where my mother still lived, and I refused. I didn't want to see how Margaux's death hurt my father; I didn't want to see him destroyed by the loss of a woman when leaving my mother hadn't hurt him at all.

HE MARRIED MARGAUX ON CHRISTMAS Day, on our beach in Montauk. It was below freezing that day, and the sand was coated in a thick layer of snow, but Margaux wore a sleeveless white dress that made her nearly indistinguishable against the heavy gray sky. The white of her arms and shoulders blurred with the snow and her black hair, hanging loose, looked like a mistake, a smudge of ink across a blank page. I loved when it snowed in Montauk; the image of snow against beach was like one photograph superimposed on another. It reminded me of a picture my father had bought for my mother's birthday the year before they divorced, a picture that was three photographs developed as one: an enormous volcano sprouting up from a wet city sidewalk, reaching up into the sky and erupting into a violent waterfall that spilled down its sides. At the base of the volcano, a couple kissed beneath an umbrella, their eyes pressed shut, their arms clasped around each other, the waterfall inches from their bodies, about to sweep them away.

"Incongruity," my father said when he brought it home to my mother, "is what makes this beautiful. Water erupting from fire, a love story amidst destruction." He pointed to the couple. "They're facing death and they don't even know it. They're totally oblivious."

My mother studied the picture, and I knew she wanted to say something artistic, something that would impress my father. She was quiet for a long time, and then she shook her head. "They know they're going to die," she said finally. She ran a finger along the glass of the frame, leaving a greasy smudge over the arc of the couple's umbrella. "That's the point. They know everything is ending, and all they can do is hold on."

AFTER NATHAN AND I HAD dinner together, Nathan went up to our father's room to help him out of bed and downstairs into his wheelchair. "It's what he does every night," Nathan explained as he piled our dishes into the kitchen sink. "He just wheels around the house and talks. It's the only time he doesn't act like he's dying."

I could hear them upstairs together, my brother's voice low and even, my father's rising shrilly over the creaks of his bed like the protests of a child. I heard their footsteps reach the top of the stairs and start to descend, the clap of their feet slow and deliberate. I turned on the kitchen faucet and watched our dinner plates fill with water, the remains of our food swirling down into the drain.

I could hear him in the living room, settling into his wheelchair, the rubber of the wheels squeaking along the wood floors. Nathan came into the kitchen and told me he was going to rest upstairs, that I should wake him up when Dad was ready to go up to bed.

"Don't leave me alone with him," I whispered, but Nathan just shook his head and started toward the staircase.

"He's still the same person, Caroline," he told me. He smiled. "If that's any consolation."

I was still washing dishes when my father rolled into the kitchen, and he stopped in the doorway, watching me silently.

"Hi, Daddy." I leaned back against the counter, waited for him to speak. I took a sip of wine. My father just studied the blanket that was draped across his lap, twisting it between his fingers. He smiled down at the fistful of fabric, then up at me. "I don't know why you're always trying to make me wear flashy shirts," he said, and wheeled further into the room. His eyes were unfocused and a light diluted blue. "I'd go around looking like a fairy if you had your way." I didn't say anything. His long, slender hands were pale and pockmarked, the skin stretched out over his bones so thinly that I could see each vein snaking around the rise of his knuckles. His fingernails were chipped and yellowing, and they snagged on the loose threads of blanket. He held the blanket up for me to see. "These are the kind of shirts I like, Margaux," he said, his voice quiet. "Not too flashy, not too casual. Just right."

"Daddy." I crossed over to him and put my hand on his. It felt natural even though I hadn't touched him in years. His hand was cold and damp beneath mine. He looked at the wineglass in my hand, shook his head.

"I thought we had a deal," he said, and wrapped his fingers around the glass's stem. "Nothing to drink this week."

"It's me, Dad." I pried his fingers from my glass and stepped back. His eyes searched me, accusing. "Daddy. It's Caroline."

"I've been true to my word since Saturday. Not a brandy, not even a cigarette." His gaze fixed on the floor. "Benny offered me a line and I said no siree."

I went back over to the sink, looked out the kitchen window into the darkness. I could hear the low rumble of waves smacking against the shore outside, but all I could see was black. "Do you feel OK?" I asked.

I heard my father sigh behind me. "How do you think I feel? I'm about to die." He cleared his throat and it turned into a loose, rattling cough. I turned back to him and he was wheeling toward me. "You're probably counting the days." He reached up and snatched the wineglass from my hand. He rolled it between his palms, his eyes set on mine, and then smashed it on the floor. "I told you not to *drink*." He wheeled across the shards of glass and they crunched beneath his weight. "No wonder you died first."

NATHAN WAS ALREADY ASLEEP WHEN I heard my father calling out for him from his bedroom. I was lying awake in my old room, on the canopy bed my parents bought me on our first trip to Montauk. The room smelled like vacation, like unused bedsheets and cold beach air. I closed my eyes and tried not to listen to my father's voice through the walls.

"Nathan," he called, and I wondered if that would make Nathan happy, if waking to the sound of our father remembering him would make his place here seem somehow more worthwhile. We were the first ones to fade from our father's memory and sometimes I wondered if Nathan resented him for it.

"Nathan," my father shouted again, and then quieter, "Caroline." The sound of my name through the wall slammed hard against me, knocked my heart into a quick, nervous beat.

"I'm coming, Daddy," I called, and my voice was hoarse.

My father was sitting up in bed and the lamp beside him was on, spilling light onto his face so that the deep creases around his lips and eyes caught in the shadows, making him look old, used up. His hands hung limp at his sides, palms up, defeated, as if to say, *I simply don't know.*

"Are you OK?" I asked. His eyes were dark, hollowed out, and his skin looked yellow and leathery. He shook his head, slowly, and looked up at me.

"She wasn't even dead," he told me, pushing away his blankets. He was wearing a pair of pajama bottoms with candy canes on them, red and green fabric with flecks of cartoon snow swirling down the legs. He looked like a little boy. "Your mother wasn't even dead when they buried her."

I crossed over to his bed. "Mom is alive, Daddy. Mom didn't die." I smoothed the blankets back around him, covered his legs.

"Caroline," he said, louder, deliberate. "I saw her move at the funeral. I told someone but they ignored me. Her hands were trembling. I told her to open her eyes but she couldn't. She was so weak." He rubbed his hands together, pressed them to his face. "I've never seen her so weak as she was at that fucking funeral."

"Daddy," I said. I sat down on the edge of the bed beside him. "Do you mean Margaux?"

He lifted his hands from his face and looked at me, confused. "Of course I mean Margaux. She was so brave that day." I saw something change in his eyes, a flicker of memory. He looked straight at me. "Your mother was never brave like that." He placed his hand on mine and leaned back against the headboard. "Margaux loved me less than I loved her," he said, and his eyes were closed. He was smiling. "I loved her so much and she cheated on me all the time. Did you know that, sweetheart?" His hands were rough against mine, dry and calloused, and he rubbed his thumb up and down my forearm as if he were trying to soothe me. "She said I was the only lover that she *loved*. She said that made all the difference." He laughed. "Boy was she something."

I reached for the lamp switch. "It's late, Daddy."

"We had a lovely life together, though. Whether she loved me or not, it was damn lovely."

MY MOTHER STILL WORE HER wedding ring sometimes, long after my father left her. She never remarried, never went on dates or had men over to the house. We'd go shopping together and I'd wonder why she bothered, why every morning she lined her lips with red lipstick and wore expensive clothes, why she got a facial each week, who she bought silky slips and lace stockings for. I hated when she bought new dresses, pictured her alone in her closet snipping off the tags and hanging the dresses behind rows of clothes, realizing she had nowhere to wear them.

Sometimes I'd see her twirl her wedding ring frantically around her finger, lift it up toward the knuckle and then drop it down again, the habit of a woman married twenty years. She'd look down at it and I'd wonder how the feel of it on her skin didn't destroy her, how the thought of my father didn't make her hurl it against the walls. I asked her once how she could still love him. She slid the ring up over the slope of her knuckle then back into place, and she said simply, "Because I do."

The light wisps of my mother's hair had begun showing the first glimmers of gray, silvery against pale blonde. She'd tried dyeing them but they just resurfaced, like wrinkles creasing their way through layers of thick pink makeup. Still she looked young and beautiful to me. "It's easier to be left. It's out of your hands. What's impossible is choosing to lose what you love." She shrugged, pushed a hand through her hair. "So I stayed until he wasn't there anymore."

MY FATHER FELL ASLEEP WITH his hands still clasped around mine, and I stretched out next to him, listening to the rumble of his shallow breathing. His heartbeat was slow, uneven, and part of me expected it to taper off, to grow lighter and lighter like retreating footsteps until it rested silent in his chest. But it kept going, vibrating hard against me.

I fell asleep next to him, and in the middle of the night we awoke at the same time. He looked at me, his eyes bright and blue and clear, the eyes of someone young. He gripped my hand in his, held on tight until my fingers were nearly numb. I knew that the memory of me had died away again. He watched me and I let him, my eyes never breaking from his, until something in his face changed and he looked relieved, calmed, as if he just had to be sure that anyone was there at all.

Trasi Johnson

The Cigar Box Collector

TRASI JOHNSON was born in Washington, D.C. She is a graduate of
the University of Maryland. She spent many formative years as a writer
in Boston, Massachusetts, where she published her first stories in *Callaloo*,
the *Agni Review*, *Testimony*, *Mosaic*, and *In the Tradition*. Her work is listed
in *Ghost Stories by British and American Women: An Annotated Bibliography*.
She lived for thirteen years in Marseilles, France, where she raised her son,
Malcolm, and became fluent in French. Now she has found her way back
to her home town and works as the assistant to a French chef.

I’ve always loved the sweet, heavy smell of a cigar shop. I don't
smoke. Never have. But I love the smell of cigars. It's an old
smell, harkening back to a lost world of black and white movies
where men and women always wore hats out of doors. When I was a little
girl visiting my grandmother in Northwest D.C. she had a neighbor, Mr.
Harper, who smoked a cigar on his porch every evening after dinner. In
summer, that cigar smell would waft through the screen door into the living
room. The first time I smelled it, I didn't know what it was. That's a rare
kind of memory—the memory of a new smell, that instant when it was
unidentifiable. Strange. Mysterious. Suddenly filling a room. Overwhelming. I followed the smell to the screen door and stepping out on the porch
saw the back of Mr. Harper's head all stubbly gray, the smoke swirling
around him, gathering under the porch roof in billowy clouds. It was an
old people's smell, like mothballs or foot ointment.

So when I smell a cigar, it's heavy with memories of summer evenings
and my grandmother and the swinging clap of the screen door. That's why
I started collecting the boxes. There was always something of the smell
left in them bridging the years.

It was on one of my first excursions into the city on my own that I
discovered cigar boxes. I was in Georgetown playing grown-up. I was

fifteen. I had taken the bus from our Maryland suburb into D.C., my parents' warnings echoing in my head. "Always have change for a phone call." "Don't talk to strangers." "Don't hitchhike." "Don't pull your money out on the street." Those were the years before cell phones. D.C. was a dangerous city. That's why our parents moved out so far in the first place. Traffic and people and stores were everywhere. Every space was filled, crammed. Even the trees that lined the sidewalks were barely contained, pushing up slabs of concrete with stubborn roots. I walked in a daze, a big silly grin on my face, more at ease in all this confusion than I had ever been in the orderly calm of the suburbs.

I smelled the cigar shop before I saw it. I was on M Street gawking at windows, wandering in and out of shops—a second-hand bookstore, an expensive boutique, an ice cream parlor—I had never seen any of them at the mall. Then I caught a faint whiff of cigar and I looked around for the smoker. I continued up M Street and the smell got stronger, more complex. It seemed to fill the street. I finally arrived at a spot where the smell was overwhelming. I looked up, and I was in front of a cigar shop. As I pushed through the door, a bell tinkled. Everything dimmed. My steps were hollow thuds on the wood floor. It was a long narrow space with a long wood and glass counter stretching as far back as the dim light permitted me to see. Towards the back there was a haziness through which I could just barely perceive puffing clouds of smoke rising up from shadowy silhouettes seated in old-fashioned high-backed wing chairs—dark leather, trimmed with shiny brass studs. Wooden shelves full of boxes lined the walls—a mosaic of rich varying woods punctuated with bright reds, oranges, greens.

One of the shadows rose up from its high-backed seat and drifted out of the haze of the back of the shop along the counter towards me. The figure resolved itself into the form of a tall, bearded man. He said, "Hello, we don't get many strangers here. How can I help you, young lady?" I said, "Oh, I don't um…smoke. I just like the…" I felt suddenly silly. I didn't want to admit I had come in simply for the smell. I said, "What are all these boxes? They're beautiful." He smiled and said, "That's how they pack cigars. Keeps them fresh. If all you want are the boxes, the empties are stacked in that corner. Take your pick and make a donation of a dollar each."

That's how I started collecting. They were perfect for storing odds and ends, pens and stationary and loose change. They were both decorative and practical. I thought they added an antique-ish, citified air to my suburban square of a bedroom.

Every time I went to Georgetown, I'd come back with a few boxes. There were so many sizes and shapes and colors with names like Maduro and Avo Uvezian and Perdomo Reserve etched in the lids. I had not been anywhere yet, but the boxes told me there were other places out there somewhere beyond the suburbs, even beyond D.C., where they rolled cigars and made these exquisite wooden boxes just to keep them fresh.

I would always go alone. None of my friends liked going to the city. They preferred the safe, climate-controlled environment of the mall. I'd go alone and have ice cream and pick up a used book and sniff my way to the cigar shop, to its dim interior, to the hollow knock of its wood floor, to its shadows mingling in the haze. The bearded man always looked at me strangely. As if he were surprised every time I came back.

One day a friend finally decided to join me on one of my treks into the city. I was always bragging about my adventures, all my rare finds, exaggerating a bit. She wanted to see what it was all about. She especially wanted to pick up one of those beautiful cigar boxes like the ones I had strewn all over my room. I had been going to the city alone for over a year and I felt that I had become an authority. I knew my way around all the museums and which buses to take and where to get lunch that wasn't fast food. When we got to Georgetown, I couldn't help bragging about the cigar shop. I said, "You'll start to smell it when we get on M Street. You can't mistake it. It's kind of a sweet, musky smell. Kind of clingy. It sticks in your throat a little. There is something of dusk in it." We passed the used bookstore and the ice cream parlor, and I said, "Do you smell that?" She sniffed a bit and said, "No." I said, "Well, I'm sensitive to it. You'll smell it soon." She kept sniffing and not smelling anything as we walked up the street. I figured too many years stuck in suburbs and at the mall had dulled her senses. I didn't care. I was in my element breezily weaving my way along the narrow, crowded sidewalk, pointing out street lamps and bus stops and the odd bit of graffiti as she dashed and dodged behind me trying to keep up.

We got to the place where the smell was strongest, almost stifling. I said, "Well, here it is," and turning to push open the door, smacked my palms into a solid red brick wall, scraping my fingers and nearly breaking a wrist.

My friend laughed, "What are you doing to that wall?" I looked up. There was nothing but wall. I could smell the shop, but it wasn't there. My friend said, "Look at you. You're lost. Little miss-know-it-all has lost her precious little shop. Wait till I tell everybody we got lost." She couldn't stop laughing. She really wasn't much of a friend.

Of course, I figured out later it was all her fault. Her senses were so messed up she couldn't perceive the shop and that messed things up for me too. I ended up being blocked out, unable to find the door. The next weekend, when I went back by myself, I had no problem getting in. The door was where it should have been, the shadows and the smokers as well. The doorbell tinkled as it always had, and I continued to collect my boxes and bask in that beautiful old smell, alone.

Stephanie Joyce

Stones

STEPHANIE JOYCE had written about science, health, art, plants, and country music before a character stopped her on the street and insisted that she listen. This is her first published story.

The bus ride to the madhouse crossed desert and green plains all across Tamil Nadu, nearly as far as the Bay of Bengal. Rafiq's mother huddled by the window, muttering now and then in Malayali. His father snored, his mouth fallen open like a dead man's. Rafiq, squashed between them, stared out to where hills and fields rolled away behind, and thought of stones.

When they stopped in Kadaladi his father took them all—in a taxi!—to the white-walled compound of a mosque. He had the taxi wait while he unpacked Rafiq and his mother and then the bag of mangoes, Rafiq's small bundle, and his mother's only slightly larger one. His mother began to shake all over. She was mad, but she was not stupid. When Rafiq's father banged on the metal gate, she turned her face to the sky and keened like a jackal.

His father peeled her fingers from his arm and wrapped them round Rafiq's wrist, and then he took hold of Rafiq's shoulder and his oily black eyes looked into his son's. Rafiq thought that now he would finally explain why it was he who had to stay with his mother in the madhouse. He was sure it was a punishment because he had thrown stones at the holy man who said a demon lived within his mother.

His father did not mention the holy man. He said that Rafiq was a man now, a man who could protect his mother since Rafiq's brother, who was already earning money, could not, and certainly not his sisters, who were needed to cook and clean; whereas Rafiq could protect his mother properly and besides he had been to school and could write every week to report on how much better she was. His father's forehead grew moist with perspiration as he spoke these words, and his gaze slid away from Rafiq's eyes to glance at the taxi waiting under the nungu tree and frown at the empty sky, as if a heavy rain were only instants away. When the gates to the compound creaked open, he swooped upon the three bags of provisions and, holding his laden arms out like wings, impelled Rafiq and his mother between the metal portals.

"Be good! I'll come back to see you soon!"

A dark-skinned man in a ragged white tunic looked straight at Rafiq's mother. "Come, sister," he said, and held out a hand. Rafiq's mother quaked like a bird before a snake. Rafiq glanced back at the world outside. Where the taxi had waited, there now squatted a little gang of staring children. This was just the sort of gang, Rafiq knew, that could very soon be throwing stones. Children just like this had thrown stones at his mother back home.

The children did not move, though, and the dark man waited motionless with one hand on the gate and the other reaching out. Rafiq's mother balked, uttering an awful mewing sound, and Rafiq had to haul her backward through the gates, countering his weight against hers as he would with a reluctant water buffalo. As he dragged her inside, he saw the children's eyes on him, until the gates clanged shut.

Inside were white walls, a wide dusty yard, a well. People lay under the sun or crouched in the shade of neem and acacia trees. An afternoon hush lay over the compound, but as they followed the dark man, Rafiq felt the silent music of madness roiling around them. A naked man rolled in the dust, clutching his knees to his chest; a pretty girl around eleven, Rafiq's age, wept silently as she tore at her hair; Rafiq could hear the soft popping of the strands ripping free. Yet the dark man, an imam, Rafiq knew later, nodded back encouragingly at them, and no one threw stones as they walked past, and his mother had slackened her death-grip on his hand and did not creep but walked beside him with some of her old grace, making Rafiq remember that not so long ago she had been a beautiful, loving mother, and now she was here and he was with her.

They found a good place between a neem tree and the western wall, shaded from the afternoon sun. There was rice to eat, and tea made with bitter well water. Rafiq's mother began to speak again—though sometimes only in Malayali. There were still many days when she thrashed and whipped her hair about her head and trotted around the compound, shaking her shoulders as if they were covered with bees, and Rafiq had to get up and trot behind her. Often, when the muezzin sang the call to pray, she saw a demon in Rafiq, and then she would scream and run from him and try to escape through the gate. Rafiq wanted to let her run, but she could not run mad alone in this strange place, could she? When he caught her, she screamed even louder, and the people in the compound watched silently as Rafiq wrestled her back to the mosque.

Sometimes Rafiq thought there might be a demon in him because he was so angry with his mother, and with his father, who did not come to see them, and with the imam, though he was kind, and with the staring children outside the walls, and the terrifying souls within them. This was his family now: his mother and her demon, and the demons living inside Suhaila the somersaulting girl; Madhu, a fat cobra-black woman who spoke only Telugu; Jaldev, his brother's age, who lay on the ground and ate dirt; Thara who tore her hair; Kalani who never stopped her silent weeping.

Rafiq wanted to avoid Kalani because something deeper than anger and sorrow threatened to well up in him when he looked into her shadowed eyes, but there was no avoiding her. His mother liked Kalani. She would sit with her, chatting one-sidedly in Malayali, braiding vines and weeds into Kalani's thick hair. And Kalani's husband, Walif, showed Rafiq how to coax spinach and potatoes out of the hard soil behind the mosque. He talked to Rafiq in Malayali, because Rafiq didn't know Kannada and Walif didn't speak Tamil. Children back in Rafiq's village would have thrown stones at him for his face, whose left side seemed to have melted; once, Rafiq might have thrown stones himself. Walif was not mad or possessed, though: only deeply, endlessly sad.

"Five years she's like this," he said to Rafiq in his broken Malayali as he pulled strings of bindweed from the vegetable rows. "She can't work, she can't cook. The doctors are not helping. I'm think she have a demon. All day she cry, she sleep, she not want to eat, but she is my wife. I think I'm stay with her forever. How can I leave her alone?"

Rafiq looked at his mother, who smiled beautifully at him as she threaded bindweed into the hair of the weeping woman, and he wondered if he too would stay with his mother forever, and who would throw stones at him if he ever left this place.

Jacqueline Jules

Be Thankful Your Mother Isn't Edna Stein

JACQUELINE JULES is the author of over two dozen children's books including *Zapato Power* and *Unite or Die: How Thirteen States Became a Nation*. Her poetry has appeared in numerous journals including *Pirene's Fountain, Lines and Stars, Inkwell, Rkvry Quarterly Literary Journal, Potomac Review, Little Patuxent Review, Connecticut River Review, Minimus,* and *Imitation Fruit*. Her poetry chapbook, *Field Trip to the Museum,* is forthcoming from Finishing Line Press. Visit her online at www.jacquelinejules.com.

My dad must have said it at least a thousand times my seventh grade year. "Be thankful your mother isn't Edna Stein."

It was his standard advice every time he heard me arguing with Mom about what time I had to be home from the movies or whether or not I could go to the mall.

"If Edna was your mother, you wouldn't be allowed to go anywhere. Think about poor Shirley."

Holding back his buck-toothed smile like a walrus trying to hide his tusks, Dad loved to remind me how lucky I was not to be Shirley, the daughter of my mother's friend, Edna Stein.

"Edna hides in the backseat when Shirley goes out on dates."

Shirley was eighteen, five years older than I was.

"She still has to hold her mommy's hand when she crosses the street."

"Be quiet, Harry!" Mom would swat Dad's arm at the dinner table. "It's not nice to make fun of people."

But like a talk show host who can't resist making jokes about the president, my father couldn't stop when it came to Edna Stein.

"Now that her kids are teenagers, Edna has calmed down. She only calls the pediatrician twelve times a day instead of twenty."

Sometimes I wondered if Dad didn't like to poke at Edna Stein as a way of pushing Mom to worry less about me. A national ranking of over-protective mothers would have given my mother second place. She paced like a caged tiger if I was fifteen minutes late. And when I walked in, she pounced on me with a roar.

"Where have you been? I've been going crazy, worrying if you were dead or alive."

The time she caught me taking a nature walk in a wooded area behind the cemetery, her hysteria must have been heard in Alaska.

"Perverts lurk in the woods! Promise me you'll never go there again!"

It was one of a hundred weekly safety promises Mom pleaded for with wringing hands and frantic blue eyes—don't lean over balconies, keep the hair dryer out of the toilet, don't eat rare hamburgers.

"Do you make lists of dangerous activities while I'm at school? Is that how you amuse yourself?"

Of course that perfectly honest question turned into another shouting match over how little I loved her and my general unworthiness as a daughter. Everything was fodder for a fight—towels on the bathroom floor, my unmade bed, my somehow unnatural desire to spend more time with my friends than my parents. But the one thing that topped all other sins was being late for Edna Stein's carpool.

"Five minutes! Edna's coming in five minutes!" Mom hollered up the stairs as I took off the yellow low-cut sweater I tried on every morning, hoping that morning I'd have the nerve to wear something that tight.

"Why do you keep doing this to me?" Mom whined.

I probably changed clothes an average of six times, throwing off each rejected outfit for a different reason. The red skirt had a droopy hem. The cream top had a stain near my left boob. The blue flowered pants made me look fat. I wasn't trying to aggravate my mother. I was trying to keep myself from looking like a dweeb at school all day.

"Trudie! Why can't you respect my feelings?"

It was a funny question when you considered that Mom didn't seem to care how embarrassing it was for me to show up at school every day in Edna Stein's dirty white Volvo.

"Trudie! Mrs. Stein and Norman are waiting outside."

Lucky me, Edna Stein lived two blocks away and had a pimply-faced son, Norman, my age. Edna and my mother had been carpooling us to private schools since preschool. Every morning, at eight a.m., Norman sat in the front seat of Edna's dirty white Volvo, with blood-shot gray eyes. Occasionally he made snide remarks about watching my mother wring her hands at the front door, but he usually kept his puffy lips shut. Unlike Edna Stein.

"Ah! The princess has arrived!" Edna announced as I climbed in the backseat. On especially perky days, she would add other cute tidbits in her low, nasal voice. She sounded exactly like what you would expect from a cartoon elephant with a cold.

"We only waited six minutes today. An improvement. You must be getting up earlier. Your mother said she was going to set your alarm clock back."

Edna's mouth ran three times faster than her car. Even my mother got ticked off sometimes.

"Why did Edna tell you about my miscarriages? I told her that in confidence."

While the reason why I was an only child vaguely interested me, the rest of what I learned on the interminable ride to school I never cared to know.

"Two years ago, we found out that Norman has a severe allergy to blueberries. I gave him one blueberry pancake and his whole body broke out in hives. Can you imagine?"

I could imagine perfectly. Norman had such bad acne he might as well have been covered with hives. I felt sorry for the poor kid. Not only was he ugly, he had to live with Edna Stein, the woman who teamed up with my mother to protest the school ski trip.

"It's too risky," Edna pronounced as we waited at a red light, her chubby hands hugging the wheel. "If parents want to take their own kids out to break their necks, that's their business. But a ski trip isn't something the school should be offering to seventh grade students. It has no educational value."

Edna Stein thought everyone should go through life the way she drove her dirty white Volvo—with one foot on the brake, never hesitating to bring the car to a complete halt whenever the traffic was uncertain.

"Trudie! Mrs. Stein will be here any minute!"

The voice hollering up the stairs was such a part of my morning routine I hardly heard it anymore. But one Monday morning in May, I did notice when Mom wasn't calling for me to get ready. I looked at the radio alarm on my bedside table. It said 8:25 a.m. Edna Stein never arrived later than 8:02.

"Mom!" I ran down the stairs fully dressed with my backpack. "Where's Mrs. Stein? I'm going to be late for school."

My mother was in the kitchen, hanging up the telephone. Her face looked puzzled.

"I just called Edna to find out where she was. You won't believe what she said to me. She said she couldn't talk now. She was making blueberry pancakes for Norman's breakfast."

"Norman is allergic to blueberries," I said, remembering the blueberry/hive story.

"I thought so, too."

Mom picked up the telephone again. This time, she called 911.

"A friend of mine sounded very strange on the phone. Like she was frightened. Something's wrong over there."

The person on the other end didn't seem too anxious to send a police car out to a house because a woman was making blueberry pancakes. Mom turned the volume up to full blast.

"EDNA STEIN IS NEVER LATE FOR CARPOOL! SOMETHING DANGEROUS IS GOING ON THERE. I CAN FEEL IT!"

After ten minutes of arguing, my mom convinced the police to check out the blueberry-pancake-making-problem at Edna Stein's house.

They arrived at 9:05 a.m., just after Mrs. Stein had been shot.

The two armed men who broke into the Stein's house at four in the morning were drug addicts who had picked the house at random. When they found only twenty dollars in Mrs. Stein's purse, they began rifling through drawers. One of the intruders found a savings account statement. That's when they decided to hold the family hostage until the banks opened.

My mind has played the scene at least a hundred times—what it must have been like for the Steins, tied to kitchen chairs while two gunmen ransacked their house for jewelry and other valuables. I see Mrs. Stein's black curls plastered to her forehead with sweat. She's chewing her bottom lip, as her brown eyes flicker with the realization that my mom will call when the carpool doesn't arrive on time. She's had hours to think of the right thing to say. But if we don't remember Norman is allergic to blueberries, her plan has no chance.

Our memory did not save Mrs. Stein. After a night without sleep, the gunmen were nervous. The telephone call Mrs. Stein had insisted she take had made them edgier. It was time to go to the bank. They planned to take the whole family in the car for the bank withdrawal. Mrs. Stein was the last to leave the house in front of the gunmen. She hesitated at the front door, realizing her children and her husband were safely outside. Did she mean to sacrifice herself or was it just an accident—an impatient criminal waving a gun that went off? No one knows exactly what happened. But when Mrs. Stein stalled at the front door, a shot was fired. Then a police car pulled up and the two gunmen ran away.

They were apprehended immediately, before the ambulance came for Mrs. Stein. She died on the way to the hospital.

Sitting at the funeral, my fingers drummed my knees uncontrollably. I had never known someone who had died before, much less someone who'd been murdered. I kept thinking about Norman and Shirley, who had seen their mother in a pool of blood.

As many times as I had screamed in my mother's face, "Go away! Leave me alone!" I had never considered the possibility that it could happen.

"Be thankful your mother isn't Edna Stein."

Those words, so often repeated by my father, echo in my head. They have an entirely different meaning now.

Brooke Kenny

Ghost Orchid

Brooke Kenny's first novel, *Echoes of Her*, was published by All Things That Matter Press in 2011. She earned a master's degree in creative writing from Johns Hopkins in 2008. This latest work is the first chapter of a novel-in-progress, tentatively titled "Ghost Orchid." Brooke works at Friends Club of Bethesda, a nonprofit serving people with Alzheimer's disease and other forms of dementia and their families. She lives in Greenbelt, Maryland, with her husband and their new baby daughter.

I wasn't looking for anything in particular that day, or rather I wasn't looking for anything particular on any day. I was worse than lost. I was existing. I had no goals, no direction, no fulfillment, and little joy outside of the sound of a cold can of beer being popped open. It was a sad state for anyone, but it was especially pathetic for a man of only twenty-five.

I was working part time selling Duron paint and somehow managing to pull in enough to pay rent. I shared a bedroom with two other guys in the three-bedroom basement of a shitty house, although truthfully we didn't typically make it back to our official beds. There were plenty of old couches and filthy blankets to keep everyone happy.

I lived on McDonald's apple pies, cheese popcorn, and cigarettes. Most of my calories came from beer. When I dropped by my mother's house, I'd usually sneak into the bathroom and take a vitamin. I only dropped by my mother's house once every couple of months, so clearly I wasn't too concerned with my utter lack of nutrition.

I'll never forget how I felt the day that led up to the worst drinking binge of my life. Just being alive was excruciating. There was no one area of my body that plagued me. It was my whole existence. I was marginally hung over from the night before and I lay on the couch for hours trying to either go back to sleep or settle on doing something that sounded appealing. Usually the desire for coffee gave me the boost I needed to stand up, but not on that day. I also couldn't get comfortable. Whether I was on my back, side, or stomach, some part of my body was being pulled the wrong way or being violated by a lump in the blankets.

I got up and poured myself a bowl of Cap'n Crunch. I recognized the taste as "good," yet it didn't taste good. It didn't taste like anything at all. It just…was. It was like all of my pleasure sensors had been turned off.

I couldn't cope with the idea of showering, so I sat on the couch and turned on the television. It was a Wednesday afternoon and our antenna allowed us access to four channels. I settled on *Days of Our Lives*, only because the lighting made everything look soft and less bothersome than the programs on the other stations. There was a character—a pretty young woman with a round face and white-blonde hair—who had just brought home Chinese food for her son. The familiar white cartons she pulled out of the bag had no metal handles on them. I was thinking about how much more sense that makes because you can't put metal in the microwave and everyone microwaves leftover Chinese food. It was right then that Ricky walked in holding a case of beer.

Ricky was a guy that I hung out with. He was around. He was kind of funny. There's not much more to say about him than that. He didn't live in our house. Well, maybe he did for a week or two once, but he wasn't an official roommate.

"Alex, what's up?"

"Nothin' man," I said, holding my bowl of cereal.

"Come help me carry the booze in from the car. I did a liquor store run. I just won a thousand bucks on a lottery ticket."

I stood and pulled up my sweatpants. I walked outside without a shirt or shoes, though it must have been close to freezing. I brought box after box into our living room. Ricky started loading the beer into our refrigerator and then went around to the other guys' bedrooms knocking on the doors. Both Rob and Lou were home, and I heard Ricky declare from the back hallway that we were all going to "do it up."

I went to our kitchen and rinsed out a Solo cup that had been on the edge of the sink for I'm not sure how long. I filled it half full of Wild Turkey from one of the bottles Ricky had just brought in and headed to my room to change into jeans. Aside from my state of mind, I generally subscribed to the philosophy that you don't wash a pair of jeans until they're ready to come alive and walk out on their own. Combine that with a general lack of enthusiasm for all things worldly, and I wound up with three filthy pairs of jeans. I put on some old, too-tight boxers I found in the back of my underwear drawer and grabbed the pair of jeans that had the fewest visible stains. I was also inspired enough to put on a green pocketed T-shirt that I was pretty sure I'd had since high school.

We all went to hang out on the driveway—our favorite refuge that was close enough to the fridge but yet not inside and therefore an acceptable location for us, according to our landlord, to smoke cigarettes. Ricky took one of Rob's cigarettes and lit up.

"Motherfucker," Rob said with sarcasm in his voice. Ricky had, after all, just given us every reason to shut the world out for a couple of days and drink an amount of alcohol that otherwise we couldn't have afforded. And I knew from looking in all three guys' faces that we were on the same page. Their eyes had a kind of excited intensity that said they were willing to go past limits they had long ago set for themselves. We were going to create something together—crazy survival stories, crazy fun, crazy fearlessness, crazy memories. But the joke of it is that I don't remember all that much of what happened over the next three days. I'd venture to say they don't either.

What I do remember is a collage of movie-like clips, out of sequence and disconcerting. I recall that first night fairly well. We tired of standing around and decided to take one of the metal barrel trash cans outside and use it to build a bonfire. It was chilly and we needed a little warmth until the alcohol warmed us. Lou was a welder and had a plasma cutter that we used to carve a pumpkin face in the side of the barrel. We burned everything in the yard—leaves, sticks, garbage, copies of the free paper left at the end of neighbors' driveways and even scraps from the next-door-neighbor's home improvement project. I remember running out of things to burn that night and resorting to sawdust from the next-door-neighbor's trash pile. One of us would throw in a handful and would be rewarded with a dramatic upshot of embers. We'd all ooh and ah over it like kids watching fireworks. It gave us something to keep our hands busy while we drank.

I remember drinking everything I wanted. I sampled peach-flavored liquor, gin that tasted like pine needles, a Chilean cabernet, an extremely smooth Mexican tequila, Baileys on ice, lime-flavored beer, and even white zinfandel. But after I stopped wanting to drink, I kept going. I remembered hoping that I would pass out so I could take a break, but that didn't happen.

Instead, I called a cab company and it took me at least fifteen minutes to communicate to the guy on the other line where we lived and at what address we needed a pickup. He had some kind of accent, and I was aware that I was slurring badly. I kept saying "Flower Avenue" and he kept hearing and repeating it as "Sour Avenue." What kind of idiot would name a street "Sour" I don't know, but that's what the guy heard.

We took the cab downtown to a club and it was an ordeal to find enough cash for all of our cover charges. Once inside, of course, we could put drinks on our credit cards. I was dancing in the strobe light–covered trance room for what simultaneously seemed like five seconds and five hours.

At some point, the silhouette of a brunette appeared, haloed by the changing colors of the lights around us. We danced and I gave her a sweaty, desperate kiss. I presume she was the one I remember being on top of me back at our apartment, but it's possible that was another girl I picked up at the club. Whoever she was, she was gone by the time I woke up in pool of my own puke.

When I came to, I had a strange sort of perception that I'd only had once before. That was the time I passed out while getting blood taken. I opened my eyes and panicked because I could see all the faces of the nurses and doctors talking to me, staring at me, but despite my best efforts, I couldn't recognize anything about anyone. This was that same feeling, only it was more pathetic because there was no one around. Who knows where my idiot roommates all were—probably still partying somewhere, unaware that I was no longer with them. It took me a minute to grasp that I was on my side on the floor. It took me another minute or so to realize that I was lying in a puddle of cold vomit and yet another minute to figure that vomit had to be my own. I righted myself by first pushing up onto my knees. That was when I discovered that my jeans (I no longer had on underwear) were around my knees. I sat back on my butt and pulled them all the way off.

My ears were ringing and I felt both hot and cold at the same time. At this point, I was still very confused about what had gotten me so out of sorts. It hadn't yet occurred to me that this was the result of a terrible binge. I recognized my room and knew I was in it, but beyond that, I didn't know where I was on the timeline of my life.

I wandered over to the bathroom and caught sight of my face in the mirror. Some addicts recall times of not recognizing themselves. I recognized myself, all right. It was same old stupid me, hair a mess, unshaven, skinny face. The only difference was that my cheek was split wide open and the bloody gash was covered in crusted vomit. If I hadn't hit rock bottom, I had certainly hit a landing on the way down.

I should have called 911, I suppose, but it made more sense to walk the four blocks to the hospital because I'd get there faster than by ambulance. Unless, of course, I passed out on the way and didn't make it. But that didn't happen. I now count that as one of the many times my higher power was looking after me.

The ladies at the hospital did me up right. I got cleaned up, stitched up, hydrated, and I even got a free meal. When they turned me loose ten hours later, the sun was coming back up again. I walked back to the shitty basement I called home and stood for a moment, surveying the place.

One of the Mexican-style blankets we had pinned up over the window was falling down, and I could see a sea of light green from the leaves outside. My ears were no longer ringing, and for the first time in I don't know how long, I heard silence.

I pulled the coffee machine out of the bottom drawer in the kitchen and found a half-empty can of Folgers on top of the refrigerator. I scraped the dead cockroach off the top and set a pot to brew. I cleared the kitchen table of beer cans and dirty dishes and wiped it clean with a wet paper towel. Someone had left a two-day-old newspaper on the couch, and I grabbed it, desperate for something to do that would make me feel more like a functioning member of society.

I flipped to the employment section. A laundromat was looking for a manager. Fabulous news! American University needed a maintenance man. How 'bout it?! And then my eyes landed on an ad looking for a writer.

"Talented and ambitious writer needed for new book project. Solid pay and great experience. Must be willing to travel. Call 301-555-1259."

It was under the "miscellaneous" section of the help wanted ads.

I called the telephone number and got a recorded message, telling me where to send my résumé and writing samples. It was a P.O. box in Rockville. Has it really come to this? I wondered. People could no longer be bothered to pick up the telephone? I was annoyed that they wanted everything sent to a P.O. box, as if their office would be flooded with drop-ins salivating at the job opportunity. They wanted nothing but a stack of applications that they could ruthlessly sort into "possible" and "hell no" piles. I was annoyed. I was annoyed but I was also desperate.

I made some quick changes to an old résumé I had on my computer, highlighting my internship at a local paper and my degree in journalism, and minimizing my current job selling paint. I printed it and put it in a manila envelope. I found five stamps in a book on my shelf and put all five on the envelope before walking it out to the mailbox on the corner. For the first time in my life, I prayed. I prayed that the envelope would reach the right person and that I'd get a job I could feel good about.

That night, I decided to set my alarm for 7:15. You know what they say about early to bed, early to rise.

Two days later, my cell phone rang before my alarm went off. I answered it before I was awake.

"Mr. Cortane?"

"Yes."

"This is Mario Ellis from Ghost Orchid Media."

Oh shit. I cleared my throat into my pillow. Good prospective employees had already been up for at least an hour. Jogging with the dog or whatever.

"Yes, hello Mr. Ellis," I said, deepening my voice.

He wanted me to come in for an interview. That afternoon. He said his client was very eager to get the project started. I was to be at 1 Metro Center, sixth floor, at one p.m.

I hung up the phone and looked over at my closet. Both of my suits were in wrinkled lumps next to my shoes. Fuck.

I went into Rob's room and searched his closet. Much to my own surprise, he had a clean navy blue suit on a hanger. He was about my size, thank god.

Now, I've been in some strange situations in my life (all of my own doing), but I can genuinely say the interview for this job was the most bizarre experience I have ever been party to.

Mario met me in the lobby of the swanky office building in downtown Bethesda. He was tall and beefy with almost black hair and a set of thick eyebrows to match. His skin—pasty white and vein ridden—looked to be a terrible mismatch to the rest of him. He wore an Armani suit with rubber-soled shoes that looked just like the ones my grandfather got at Easy Spirit. A beefcake with fussy feet and a history of skin cancer?

"Let's go upstairs," he said in a deep voice. He towered over me, and I suddenly felt like he was trying to bamboozle me into starring in a gay porno.

As we rode the glass elevator, I looked out over all of the people hustling through the lobby and felt a sudden rush of embarrassment. I wasn't qualified to be among them. Instead of a regular job, I was following some vampire up to Office 666 where he was going to tell me that the job I was interviewing for involved leather and farm animals.

Mario's upper lip was sweating.

He opened the door, led me past a woman sitting behind a desk and into a conference room with a long oval table and too many gray chairs to count. He excused himself for a moment, saying he needed to use the rest room. I was certain he was going to get the syringe.

I checked my email from my phone and was not surprised to find that I had won the lottery and qualified for a free sample of Cialis.

Mario walked back in, seeming much less creepy than he had just a moment before. He had dried off his upper lip and his voice was different—no less booming, but somehow more pleasant sounding.

"So tell me about yourself, Mr. Cortane."

Thinking back now, I realize that was the only thing he asked of me during the entire interview, and it wasn't even really a question.

I started talking about all I had learned in journalism school and explained that, even though the market seemed to be changing drastically, I was sure there would always be a place in the world for a good writer, blah, blah, blah. It wasn't so much what I wanted to say, but what I had felt was expected of me.

To my surprise, Mario told me a little bit about himself, too. He was born in Panama and lived there until he was six, when his family moved to Brooklyn. He played the guitar, drove a Mercedes, and grew poblano peppers in pots on his back porch. He had a girlfriend and his father was dead. All in all, he seemed to be a pretty resourceful guy. I wondered how much he was making from Ghost Orchid Media. He couldn't have been older than thirty-five.

At this point, I wasn't quite so nervous, so I started to ramble on about whatever came to mind. It felt much more like we were enjoying in a beer after work.

That was when he reached into his jacket pocket and pulled out a heavy, unsealed envelope. He handed it to me, and before I could say a word about the cash inside, he said, "This is for your plane ticket to Singapore. Take the flight out of Dulles tonight. There is one seat left in first class. From Singapore, you'll travel to an island."

"But I don't even know what—"

"You'll be writing the memoirs of an extremely rich and reclusive woman whose connection to the world you'll learn more about while visiting her." Mario spoke sharply, as if had he stopped to listen to himself, he would burst out in laughter. He stood up still talking and made his way to the door, motioning for me to follow. "You'll be there for about four months. Don't worry about bringing too much clothing. That kind of thing will all be provided. If, however, you take any kind of medication, you'll need enough for the duration." We were in the hallway and he held out his hand to the right to show me the way back to the elevators.

"All right, who put you up to this? Was it Danny? If so, he just took it to the next level because I—"

"Only one person put me up to this, and that's the woman who wants her story written. She wants someone with a decent background in writing but who hasn't been around long enough to let his drive to get the story first crush anything resembling altruism."

"So a naïve and sympathetic ear?"

"Maybe. Mostly she's just looking for someone crazy enough to go to an island for four months to live with her."

"Exactly. You'd have to be craz—Why am I still having this conversation?" I was talking more to myself than Mario. The whole situation had gotten really weird really fast. I started for the door.

"You're either the man for the job or you're not. I can't do anything about that."

I'm sure that a therapist would be able to get me to admit to myself why I really took the envelope filled with cash that day and walked out the door, but to tell you the truth, I think it was just because I was broke. It doesn't really matter, as I prefer to accept that I did what I did. But I can tell you that for every minute I spent packing my bags, I spent two minutes questioning my actions. By the time I got to the airport ticket counter, I had yielded to what was clearly a compulsion.

I was going to Singapore not because I cared to go to Singapore, but because I was afraid of what would happen to my life if I stayed in Maryland.

p. m. korkinsky

Late-Night Jazz

P. M. KORKINSKY lives in a small apartment with a large dog of indeterminate heritage. The poet and dog live in D.C. and spend many hours wandering the city in search of words. When not writing poetry, Korkinsky blogs about dogs with separation anxiety at www.zendogjourney.com. *Late Night Jazz*, a collection of experimental prose poetry, is being indie published by iUniverse and will be available in 2014.

1968 DC:
    cities unravel
burn
    deconstruct…

ભ

She stops reading. Places the hallucination back into the painting above her bed. The painting:

A jazz silhouette wandering through portraits in the city.
    The city shuffles and shifts the focus to pictures of missing persons
        taped to damaged walls.
Echoes and smoke in large hallways of the city morphed museum.
A whisper in his wife's ear: *I was here*, he says. *Listen…*

ભ

Her husband disappeared. Gone the right word. She begins to unravel. Shedding layers of herself.
    Gone.

ભ

Hallucinations follow, picking at threads and pulling her further apart. The hospital room. She rocks back and forth. Thorazine agitated and still the leftover sounds.

She sits on the bed and looks at the chess game on the table. Own world. Still the leftover sounds of moving pieces pawning the king into the streets. And gone.

Move forward and speak wrong word and back. Sounds in feral dreams. Ghost-driven horses on a black and white board. Madly charge and pace— up two and over one.

    Everything. Where gone.

The king escapes the castle. Where safe. No safe the forward gone.

She lies down and closes her eyes. Voices and sounds hollow from the hallways.

    Move
        forward—
the sounds through the night in jazz
    in octaves
the staccato stairways
    winding
        through a home now
    Gone.

☙

He comes to her in dreams. A single note held in an eternal fermata. The soft touch of minor keys whispering to hold on.

The beautiful forgotten. She remembers him drifting away in landscapes darkened in the shadow of the skull. The echo. The echo meaning future as sound moving
    forward or gone.

⌒

She remembers the clubs. Before the fires. The light weakens as the sound grows. Gone the city pieces the king together and moves him to the safe no sane. Frozen in stalemate the waiting begins.

Missing pictures on burning streets the chaos weakens the focus. She remembers the walks at night with others to find the ashes and the ghosts. She saw him once on a walk or in a dream she reaches her hand and caresses the night like shadows they grow strong and then fade.

The city is not simple or easy. Years of tension trapped in city walls. Waiting for a weakness the light weakens as the sound grows.

And stop—

I was here. Listen…

⌒

She remembers him in music replaying inside her head. She hums a melody quietly to herself and rocks back and forth in a space of darkness replacing time.

She remembers the band
the tenor sax
the growling voice
the tap stuttering tap
the drumming of city tantrums
held steady with a deep sound
of a bass
of sound
taking over
Still the sound weakens as the city ignites.
Yes.

She remembers the band the sax the drums the bass against the city walls. Too weak against the fires dimming the sound. Compose or de-compose the castle walls the echo faint and falls.

Faint and fainter still the sounds outside the clubs. More quickly the forward comes. Never seen again except in missing posters. Or nocturnal walks inside the skull.

℘

Two days go by. Maybe a week. A month perhaps.

They have different drugs to give her. So she will be realized in the world of the normal.
 The mind clearing
open
 not numb
not shadows.

They stop in to check on her. Medication the lithium of lesser the insane. Her hands tremble. She will move on they say and less and less. At some point the light is turned off and on the melody moves forward.

The room shifts into warehouse empty the normal is less and less. More worry. More fear. More empty.

℘

Less the medication more the dreams. The nocturnal walks inside the skull. The masterpiece of deception to be real again. The feel of falling
 inside minor chords
  the shift of medications
   altered scales to drifting voices
Of crowded jazz-filled rooms of rain syncopated against the sway of people dancing. The glow of fire building, syncing, screaming—
 The king can only move one square at a time. Limited sound of game
  and movement
 The queen glides through
  the crescendo of time and exits
   the board

and waits the trade.

No sane the forward and gone.

✌

She thinks the city collapsed. Swallowed whole. But no. The forward as the future as moving.

She sits in her room and imagines people passing. She waits for him.

In sounds through nights in jazz. In nocturnal walks inside the skull. She stays inside this nocturnal fermata

in octaves

the staccato stairways

winding

through a home

Not gone. Not forward. Not forgotten.

The beautiful forgotten. Remembered. The coda returning the sound. A whisper of a tenor saxophone.

I was here, he says. *Listen…*

She softly drums her fingers on the arms of the chair. Closes her eyes.

A whisper.

I was, he says and is—hear.

Anne Levy-Lavigne

Crossing Stars

ANNE LEVY-LAVIGNE holds an MA in writing from Johns Hopkins University. Her short fiction has appeared in *REAL,* the *Potomac Review,* and *Phoebe,* and she is an assistant editor for *Narrative Magazine.* She is a recovering lawyer and clinical social worker. A fugitive from Pittsburgh and a long-time resident of the Washington, D.C., area, she now lives and writes in New Orleans.

Some people live their lives in patterns that begin early, last long, and change little, patterns that recur with the constancy of the Earth's orbit around the sun. People like Lina Taylor. Everyone knew this about her—her family, her friends, her acquaintances—everyone but Lina Taylor herself. Her daughter, Kayla Reilly, had sensed it in childhood, known it by early adolescence. Now thirty, Kayla climbs into an airport taxi in New Orleans, here to attend her mother's wedding. Her mother's fifth wedding. A stinging reminder of Lina's years-long pattern of serial monogamy. Already divorced and remarried herself, Kayla harbors a fear of reliving Lina's pattern, as if it were a congenital aberration whose presence seals her fate. But that time was different. It won't, it can't, happen again.

She gives the driver the French Quarter address where she and her husband Damon are staying, and twenty minutes later, the taxi turns off Rue Chartres into the cobblestone drive of the Hôtel Provincial. She wheels her suitcase to the reservations desk to register, and she's strolling through the sunlit lobby examining the period furnishings when her cell phone rings from deep within her handbag.

It's Damon, his words spilling out in a rush: he's calling from Chicago, had to make a last-minute business trip there this morning and something came up that can't wait so he can't leave till tomorrow he'll come in then. He can't talk now, he'll explain later.

Chicago? He'd never mentioned business in Chicago. He sounded—Kayla can't pinpoint it—excited, or edgy, or upset? Far from his usual unruffled self, cool through crises, cool even with the specter of unemployment looming over him. Why not now? She sinks onto the arm of a brocade sofa and picks up a French Creole statuette from a nearby table, too absorbed in analyzing Damon's call to appreciate the object.

Or to notice the double entrance doors swing open and Lina Taylor sweep in. Lina, a petite, chic woman of fifty-two, spots Kayla and rushes over, singing *Kay-la*. Standing on tiptoes to embrace her willowy, much taller daughter, she exclaims, "So glad you came…after all."

Surprised by her mother's in-person welcome, Kayla ignores the allusion to her initial refusal to come. She steps back to arm's length and regards her mother. Lina still has the alabaster skin, trim curves, and dazzling smile of years before, when rooms lit up and heads turned the minute she walked in. But her eyes, an intense, startling green, show signs of weariness.

Kayla has neither seen nor heard from her mother in nearly five years, since Lina up and moved to New Orleans two years after Hurricane Katrina. Odd, Kayla had thought—a storm-torn city she'd never even seen. Where else, Lina says now, but in a city where *laissez les bons temps rouler* is creed would the man of her dreams have flashed into her universe?

The invitation had materialized in Kayla's mailbox out of nowhere. She'd glanced at it briefly, grimaced, and left it to languish in a growing stack of mail, where it would languish still if her mother hadn't phoned two weeks ago to say, "You *are* coming to my wedding, aren't you?"

To Kayla's firm *no*, Lina responded, "But you're my only child…my only *family*."

Which, strictly speaking, was not the case. But Lina's terminally alcoholic father, aside from lacking any interest in his daughter's marital affairs, was too infirm to travel, and her sisters had flatly refused. That left Kayla standing in the lobby of a New Orleans hotel, embarrassed to have succumbed to her mother's cajoling. How, she wonders, can a flighty, rarely there mother exert such leverage?

"Now, about the wedding festivities…" Scanning the lobby, Lina says, "Where's…Rob?"

"Damon, you mean. Rob and I were divorced more than five years ago." Soon after she met Damon, at the mailboxes of the townhouse complex where they both lived, within weeks of her move to the D.C. area from Atlanta.

"Oh! The excitement of the wedding…I just forgot, momentarily." She laughs, sheepishly.

"Damon's delayed till tomorrow, some urgent last-minute business." Her cheeks burn. She'd wheedled Damon into coming—he'd never even met Lina—and he'd agreed, reluctantly, only to please Kayla. And Lina barely remembers he exists.

"Anyway, the wedding is tomorrow evening in the garden of Napoleon House on Chartres. Tonight is a small family dinner at Galatoire's, in the French Quarter." Pulling a street map and a highlighter from a large silver tote, she traces a yellow line along the route to the destination and circles it. "Two-oh-nine Bourbon Street, an easy walk from here. Seven-thirty."

She kisses Kayla on both cheeks. "I can't wait for you to meet Ray, the blazing comet in my firmament! *And* a Taurus." She pauses, her expression solemn: "The ideal Pisces match"—sensuous and sensible and a giver of extravagant gifts.

She moves to the window and tilts her left hand toward the glass, displaying a large opal rimmed with diamonds. "See how it catches the light? Finally, the right one!"

Whether she means the ring or the man, she doesn't say.

After a five-minute visit, Lina tosses her auburn waves, sweeps back out to the driveway, and slides behind the wheel of a gleaming new Corvette, no doubt from the giver of extravagant gifts; she smiles, flashing a row of perfectly even, pearl-white teeth, and flutters her fingers in a wave as she backs out onto Chartres. Kayla watches the car disappear down the street, a streak of red like a flaming arrow. The image of another leave-taking supplants itself in Kayla's mind: herself at five, standing with her father in their front doorway on a bright Saturday afternoon, watching her mother ride away in a silver convertible beside a strange man. Her stomach knots. Once again, Kayla will witness the ceremonial validation of Lina's fast-track romance and, if the past foreshadows the future, another marital fiasco.

Kayla follows the bellhop into the glittering May sunshine and around the perimeter of a lush courtyard fragrant with vibrant tropical blossoms. Stopping in front of a room facing the pool, he unlocks the door to a large room furnished with a period reproduction four-poster bed and an overstuffed velvet settee. Although Kayla, an interior designer, specializes in contemporary design, she finds a quaint charm in the faded elegance of this room.

She tosses her suitcase on the bed and begins unpacking, wondering whether his job situation accounts for Damon's earlier abruptness. Ten months ago, he was up for partnership with his law firm; with new clients to his credit and the solid backing of the partners in his practice group, or so he'd thought, he'd expected to get it. But he hadn't, and under the firm's "up-or-out" policy, an associate passed over for partnership had a year to find another job.

The shock of not making partner without a glimmer of warning stunned him into inaction for weeks before he could rally enough to begin a full-scale search. Early on, he was unconcerned—Washington was the hub of national legal practice, he'd said, a legal land of opportunity, and he'd developed a solid reputation in his field.

"You do plan to stay here, don't you?" she'd asked. "Because…"

"Because you don't want to leave your job. Of course not. You're moving ahead fast there. I'm all for that job—we'd never have met without it."

"So no living changes, right? You'll look here."

"Absolutely. It never occurred to me to do otherwise. I know how much your job means to you, Kay. Besides, all my contacts are here. It's my best shot."

She'd released a held breath. This wasn't just any job. It was a top cutting-edge firm, sheer serendipity, a magnum leap forward, the career boost she'd moved to D.C. for and left her then-husband behind for before she'd ever so much as laid eyes on Damon. He'd known from the start what Kayla's job, what her career, meant to her.

He'd expected to find a job comparable to his current one within three, four months at most. He had, in fact, attracted offers from the beginning, but none the right fit. With the deadline closing in and calls for interviews slowing down, Kayla suspects his nerves are fraying.

❧

THAT EVENING, KAYLA LEAVES THE hotel at close to seven-thirty, Lina's map in hand. She strolls down Chartres and across Jackson Square, stopping to admire St. Louis Cathedral, a majestic white apparition overlooking the square. Farther up, she pauses to peer into the patio gate at Napoleon House, the site of tomorrow's wedding. She checks the map before turning right on Rue St. Louis and again before turning left on Bourbon, though she had located both streets walking through the Quarter this afternoon.

Wending her way through a throng of tourists, she makes her way to the entrance of 209 Bourbon. The host leads her across a black and white tile floor to the back of the large dining room, where the sounds of drinking and mingling reverberate from an area screened off for the party. She's twenty minutes late. She inhales deeply, lets it out, and glides in, wishing Damon were here. With his lanky drop-dead good looks, the curly hair that springs from his head like electrified corkscrews, his quick smile and warm brown eyes, he's the perfect buffer.

Lina is standing in the center of a circle of guests gathered a short distance from the entrance near a long marble table set for ten. Catching Kayla's eye, she waves her over. A darkly handsome man, late fiftyish, stands beside her, his arm around her waist, smiling and gesturing to a man on his other side. A black patch covers his right eye.

"Here you are, Kayla," Lina says. "Come meet the light of my life." Ray steps forward, a wide smile like a beam of light opening his craggy face. He's tall and broad shouldered, not heavy, as he seems at first, but muscular and solidly built; beside Lina, he projects the image of the great protector. He extends his right hand to Kayla, revealing two stumps in place of the index and middle fingers. Kayla involuntarily blinks.

He smiles, raising the hand aloft. "A past misadventure." Many moons ago, he explains, he kept and trained a cougar to star in bygone Mercury commercials. "She performed right on cue, never missed a beat. Good cat, sold a lot of cars for us. One day she suddenly snarls and leaps at me. Which accounts for the missing fingers and eye." He shrugs.

Now he holds a part-ownership interest in a riverboat casino and invests in foreclosed properties, the major part of his business since Katrina. "Less exotic but safer." His laugh, a melodious baritone, peals out, and Kayla wonders if he and Lina sing together, whether they share a love for music. Years ago Lina, a gifted soprano, left Juilliard and a promising career in opera behind to marry Kayla's father and subsequent others. She teaches voice occasionally now when the need arises.

Ray draws Lina close and gazes down at her as if he holds the Hope Diamond in his palm. "This little redhead is wildcat enough for me." He winks, and his smoke-gray eye glimmers. "Knew it the day we met."

At Café du Monde, Lina explains, over coffee and beignets at adjacent tables, until he sidled over and slid into the chair opposite hers. Within days, they realized they belonged together; within weeks, they'd arranged the wedding.

Ray takes Kayla's arm and escorts her around the group, introducing her to the other guests, all long-time friends or members of Ray's family. When dinner is announced, he seats Lina and Kayla on either side of him.

Leaning toward Kayla, he says, "This will give us a chance to get to know each other," and a rapid succession of questions ensues: "What kind of work do you do? What does your husband do? How long have y'all been married? Where in the East d'you live?"

Trying to mask her annoyance—hasn't Lina told him anything about her?—she wonders why she's sitting here, preparing to answer this man's questions about things he should already know if she's so damned important a presence here, this man who, though charming, is but one in a string of husbands and unlikely to last very long in her mother's life.

She's gotten as far as "We've been married for five…" when waiters converge, setting down heaping platters of oysters and shrimp, pouring wine, exchanging quips with the guests. The volume of chatter and clanking silverware picks up, and Ray joins the general group banter. As stories about local doings fly back and forth, Kayla retreats into visually designing her newest project, a residential loft condo.

She's configuring a third alternative layout for the living area when a deep voice beside her jolts her back to the present. "Your mama tells me you lived with your daddy growing up," Ray says, filling her plate with oysters and shrimp. He looks at her quizzically as she dips a fried oyster in rémoulade and pops it into her mouth. "How come?"

Surprised by so personal a question from a near stranger, Kayla's brows lift and she falls silent. Lina has obviously told him the outcome but no more. Kayla can hardly blame her. It was a dark time, and Lina, like a butterfly, gravitates to the light.

"I was told…I was only about seven at the time…that my mother had a demanding job that required travel, sometimes last-minute trips. My father had remarried, and when he and my stepmother had their first child, she quit work and stayed home. She was more available, so it seemed that arrangement would work better."

What she doesn't tell him is her father sued for sole custody; Lina's estranged second husband testified that living with Lina was like "living in the eye of a hurricane"; and the judge, finding Lina "loving but unstable," awarded custody to her father.

"I saw my mother on weekends. She took me to concerts and fancy restaurants and parties with her musician friends," usually with a male companion. Kayla rarely saw her mother alone. The visits, which started as monthly, dwindled in frequency over time.

"She's real happy you came, says she doesn't see you much anymore. But that's life nowadays, right? Families scattered everywhere. Except the Broussards, all of us still here in New Orleans. Just like back in the day." He laughs, that rich wave of cascading notes.

"My husband's family is like that, too. It's not how I grew up."

As her father and stepmother's children grew, the demands on their time grew; Kayla hovered at the sidelines of her family's life. At ten, she began browsing through her stepmother's collection of design magazines, intrigued by the before-and-after pictures: what had been versus what could be. Cloistering herself in her room, she drew one design after another, only vaguely aware that her longing for a refuge that expressed her inner self underlay this passion.

Entrees are served and wineglasses refilled. The clamor of a restaurant filled with lively tables echoes throughout the space, seeming to converge on the Taylor-Broussard party, and Kayla's historical account of her hapless childhood falls victim to the din. But the tension of recalling those years, and the sight of bony shrimp tails, limp gray oysters, jagged-edged crab claw shells remaining on the diners' plates leaves her feeling queasy.

By the time Kayla slips away after a boisterous round of thank you's and good nights, her head is about to explode. She walks back to the hotel through the narrow, still-crowded streets, past funky clothing and jewelry shops, small art galleries and restaurants, through lamp-lit Jackson Square and St. Louis Cathedral, its lofty spires bathed silver in moon-glow. She sits on a metal bench, intrigued by the play of light on the cathedral spires and by the people strolling through the square. The pounding in her head eases in the gentle night air.

In her hotel room, she turns her cell phone back on to find a message from Damon. "Arriving early tomorrow afternoon. See you at the hotel...Interesting trip."

A series of cryptic, clipped phrases, an abrupt stop—like a telegram. Collapsing into bed, the thought *Whatever interesting means* skims across her mind as she drifts into sleep.

↭

THE NEXT MORNING, BOTH THE day and Kayla dawn clear and bright, and what Damon meant by "interesting" now interests Kayla keenly. She queries him about his calls as they walk to Jackson Square for lunch.

"You sounded brusque or hurried every time. I couldn't tell whether you were nervous or excited, but either way, you never sound like that. Plus, why were you in Chicago? Most of your clients are in the Northwest. Were you pinch-hitting for someone else? It couldn't be a new case at this late date, could it?"

"Let's order, then we'll talk. I'm starving." He spreads the menu open.

They're seated at a window table in a small sandwich place at the edge of Jackson Square. Damon usually decides quickly, but he's taking so long now that Kayla starts fidgeting.

After they order, she shakes her head. "You could have bought a house and three cars in the time it took you to pick a sandwich."

Damon turns to the window, watching the stream of pedestrians passing by. His face looks drawn and a hint of anxiety dulls his eyes. "It's too noisy to talk in here. Maybe later…"

"Why are you stalling, Damon?"

Like she did when she left the hotel late for last night's dinner yet strolled at a lackadaisical pace.

"It's kind of complicated."

ↄ

AFTER LUNCH, THEY WALK ALONG the riverfront, stopping at the Steamboat Natchez and continuing on to Woldenberg Park. A vague sense of fear nags at Kayla.

He smiles guardedly. "The trip was personal business, not firm business."

"Personal business? What kind?" They spot an empty bench and sit down, looking out at the water, the ducks skimming past, people passing by. A warning, the phrase *something is wrong*, circles through her mind. Her neck muscles tauten, like strings about to break.

"A job interview. Something that just happened to land in my lap. One of the partners in my practice group has a friend there who told him they were looking for someone. I told you I talked to them when they contacted me, a while ago."

"You said you weren't interested."

"I wasn't. Then I checked them out. Everything about the firm—their environmental practice, their reputation, the people, the money—is great. We met all day yesterday, interviews with different members of the firm, segued into dinner, and met again early this morning." They'd discussed terms and made him an offer right then.

"After one day-long interview?"

"Well, a couple of others, phone and teleconference," he mutters.

"All these interviews without telling me? With my career at stake, too? But now that you have an offer, you'll discuss it?"

He leans forward, propping his elbows on his thighs, his head in his hands. Several minutes pass before he speaks. "Not exactly. I accepted already. Please understand, honey. This is a prestigious firm with several satellite offices, too good to pass up. Time was closing in. I'm ashamed to say it, but I panicked."

"I'm your *wife*. Isn't sharing what marriage is about? It sure the *fuck* isn't about keeping secrets and dropping bombshells, is it? How *could* you?" Within the white heat of her grief, a cold anger seeps in.

"I didn't know how long we could hold out, moneywise. I didn't want to worry you or upset you. They might have dropped me at any point. Happens all the time."

"But they didn't. You said they've got satellite offices. Then you'll be in their D.C. office? That makes some difference."

He rakes his fingers through his hair. "They don't have a D.C. office, Kay," he says quietly. "The job is at the main office, in Chicago." He sucks in a breath and falls silent.

She can barely stand for the shock charging through her body. *Something* is *wrong. Very wrong.* She fixes her eyes on his face, and he squirms under her stare.

"Honey, I know I promised we'd definitely stay in D.C., and I meant it," he says. "But after months of nothing working out I felt backed into a corner. You must have realized that. This isn't for me, it's for us."

"You had two more months plus six months' severance pay at your current income level with full benefits," she says, her voice hushed. "You didn't have to do this, not this way."

"You're right...But I thought, I hoped, you'd understand. Please let's talk it out, explore the possibilities. It's a great city. Especially for the arts and architecture and design. You might find an even better job."

"That's not the point, Damon. The point is that you deceived me, deliberately hid this from me. Because you were hell-bent on doing what you wanted. I never thought you were capable of such a thing. I trusted you. I thought I knew you. But...who *are* you? I don't know."

"You *do* know me. I just...lost it, didn't think straight. Not like myself. I never wanted to hurt you. I love you. I'll make it up to you, I promise."

She raises her arms, palms turned upward, fingers outspread, opens her mouth to speak, then closes it and drops her arms to her side. Turning away, she strides toward Chartres.

え

THAT EVENING, KAYLA AND DAMON Reilly walk the five blocks from the hotel to the wedding, locked in near silence. At the side gate of Napoleon House, the melodic notes of a flute draw arriving guests down a narrow passageway opening into a large stone courtyard. Wire flower baskets hanging from wrought-iron balconies, a golden-eyed cement owl atop a brick wall, the peeling yellow-beige paint on the centuries-old building, the tinge of violet-pink light—all coalesce to create an aura of enchantment.

At another time, Kayla would have appreciated the romance of the setting. But Damon's announcement, its finality, has left her emotionally shell-shocked, and an afternoon of recriminations, apologies, tears, and attempts to persuade—she, to change his decision and he, to justify its rightness—has left them depleted and impervious to enchantment.

They talk quietly at the edge of the courtyard, trying to bolster themselves for the celebrating ahead, feeling more downcast than festive but determined not to let it interfere. They would appear to be a together couple. To Kayla, it's a necessary but temporary truce; to Damon, it evokes resolution. He knows he blew it, seriously blew it, stupidly blew it. He'll do whatever it takes to regain her confidence.

They cross to the center of the courtyard to where Lina stands welcoming guests. She's dressed in airy pale pink chiffon that floats around her; the emerald eyes shine; the megawatt smile glows. A déjà vu feeling washes over Kayla: other times, other weddings.

Kayla approaches her mother, Damon beside her. "Charming setting, Mom." Glancing at Damon, she angles her open hand toward him. "This is Damon. He got in this afternoon."

"Wonderful—at last we meet!"

"The pleasure is mine," Damon replies, producing a smile.

"Ray," Lina calls, extending her arm toward Kayla, then Damon.

Ray saunters over and grabs Damon's hand, pumping it vigorously. "Great to…"

"Darling," Lina interjects, "I was about to tell them how you decided on Napoleon House and how I chose the date."

Her past passions, she explains, were ruled by cosmic imbalance, dooming her prior marriages to failure. This time, having learned that the alignment of the stars will determine her future happiness, she charted their position for the entire month, day by day. On this night, and this night alone, the heavenly bodies move into total synchronicity.

"Everything is right!"

The right astrological signs, the right planetary positions—virtually a marital warranty.

Kayla smiles, laughing to herself. On the way here, she spotted a corner newspaper machine displaying the local paper with the bold headline, "STARS ALIGN"; underneath, small letters qualified, "For Jazz Fest." Here then gone, with a catch.

Twilight falls, and Lina and Ray take their places before the judge. The guests cluster around them as Ray jokes with the judge about keeping the ceremony short "so we can get to the important stuff." Lina, cradling a bouquet of pink tulips, toys with the ribbon. Kayla and Damon move to the side, at a distance from each other.

As the judge begins to read, his words carry Kayla back to her and Damon's wedding. That evening at the townhouse mailboxes, a light exchange of remarks had sparked an instant connection, a feeling they'd known each other always. They'd been inseparable since that night, read each other's thoughts, intuited each other's needs. Always on the same wavelength. She'd never known anyone like him, so exciting, attractive, understanding, loving, so good.

She'd divorced Rob with frightening speed. A youthful mistake, she'd reasoned. She could forgive herself just that once. Rob would understand, wouldn't he? Days after her divorce became final she and Damon were married. They knew they were moving quickly. But this was something rare, a love that comes but once in a lifetime, if that. They had to be together. It hits her now that that's exactly how Lina feels each time she rushes into marriage, and that every couple in love revels in its own specialness.

She glances at Damon, several feet away, and finds him gazing at her. He lifts his eyebrows, as if asking, "Will we be OK?" She knits her brow and looks away. *No.* Who is this stranger? Is he the man she thought he was, or the man she wanted him to be, a figment of her desires? She feels lost, as if she's been suddenly, shockingly widowed.

The judge calls, "I now pronounce you man and wife!"

The newlyweds lock into a protracted kiss, then turn to embrace everyone around them. Waiters appear with trays of champagne and canapés, and Lina disappears into a sea of well-wishing arms before Kayla can congratulate her.

Ray ambles over, kisses Kayla's cheek, hands her a flute of champagne. Damon joins them and shakes Ray's hand. How long will he be around? His predecessor, the love-struck cellist, had lasted four months. In six months, more or less, Kayla would pick up the phone to a tearful litany of Ray's failings: his Taurean bullheadedness and the ascending Aquarius moods that trigger Jekyll-Hyde transformations—Taurean potentialities that Lina had known about but disregarded, believing he was different. She should have realized, she would conclude, that opals brought bad luck.

As if telepathic, Ray murmurs in Kayla's ear, "I know you think this marriage is just another one of your mama's fly-by-nights." Kayla's lips part in surprise. "But not this time. I got a past packed with mistakes, stupid mistakes, but I finally caught on. So's your mama. We're in this for the duration." He winks and turns away. The words *for the duration* send a shiver through Kayla.

She rejoins Damon and introduces him to the friends and relatives she met last night, all of them in the same partying spirit, effusively praising the twice-married Ray's choice of Kayla's vivacious mother, a pepper if they ever knew one. They're draining another round of champagne in the bridal pair's honor when a gong sounds.

Lina summons Kayla and Damon to a large round table beneath a pecan tree. She takes a seat, places Ray beside her with Kayla on Ray's right and Damon on Kayla's other side. Ray's family completes the table, assuring an evening of hilarity. Darkness has fallen, and the courtyard glows under the light of brightly colored paper lanterns.

A multicourse wedding feast begins and wine flows liberally. Damon leans toward Kayla and whispers, "You look beautiful tonight. You know that's my favorite dress?" She nods, inwardly shrugging. She's wearing a figure-skimming column of crimson silk, and she's twisted her thick honey-blonde hair into a figure eight. Usually, it's her feel-good, live-wire look.

A jazz band is playing "Sweet Georgia Brown," and the courtyard pulsates with rhythm. When the tempo slows to a ballad, Ray gathers Lina in his arms and they glide around the dance area. Damon takes Kayla's hand and leads her in a slow dance, holding her just close enough to keep their words out of earshot.

"I know you're upset, Kay, but can't you at least *try* to look at this job thing from my perspective? Look at the situation I'm in. Considering that, I'm lucky to get an opportunity like this. It isn't just about money—being unemployed means a black hole on my résumé. How am I supposed to get another job with that? You aren't being entirely reasonable. I did what I felt I had to. Except I should have talked to you first."

"That's a pretty big 'except.' A secret, unilateral decision, not just about your career but about mine, knowing how important my job is to me. Sneaking it past me so I couldn't fight you over it."

"Kay, I fell in love with you the minute we met. What we have has been special from the start. If I withdraw my acceptance, will that put us back where we were?"

"I don't know. Lines were crossed. Everything has changed. I don't know my own heart anymore. But after this, I don't see how we can go on."

They drift over to where the ceremonial cutting of the wedding cake, a many-tiered pink and white confection, is beginning. A long succession of toasts follows. The newlyweds' faces flush with joy and champagne. Kayla approaches her mother to say good night but Lina is too absorbed to respond. Under an indigo-blue sky dotted with pinpoint glints of starlight, perfectly aligned, Kayla crosses the courtyard. Damon follows, and they slip out through the side gate.

⁓

ON SUNDAY MORNING, KAYLA SETTLES at a wrought iron table under a magnolia tree outside their hotel room with a cup of coffee and the latest *Interior Design*, dressed and packed for the flight home, a cab ordered for nine o'clock. Inside, Damon still sleeps. When he rearranged his itinerary for the Chicago trip, his return flight shifted to a later time. She'll welcome the time alone to sort her jumbled thoughts, picture her life without Damon. She can do it, she can make a new start on her own.

In the air, she gazes out the window from her seat in Row 10, pondering what to do, rehashing the same thoughts over and over, until the recognition jolts her that she has no decision to make. Years ago, watching her mother take vows yet again, Kayla made her own: she would never follow that path. She is not her mother. Ray's words, "for the duration," grip her. Once is enough. She won't leave Damon. Not because it's best, not because she doesn't want to, but because she can't.

Veronica Li
The Number One Virtue

VERONICA LI was born in Bangkok, spent most of her childhood in Hong Kong, and immigrated to the United States as a teenager. She received her BA in English from the University of California, Berkeley and her master's degree in international affairs from Johns Hopkins University. In her first career, journalism, she wrote for *Agence France-Presse*, the *Asian Wall Street Journal*, and *Congressional Quarterly*. In her second career, international development, she traveled for the World Bank to Asia and Africa on aid projects. Since leaving the Bank, Li has been a writer and caregiver to elderly parents. Her first novel, *Nightfall in Mogadishu*, is a thriller set in Somalia. Her second book, *Journey across the Four Seas: A Chinese Woman's Search for Home*, is a true story of her mother's life. "The Number One Virtue" is adapted from her next novel, a comedy about caregiving for aged parents.

The woman strides up to the receptionist, her hard heels click-clacking on the floor. She's dressed in a navy blue suit, a sort of civilian uniform without the stripes and chevron. The strap of a black bag cuts into her right shoulder, indicating the weight of the equipment she's carrying. She states her name and purpose and is issued a badge. The guard pushes a button, the double doors open, and she steps into the restricted area.

The badge on her chest reads, "Amy Kwan." As she marches toward her destination, people in color-coded uniforms duck out of her way. They can see and hear that this visitor is on a mission. She looks at them yet doesn't see. Her mind, which normally juggles a dozen tasks at a time, is now whirring around only two. One is to prepare a U.S. response in the event of an Israeli attack on Iran, and the other is to find room number 6. Ah, there it is.

"Mom, have you been playing with your pills again?" she says to the elderly woman reclining on the bed.

The woman raises a gnarled tree root hand and waves frantically.

Amy shakes her head, the tips of her wavy black hair sweeping her shoulders. She presses her lips together in an expression of annoyance, resignation, and despair. How many times has she told her mother not to flap her hand like that? The gesture means "Come" in Chinese, but in English, it means "Bye." It's no wonder that the nursing aides at the home ignore her.

"What took you so long?" Mom extends her customary greeting in Chinese.

"I was in the middle of a meeting," Amy replies in English.

"Beating? Are you all right?" Mom says with concern.

The daughter repeats the ritual of head shaking and lip pressing. She draws in a lungful of air and bellows the message again. The loudness hurts her own ears, and yet there's no other way to communicate with Mom. A test at the audiologist's office showed she couldn't hear unless the volume reached the decibels of a jet plane taking off.

A nurse barges in. Amy wants to explain why she has to shout, and that she's not angry or abusive.

"Hi, I'm Hidayah, your nurse this morning," she says cheerfully. "Mama, how are you doing?"

Mama manages a little smile.

Judging by the head scarf and guttural accent, Amy ventures, "As-salam alaykum."

The nurse looks at her with pleasant surprise and says, "Wa alaykum e-salam."

From her worldwide contacts, Amy has found that the best way to connect with strangers is through their mother tongue. Even if it's a phrase or two, the effort usually triggers a flood of goodwill.

"The doctor will be here shortly. In the meantime, please have her take off her clothes and change into a gown." Hidayah points to a stack of green fabrics in a bin.

"How about underwear?" Amy doesn't want to strip her mother more than necessary.

"Everything off. And the gown should open at the back."

Amy nods good-to-know. Some gowns open in the front, others at the back. "Can you ask the doctor to come as soon as possible? I have a very important report to write and the *President*—" she repeats the title to make sure that the capital P stands out—"is waiting for it."

"I'll let the doctor know," Hidayah says as if the President is just another patient.

She's probably heard this line before, Amy thinks while closing the door. Located in the Virginia suburbs of the nation's capital, this ER must have seen its share of bigger shots than a mere foreign policy analyst such as her. Amy helps her mother off the bed and starts to undress her. The blouse slips off easily. The next step, however, involves a few complex maneuvers. She pauses to think of a strategy.

"Raise your arms," she says, and slowly pulls up the undershirt. A bowl of cream-colored jelly appears. She should have averted her eyes at this point. A split second later is too late. Two withered pears stare at her, and she can't stop from staring back.

It's not that she's never seen her mother's body before; and it's not that her mother has transformed from a pretty young thing to an old woman overnight. The changes have occurred one spot, one lump, one hair at a time. Yet every time she looks at her mother's bloated belly and shrunken breasts, she goes into shock. Her breathing quickens, heart palpitates, and she sucks in her abdomen. At fifty-two, she looks forty-two, thanks to yoga classes and gym workouts three times a week. Since menopause started, however, her body has turned against her. In spite of her best efforts, the parts that should be full are sagging, and those that should be spare are filling. All her life she's believed that a person can steer his fate through hard work and will power. Now the truth is out. A person is nothing but hormones.

Amy drapes the gown like a curtain over the frightening body and blind touches the rest of the stripping. Winded by the exertion of stepping out of her pants, Mom starts panting. Her lungs whistle and her cheeks are dangerously rosy. She holds up a hand to signal time out. Amy sits her down on the edge of the bed and waits. Her fidgety eyes land on the black bag on the chair, a somber reminder that the President is waiting. A heat wave hits her. She swings around to see who's tampering with the thermostat, and then remembers that it's her internal device going haywire again. She tears off her jacket and throws it on the chair.

It's all Mom's fault! If she'd taken better care of herself, she wouldn't have fallen to this degree of decrepitude. She wouldn't be so weak and needy. Amy can't help contrasting her mom with her neighbor Ruth. The woman is in her eighties too and is managing with minimal help from her son. She always has a smile on her face and a cheerful attitude, "I thank the Lord for every day I can get out of bed." Mom's mantra, on the other hand, is "I'm so miserable I want to die." Her greeting to her children is a scowl and a "Where have you been?" followed by a vivid description of the pain in her arthritic knee. "It's like if somebody sticks a looong needle under my kneecap and whips it around." A finger from each hand is required to measure the length of this needle.

Amy puffs three yoga breaths. The urge to grab her mother's shoulders and shove them into bed dissipates.

"OK, you take a nap now. I've got work to do." Finally, Amy gets to her bag and pulls out the laptop, an unfashionably large government issue.

"Why isn't the doctor here yet? Why don't you go get him?"

Mom has done it again, putting her finger on Amy's sorest spot. Raising hell on the slow service is precisely what Amy wants to do. At the same time she knows she can't, which is most frustrating for a can-do person.

"You have to be patient." Amy realizes the pun. Perhaps that's why a sick person is called a patient. "You're not the only sick person around here. Not everyone is at your beck and call." She's pretty sure Mom won't hear her last remark.

"Beck and call. What you mean?"

Amy knows that her mom knows exactly what the idiom means. "Nothing," she says and enters the password for her computer. She clicks on the folder named Iran and scrolls through the files, all unclassified, of course.

"Of all the virtues, *Xiao* is number one," Mom says in a scratchy voice.

"Mmm." Amy ignores the muttering and clicks on the file entitled Israelstrikeoptions.

"You know how to write *Xiao*? The top part means old." Mom scribbles with her finger on the bed. "The bottom means child." She completes the invisible character 孝. "The child carries his parents on his shoulders."

Amy hitches her shoulders up to her ears and drops them with an exaggerated "Hmmmm."

"*Xiao* is the root of virtue, and the source of teachings—"

"Mom, pleeease, I'm trying to work. I have to brief the President, I mean the *President* on a very important subject. I'm the team leader, so the responsibility is on *my shoulders*."

Mom flicks her hand. "Go ahead. I won't bother you anymore." Her brows knit together as if the *looong* needle in her knee is whipping away.

Amy seethes. What's her mom implying—that she's not *xiao* enough? She's here, isn't she? She could have stayed in the office and worked on world peace and her career, yet she's jeopardizing both to sit by her mother's side, hopefully not for much longer.

The latest F-15 model appears on the screen. The next diagram shows it dropping a bunker-busting bomb into a box labeled "nuclear lab."

"Hi, I'm Dr. Morrison. Your mother was brought here by ambulance because of elevated blood pressure. Is she taking medication for hypertension?" the doctor says the big words in a little girl's voice.

Amy eyes the young woman about the age of her daughter. "She's been on medication for the last twenty years. She used to be on Hyzaar, and when she started having constipation, the doctor thought it could be a side effect of the Hyzaar. He switched her to Norvasc, and she seems to tolerate it well." Amy is quite pleased with herself for rattling off the drug names. "The problem is—" she angles her body away from Mom so she can't read her lips. "I've caught her playing with her pills. Every week I put her pills in an organizer—four in the morning, four in the afternoon, and two in the evening. One time I saw her reorganizing the pills by color—the reds with other reds, whites with whites, and so on. I told her that's a dangerous game to play. If she got a stroke she might lose her ability to speak. That really scared her, and she promised not to do it again."

The doctor looks up from the chart. "I see she lives in an assisted living home."

"Oh yes, it's a very good one, and I visit her at least twice a week." Amy catches herself bragging and apologizing all at once. Her mother has been begging to live with her.

"Some homes administer medications to the residents. Does her home offer that service?"

"They offer the option. We didn't take it because we thought since she was still lucid it would be good for her to do something for herself." Amy invokes the "we" that includes her three brothers.

"Most homes charge a fee for the service," the doctor says. "I understand why you don't want to use it unless you have to."

Is she implying they're cheap?

"In your mother's case, I think it's time that she gets the extra care. From what you described, she most likely has some level of dementia."

Amy maintains her right to silence while her mind exclaims, "No way! My mom's problem is the opposite. She's too lucid. She knows exactly how to get her children's attention."

"Our immediate goal is to get her blood pressure down," the doctor says. "I'm going to give her the medicine through an IV. After she's released, you'll have to follow up with her family doctor."

Out goes the white coat and in come the baby blue pants and flowery top. The black head scarf must not be part of the uniform.

"Mama, we have to put an IV in you. It will be just a little stick, OK?"

Hidayah snaps on a pair of thin rubber gloves and breaks off the tip on the index finger. She presses her naked finger on the inside of the patient's elbow, tracing a bluish thread. The nurse taps it several times, gives up, and goes for the other arm. The situation is the same there. Amy is getting nervous. Hidayah's face is deadpan. She ties a rubber tube tightly on the patient's right arm and tells her to squeeze her hand. The patient pumps like a champ.

Hidayah tears open a little packet. A needle half a finger long appears. *"You're going to feel a little stick,"* Hidayah shrills.

The tip of the needle disappears into the tofu flesh. Amy fixes her gaze on the buried needle as it squirms around and around. She'd rather watch this than her mother's face. Hidayah presses a cotton ball on the point of entry and aborts.

"I'm sorry, you have little veins," she says. "Did you have anything to drink this morning?"

"I had tea," the patient says weakly.

"Next time you should drink lots of water. Let me try again… *You're going to feel a little stick."* Her voice jumps an octave once more.

Amy twines her fingers around Mom's free hand. The ten digits clench until every one is a striation of red and white.

The nurse straightens up and pulls her shoulders back. Mission aborted again.

"I'll try it once more," she says to Amy. "If I still can't get it, I'll find somebody else… *You're going to feel a little stick.*"

This time Amy twists her neck toward the wall to make a show of not looking. Perhaps her watchfulness is jinxing the nurse's touch.

Hidayah gets up. "Please give her plenty of water. Paper cups are over there." She points to the counter and disappears.

Amy plies her mother with water, one cup, two, until Mom clamps her lips together. It will take a while for the liquid to percolate into her bloodstream. Meanwhile they can only wait. Amy goes back to her computer and clicks on the next file, Iranresponse. She skims the headings: Direct Missile Attack, Strait of Hormuz Blockade, Terrorist Action—

Amy looks up and sees a nurse name-tagged Cindy walk in. She's blonde, apple cheeked, and looks too young to have drawn much blood. Amy tells herself to keep an open mind. For all she knows, Cindy may be the world's leading expert on small veins.

"Let me take a look at the teeny veins," she croons in a kindergarten teacher voice. She picks up the right arm, sees the bruises there, and goes for the left. After digging around the soft flesh, she turns to Amy. Her voice is grave. "Your mother has small veins, and on top of that they've grown stiff with age." The needle has gone in by the time she finishes her sentence. "You see how the needle is chasing the vein? It can't get through the thick wall." Switching to her other persona, she sings, "I'm sorry, sweetie. Yes, yes, I know it hurts. Bear with me, sweetie."

The needle is out. "You see what I mean?" she says to Amy. "Let me give it another try…OK, sweetie, squeeze your hand real tight now."

Amy feels the sting of salt in her eyes. She lowers her head to hide the large drop clinging to her eyeballs. Why on earth did she think she could do this alone? Her brothers have "volunteered" her for the job because her two children have flown the roost, and so has her husband. She also has an "easy" government job. They picture her moseying into her office at nine, answering a few emails, taking a long lunch break, going to a few meetings, and dashing out of the office at five minutes to five. They believe that of all four of them, she's got the most time on her hands.

She was naive too, thinking the six-thousand-dollar-a-month home would take care of Mom's every need. She thought all she had to do was bring Mom some greasy Chinese takeout once in a while, help her at bingo, and bribe the staff. Although the home forbids cash incentives, flowers and candies are welcome. It has taken her the whole six months to fully realize her stupidity. Her mother isn't a poodle. A warm bed, meals and treats, and two walks a day don't add up to happiness. Her demands are many, and she's constantly recycling them as well as creating new ones.

Her brothers have told her they would support her in every way they can. Where are they now? Are they going to drive in from New York City, Trenton, or Philadelphia to hold Mom's hand? Are they going to hang around while people take turns torturing their mother?

Cindy straightens up. "You've got such baby veins," she coos, her fingers twitching as if dying to pinch the flabby cheeks.

"I have to go to the bathroom," Mom says, wiggling to get out of bed.

"Don't move, stay there. You can't get up yet." Cindy swings around, opens the cabinet, and grabs a package. A long, thin snake emerges from the plastic wrap.

"I'm going to put this catheter in her," the nurse says.

"Hey, Mom," Amy shouts. She cups her mother's face with both hands and gently turns it until their eyes meet. She wants Mom's undivided attention. Her mother must *not* know, must *not* feel what's going to happen.

"Let's recite from the Book of *Xiao*." She switches to Chinese: '*Xiao* begins with service to parents…continues in service to the ruler…and ends with establishing oneself in the world.'"

"You remember!" Mom smiles widely, baring all her teeth, fillings, caps, and implants.

"How can I forget? That time I cut school and faked your signature, you made me write those lines a hundred times."

"*Xiao* is the root of virtue, the Way to establish oneself in the world. You know how to establish yourself in the world?"

Amy reaches into the bottom drawers of her mental cabinet, where the lessons of Mommy's Chinese school are filed. When her non-Chinese friends watched cartoons on Saturday, she studied The Analects and The Great Learning. She hated it then but loved it when her language ability launched her foreign service career.

"Let me see. To establish oneself is to be a good person. Don't lie, don't cheat. Be kind to others, especially your parents," she says what Mom wants to hear. "If you can be nice to your parents you can be nice to anybody," she adds tongue in cheek.

"Work hard, do your best, save your money," Mom adds to the list.

Amy's heart thumps at the mention of work. *The country is about to go to war again, the Middle East is on the verge of self-destruction, oil shortage will send the global economy into a tailspin, markets will crash, the world will burn, and I'm here discussing Confucianism with my mother?*

"Aah," Mom gives a deep sigh of satisfaction. Every tension in her body melts.

Amy's eyes jump over the forbidden parts of her mother's anatomy to the tube. A yellow fluid trickles in. "Aah" echoes inside Amy as if her bladder is the one getting relief.

"I love going out with you," Mom says. "You always know where the bathroom is."

Amy is first surprised, then amused, then touched. "I love going out with you too, Mom," she says, patting her mother's anemic hair.

Another nurse walks in. Her yellow face is reassuring and even more so the name pinned to her chest. Jennifer Zhou. Amy can tell from the last name that the young woman is from China. Only those who have lived under the communists use this system of Romanization. The broad face and high cheekbones suggest northern origins.

"Are you from China?" Amy says.

"Yes, from Beijing."

"Really? My mother is from Beijing too."

Amy shouts the information to her mother. Mom immediately wants to know which street the nurse has lived on, how old she is, whether she's married, and if so, how many children she has.

"Mom, you're keeping her from her job," Amy interrupts. This nurse from the same hometown as Mom is going to succeed, she's sure of it.

With a steady hand, the nurse holds up the needle in a perpendicular position. While the other nurses attacked from the side, Jennifer Zhou favors an aerial strike. The needle goes right into the top of the vein—a direct hit. Amy is sure of it. Eyes don't lie.

The nurse jiggles the tiny tube. Nothing. Jennifer shakes her head and clucks her tongue. She takes her position and attacks again. This time Amy turns her eyes away from the needle. She devotes her energy on Mom's free hand, stroking it, patting it, and squeezing it back. Everything she's wanted to say to her mother, the words that would sound maudlin or insincere, is expressed with poetic precision by her fingers.

When the fourth nurse walks in, the atmosphere in the room is as sober as a funeral parlor. There's no introduction, just a grim exchange of nods. The African American nurse by the name of Chantella completes the racial spectrum. From black to white and the colors in between, Mom has experienced them all. If Chantella fails, the next nurse would have to hail from another planet.

Snap go the rubber gloves. *Zeeep*, the foil packet opens up its frightful content. *Vrooom*, the nurse's chair rolls forward. The needle goes in without a sound. Amy can no longer think of the black and blue surface as her mother's flesh, alive with nerve endings. It has become a dead object, like a sponge or pin cushion. And she's stopped looking at Mom's face.

The needle burrows straight ahead and stops. All eyes stare unblinking at the same spot, all hearts murmur the same prayer. A dark red fluid seeps into the tube.

"Don't you have work to do?" Mom says. "You better go now."

Amy smiles fondly at her mother and strokes her cheek. "I'll stay until your blood pressure is stable…The President can wait."

Katharine A. Lorr

Night Walking

KATHARINE A. LORR has published poems and short stories in numerous small magazines. Her mystery, "Blindside of the Border," which
takes place in South Texas against the background of Mexican drug cartel
violence, is with an agent seeking publication. She is working on a second
novel in which the story in this collection, "Night Walking," will be a
chapter. She is retired from a federal career that included work on a range
of international and domestic immigration law and policy issues. Born and
raised in Upstate New York, she lives in Silver Spring, Maryland.

*A*ileen heard the steady thrum of Shiva's fingers on his laptop
as she passed the crack of light glaring from under the study
door. He'd bitched all week about the brief he had to file, and
the research, statistics, and arguments he needed to develop. In typical
Shiva fashion, he'd put it off until the last minute, and now that it was due
in the morning, spent the evening cursing his clients, staff, and the chaotic
immigration practice he was trying to build. He'd be up all night again
and demanded sympathy. If she made a suggestion or pointed out this was
happening a lot, he'd scream that she didn't understand. Well, fuck him.
She was desperate to get out of the house anyway. Her head ached, and
she couldn't stand to think about the argument they'd had at dinner. She
scooped up her running shoes and tiptoed down the stairs.

"Come on, baby," she whispered in the dog's ear. "Let's go."

Jack jumped to attention, his ears twitching like satellite dishes, alert
to motions signaling his release into the galloping outdoors. She tied her
shoes, grabbed her hair in a ponytail, and mashed it under a black baseball
cap. The dog stretched back on his hind legs, moaned, and wagged his
tail, eager to depart. She glanced at her watch—it was late, barely still
Thursday—and clicked the thick leash into place on his collar.

The front door shut behind her as she stepped out into the darkness. She hunched her shoulders and flexed the muscles in her arms, back, and legs, glad she was strong from the weights she had been lifting at the Y. Turning right she headed down Emerson Street, through her silent neighborhood toward the jogging track that ringed the field behind the school at the far end of the street. She walked past her neighbors' houses, noting the blue flicker of television lights and the scattered recycling containers at the curb ready for the pickup the next day. Under the shadowy trees, yards were tidy or scraggly, steps and walkways bare or strewn with children's toys, abandoned rakes, the flotsam of the day. In a few hours newspapers would be thrown up various driveways, and crows would flap down to scrounge for delicacies around the trash cans.

She and Shiva usually told each other when they went out night walking, but tonight she didn't. Halfway down the block she realized she'd left her cell phone in the charger. She tossed her head and stretched her jaws wide as she gulped in the cool air, hoping to diminish the burn that raked her forehead. *Don't mess with me*, she thought to herself, striding firmly, keeping the dog close. *Tonight I am the mean queen*, Shiva's name for her in certain moods. *If anybody gets in my way, look out.*

"Jesus, Jack." She yanked the dog off a huge, green bag of garbage. A cool night breeze hit her and she exhaled. The conversation about Rowan at dinner had made her feel trapped and enraged. Fuck Shiva for bringing it up. Thinking about her brother's death would fuel dark thoughts if she didn't shake them off fast. The house was clogged with dark thoughts these days, and she felt better the instant she stepped outside.

Walking the dog kept everyone sane. Shiva wanted the exercise and often ran with Jack, doing up to eight or ten miles a day, depending on time available and weather conditions. Aileen just sought release and distraction. Oh, she believed in exercise and stayed in shape, but that was for the gym. Outside, she took her time and opened up to the solitude, noticing the dog's intense preoccupation with scents and smells. Seeing Jack's feet planted, nose riveted on a branch, tree, or fence as he fretted over another dog's urine reminded her that humans might look just as silly in the grand scheme of things. Could you see yourself as an alien would? Walking Jack she was absorbed by the foliage, insect noise, sky, light, windy shadow, and the earth's state of decay. The neighborhood looked different in darkness, unfathomable and mysterious.

"Come on, Jack," she whispered again, wired to the dog's muscular energy. The dog was frozen, hackles raised, and retriever instincts kicked into high alert, scanning the air for undomesticated, nocturnal wildness. But at the sound of her voice, the dog relaxed and moved on. The enclave of small brick colonial-style houses lying on the north side of Sligo Creek Park was generally peaceful, but trouble could lurk or pounce anytime. As part of the D.C. metropolitan area, neighborhood houses were often broken into and robbed if a window was left open or a door unlocked. A car left unlocked overnight would be rummaged through and ransacked, anything of value taken.

Aileen liked to tell the story of the elderly couple across the street who'd returned from a trip to Florida, gone inside, and fallen asleep. When she'd stepped outside the next morning to get her newspaper, Aileen had found the trunk of their car wide open and three suitcases lined up in the street where they'd left them. Nothing was touched. But a few nights later a heated argument in Spanish in the middle of the night was followed by the roar of car engines, the screech of tires, and a shoot-out in front of the same house; someone apparently had not paid for their drugs in the park. Ninety percent of the time nothing happened, but anything could and sometimes did. Shiva showed her stories about gangs, crimes, and police activity in the local paper. Aileen thought these were overwrought. Of course, bad things *could* happen, but the likelihood was small. Anyway, where could you live where that would not be true?

"Jack," she said to the darkness at the end of the leash. "Let's go to the track."

Big, black, and invisible unless he was right next to her, Jack jolted up from whatever he was sniffing and charged down the steep hill toward the track, tugging at the leash. He pulled her left and right, mesmerized by animal shuffles in the bushes, jungle smells, and the promise he'd be loosed at the track. At the huge field inside and around it, Aileen would let him off leash, so he could run hard and wild, and tire out before they walked north along the creek to the golf course. The laws prohibited unleashing dogs, but she trusted Jack to stay close and obedient, and she would not let him off leash for long. Jack unleashed would disturb no one at this time of night except errant cats or other dog owners with similarly well-controlled animals.

For days she'd promised herself she'd take Jack up to the golf course and surreptitiously watch the sharpshooters hired to gun down the exploding deer population at night. Shiva hated the idea that deer were being killed right in their neighborhood, but Aileen had grown up in upstate New York and was more pragmatic. Deer were everywhere these days, starving, triggers for Lyme disease, and dangerous to drivers. Something had to be done. The county's deer management program was controversial but effective, and she just wanted to see how they did it. If she and Jack stayed hidden in the trees and shadows near the parkway, which was closed at night up there near the raised platforms, she hoped to see if they had lights or worked in the dark with night-vision equipment, if they enticed the deer to come within range, or the deer were completely oblivious when shot.

At the corner of Jackson and Quinn, a dirt foot path veered off to the left down to the track. There she bent over the dog's collar and unsnapped his leash. Ecstatic, Jack disappeared into the dark, overgrown terrain between the street and the field. What prey was he tracking? Beyond the track and field, she could hear Sligo Creek rushing through the woods, and beyond that was a parkway and a low-income housing project surrounded by lots filled with cars. She stood, silent in the insect-filled night.

"Jack." Her voice was snappy as a stick on a tin can. Instantly the dog leaped out at her, checking in as if to say, *hurry up and join me*, before darting off again, following the pathway nose down in a fierce zigzag, and turning sharply right at the entrance to the field.

The field was lit to discourage crime, she supposed, but she could only dimly make out the dark, tarred surface circling it. No one was running on the track. Casting a glance all around to be sure the field was empty, she headed out toward its center, Jack now in a frenzy of running, stopping to sniff, and flying off again. During the school day the high school's gym classes sprinted and careened around orange cones; in the afternoon pickup soccer players sorted themselves into teams. Inside the far corner of the jogging track sprawled a baseball diamond banked by bleachers and fencing behind the batter's box.

People often walked across the jogging track from Wayne Avenue, a busy street at rush hour with a bus stop near that end of the school. So Aileen surveyed the far side of the field to see if anyone might be down there. Under the hazy light someone—likely school authorities discouraging use of their inside facilities by the pickup soccer players—had placed a large, green plastic portable toilet on the concrete.

"Wow." Aileen stood with her hands on her hips and breathed, surveying the vast, empty field and inhaling the cool air. A sense of life stirred her, crowding out her sadness and frustration. For the first time since her brother's death, she felt whole, and she hugged herself, savoring a rare sense of wellness and possibility. For a fleeting moment she let it all go: the loss of Rowan, the difficulty of communicating about it with her husband, the constant worry about who she was now that her brother's death had passed its dark shadow over her. Rowan had been a good, if troubled, younger brother. He'd have liked it here, outside, in the center of the field. As kids, they'd roamed the countryside, sometimes at night, and she could feel his presence, his shared joy in seeing the dark field and the stars. He'd have told her to let go of her sadness; indeed, he would not have wanted his death to leave her so devastated. He'd have told her to buck up, be strong, and get over it. *I'm trying*, she thought, talking back to him in her mind. She smiled at this exchange, a gift in the night. But she also wanted to say *fuck you, Rowan, why, why, why?*

Standing still she could hear the cars rushing by on Wayne Avenue, Sligo Creek Parkway, and even as far away as the Washington Beltway, a sound like wind or someone humming. From across the jogging field she heard a muffled thump in the direction of the portable outhouse. From where she stood, she could not see the door to the outhouse, only the back of it, which held a large sign, unreadable in the dim light. Perhaps someone had gone inside to use it.

She stood and waited. Silence. She thought about Rowan again, his stupid grin.

Muffled screams broke the silence. Moans, followed by a sharp voice, filtered across the great expanse: a command or a threat, perhaps in Spanish, she was not sure. She waited, wondering what to do.

She cursed quietly her failure to bring her cell phone. How to see the originators of the threats or cries, which came now, intermittent, sharp, jagged, terrified?

Rumbling or thumping came from the outhouse wall. She saw the outhouse itself was rocking back and forth.

As if magnetized, she started toward the sounds. Someone was being attacked, someone was attacking someone. Where? Inside the portable toilet? Or in front of it, on the side she could not see? Where the hell was Jack? She couldn't call him now without announcing her presence, and hoped to God he wasn't rolling around on some dead animal somewhere. To see what was happening, she'd have to circle around to the south side where the door was. She did not want Jack rushing up, or barking and warning people she was there. And she might not be able to see in the darkness. Slipping across the field, she debated how close was safe, what would happen if she observed the attacker, what her response would be.

Hearing desperate pleas, she ran toward the sounds. Nearing the back of the toilet, she read the sign, "Don's Johns," heard a man's voice inside, no words, just harsh, guttural, insistent, crazed, urgent sounds in time with the rocking of the portable toilet. Shove, shove, shove.

Jack came up next to Aileen and looked at her. She signaled to the dog to be quiet.

A woman was begging. "No, no."

Touching the cold plastic side of the portable outhouse, Aileen rounded the corner and approached the door, which flapped open with each violent thrust. Suddenly, the door was flung open as the outhouse tilted, and she saw the rear end of a man between the knees of a woman sprawled across the toilet. The smell was unbearable. A man was nearing his climax, eyes shut, head back, riding the woman harder and harder and harder.

Without thinking, Aileen took both ends of Jack's leash from where it hung around her shoulders, lifted it over her head, and slung it over the man's head and under his neck just as he was groaning. She tightened her grip, braced herself, and jerked it hard and back with all her strength.

The man fell back, sperm spitting into the darkness. She heard a loud crack as his head hit the pavement. What had happened?

The woman clutched herself and sobbed, naked from the waist down, her blouse around her shoulders, her whole body heaving.

"Are you OK?" Aileen asked.

"*Dios, Dios mío*." The woman shook her head.

Aileen helped the woman up, and the outhouse door slammed shut, separating them from the smells emanating from it. She gasped, choking on the fresh air that had soothed her.

The attacker lay outstretched on the ground in front of the outhouse. The woman stood, staring at him, hand over her mouth, stifling a scream. She had long, dark, tangled hair, and a face streaked and swollen from crying. Her hand fell away, revealing a mouth twisted like a crushed plum. Struggling to cover herself, the woman pulled her bra over her breasts, yanked a dirty white blouse over her hips, and picked up a torn dark skirt.

"You're safe, you're safe," Aileen said. She sucked in the night air, shocked and trembling. Heaving huge sobs, the woman buried her face in her hands. If Jack moved, the woman sobbed harder, so Aileen grabbed the dog, made him sit down next to her and fumbled to leash him, trying to explain he was friendly. But the woman recoiled and sank to her knees, rolling her eyes in terror. *What do I do?* Aileen thought. *I don't know this woman.* She tugged the woman to her feet, warning the dog to stay put. To her surprise, the woman smelled sweet, soapy. She summoned her high school Spanish.

"*Como se llama?*" Aileen asked. "What is your name?"

"Rosa." The woman whispered as if someone might hear her.

"Who is he?" Aileen studied the motionless body for any sign of life. Suddenly the night air seemed cold. Aileen hugged herself. What had she done?

"He steal me many months, hide me, threat me, give me to men I no want," Rosa said in broken English. She wiped her wet face and spat out the word, "*Malo.*"

Aileen thought he might be dead. She shivered, appalled at her own violence, but strangely observant: she had done this. Fuck it. Whatever happened, she would explain it and Shiva would know what to do, who to call, how to handle the situation. Thank God for Shiva.

The woman named Rosa turned, her eyes looking for a way to escape. Aileen grabbed her.

"How long was it going on?" Aileen knew Shiva would ask that kind of question.

"Since he bring me here." Rosa stared at the man on the ground as if he might leap up at any moment.

"Here?" Aileen's hands were shaking so hard she had to let go of Rosa. She tried to clench and unclench her fist.

The woman gazed around her, the whites of her eyes seeking a way out of this field. Aileen followed her gaze and looked again at the woman, this Rosa, as if seeing her for the first time. "From?"

"Mexico." Stepping toward Wayne Avenue, Rosa seemed ready to flee to the bus stop.

Aileen blocked her. She'd heard about this. Trafficking, human trafficking. Didn't Shiva go to a conference on this? Where had he gone? Colombia? Ecuador? Mexico? Oh, Christ, would Shiva even believe this story? He always said people could make up stories so easily it was hard to ferret out fraud.

Thinking about Shiva's skepticism made her ask, "Why, why was he doing that in the toilet? Why there? It seems…crazy."

"He crazy, loco. I escape across the park from over there." The woman pointed with her hand across the other side of Wayne Avenue. "Hide. But he find me here, was going to kill me."

The man suddenly convulsed. Jack sprang up next to Aileen and growled, but Aileen held him back. "We better get going."

Rosita started to run in the direction of Wayne Avenue, but Aileen grabbed her wrist tightly and pulled her in the opposite direction. "Come to my house and we'll tell my husband. He'll know what to do." She shivered, sweating, trying not to look at the man lying on the ground. *Oh, my God*, she thought. *He's not dead. If he moves again, or gets up, I'll die. Help me.* She suddenly wanted to pray, cry, scream. She looked around desperately and saw the moon. The moon! It was dented, wobbled on one side, as if someone had pushed it in. She'd never made it to the golf course to watch the sharpshooters take aim. The air pulsed around her and the insects buzzed. Dirty, proud, and terrified, she wanted only to go home to Shiva, to have him fix this and help her understand what had just happened. He'd know what to do, he always did.

Kate Lu

Ink

KATE LU is a native New Yorker who now lives and works in Virginia. She holds a degree in creative writing from the George Washington University, where she was the editor-in-chief of the *G.W. Review*. Her work has previously appeared in literary journals including *Ellipsis...Literature and Art* and the *Missing Slate*, and is forthcoming in the 2014 edition of the *Labletter*.

*E*ven eight months after her death, there are evenings when I find myself in front of the bar where I ran into Carly on the hottest night of last summer. Tonight, after the rain stops, I loosen my tie and roll up my sleeves, wander the damp streets until I find the shuttered building, the lights out and the noise silenced. The barred windows stare at me blankly like dead eyes, the doorway cluttered with broken bottles and an abandoned sleeping bag. I think about Carly, dead in a body bag, her eyes sightless, her mouth slightly open, a gash of red in her side. I never saw her body, but when I think about her, I often think about her like that, the memories of her smile at seventeen, and later, her resigned grimace at twenty-eight, scrubbed away in favor of a pale corpse.

Almost everything I know about Carly are things that anyone who came into contact with her would know. I know that she had grown up on the same street as I did, that we had gone to the same high school and had been in the same English class junior year, that she had been a second-string cheerleader whose eyes are blank in the yearbook photos, that she had wanted to be a painter but failed. I know that while we had been aware of each other during high school, we never spoke, and that the last time I had seen her, before running into her at that bar, was graduation. I know that during my junior year of high school, I had been completely infatuated with her, but she had hardly known who I was.

It was those things that returned to me when I found her in this bar last July, sitting at the counter, staring into her glass, one hand pushed into her long, dirty blonde hair. She almost didn't recognize me when I approached her, but I would know her face anywhere, no matter how pale, how tired, even with the lines beginning to form around the sides of her mouth, under her eyes. My stomach still dropped when she smiled; I felt like I was seventeen again, trying to find the right things to say to a teenage crush. When she came back with me to my apartment, it was like receiving the answer to *What if?* I thought I would understand everything if she kept her body curled against mine, that I could fill in the missing spaces where my high school regrets, the things I never could find the courage to do, left blanks.

But she left in the morning, an answer that slipped away from me. When she stepped out of the back door of my apartment, she was murdered by a man who had been waiting there, and she became another name, another picture on the list of women that he killed all through that summer.

There are the things that maybe only I know about her: the way she slept with her right leg bent, the way her paleness made her recede into the dark so that she was almost invisible. The fact that she was sad, and that it was the sadness I was drawn to. When I think about her, among other things, I always think about the sadness.

I look back at the bar, thinking about Carly's mess of hair on the pillow beside me on that night in July, the smooth line of skin where her ribs protruded slightly, her long, skinny legs, her distant eyes. I think about the ways that her sadness has become mine, the ways that I carry it around with me, pocketed, close to my skin; when I'm breathing in the darkness of my bedroom, I often think of her.

THE BAR IS LOCATED A few blocks from a tattoo parlor, and tonight, I decide to go in, the tiny image of imagined text that I have been considering for months now at the forefront of my mind.

The inside of the tattoo parlor is a sterile white, the kind that bounces bright florescent light around in a way that makes the room seem smaller. I swallow and wind my fingers together behind my back, examining the framed designs that hang on the walls while I wait. Outside, cars hiss over the dark, rain-slick streets, appearing under the glow of street lamps before disappearing again into the night.

"Can I help you, sir?"

I jump and turn around, the skin on the back of my neck prickling. A girl with big brown eyes and curly black hair stands at the counter, watching me. Her skin is free of blemishes, including ink.

"Hi," I say. My voice creaks and I clear my throat. "I'm here for…" I wave my hands around, feeling silly; what else do people go to tattoo parlors for?

"Come to the back, then," she says, heading toward a heavy white curtain to the left of the counter, which obscures a back room. She doesn't bat an eye at my awkwardness, either because she doesn't notice it, or because she chooses to ignore it; her expression doesn't change and I can't tell which.

The back room is well lit, but less blindingly white. On the right side is a table with a number of instruments and supplies, and next to it is a large black chair. She gestures toward it and I sit while she pulls up a stool next to me. The entire parlor is empty except for the girl and me.

"So what were you thinking of?" she asks as she ties back her hair.

"A date," I say, "in Roman numerals, here." I draw my finger along a space on my inner arm, close to my elbow.

"How big?" She rolls the stool closer to the table to examine the gleaming array of instruments there. "What color?"

"Black, this big." I hold two fingers about a centimeter apart.

"OK," she says. "And the date?"

"July 21st, 2006."

She gets to work, leaning over me with the needle, my arm laid out on the arm of the chair. I feel pinching in my skin, but I try not to concentrate on it.

"Whom is this for?" the girl asks. Her voice lifts with interest, and I'm grateful for the conversation.

"Someone I knew." I feel the need to add, "She's dead now."

"I'm sorry." Her eyes are soft, but she's frowning.

"Her name was Carly." My mouth is moving now without my intending it to. "I knew her in high school. She was killed last summer, after leaving my apartment. I'd run into her at a bar. And I—" I stop myself; I'm not even sure of how to finish the sentence. The girl stiffens slightly but her hands keep moving across my arm steadily; she says nothing. My mouth feels like it's full of flour, damp, chalky, and half dry. "I guess sometimes you can't help but wonder 'What if?'" I finally mutter.

The girl is looking at me now, the needle stopped, her dark eyes examining my face as if searching for something.

"What?" I ask her.

She shakes her head and goes back to working on my arm. "If I were you, I would not be getting this tattoo," she says.

"Why not?"

"It just seems like bad luck. That's all." Her eyes seem larger, fiercer, like she is pushing even her body into conviction. "The dead can follow you around if you let them."

"What's your name?" I ask her as a sudden stab of curiosity finds me.

"Corinne," she says without looking at me; her focus is on my arm.

"I'm Ed."

She nods in response and says nothing more, just moves the needle along my skin and watches it jab black beneath the surface. When she finishes, she wraps my arm up in long bandages so I can't see the tattoo, pausing for a moment before hiding the numbers, giving them one last glance, her fingertips brushing my skin. I like the way it looked when it was done, the date stamped in crisp, black letters, the whole thing edged in blood. I realize only now how permanent it is, how permanent I want it to be—it, and all the things I don't want to forget.

THE NEXT DAY IS SUNDAY, and when the afternoon sun gets through the missing space in my bedroom window's blinds and wakes me up, I find myself curious to see both the bar and the tattoo parlor in daylight.

The bar has lost all the magnetic qualities it has at night; it looks only like an abandoned building, the stark sunlight emphasizing the heaps of trash around it, the notice on the door that says it's been closed by order of the health department. It could be any of the other empty storefronts that line the street. When I get to the tattoo parlor, though, I can see Corinne framed in the large glass window, foregrounded by the white walls; she is sitting at the counter, paging through a hardcover book with no dust jacket.

She doesn't look up when I enter the parlor, but her eyes stop moving along the page. The place is just as empty as it was last night, and the walls seem less bright than they did before. I stand in front of the counter with my hands in my pockets, a knot of awkwardness forming in my stomach.

"Hi," I say. My voice comes out hoarse.

She looks up at me but doesn't close the book. "Hello," she says. There is a long pause where neither of us speak; she seems unruffled, but I can feel my palms grow damp. She rests her arms on the counter and leans her body toward me. "Is there a problem with the tattoo?" she asks.

"Oh, no," I say. A spark of pain stutters across the inside of my arm, but I ignore it. "I was just taking a walk, and I found myself back here." I realize how lame this sounds as soon as I say it and try to change the subject. "Are you always the only one here?"

"On the weekends, yes. We used to get more customers, but that's all changed in the past year or so. There's less foot traffic now that everything else around us is closed." She uses one of the parlor's business cards to mark her page in the book and closes it. "Why are you really here?" she asks as she sets it aside.

My shoulders jump a little; while there is no accusation in her voice, she surprises me with her directness. "There's a place nearby that was important to me," I say. "Sometimes I feel like walking past it."

"If it was important to you, why walk past it?"

I stare at her. "What do you mean?"

"You said it *was* important to you. Why dredge up that old hurt?" Her head is tilted slightly to the side, and she studies me like someone might look at a microscope slide.

I try to determine how she could possibly be figuring me out so quickly, but I can't get past those unflappably discerning eyes. "I don't know that it's hurt," I say.

"Then why get a tattoo?"

She's sharp; her intuition slices through me and makes me curious. "When are you off from work?" I ask, avoiding the question.

"Why?" She looks amused now, a small smile playing around her lips.

I shrug. "I just thought we could get coffee sometime." I want to tell her that I think she's interesting, but that makes her sound like an insect.

"I haven't been getting out much lately," I say instead, even though the excuse sounds flat.

"Maybe," she says, but she pulls another business card out of the display on the counter and begins scribbling on the back of it. She smiles slightly when she flips the card back over and pushes it across the counter toward me.

I take the card and pocket it without looking at the back. "Saturday," I say.

When I get back outside and look at the card, I see that she has written her phone number and edged the sides with a simple sketch of vines.

THE WORK WEEK COMES AND goes in a blur of paper being pushed across my desk; I spend my days stacking, sorting, and processing legal briefs. I call Corinne on Friday and ask her if she's still free on Saturday.

"Yes," she says, "I haven't forgotten." Her voice lilts more than usual; she's laughing at me.

We agree to meet at a coffee shop near my apartment, and on Saturday I find her sitting next to the window, her gloves set neatly on the table in front of her. She doesn't notice me—or pretends not to—until I sit down across from her.

"Hi," I say.

"Hello," she says, the corners of her mouth quirking up. The late afternoon sun catches the red in her thick hair; the shine makes it almost difficult to look at her.

"How has your week been?" I ask, taking off my coat and throwing it over the back of the chair.

"Quiet," she says. She doesn't offer anything more, and there is a brief silence, which feels awkward on my end but doesn't seem to bother her. I feel relieved when a waitress comes to take our orders.

"How is your tattoo healing?" Corinne asks after the waitress walks away. She rests her chin in her palm and watches me.

"It feels a little itchy, but it's fine." It twinges now, as if to remind me that it's there. The waitress returns with my coffee and Corinne's scone. "Do you have any tattoos?" I ask.

Corinne smiles. "No," she says, "I don't. Not yet."

"Really?" I ask. "Why not?"

"I haven't found the right one yet," she says as she stirs milk into her coffee, watches the swirls of white dissipate into the brown.

"Do you think you'll ever get one?"

"Maybe," she says, shrugging. "There is one design that I have been working on for a long time. Some day it might be ready." She takes the scone apart with her fingers and eats it piece by piece, offering no further details about the tattoo design. I decide to let it go.

"What's your favorite thing to tattoo on people?" I ask instead. It sounds like a filler question, but I find myself curious to know more about her art.

"Flowers," she says. "Always flowers."

We fall into silence again, but this time it's a thoughtful one. I try to settle into Corinne's quiet, the way she doesn't speak unless spoken to, the way she likes to sit and watch and listen.

I pay for the meal, and afterward, we spend the rest of the afternoon and early evening walking, sometimes talking, sometimes not. I tell her about my job as a paralegal, my failed attempts at completing law school, and she tells me, in bits and pieces, about her time at art school, her apprenticeship with her father, who was also a tattoo artist. The parlor isn't hers, but it is her life; when she isn't in the shop, she spends most of her days sketching new designs.

At dusk, I walk her back to the parlor so she can start her shift.

"It was nice to see you," I tell her when we reach the door. I shove my hands in my pockets and look at my feet. "Maybe we can do this again sometime?"

She smiles and reaches for one of my hands, hesitates briefly before touching me, like a hiccup, a blush rising in her cheeks, her face almost shy; her leather gloves are cool against my skin. I take it as permission to call her again.

I WAIT THREE MONTHS BEFORE inviting Corinne back to my apartment, but after that, she is over almost every night she isn't working. The floor of my bedroom becomes littered with bits of paper, on which she outlines new tattoo ideas before scrapping most of them; when she's gone, I smooth them out and stack them in my nightstand drawer. She lights candles during thunderstorms and avoids the cracks between the tiles in my apartment building's hallway, sometimes sliding into me in a sudden stop to avoid a line, her arms around my waist, taking several long moments to let go. Sometimes we go to bed together but she'll be gone in the morning, leaving only a few long, dark hairs on her pillow, the smell of her soap in the sheets. It all reminds me of Carly.

One night in late spring, Corinne and I are in bed, listening to the traffic sounds that filter in through the window, whose frame is so rusty I have to prop it open with a stack of books. The streetlights make patterns on the oatmeal-colored walls, and for a moment, I'm reminded of a cheap motel. We are lying on our own sides of the bed, hands folded over our stomachs, staring at the stucco ceiling.

"Do you ever think of her now?" she asks, breaking our long silence. She doesn't have to look over at me to know I'm awake.

"Sometimes," I say, trying to be vague and knowing she can tell, probably, exactly how much I think about Carly.

"You shouldn't," she says. "Not when there is so much else to think of. So much other life." She hesitates for a moment before saying, "I love you." One of her slim, cool hands finds mine, squeezes my fingers so hard that they smart. I don't say anything, only take her wrist and pull her closer, as if friction on skin will make up for my silence. Although she doesn't repeat the words, we both feel them hanging in the air over us, a heavy thing ready to drop.

Later, while she's dozing, lying on her stomach, I see a tiny knot of dark, spiky flowers on her shoulder—purple with yellow centers. I run my fingers over them and feel only her marble-cool skin.

"When did you get this?" I ask her.

"A few weeks ago," she says, her voice thick with what I assume is sleepiness. "I asked one of the other artists at the shop to do it, but I've been working on the design for a very long time."

"What is it?"

"Flowers," she says.

My chest tightens a little with an impatience that surprises me. "But what kind?"

"Belladonna," she says. "Nightshade."

I snatch my fingers back quickly, as though the ink itself might be toxic. She looks almost amused by this, and falls asleep with her body curled around mine, the shadow of a smile on her face; I wake up in a cold sweat the next morning, the date on my skin glaring at me when I lift my arm from my eyes.

I TRY NOT TO THINK about Carly when I'm with Corinne, but sometimes the two slide together: hair on pillow, soft smile, angular limbs. The ink on my arm dissolves; the date is any other date, devoid of sinister meaning. When I'm on the verge of falling asleep, Carly swims through my half-collected thoughts, her sad smile the last thing I remember before I drift off. In my dreams I wish my arms were lighter, that I could reach out and touch her, even as I press myself closer to Corinne, bury my face in her hair, feel the heat of her body, wanting something from her I can't name, my mouth filling with the metallic taste of guilt.

There are still days when I almost call Corinne by Carly's name, usually in the morning before I'm fully awake, or right before I fall asleep at night. The syllables—the women—get mixed up in my mind, one blending into the other, Carly with dark hair or Corinne with blue eyes, the same limbs, the same warm weight next to me. Sometimes I dream about Carly painting flowers, massive swaths of purple and yellow that become deadly nightshade, before the paint leaps off her palette and swallows her up and she disappears, drowning in purple, becoming a splotch that then becomes Corinne, but only the back of her, only recognizable by the poison-dark ink on her shoulder.

ON A SATURDAY NIGHT IN late June, I sit alone in my living room, unable to sleep, while Corinne works her shift at the tattoo parlor. The lights are off, and the street lamps cast long shadows across the hardwood floor. I wiggle my toes to feel the varnished coolness of the planks, to remind myself that my feet are still there. I doze in the armchair; across my legs is the jacket that Carly had left on the back of my front door the night she stayed here. I sometimes still use the leather to fight off the cold of chilly nights, but never when Corinne is here.

That night last July, I asked Carly why she had brought the jacket with her.

"I get cold easily," she said. She put her hand to my face; in spite of the heat, her fingers were icy, and I shivered. I took her thin, pale fingers between my own and thought about how skinny she looked, how narrow her shoulders were, how I could almost count each of her bones. I thought about fitting my hands against her sides, one finger between each rib.

I hear the click of my front door, the soft sound of Corinne slipping her sandals off and padding toward the living room. I wake fully and whisk the jacket off my legs, but not fast enough.

"You're off early," I say. My voice is too loud. "I wasn't expecting you tonight." The jacket is like a dead animal in my hands.

"Why are you still sitting up?" Corinne asks me as she steps closer. She sees the jacket I'm clutching; I think if I hold onto it tightly enough, it will disappear.

She reaches out and whisks it from me as I flinch, holds it out in front of her by the collar. The brown leather glows dully in the ambient light. Corinne doesn't have to ask whose it is. Her jaw tightens.

"Good night, Ed," she says, stalking off toward the bedroom, her shoulders bunched up about her ears. Fifteen minutes later, when I go lie down next to her, she doesn't react; her body faces away from me, held in a tight ball, the muscles wound, ready to spring, flee. She's pretending to be asleep, but while I stare at the ceiling I can hear her shallow, hitched breathing, and when I look at her face, her eyelashes are shiny with tears. I can't remember the time that I finally fall asleep, but when I wake, she's gone, and I feel like I can breathe.

MY MOTHER KNEW CARLY BECAUSE she was the girl who lived up the block, but the two never actually met, never spoke to each other. Sometimes, when I have nothing else to think about, I wonder if they might have liked each other, if my mother would have fretted over Carly's tired skin and the circles under her eyes, if Carly would have been stifled by the attention.

When my mother asks to meet Corinne, though, I worry about other things.

"I'm not sure that would be a good idea right now," I say to her. We're on the phone, and my mother is pleading. I try to keep my voice low so my coworkers don't hear me arguing with her.

"Well, you've been seeing her for four months," she says. "You talk about her all the time. When exactly is it going to be a good idea?"

"I don't know." I don't tell her that I'm worried about the impression Corinne will make with her long silences and her short answers, that I'm worried she will start talking about the poisonous plant that she has tattooed on her shoulder. My mother doesn't even know that I myself have a tattoo, or that I still think about Carly when I'm lying next to Corinne.

"I was thinking about going into the city on Sunday anyway, to visit some friends," she says now. "Would it be so bad for you and Corinne to have dinner with me?"

I rub my hand over my face and hold back a groan. The office is an oven; the walls trap the midsummer heat, and even the small fan on my desk can't keep the air around me circulating fast enough.

"Ed?"

"All right, fine," I say, defeated.

She tells me that she'll meet us at the Italian restaurant that I always take her to when she comes to visit me. "Don't be late," she says before hanging up.

I reach up to the calendar hanging above my desk to scribble in the obligation. My eyes fall on the date, and I immediately feel as though I'm being plunged into ice-cold water. My skin breaks out into goose bumps. I roll the sleeve on my right arm higher and look from the date there to the one above me; they are exactly the same, though one year apart. The skin suddenly itches, and I try to shake off the feeling that something is creeping up my shoulders, coming to get me.

CORINNE IS SKETCHING WHEN I get home from work. She perches on a chair at the desk in my bedroom, using only the fading evening sun as a light source. I put my bag down by the door and go over to her, bending to lean my head on her shoulder; she's drawing more flowers, ones I can't name.

"Hello," she says without stopping her pencil.

"My mother wants to meet you," I say.

"Oh?"

"She'll be in the city on Sunday. She wants us to have dinner with her."

"Sunday?" She stops drawing, turns around in her chair to look at me. Her eyes drift to the tattoo on my arm, which is partially covered by my rolled-up shirt sleeve. "I have a shift on Sunday."

"Oh, right. You couldn't just get someone to fill in for you?"

She frowns slightly, but she says, "I can ask. If this is important to you."

"Well, it's important to my mother, so she thinks it should be important to me." The joke falls flat; Corinne's face is serious, her eyes clouded. "It would be nice if you met her," I say. "She would appreciate it." I want to say *She would like you*, but I'm not sure if that's true, so I don't.

"I'll think about it," she says, turning back around and returning to her sketch. She sighs and sinks her chin into her palm, staring into the paper without moving her pencil, still as stone.

ON SUNDAY, CORINNE MEETS ME at my apartment before we head off to dinner. She is wearing a magenta dress that seems to be made only of folds; the loud color belies her grim face. She looks like she has just swallowed something sour. When she walks out of the apartment ahead of me, I can see her tattoo peeking out through the straps of her dress.

The inside of my right arm has been itching all day, as if daring me to look down at it and be reminded what the date is. Walking out into the heat makes the stinging worse; the entire area prickles.

My mother is waiting for us in front of the restaurant when we arrive. She hugs me first, then kisses Corinne on the cheek. Corinne only smiles, but her eyes are serious and slightly narrowed, as if she's waiting for something to strike. As we go inside, I can feel the unease radiate off her skin like heat.

Corinne remains quiet through dinner, only speaking when my mother asks her questions. My mother frowns slightly when Corinne tells her that she's a tattoo artist, but to my relief, she doesn't linger on that point. Corinne looks like a wind-up toy ready to spring, her limbs held tight to her body. She traces patterns on the tablecloth with her finger, telling me silently that she would rather be sketching. I try to figure out what, besides my mother, could be making her so uncomfortable; I can see her being her impassive self even through the apocalypse, so her behavior confuses me.

The inside of the restaurant is warm in spite of the air conditioning. I roll my sleeves up, then reach for my water glass.

"Ed, what's that on your arm?" my mother asks.

I freeze with my hand around my glass, which is still on the table. "Um," I say.

"It's a tattoo," Corinne says. She doesn't look up, just keeps picking at her salad. I grind my teeth together to stop myself from snapping at her.

"When did you get this?" my mother asks. Her eyes are wide with surprise. "In March," I say.

"I see," she says, looking at Corinne. Corinne ignores her.

"Carly did it for me."

There is a silence that lasts for a moment too long. I look up, and then I realize my mistake. My stomach clenches and my insides feel cold. Corinne doesn't move. My mother stares at me, confused, but doesn't say anything.

"Corinne," I mutter. "Corinne did it for me." My head buzzes loudly and everything looks fuzzy.

The rest of the dinner drags on, mostly in silence. Corinne pushes her food around her plate without eating it and I do the same thing, while my mother's brows remain furrowed in disapproval. She hugs me and gives Corinne a passing peck on the cheek before leaving both of us in the entrance of the restaurant.

Corinne's arms are crossed, and she stares at a potted plant in the corner of the room. Her jaw is set and her eyes are narrow with fury.

"Corinne—"

"Please don't," she says thickly.

"I'm sorry," I say.

She whirls around to look at me, her eyes shining. "I thought—I thought I could prove myself wrong. I wanted to be wrong about you, about what I could see in you." She grabs my arm, her thumb burning into the middle of the tattoo there. "But I knew already what your fate would be. What it is. I knew it when I put this tattoo on you. I'm sorry, Ed."

She lets go of my arm and walks out of the restaurant, her heels clacking loudly on the tiled floor. When I can think to follow her out, I stand on the street looking both ways, but she's nowhere to be found.

THE NIGHT BEFORE CARLY DIED, we met at a bar. We walked down to the pier, then back to my apartment. We slept together, and in the morning, she left. She went downstairs, and when she got outside, she was accosted and killed by a man waiting in my alley; he was wanted for the murders of two other women at the time, a number that would grow over the course of that summer. I was the first person the police questioned. Those are the facts; I know them as well as I know my childhood phone number or my parents' names.

But I also know that woman and that man, the people that Carly and I were that night, the person that Carly will always be, now that she is only the fading ghost in my imagination, the one with the sad smile and the dirty blonde hair, the hopeless hunch to her shoulders and the already dead gaze. Sometimes, when I wake up, I think I only dreamed what happened last July.

And then I see the tattoo on my arm, the date in bold black ink, the places where Corinne's needle touched me, where she herself gripped me while her large eyes lit up in rage and disappointment. I know now that her warning against my memorial to the dead was not merely superstition, that she could see already all the longing wrapped up in it. I know that if I told people what those numbers mean, maybe no one else would ever touch me again, that I could die with only those memories, that ink, this phantom—the things in me that will never fade away.

Mary Claire Mahaney

Laurel's Song

MARY CLAIRE MAHANEY is the author of the novel *Osaka Heat* (AuthorHouse, 2007), which has won Independent Publisher gold and silver medals in romance and multicultural fiction, respectively. A retired lawyer, Mahaney writes poetry, fiction, and essays; her most recent works have been published in *Gargoyle Magazine* and *Legal Studies Forum*. Mahaney is an editor and book coach as well as a painter and photographer. She lives in McLean, Virginia, and enjoys finding typographical errors in restaurant menus. Her website can be found at www.maryclairemahaney.com.

These events always put Laurel in a foul mood. She goes because she loves her son and because of her maternal duties, although she wonders if these are two reasons or one. That her long-suffering husband, Johnny, the boy's dad, always accompanies her without complaint just increases her anguish. Johnny offered to bring Saul alone so Laurel could stay home, but she rejected his offer even though she fantasized an evening alone with her books.

The party celebrates the end of the year for the tennis team. Saul played a mediocre season, but two of the seniors are headed to college with athletic scholarships. Saul is only a sophomore, and if he doesn't continue with tennis over the next two years then surely he'll try something else—a placid sport like golf, or raucous rugby, or even javelin throwing, for crying out loud. (The parents of javelin throwers might be a more interesting crowd.) He isn't inclined to have a fall, winter, *and* spring sport, much to his mother's relief. But her boy has a lot of energy to expend, and sports are a better outlet than other things he could be doing, things Laurel doesn't want to think about. Even so, there wouldn't be an end-of-season party that included parents of graffiti-taggers or subversive roller-bladers, and that would be a good thing to go along with a bad thing.

Via email invitation, the party organizers assigned Saul's family an appetizer, and Laurel gave her son responsibility for it. That's what the school counselors advise—give your son or daughter RESPONSIBILITY. Laurel drove Saul to the grocery store and parked a twenty-dollar bill in his palm. She waited in the car and read the *Atlantic*, and Saul came out with three kinds of chips, as well as containers of guacamole, onion dip, and two salsas (mild and extra hot) and a nickel in change. Saul has decided to pass the chips in a plastic Kmart bowl that holds all three bags at once and to serve the dips in their containers.

In the car on the way to the party, Saul says one thing: "If you do anything embarrassing, Mom, you'll ruin my life. I'll never speak to you again." Laurel has foreign-born friends whose kids tell them not to show up at school or to speak English in public, for it embarrasses their children. Laurel thinks this is an unfounded and unfair worry on a child's part and counsels her friends to speak and to show up whenever they want. Laurel's English is native and impeccable.

The party is at a posh home. There's a sign on the side door: "Let yourself in." Blonde women populate the high-end kitchen, their voices slicing the room's fennel-scented air as they buzz around silver holloware and ceramic serving bowls. Phyllo-wrapped tidbits are being pulled from the oven, zigzag-cut fresh vegetables sit arranged in circles on trays, women's sterling arm jewelry jangles along tanned forearms, but at the door of the kitchen nobody comes up to Laurel and Johnny to say "Hello" or "Welcome" or "Make yourself at home." The kitchen blondes, dressed in bright blue or white shirts and slim-legged khaki trousers, mass together as if they're all speakers of the same foreign tongue. They *could* all be of Scandinavian descent, though that's a possibility with little likelihood.

Laurel, wearing a gauzy dress in her favorite color, aubergine, follows her husband into the dining room, having paused to witness their efficient son, smack among the glamorous women, rip open the chip bags, dump the contents into his mint green bowl, fold the empty bags and stick them in his jeans pockets, and ferry the bowl and the dips, lids on, down the basement stairs. Johnny offers Laurel an iced beer from the stainless steel party tub, and Laurel drinks from the bottle as the men do. Another couple drifts over; the female, the only woman besides Laurel not in the kitchen, isn't blonde but darker even than Laurel. She blathers on for some time, in an accented English Laurel can't quite place, her voice reverberating with her husband's even more exotic tones, about their older offspring, a daughter, and her numerous successes at Princeton and how they expect their son, in his junior year at the high school, to follow his sister. Laurel and Johnny have only Saul, and long ago they put the Princeton league out of their minds. As this other couple spills their confidence and pride out and over onto themselves, Laurel would like to wish ill to them, although not to their daughter, for she might not be the bore her parents are. Laurel is on the edge of blurting, "I hope your daughter drops out of school and joins the circus!" but damps the comment.

Laurel's eyes escape, beyond this throaty couple, beyond the staid dining room with its Queen Anne suite of furniture, through the mullioned windows, to the grounds beyond. A martin house stands on the wide lawn next to a brilliant but deserted swimming pool. Inside the house, to Laurel's right, hides a corner of the living room, the holy of holies, twin upholstered wing chairs flanking a fireplace.

The other couple wanders away amid Laurel and Johnny's lukewarm responses. There's no purpose in keeping up with the Joneses in the college world. Johnny and Laurel are simply hoping that Saul, when the time comes, finds a fit for his educational and social needs, not a feather for their cap, but this view, they've learned, is heresy among this crowd. Right now Saul's parents stand alone, indeed the only people who are alone, and they are still unaware who their hosts are. Laurel tells Johnny she feels invisible. Johnny offers to run her home and return to the party alone, but no, she'll stick it out. You never know, Saul could win an award for Most Improved Player, and missing that would be worse than staying, at least worse for Laurel. Laurel has stayed at bad parties before, though, and bad things have happened. Twice she threw up, three times she had diarrhea, and once she told off a widower who was monopolizing the conversation with his around-the-world sailing tales. She asked him if he thought his listeners really cared.

At Saul's tenth birthday party she spoke only in rhyme; at his twelfth she wore a Peter Rabbit mask. Both these episodes, and others, Saul complained about. There was also the incident—after her doctor prescribed a sedative for her, but before Laurel learned the dose she could tolerate and that she probably shouldn't have a drink along with the medicine—when she fell headlong over an ottoman. The good news: it was an adult party, so Saul wasn't there; the bad news: it was a retirement party for Johnny's boss, so all her husband's coworkers, and their guests, witnessed her cascade. She has yet to see another office party. This likely won't be her last end-of-season sports party, however, and with Saul's warning in her ears, she's resolved to make it through this party on her best behavior.

Johnny steps away to grab a couple of dolmades and gets wrapped up in a football conversation with one of the dads—something about the new defensive coach switching from the cross-town rival to turn the team around next season. Laurel moves to the threshold of the living room, which, unlike the foyer, kitchen, and dining room, is shady, cool, hushed. The room is unoccupied, but smack in the middle of the room, antiqued in a green that matches the foliage in the damask draperies, she finds a concert grand. The lid is closed, as is the fallboard, hiding the keys.

Laurel's own piano, a third-hand upright with a musty smell, stands against a wall in their small great room. Laurel plays it every day, once Saul leaves for school and Johnny for the office, withholding from her husband and son the number of hours she spends at it. The family's finances would ease if she approached her home-based graphic design business as aggressively as she does the piano. Her early training was in the works of Mozart and Schubert, beginning way before her feet reached the pedals, and later, as her hands grew so that she could find an octave, a ninth, and finally a good, deep, tenth, she moved to more modern work: Debussy, Rachmaninoff, Joplin, Monk. But her training and talent didn't get Laurel into a top music program, so instead of pursuing what she wanted, she settled for the business of graphic art.

Does anyone in this household play the green piano? Some people invest in a piano with hopes their children will play; others wish to add panache to the most formal room of their home, although a green grand goes somewhere beyond panache. The piano might be an heirloom, its original players long dead, this family stuck with it. The green object resembles a moldy easel, looking as if it had spent years in a cellar, waiting for its lid to be raised so a canvas could be propped against its far side. Laurel strokes the instrument's surfaces as one would a lover. Then she braces herself, heaves the lid to its full height, and sets the prop.

Inside the piano a man's twill tie lies on the cast-iron plate, the tie helter-skelter, overtwined onto itself as if tossed into hiding. Laurel lifts the tie, fingers it, checks the label: silk. She holds the tie to her nose and breathes in a dose of sandalwood, the scent androgynous, maybe a man's fragrance, maybe a woman's. She saw a tie like this—its design comes from Paul Klee's painting *New Harmony*—in the gift shop at the Guggenheim Museum several years ago. Johnny and Saul were away on a weekend camping trip with the Scouts, and Laurel had a Saturday to herself. She paid cash for a train ticket to New York City, leaving home early in the morning and arriving in the city before lunch. She spent the day at the museum and caught the train home that evening, never mentioning the trip to her family. So much dust has settled on the piano plate that Laurel is drawn to write her name in the powdery dirt, flicking the colossal yet weightless dust ball from her finger onto the Oriental rug.

Alone in the living room but for large, old-looking portraits that hang in gilt frames on the canary yellow walls, Laurel drapes the tie over her shoulders, sits at the piano, and opens the fallboard. The striations of sage green over cool white have obscured the manufacturer's name. With a few soft E major arpeggios—*E* for *excellent*—the grand sounds a bright tone, tending toward a harpsichord. Even without the gift of perfect pitch, Laurel can tell this instrument hasn't been tuned in some time, but the out-of-tune keys are like quirks and foibles of loved ones: while crotchety overtones crop up now and then in relationships, lack of perfection reflects the fullness of the human spirit.

The necktie from the Guggenheim has determined Laurel's course. She'll play Debussy's First Arabesque. The piece's ups and downs, its repetitions, its curlicues—they echo her visit to the helixed building. The notes on Laurel's sheet music, waiting for her at home, are like pictures on walls, visual signs of the artist's intent. Relationships of notes, their importance to each other, their priority in the musical scheme of a composition, these things correspond to the features of a painting—how the composition is ordered, where the eye is drawn, the location of transitional passages.

Laurel does not possess a photographic memory. To what she does see, she adds muscle memory and an urge, a commitment, to advance Debussy's composition—the gentle introductory measures with their light arpeggios, the triplet melody's gradual fall and rise, the later spots calling for a bigger sound, and the insistent quarter note build-up in both hands. The music spirals, winds, twists up and down and around itself, and Laurel, as at the museum, goes up the spiral, down again, gets her footing, adjusts her pace, finds spaces for lingering, takes breaths, and is on her way once more. Melodies and harmonies, rhythms and tempos, appear and reappear the way a painter, Kandinsky, for example, explores hairy, fuzzy lines; circles and semicircles; twisted oblongs; and in the way each viewer of his paintings investigates them anew. Laurel pored over many Kandinskys that Saturday at the museum. Today, music and painting come together for Laurel, creating a sanctuary-in-motion for her, allowing her to take flight with her friends, the way she took wing to New York and lost herself in art.

Again and again the motifs appear, in the arabesque, at the Guggenheim, in Laurel's mind, and she finds herself in the coil, the snare, of art, in creation's endless capacity for expression, for wonder, for exploration. The sound is big, the room is big, and Laurel can't imagine a better place to be. She brings her entire being—her conscious and subconscious selves—to the work. She has *studied* the music but above all *feels* it, where to take a ritardando, when to return to the initial tempo, how deeply to press the damper pedal. Here she might miss an eighth note, there she might play G sharp when she should play G natural, but no one can say Laurel plays without expression. Within her music Laurel finds her voice, so hard to come by in casual conversation that often she is rendered mute. It's here, in her art, that Laurel expresses herself.

Laurel's thoughts shift to van Gogh, her most beloved painter, who completed *The Night Café* in 1888, the published date of Debussy's First Arabesque. Possibly he'd heard this music and kept it in his head as he painted. Laurel had no idea she'd enjoy this party, but the enigmatic piano connects her to van Gogh. He put plenty of green in *The Night Café*—the pool table, the café tables, the bar, the ceiling. Who's to say there wasn't a green piano behind him, an object that didn't make it into the picture? Van Gogh used a lot of green in his final years—dying younger than Laurel is now as she brings Debussy to life: a green background in his 1888 self-portrait, the green wall and chair seat in his painting of Gauguin's chair the same year, the skin and clothes of his figures. Green was an important color to van Gogh, as it was to whoever chose it for this piano. Laurel would have missed all this if she'd stayed home with her books.

At the end, a crowd has gathered at the periphery of Laurel's eyesight. As she uses both the damper and soft pedals on the final octaves of E, releasing the pedals within four beats of striking the keys, her hands come to rest on her lap. She is motionless, the room silent. Saul is standing just within her vision, his hands in his pockets. As Laurel stands, the clapping begins, at first quiet, then filling the room, and low murmurs are interlaced with the applause. Whether they are murmurs of approval Laurel can't say for sure, but she hopes she hasn't embarrassed Saul and that someday he'll have a mother who isn't a threat of shame to him. She hopes he will speak to her again.

Jocelyn McCarthy
Light

JOCELYN MCCARTHY received her BA in English from Cornell University and her MFA in creative writing from American University. She writes fiction and nonfiction. She teaches at American University and lives in Maryland with her husband and two children.

In the house where I grew up, there was a drawer filled with candle stubs. They were left over from dinner parties. For guests we used fresh candles. The stubs had ridged bases and globs of melted wax. I loved to handle them, the way their black, burned wicks broke in my fingers, the way a line of dripped wax separated from a candle in one piece if I wedged my thumbnail under it at just the right angle. I loved their fragrance, the waxy residue they left on my hands, the dull, wooden sound they made when they jostled against one another in the drawer.

I don't know why we kept so many. Every leftover candle from every dinner party went into that drawer in the big cupboard in the dining room. Now and then we'd use the longer stubs for family dinners. Sometimes, summer storms knocked the power out for a long time and we had to resort to candles to light the house.

I was terrified of thunderstorms, though I could never let on to the other boys from school, or to my little sister, April. This was included in the things I didn't like about summer. Bees, sunburn, mosquito bites, wet sand in my swimming trunks, thunderstorms. Someone told me that lightning could electrocute you if you put your hands under the water tap during a thunderstorm. Also, phones were bad. You could die talking on the phone during a thunderstorm. I don't remember who told me these things, but I believed them. I knew it was true that water carried electricity. That was why at the pool, they let you swim in the rain but they made you get out the minute the lifeguards spotted lightning.

After electrocution, my next greatest fear during thunderstorms was blackouts. It seems to me that they were more frequent fifteen years ago. I dreaded those first few moments of sudden and complete darkness before we found the candle stubs, the flashlights, each other. We'd be going about our business, often in separate parts of the house, and then suddenly, bam! Everything. The lights, the TV, the blender went dead. It was pitch black. It must have been very quiet, aside from the storm, because everything had gone off, but somehow the darkness always seemed very loud. It would send us all scrambling for flashlights, matches, candles, in that cluttered house. My father's voice: "Goddamn it, how come the flashlights are never where they're supposed to be?" The sound of a drawer slamming shut. And when you found a flashlight, odds were the batteries were nowhere near, or they were weak, or dead, even.

That's why I always put my money on the candle stubs. The candle drawer was in the enormous china cupboard in the dining room, and the dining room was always my destination when the lights went out. If I was alone in my room, I'd have to feel my way along the walls and down the stairs. Once in the dining room, I had to feel around for matches, maybe even cross the room, arms outstretched stiffly, like a monster in an old horror movie, and feel along the mantelpiece over the fireplace. But the candle stubs were always there, sitting in that same drawer.

A lit candle stub could illuminate the whole room. When the power outages lasted a long time, we lit the whole house this way, stubs jammed in every candle holder and empty bottle.

Although I tried not to let it show, I liked the house this way, once the candles were lit. It was spooky but also cozy and festive. My family acted different. We sought out each other's company. It seemed wrong, somehow, to sit in the dark by yourself.

Often my parents sent April and me to find a board game for the family to play. April held a candle while I rummaged through the cabinets and closets. We argued about which one to play, but always ended up with Monopoly. April picked the horse to be her piece. She was horse crazy. I liked the roadster.

We put a candle at the center of the Monopoly board while we played. April giggled and shrieked each time someone jostled the board by accident, causing the flame to wobble. I liked to flick my finger back and forth through the flame, slowly. "Stop it," April said, and tried to grab my hand. "Michael, stop it."

When my mother landed on one of my father's properties, he said, "Pay up, sweetheart, or suffer the consequences," and then leaned over to kiss her. She smiled and said, "Oh, Jack," and shook her head, if she was in a good mood, or said no, that he had martini breath, if she was in a bad mood.

My father drank martinis. That was the only thing my father drank, night after night, except for the wine he and my mother had with dinner.

Then the lights came back on, making the candles look pale and inadequate. We had to go around and blow them all out. My father went to watch television, my mother went to load the dishwasher.

THERE WERE OTHER DRAWERS IN the china cupboard containing things besides candle stubs: some of our holiday decorations, some dusty, pilgrim-shaped candles for Thanksgiving, a Styrofoam advent wreath that my mother decorated with fresh greens for Christmas, a few Easter baskets with plastic green grass still in them.

Other drawers in other rooms were also filled with things. In the family room, across from the dining room, there were cabinets stuffed with toys that had been given to me and April. There were boxes jammed with parts of different toys, all mixed up—Lego pieces in the Matchbox cars box, furniture from the Tiny Tots Treehouse mixed in with Star Wars things. I had a lot of Star Wars toys. I'd had to watch the first two movies on video because I was too little to see them in the theater, but my parents let me go to see *Return of the Jedi*. I even had a blue plastic light saber.

That didn't mean anything to my mother. She said she couldn't keep all our toys straight. "If you leave everything lying around, I'll just have to put things away in whatever box is handy. I'm trying to keep this place clean. You'd think somebody would appreciate that."

Despite my mother's efforts, the family room was a mess of toys much of the time. My father hated it. It made him mad. He would pause in the door, drink in hand, on his way to the television, and say, "Christ, look at this mess." He would shake his head. "Look at this mess. Doesn't anybody ever clean up around here?" No one answered him.

A lot of things made him mad. When I asked my mother why Dad was mad so much, she said that he was under pressure at work. *Under pressure*, like the warning label said on aerosol spray cans. She said he had to make his numbers every month at work, at the Ridgeway Paper Products company.

One of the toys floating in our family room was a tambourine. I don't know where it was from, or if it was part of a set of instruments that got separated and shipwrecked in our family room. It had green magic marker scribbles on the drum.

One day, April and I were in the basement, playing. My mother and father had had the basement redone not long after I was born, seventies-style, with orange shag carpeting and stucco walls. There were closets with hollow doors and fake mahogany finish, and I shut April in one of them and locked the door. "Stop it, Michael," she yelled, pounding on the door. "Let me out! I'm going to tell Mom."

I told her I was going to count to ten, and then the zombies would come. I had the tambourine in my hand and after I slowly pronounced each number, I paused, and gave the tambourine a thump, for effect.

"One." Thump. "Two." Thump.

"Let me out! C'mon, Michael, lemme out lemme out!"

"Three." Thump.

To be honest, I don't remember how it ended. I must have let her out, because I don't remember reaching the count of ten. Maybe I felt sorry for her. I don't remember getting in trouble, so April must not have told on me. But I know I didn't walk away and leave her there in that closet, there in the dark. That I wouldn't do.

THE CANDLE STUBS WERE LEFT over from dinner parties that took place in the dining room. My parents always lowered the lights and lit new candles when it was time to sit down. Cocktail parties took place in the living room, which we never used except for company. The lights stayed on for those.

My mother was irritable when she was getting ready for a party. She spent the day of the party in the kitchen, measuring and chopping and stirring, even if it was just hors d'oeuvres and not dinner. You could hear the sound of the chopping knife against the wooden cutting board for hours, and the sound of things sizzling in a pan, and the house filled with the smell of raw onion and grilled meat and pastries in the oven. Just before the company came, she raced around the kitchen with an apron over her black cocktail dress, smelling of hairspray and perfume, putting the final touches on the spread—stuffing the mushroom caps, putting the little baby shrimp on pieces of toast. She always seemed very nervous about whether things would go all right. "Is your boss coming tonight?" she asked my father, sometimes more than once.

"Honey, I already told you. He's coming," my father said. My father was in charge of setting up the bar in the living room, which he generally did at the last minute. "You'd think he'd at least take out the garbage," my mother muttered, slamming the oven door shut with her knee as she removed a tray of cheese puffs.

During the party, I never saw my mother eat anything or sit down. She always had a bowl of fresh bread sticks or a towel or a pitcher in her hand. "Oh, it's nothing," she would say, smiling, when someone praised the tenderness of the Swedish meatballs or the lightness of the pastries.

The men wore ties and the women wore lipstick that came off on the wineglasses they held. The men didn't hold wineglasses. They held short, fat glasses with just a little dark liquid, or martini glasses, cone shaped and oddly flowerlike, like my father's.

April and I wandered among the guests, like wayfarers in a forest of rough, tweedy jackets, and white necks smelling of perfume.

I didn't know them all, but I knew that a lot of them worked for the same company as my father. I'd been in his office at work. It looked just like all the other offices off the hallway: a few windows, a fake-wood desk. The men called the secretaries "the girls," even though they were grown-ups, and kept photographs of their wives and children in hinged, three-paneled frames on their desks. My father let me play with the tape dispenser and the paper clips, and run my Matchbox cars over his desk. Sometimes he had to go in on Saturdays, which my mother didn't like, but he said he had to make his numbers every month. He also said that maybe she didn't understand because she'd never had to work.

"I worked," she'd say. "I worked at my father's company."

"In the summers. Answering phones," my father replied. My mother married my father right out of college. There was a wedding photo of them on one of the tables in the living room. My mother was thinner and my father's hair was darker.

What I didn't understand until I was grown was that my father hated his job and his boss. When I asked him, years later, if he ever thought of quitting, he looked puzzled. "No, I didn't." When I asked why not, he said, "We had you kids to think of."

At my parents' parties, the men from the office brought the wives from the photographs. I liked to listen to their voices, the men's voices gruff and the women's singsongy.

"So I said, come on Fred, do you want that guy to walk out the door? He's one of the best salesmen we've got."

"Martha's Vineyard? We went to Martha's Vineyard last year, and it was marvelous. We didn't take the kids, though. We hired the Hodges girl to stay and look after them. She was on break from school."

My parents had a few friends who were divorced, and people talked about them a lot when they weren't around. But mostly people came and left the parties in pairs. Sometimes I helped get their coats, if we hadn't been sent to bed yet. We kept the coats in the family room, and for this reason, it had to be made presentable on those occasions. Also, sometimes one of the men at the party went in to check the sports scores on the television, or my mother would talk someone into looking at the photo album of our last trip to the beach.

Once I was in the family room, playing with my Star Wars toys, and my father came in with some men, to get their wives' coats. He picked up one of my X-wing fighters. "What's this?" he asked, as if he'd never seen it before. His eyes were a little glassy. "Why, that's a goddamn space ship."

He lunged a little as he turned to face one of the men. "Chuck, this is a goddamn space ship." His voice was too loud.

"Yep, Jack, it sure is," said the man named Chuck.

"It's an X-wing," I said quietly, "it's from Star Wars."

The man named Chuck reached out and took the ship gently from my father. "Jack, let's put this down and let Michael play. I need to get Margery's coat. We have to leave for her mother's real early tomorrow."

I HAD A DREAM THAT I was trying to get to the candle stubs in the dark. It wasn't a blackout. It was night. I was walking along the downstairs hall, headed for the dining room. The dark was cloudy. Shadows gathered and spread. Each step I took was slow and fluid, as if I were walking through water. As I neared the door of the dining room, I saw ghosts and they were blocking my path to the candle stubs. I knew they would notice me and come after me any minute, so I froze, thinking that they wouldn't see me if I stayed perfectly still. Then I woke up.

I had a lot of dreams about that house. In one, there was an extra room that wasn't there in real life. The entrance to the room was off the hall that led to my parents' room. It was a bedroom with twin beds. On the nightstand between them was a lamp with a white lampshade covered in red rosebuds. A soft, pink light filled the room. The beds had thick, soft covers. My parents and April were there and we were all dressed in our pajamas, ready for bed. April smelled like baby powder.

I think the room came from one of the houses my family rented in the summer when we vacationed at the beach. They were always musty-smelling houses, with scratchy thin bedspreads and yellow water stains in the corners of the walls and ceilings. The first thing my mother did was wipe down the chipped countertops in the kitchen and go down to the corner store in her flip-flops to buy cereal and instant coffee. In the mornings, she'd pour hot water into the instant coffee and my parents would sit and drink it in their bathing suits in the kitchen. "Surf's up," my mother would say after breakfast, and put on her beach hat and sunglasses with a smile. She'd pack up our toys and towels before we headed to the beach, and when we came back she always made us wash our feet under the spigot outside so we wouldn't track sand in the house.

My father was different there, happier. Sometimes he and I walked down the beach to where the bay met the ocean—the inlet, my father called it. There were sandbars, and shallow pools of ocean water. We found little crabs sometimes in the pools. "Look, Michael," he'd said once, holding a crab up by its claw with a stick. "He's a little one. Not big enough for dinner." He was smiling, and he let me hold the crab by the stick. I stooped over and looked at it closely, at the alien, antenna eyes, the smooth, brown-speckled shell. Close up, it was more delicate than I had imagined it would be.

"C'mon," my father said. "It's getting late. We'd better get back to your mother and April." I dropped the crab back into the pool, and it scurried away.

I WAS ALLOWED TO TOUCH the candle stubs. There were other things in the cupboard that I wasn't allowed to touch, like my mother's good plates and her collection of little porcelain Hummel figurines lined up on the top shelf. They were very special, she explained to me, because they had stopped making most of them, and only came out with new ones once a year. Her own mother had collected them, and passed her collection on before she died. April wasn't allowed to touch them, either, and we couldn't reach them anyway. I didn't see why the figurines were so special just because they had stopped making them. They were mostly doe-eyed children in old-fashioned clothes, holding baskets or kites or farm animals. But I knew they were important to my mother.

A few of them did get broken once.

I had been outside in the yard one day, playing. The back door was open but the storm door was shut. As I came through it, I heard voices, angry but hushed. It was my mother and father, in the dining room. The only thing I could make out was my mother saying, "You think I don't work hard, too? Your problem is that you never think of anyone but yourself." As I quietly closed the storm door, I thought I heard a smack. Skin on skin. A slap? Then silence.

I crept past the washer and dryer in the mud room and approached the kitchen. The dining room was visible beyond the doorway.

I could see them, through the door to the dining room, framed. They were facing each other, my mother backed up against one of the extra dining room chairs we kept against the wall for when company came. My father's mouth was set, his eyes hard. My mother had put her hand to her face. She was looking down.

"My mother gave these to me," she said. There were chunks of broken porcelain near her feet. My father grabbed her by the shoulders and shoved her into the chair.

I backed out of the kitchen, back to the mud room. I shut the storm door quietly behind me, then headed around toward the front of the house and the street, away from the dining room windows.

When I came back, my father was watching the news, stony-faced, with a martini in his hand. My mother was getting dinner ready. She asked me, a little sharply, where I'd been. "At Jed's house," I said, hoping I wouldn't be found out. I had gone to the park, to sit by the creek and catch my breath.

"I thought I'd make some iced tea," she said without looking up. "Would you go and pick some mint from the garden, please?" I grabbed a colander and scurried out. Later, when I was sitting down for dinner, I looked up at the top of the china cupboard. It looked like there were a couple of Hummels missing.

My father was quiet and grumpy that night. I avoided him after dinner.

MY CHAIR AT THE DINNER table stood directly in front of the drawer with the candle stubs, my little sister's to the right and both my parents' across the table. My mother sat closest to the kitchen so she could get up and down quickly while she served us dinner. Sometimes I got in trouble with my father when he came home from work. On those nights, my chair was empty during dinner until I came down from my room. I sat with one elbow on the table, fingers resting on my temple, shielding my red face from April's view. Sometimes she teased me to try to get my attention. "Michael," she called softly, as if over a great distance. "Hello, Michael." She cupped her hands to her mouth like a megaphone. "Earth calling Michael. Are you in there, Michael?"

April got me in trouble sometimes. I love her now, and I loved her then, but she got away with things as a child, and I didn't. Once I got in trouble for knocking over a cup of juice that she had left on the floor. My mother was at the stove, busy with dinner, and my father was sitting at the kitchen table, staring straight ahead, with a drink in his hand. It must have been after my mother started talking about going back to school, because April was using one of my mother's course catalogues as a mat for her jars of finger paint. She was on the floor, three of the fingers on her right hand bright with a primary color.

Since my mother had been talking about school, my father had been extra grumpy, speaking to my mother less and drinking more. My mother didn't seem to mind this arrangement, and spent her time poring over course catalogues and talking on the phone with people from programs while my father scowled in the background. I couldn't understand why anyone who didn't have to go to school would want to. So far, I'd managed to stay out of my father's way.

I was crossing the room and didn't see the cup of juice April had set on the floor. My foot brushed it and it tipped, spilling its bright red contents in a long stream across the white linoleum floor, just reaching the toe of my father's socked foot. "Michael!" April yelled.

My father put his drink down suddenly, sloppily, the clear liquid sloshing over the sides. He stood up, looking first at the trail of red juice across the floor, and then at the dark gray sock on his foot. He picked up his foot and shook it, as if that would get rid of the juice now seeping into the fabric.

"Michael, what did you do?"

"It's not my fault. It was an accident. April left her stupid cup lying in the middle of the floor."

My mother went for the paper towels, but the juice had already seeped into the edge of April's painting, and the corner of my mother's catalogue. "Mom, it's getting my painting wet!"

"Just a minute, April, I'm coming."

"Mom, it's getting your book wet!"

I thought my mother would be angry, but she wasn't. She started to sop up the red juice on the floor. One whole side of April's painting was blotted with red, and the corner of my mother's catalogue was pinkish and the pages were puckering. My mother lifted the catalogue from the puddle and tossed it aside. April was winding up for a sob.

"Would you two pipe down? Christ," my father muttered. He sank back into his chair and leaned over to peel off his sock.

"But it was an accident," I said. "It was April's fault for leaving her cup on the floor."

"It was not!" April screeched. "You kicked over my cup. You did it on purpose."

"Would you two pipe down, for Chrissake?" my father said again, from where he was hunched over. His face was flushed.

"I did not!" I yelled at April. "Why don't you just shut up, you big baby."

"All right. That's it." My father threw his sock on the floor, and started for me, one foot bare.

"But it was an accident. It's not my fault!"

He grabbed me roughly, half by the shoulder, half by the shirt, and started to drag me out of the room.

My face went hot. My feet stumbled, not able to keep up. I looked over my shoulder at my mother, but she was kneeling on the floor, blotting the corner of April's painting with the paper towels, the skin on her face tight.

My mother never spanked me. Only my father. She didn't believe in it, she said. *Believe in.* Like in God or Santa Claus.

My father dragged me down the hallway and up the stairs. He fumbled a little on the steps and I slipped on the carpeting. He picked me up by the upper arm, nearly lifting me off my feet. He hauled me to the bathroom, pulling me by the shirt. The neckband cut into my neck. I was off balance when he yanked me through the bathroom door and I hit my head on the door jamb.

"Dad!" I wailed, my eyes filling with tears. I thought for sure he'd stop then, and ask me if my head was all right, but he didn't.

He sat on the closed toilet seat lid and spanked me. I was over his knees, the breath squeezed out of my lungs, my head throbbing in the place where I'd hit it. Tears welled in my eyes and dropped to the floor. I was almost too big now for this. My feet reached the ground.

When he was finished, he pushed me off his lap and I scrambled to my feet. I kept my head lowered. My face stung.

He passed his hand over his face. He looked tired, defeated. "Go to your room," he said. His speech was a little slurred. As I turned to go, he planted his foot on my butt and gave me a shove. I yelped with surprise. When I reached my room, I locked the door.

I didn't go down for dinner that night. I was hungry, but I waited until I knew that dinner was over. I waited for the sound of the dishes in the sink, the sound of the water running in the kitchen below. I knew my father would be firmly planted in front of the television by then.

I crept down the stairs, careful not to creak any loose floorboards. I padded softly down the hallway. The sound of the television came from the family room, and I guessed that my father was in front of it. I didn't know where April was. It would be her bedtime soon.

I went through the dining room into the kitchen. My mother looked up from the sink, where she was doing the dishes.

"Hi, honey." She said it consolingly, like I'd been sick, but her face was questioning.

I paused in the doorway, outside the pool of light that fell from the lamp hanging above the kitchen table. I didn't want her to see that I'd been crying.

She turned the water off, dried her hands, and turned around to look at me. She sighed and folded her arms in front of her. She looked tired, like my father.

"Are you hungry? I saved you a plate."

I nodded. She went to the refrigerator and got out a full plate, covered with plastic wrap, and put it in the microwave. I closed my eyes for a moment and listened to the familiar, vibrating hum of the microwave. I opened them when I heard my mother rummaging in the silverware drawer. She put a knife and fork on the table and went back to the microwave to wait for it to finish. I was sorry when the bell went off and the humming ended.

I approached the table, keeping my eyes down. There was a small puddle of water on the surface of the table, the size of April's palm. I put my finger in it and slowly drew it away, making a tadpole shape.

My mother removed the plastic from the plate and placed it on the table in front of me. Steam rose from the food, carrying its smell. It was a piece of chicken, a drumstick—my favorite part, and peas and carrots.

She sat down near me. I looked up at her face. There was a crease in her forehead, and her lips were drawn together in a pout. "It wasn't so bad," I said. She paused, spread her fingers out on the table and looked at them.

AFTER THAT NIGHT I BEGAN to have stomach aches. Sometimes they were so severe that I couldn't sleep. Sometimes I couldn't go to the bathroom for what seemed like days. Later that year I was rushed to the hospital in the early morning. I could barely stand. The doctors who cut me open discovered that my appendix wasn't inflamed, but they said that it was a common misdiagnosis.

Things changed later, when I was in junior high school, I think. I had a growth spurt and sprang up taller than my father. Then the year of the operation and the years just after grew dim in my mind, and slowly receded in my memory, like the foamy edge of a wave as it's drawn back to the ocean. By the time I left for college, I hardly thought about those times, and couldn't remember much.

The house I live in now has no drawer with candle stubs, only a dining room with a Ping Pong table and newspapers stacked in the corner, a recycling bin full of sticky beer bottles, and three other struggling college graduates like myself, marooned in the same city in jobs we don't like.

Even now, I forget things. Current events, which countries have dictators, the title of the movie that won the Oscar, the number of cups in a quart, the names of people I meet at parties. I forget right away, with great efficiency. Information makes no impression on me, like a rough blanket pressed momentarily against the skin.

After the latest in a string of short-lived relationships ended, I got to drinking too much. Six months ago, I woke up on the bathroom floor one morning, stumbled to the phone, and called, of all people, my sister.

April was living in a hippie co-op at Hampshire College. She was studying psychology, and had been involved in peer counseling since she got to college. I had dismissed this activity, and told her she made too big a deal about what she called "the scars" of our childhood. But this time, I found myself comforted by her attentive listening. After she had listened for a long time, she said she thought I ought to get help. "You need to talk to someone, Michael. You need to sort things out." There I began this journey of circles.

I DON'T KNOW WHY MY mother kept the candle stubs, but she did. She kept things. Our old watercolor pictures, collecting on the walls, wrinkling like dried leaves, the white edges going dull with age. The little paper parasols and the little plastic swords from drinks she and my father had when they were out. Bottle caps that smelled faintly of ketchup, wide rubber bands with something powdery adhering to them, toothpicks, and disposable coasters and knives that were coming loose from their wooden handles and stray cards from a deck long gone. Her collection of porcelain Hummel figurines, lined up like sentinels on the top shelf of the cupboard.

That night so many years ago, the night of the spilled juice, I waited until my parents were getting ready for bed, then I tiptoed down to the dining room. I could see the cupboard by the light of the moon through the window. Beyond the window was our swing set with the rusty hinges, and the garden where my mother grew her summer vegetables. I opened the candle stub drawer very carefully, so as not to make any noise. I took handfuls of the candle stubs from the drawer, and laid them on the table next to one another. I took a box of matches from the mantelpiece. I was careful to take a box of wooden matches, since the cardboard ones were hard for me to light. I got out as many candle holders as I could find, even looking in the kitchen for a few discarded gin bottles.

I plugged about a dozen holders with candle stubs, and arranged them on the dining room table. It took me a couple of tries to light the first match. When it finally sputtered to life, illuminating the room, I held it to a candle wick and watched the flame surge between them. I lit all the candles, one by one, like I'd seen my mother light candles on a birthday cake. The flames flickered before me, filling the room with light. I could feel the warmth of the candles on my face, and the air smelled of burnt match. I had used a lot of matches.

Carrying the candles two at a time, I took some into each room: the kitchen, the dining room, the family room, the living room. I tried to arrange them in different parts of each room, so that the whole room would be lit. As I was arranging the last few in the living room, I heard footsteps on the stairs, then whispering in the hall. I had made my way across the room with the last candle when my parents appeared in the doorway, their faces two question marks in the soft light. I stopped where I was, and dropped my eyes to the flame in my hands. The tip of the wick glowed orange, like the logs in the fireplace did when they had burned for a long time. I heard my mother's voice, gentle and confused. "Michael? What are you doing?" I gazed at the blue base of the flame, the dark place at the center, and the white, flickering finger above. "Michael, honey, what is it?" In the place above the flame, everything looked liquid.

Barbara Moore
Thirty Benches Please

BARBARA MOORE studied art history at Vassar, the École du Louvre, and
the University of Michigan. She has been writing about art and producing
fiction for the last twenty years, first prompted by the 1989 anti-gay, political assault against the Robert Mapplethorpe exhibition due to open at the
Corcoran Gallery of Art when she was its curator of education. This short
story is drawn from the novel she wrote in the aftermath. Currently head
of education publications at the National Gallery of Art, Barbara lives in
Washington, D.C., with her husband and springer spaniel, Robin.

e need them."

"No we don't."

"Yes we do, it's the least we can offer the public," Jane said at
Henry's exhibition meeting. A telephone call with her mother lingering in
her mind, Jane was in the undone mood of the grown-up child at work, a
mood that made her anxious and talkative whether or not she could make
herself heard, and Henry Franchot, the museum's director, was distracted
by his recent dreamy trip to Paris to discuss an exhibition of surrealist art.

Instead of a decent discussion, Jane was getting cold, distant stares from
the other curators. The subject she had invoked was indefensibly mundane.
And it's just your luck that Teddy, who might help you, is late, Jane realized.
Teddy Flanders, the museum's deputy director, was always punctual and
often on Jane's side. *Where was he now?*

"Henry, haven't you ever wanted to sit down on a bench in front of a
fabulous picture and just stare at it for a while?" Jane reasoned. "You can't do
that here. You have to keep on walking by those Rembrandts and Vermeers.
I have to, since I represent the interests of the visitor, what's the point?"

Henry stared at Jane from his seat at the head of the long Italianate
table in his office. He leaned forward, but just a little, meaning he was
trying to figure her out.

"I know what you're thinking, Henry," Jane assessed. "You're thinking why am I bringing up an issue that costs a minimum of sixty thousand dollars to resolve, and much more in what even I would call vex time? Not to mention the obvious, that benches are a colossal bore."

"Jane, the picture galleries are the territory of the curators, so perhaps you'd like to have this discussion with them," Henry smiled and crossed his arms.

Henry's going to take the position of observer. And you're the observed one. This is bad, Jane registered.

Sit up straight and use the ramrod posture you learned at school to deflect the oncoming blow, Jane said to herself, going to upright alert.

"OK," she said, looking at Henry with the same disembodied expression she got when her husband Mack forced her into a sporting goods store, "does anyone here believe that benches are undesirable in the galleries?"

First Curator (enunciating slowly): "No, they're not undesirable." The First Curator pressed back in her chair, pointed her feet which that day rested in red leather heels contoured on the sides like roller coaster tracks. She looked down, and then squinted across the table at Jane.

Second Curator: "No, they're not undesirable, but sometimes they can affect the aesthetic mood of an installation—in which case they should be removed." The Second Curator observed Jane with dry regard from his perch in Sensitivity Central.

Third Curator: "I think benches are fine. But they have to match. If we agree we should put them in every gallery, we need at least thirty to add to our current group, and that will cost a lot." Jane took that to mean "Ditto," but with some degree of sympathy for the innocent museum visitor.

Fourth Curator: "Still, it would be a cost well worth paying. Just think of the letters of complaint we'd no longer receive."

You're dead, Jane thought, staring at the Fourth Curator. *You know that whatever the Fourth Curator likes gets splattered and trashed, especially if she's enthusiastic. She worries too much. Then we don't trust her because of the worry. It's that horrible nail-biting habit of hers.*

The Fourth Curator smiled at Jane.

Smiling. That's it. The ultimate project-buster in the art world, Jane chewed inside. She knew that if Teddy were there he'd be asking, "Jane, do we have a major project-buster on our hands here?"

She had to speak again, to see where they were.

"So, where are we on benches, then?" Jane asked, still sitting upright like a college freshman in a beanie.

The curators looked at one another. Then they looked at Jane. Then they sighed. The Eager Curator of Interpretation and Her Benches. Such a hideous bore.

"Well?" Jane asked. *You HAVE to ask,* she regretted as she put out the question.

"Can you raise the money for them?" Teddy asked back, having alighted on a chair a few seconds before. Teddy's voice had a frustrating inflection. "I don't sense any objection to benches here, and certainly I wouldn't want you to think that we're against visitor comfort, but this will take money."

"OK," Jane sighed. "I'll get a bunch of proposals ready, but I'll need Henry's help with contacts."

"I didn't need that bureaucratic air block from you in the meeting," Jane said to Teddy on the way out of Henry's office. "I mean, where's your heart? Don't you remember what Gertrude Stein, one of the greatest art collectors of the twentieth century, said about benches? She said, "When in a picture gallery, what I look for is a bench, is a bench, is a bench.""

"I don't give a damn about Gertrude Stein." Teddy barely glanced in Jane's direction as they walked across the main hall of the museum toward their offices. "I bet she never said that. And even if she did, you can see the curators don't give a damn about benches either. I thought I got you off the hook while also giving you a chance to get the goddamn benches—that is, if you can pull off a grant," Teddy teased her.

Teddy turned off in the direction of his office, and Jane walked on alone. *Face it,* she said to herself, her posture now crumbling as she grew downhearted, *no one wants to hang around with a person who brings up benches in exhibition meetings.*

Jane's department of museum interpretation was across from the bathrooms. The sound of whistling sometimes emanated from the men's room, as it did that afternoon while Jane tried to make it to her office nook through the maze of extension cords and people standing bent over phones in the space where her staff and most of her volunteers worked. She sat down at her desk, but soon, an unbearable and unnerving sound made it impossible for her to think.

"Who is whistling out there?" Jane grumbled.

"I'll see about it, Jane," said Alan, her secretary.

Alan used to whistle when he first came to work for Jane, but every time he'd feel good about something and break into song Jane would stalk into his partition and glare at him like a madwoman and ask him to *Please Stop Whistling*.

"Whistling bores into the head," Jane would ventilate, her face a frozen mask of repudiation. "It's intolerable," she would add, her eyes freezing on Alan's.

So Alan ran into the men's room to see what he could do about the whistling in a clear display of loyalty and reverence—the kind the museum staff all wished for but almost never got.

The phones never stopped ringing in the department of interpretation. All day long people called to make appointments to visit the museum, and then they called back to cancel or amend them. All day they called to sign up for lectures and workshops and internships and volunteering. And all day the staff answered the phones while conducting meetings, doing research, and executing plans based on ideology and strategy that caused the people to call all day long.

"I just can't handle a piercing interruption such as whistling when I'm trying to think!" Jane stomped around after Alan had stopped it. "Thank you for doing that," she said, as she stood beside him at the edge of his cubbyhole. "I know I'm barely clinging to civility," Jane said in the bent posture of a person who is barely clinging to civility in the wake of such an assault as whistling, which bores into the head. "But I do thank you."

"You're welcome," Alan returned.

"What shall we do about this bench problem?" Jane said to both Alan and her assistant, the Second Jane, who was in her cubby across from Alan.

"Here's the situation," the Second Jane declared as she turned in her chair to face Alan and Jane. "We love people and Henry is oblivious to them. That's why we're the department of interpretation, the department that supports people. It's our job to contradict the director's imperative. That's why I had to keep dragging benches into the Dutch painting galleries last month while Henry tried to drag them out."

"We have to stand up for people's right to sit down and look at a painting. It's our mission!" the Second Jane announced to an empty space that was widening around her. Alan crept out toward the library under the Second Jane's last word.

"Well," Jane resolved, "that means I have to fight for some money." And she removed to her office to start writing a grant proposal.

BEGGING IS THE BOTTOM LINE of museum work. No proposal, no grant, no project. Jane sat down at her table and thought more about the proposal she would write to finance thirty wooden benches, made to the specifications of the benches originally produced for the museum in 1897. *You have the plans*, she sighed contentedly.

Then she thought about the best proposals she had written.

"Culture is, after all, political," she concluded in one. *Yes*, Jane congratulated herself as she tapped some ideas for the bench request on her computer. *Put the bench request inside your proposal to fund and interpret the museum's show about official Salon art in nineteenth century Paris. Clever. Layered. Possibly even distinctive.* A show of that period literally relied on benches for authenticity, and when it closed, the benches would remain in the museum.

Yes, she nodded. *Good beggar!*

But a dark doubt entered in the form of Teddy, cruising into Jane's office in his blue shirt and red suspenders.

"Jane, a smart person would realize that having just returned from Paris, Henry might want to talk about the upcoming surrealist exhibition instead of benches for visitors."

"You're right," Jane said, leaving Teddy in a chair. "Amuse yourself while I try to repair things up front."

Jane scurried over to Henry's office to see if she could get him to talk about the surrealist show.

"Henry, have you got a minute?" she said, popping into one of the leather chairs that sat around Henry's hand-carved table. "I thought we should exchange notes on the surrealist exhibition now that you've returned from France."

"Ah. Yes!" Henry assumed a take-charge attitude, gathering piles of papers and documents from the Bibliothèque Nationale that were piled at various locations on his desk. "Work is proceeding apace, and I had one of the best meals of my life in Bougival with the curator. How did your end go with the Cahuns?" he asked Jane. Claude Cahun made photo self-portraits that challenged sexual identity.

"Henry, I got the Cahuns, but at a very high personal price," Jane said, her voice like charcoal.

"Don't fuss over it, Jane. If you got them, you got them," Henry said, dismissing her melodrama with a commanding sweep of the hand as he walked over to stand by a window. "Let's concentrate on the up side of this project. Imagine this," Henry lifted his arms:

"Bougival—site beloved by the French impressionists.

"An artistic afternoon—speaking learnedly of the impressionists while strolling along the Seine, where they actually set up their easels and worked.

"Le Coq Hardi—a stone farmhouse, now a restaurant, sitting just across the road from the Seine.

"A memorable lunch—Loup St. Jean on a bed of green vegetable concasse, wonderful white burgundy.

"Brilliant and amusing conversation."

Henry is now completely absorbed in himself, Jane observed.

He continued.

"The restaurant has a series of outdoor terraces that rise on the hill that climbs behind the inn. Each terrace has a rounded stone wall planted with flower beds overflowing with dusty violet hyacinths to which the linens are matched precisely. The atmosphere is layered in the most wonderful way, because its cheerful weekend mood is juxtaposed by the true purpose of the individual bowers on the terrace—businessmen's weekday trysts with their 'nieces.'"

Henry's eyes danced with recognition that he had sniffed out one of France's *endroits amoureux*. Jane knew he wanted her to admire his astute sophistication, but all she could think of was the promise her best friend Eloise had made to herself after reading almost every nineteenth century French novel ever written in her French 326 class at NYU: *Never marry a petit bourgeois!*

"Henry, it sounds great," Jane said, her voice as flat as an ironing board.

"Your enthusiasm is duly noted," Henry said looking down at her with a thin gust of disapproval at her lack of pep after he'd delivered one of his stirring descriptions of *la vie en rose*.

"What can I do to enlighten you further?" Henry asked, his voice drifting off his nostrils.

"Tell me about the images the curator is gathering for the photography show. Are we into scandal, fetishism, voyeurism, sex? That's what I want to know," Jane announced, "because I'll need to explain it."

She felt brave.

"Well, here's what I want to know," Henry stated. "Why are you in such a dreadful mood? I can't possibly discuss the surrealist show with you when you're in a dreadful mood like this."

"I'm not in a dreadful mood," Jane said.

Then she felt testy. And challenged to truth.

"I'm in a perfectly fine mood," she advanced, "for a person whose boss has been off on a junket to meet up with a curator in France, and who's been left alone on an emotionally devastating mission to retrieve exhibition loans from a man she humiliated twenty-one years ago."

"A man she humiliated twenty-one years ago?"

Henry looked at Jane, incredulous.

Then, he got it.

"Why didn't you tell me your contact in New York was personal before you went there to see about getting them in the show? I would have sent Teddy," said Henry, in a warm, concerned voice as he took a seat at the table.

"No you wouldn't have," Jane said, looking Henry straight in the eye.

"You're right. I wouldn't have," said Henry, when he actually considered it.

They shared the kind of smile people hate to admit to later. Then they turned to the art, rife with fetishism, voyeurism, and sex. Images made by the surrealists in the 1920s and '30s. Cunt on a plate, the face of a woman in mid-orgasm, lesbian cunnilingus, female masturbation photographed from below, and nudes tied up with ropes or headless and armless.

Henry wants you, Jane felt as she looked at the images of dark sex and demi-violence while Henry sat, watching her review the images.

"Henry, are Hans Bellmer photographs in this exhibition?" she asked, flipping through a stack of reproductions. A group of doll photographs was piled up next to a stack of slide sleeves. Jane picked one up and studied it.

It was a photo of a naked doll without arms, lying on a flower-printed rug in an overturned chair. She had dark hair and a big bow on the top of her head. Jane lurched from one realization to the next.

Even though she's a little girl doll, she has two big, round breasts without nipples that sit up so high that they hide half of her face. And under them is a round, little girl kind of stomach.

The photograph cuts off the doll body just beneath her vulva and thighs. But when you look down at them your eye is forced back up her body where, between her breasts, is a second vulva.

This vulva is bigger than the other one and has spread lips and is right in front of the doll's mouth.

Scary, Jane thought.

All together there were about ten Bellmer photographs featuring girl dolls. Jane inhaled and went through the rest.

White socks and black patent leather Mary Janes on the feet, she saw, alarmed at Bellmer's proximity to her own wardrobe. Jane liked to wear clothes with children's silhouettes.

Some of Bellmer's figures lay on grass outdoors or on a messed-up bed in an interior, or leaned up against a tree, and in these images Bellmer knocked off the limbs below the knee and then screwed small wooden balls to the torsos.

Jane held the last Bellmer image, feeling aroused and conflicted. She knew better than to think of Bellmer's art as marginal. The manipulated, dismembered, and violated female image was considered the mojo of dreams by a number of the surrealists.

Just then Teddy appeared in Henry's office.

"Oh, I see we're into female bondage this week," he observed as he looked at the image in Jane's hands. Teddy had unconditional access to Henry's office, which he massaged vigorously.

"Don't speak before you study, sir," Henry advised without looking up. Translation, as Teddy and Jane interpreted it: *Don't judge what our brilliant curator in France is doing before it is done.*

Forget discussion of a slaughterhouse of women's rights where this show is concerned, Jane said to herself. *Teddy won't bring it up unless he's become suicidal.*

The Third Curator saw her ideological life spared by the possibility of a Bellmer show, so she'll be only too delighted to see selections of Bellmer's work appear at the museum.

The Fourth Curator can stop worrying now that a major exhibition including photography—her area of expertise—was coming up.

And the First Curator won't dare disparage the intentions of the brilliant curator in France because she takes her vacation in France every summer and wants to keep on going there in the future. Only a curator who has a second career bad-mouthing her colleagues knows how very much she doesn't want a brilliant curator in France bad-mouthing her in her favorite foreign country.

Besides, Jane concluded, *you like this exhibition. Its dark side might bring the issue of female oppression into open debate.*

OVER THE NEXT SEVERAL MONTHS Henry's office grew heavy with reproductions of surrealist art. The signature calendars in departments throughout the museum turned from American landscapes (fall) to French impressions of the garden (summer), and the surrealist show passed into its own season of typical museum anguish.

"She won't return my phone calls!" Teddy telephoned Jane from the curatorial offices one afternoon to complain about the brilliant curator in France who was the only person who knew how many works of art she planned to include in the show.

"I need to know how many objects there are or else I can't insure them, Jane. And if I can't insure them, they can't go to Paris for the opening, Jane. And every curator in the world knows that, Jane. So, what the hell am I going to do?"

"Teddy, when you get this undone by a single impediment in your day, things must be very bad," Jane crooned over the line. *You're Henry's deputy. Every day you have hellish nightmares like this. The leering trustee who offends a new recruit to the board. The truck transporting works of art that loses its air conditioning. Why is this worse than your typical message on the half hour?*

"You're becoming unhinged." Jane observed mischievously. "Ask Henry to call the curator," Jane suggested.

The suggestion caused Teddy to align his head and neck, producing a peppy breathing sound on the line.

"That's a very good idea, Jane, a very good idea." Brightening, Teddy skittered over to Henry's digs.

"NOW SHE WON'T RETURN MY telephone messages!" The sound of Jane's voice complaining about the brilliant curator in France through clenched teeth was not pleasant. Jane had heard from the Fourth Curator that Teddy often imitated her when she wasn't around. The Fourth Curator also admitted that Jane's nickname at the museum was "Oz" after the wizard who, discovered behind his throne of towering smoke and bellowing pronouncements, turned out to be a tiny little man working wheels and pulleys.

"Well, well," Teddy chuckled from his office while he leaned back toward his window overlooking the west end of the National Mall and crossed his arms behind his head, "your turn now, eh?"

"Awfully calm now that you've got the information you need, aren't you?" Jane steamed over the interoffice line. "I'm not calling her again," Jane steamed. "I told her in my last message that if I didn't get a résumé from her I'd just make her life up. I need her résumé so I can raise some money for the show. I mean, who does she think is paying for this project, André Breton? We are, Teddy, we are—one way or another—and if I don't get the money for at least part of it Henry will kill me!"

"Nonsense, Jane," Teddy consoled from the other end of the wire, "this is where your ego LIVES." He giggled. "You'll get the money. Suggesting that you'd make up her résumé is a brilliant idea."

AT THE NEXT WEDNESDAY AFTERNOON meeting with Henry, at which illustrations from the surrealist exhibition were passed around, the First Curator criticized.

"There are too many photographs in this show," she said, with an ugly glare at her colleagues.

"It doesn't matter whether there are too many or not, in our view," Henry said. He turned his chair toward the tall window at the end of his office, and the staff all turned to follow his gaze across the street where cherry blossom trees lined the avenue. "Allow me to remind you. This is not our show. It is a show we have commissioned from France, and the organization of the material is at the sole discretion of the curator."

The First Curator and the Third Curator are not pleased, Jane began to diagnose the situation.

The Second Curator is suspicious of a director who steps all over his own staff but gives free reign to an outsider.

The Fourth Curator is thrilled to see the other curators trashed.

When the installation plans for the show were complete, the surrealist exhibition designer made several outsized hanging panels that repeated a blown-up image of two nude women, one leaning over to kiss the other on a bed. Jane went into the carpenter's studio where they leaned against the wall.

This looks like a moment of lesbian intimacy, Jane said to herself at first. Then she examined the blow-up, carefully. *But I wonder if anyone noticed this,* she thought, staring at the pop-up breasts and shaded thighs of the woman lying on her back. *I think it might be a real woman bending over to kiss a mannequin. Time to call Henry before this backfires on us. But then you can do what you want to women in art. Just try it on a man.*

Brighid Moret

Monsoon Season

BRIGHID MORET holds an MA in writing from Johns Hopkins University and writes fiction and nonfiction. Aside from her weekly columns for the *Communities at the Washington Times*, her work has appeared in *Renaissance Magazine*, *SageWoman*, and the *International Examiner*, among others.

Over time, Sister Marie Grace had come to realize that in America a nun dressed in her habit was a rare sight. With the brown dress nearly matching her brown skin, the white headband of the veil stood out. In public places, her appearance drew sideways glances and double takes.

A small leather bag clutched to her chest contained all her personal effects—her ticket and the cash the Mother Superior had given her to get to the small hospice in Boston. Sister Marie tried not to look nervous. As the leather started to stick to the sweat on her palms, she told her fingers they could uncurl just a bit. The crush of people was natural to her, the streets of Bombay had been far more crowded than the airport terminal, but the security guards' eyes said a dark-skinned woman in a nun's habit was more likely hiding something than a woman wearing a burka.

A man ran down the corridor and darted in front of her, causing Sister Marie Grace to stop short. A woman following behind knocked into her, causing Sister Marie to stumble. The nun reached out a hand to brace herself from the fall and found that it had landed on the back of a man in a business jacket and slacks.

"Watch it," the man said, as he turned. The he saw the veil. "So sorry, Sister." He hurried away, casting one last glance over his shoulder. As she navigated her way through the frenzy of the terminal, she was careful not to bump into anyone else.

The stares were beginning to wear her down.

ALMOST THIRTY, AND TWELVE YEARS after entering the order as a novice, Sister Marie Grace still wore the brown habit. She struggled with discipline, but her only rebellions were a pair of black sling-back heels and her secret belief in Ganesh. For the last several years, she had lived in the Midwest, cloistered with the more penitent of her order, but while she had left Bombay behind, it hadn't let go of her. The voice that spoke to her when she prayed was Shiva's, and her dreams were filled with the chants of the Brahmin priests, not the Latin mass. The laughter of the nuns reminded her of the laughter of children playing in the dusty streets. The scent of the lotus flower was forever floating on the wind, and on humid summer days she always looked for a coming monsoon.

"Your time here is finished," said the Mother Superior, drawing an envelope from the depths of her habit. She dropped the packet on the desk in front of her. Nodding towards it, her wizened eyes suggested it contained Sister Marie Grace's future. Sister Marie reached out, her hand shaking, and took the letter from the Immigration and Naturalization Service. She shut her eyes and sent out a silent prayer, even though she knew it couldn't change the contents of the letter. It would determine whether she would be returned to the poverty of her childhood.

She opened the envelope and gasped, then realized the Mother Superior was regarding her with curiosity. It was only then she realized an old habit had surfaced, and the traditional words of thanks to Ganesh had tumbled out of her mouth. Sister Marie quickly crossed herself.

"God blesses me this day," she said, trying to recover from the Marathi slip she knew the woman in front of her couldn't fully understand. The other nun let a reluctant smile spread halfway across her face. Inside, Sister Marie found a letter and other documents conferring status as a legal citizen. With citizenship of the United States, she would never have to go back to life in the poorest section of Bombay. However, she was eager to leave the convent, kneeling made her knees ache.

"Yes, He blesses us all." The Mother Superior pulled open a drawer and removed a folder. She flipped through the contents before shifting a letter to cover a pamphlet. Sister Marie caught a glimpse of a smiling face before the photo had been covered by the movement of papers. Her heart danced. She knew she wouldn't be sent back to her children in India, but perhaps one of the schools. She held her breath and asked her heart to stop racing. Displaying a preference would not be looked upon favorably—God's servants did His work without question or complaint.

"As I said, your time with us is finished. Solitude doesn't suit you, monastic life doesn't suit you. Although I do hope you gained some benefit from being with us. Mother Angela was so concerned for you when she sent you to us dancing at a pagan festival…" The last was said in a whisper of disgrace not intended for Sister Marie to hear. The words made her heart pause. The Mother Superior rearranged the papers in the folder until she withdrew the pamphlet and held it out Sister Marie Grace.

Sister Marie took the paper, hoping to see children on the cover.

"Our sisters here have reflective souls. Yours is a healing soul."

The brochure was for a hospice run by and for the elderly members of several different religious communities. Sister Marie looked into the dull eyes of the people on the cover and felt a piece of herself fade. She recognized the look of drug-induced peace. She was to be an ambassador for death. Was she being punished for her mistake? What did she know about the old, and how could she possibly help them? She had been a teacher, not a nurse. Sister Marie Grace stopped her thoughts, startled that she had reverted to the old caste thinking in which she had been raised. She was a minister of the Lord, and all stations of life were equal under the eyes of God.

After the meeting with the Mother Superior, Sister Marie Grace quelled her tears as she stepped into the cloistered gardens to clear her head. The wind tore at the pamphlet in her hand and billowed her skirt.

EVEN THOUGH IT WAS A Thursday afternoon, the crowds at the gates had overflowed into the corridors separating the waiting areas. The din of conversation was punctuated with the occasional raised voice of a dis-gruntled passenger yelling at the ticketing counters and the high-pitched beep of the passing security carts moving the handicapped through the sea of delayed travelers. On the first leg of her flight, she had been squeezed into a seat between two broad-shouldered men and had to sit folded into herself to avoid pressing uncomfortably against either stranger. Now the terminal made her feel the same way. She had to navigate through the throng of people, carefully choosing her steps as if she were trying to cross a river on scattered stones that peaked precariously above a current that could sweep her away.

A quick scan of the waiting area told her she would be standing. She tried to find a spot along the wall or at a pillar where she would be out of the way. As she passed through the crowd, she noticed as people looked away, but she could feel their eyes return as soon as she passed. Others stared her down, defending their seats the way an animal defends its kill. As she was walking down the farthest row from the gate, a man rose and offered his seat to Sister Marie Grace. She thought he was being chivalrous until he said, "My flight's been delayed two hours. I think I'll pass them at the bar," then winked at her as he reached for the handle of his carry-on and rolled away.

To pass the hour layover, she flipped open the small red hardcover book to where a prayer card marked the page. The card's edges were slightly worn, and the picture was starting to fade in a few places. The light caught the gold foil border surrounding the portrait of St. Jerome Emiliani, calling Sister Marie's attention away from the words she was supposed to be reading. The picture was rendered in the two-dimensional style of medieval iconography. The saint stood in brown monastic robes, a rope tied at the waist, hands raised in benediction, and a flock of children pulling at his skirts.

THE WIND ALWAYS BLEW MORE in the summer; it was the bringer of life and death, the rains and monsoons, the fertile fields and the floods. On a windy day in April, Sister Marie Grace was told she was leaving India. She had anticipated the decision after she was caught dancing at the Ganapati Festival in September with a jubilant group of children and had been cautious about her actions since.

Before heading for the United States, she walked down a side street, one that crossed Falkland Road, and stopped outside a building with its blue wooden shutters pulled closed. She had only ventured down this street three times in the last fifteen years. There was no sign describing the business that resided here, the opium-laden smoke drifting out the slats and floating on the wind was advertisement enough. The door stood open. Inside, Sister Marie found a woman in her early fifties, serving patrons. The woman's stringy hair was pulled back, and she wore clothes that might have fit her if she had eaten more. The waist of her *pavaada* hung low, barely clinging to her hips, and every few steps she took she reached down and tugged the waistband up. The *choli* was splattered with remnants of the meals she was serving to the patrons. The hem was discolored from years of brushing against wet tables and counters, absorbing water and fluids that lay on top. The shadows of the building shrouded her face, but Sister Marie recognized the signs of a person strung out on morphine. Addiction kept servants and slaves loyal.

Noticing someone at the door, the woman turned to face Sister Marie. In that moment, Sister Marie Grace saw her future if she were to stay. She stepped through the doorway, her eyes taking a moment to adjust. A flash of recognition shone for one brief instant in the server's eyes, but she quickly went back to her work clearing the table in front of her. Sister Marie walked toward the other woman, questioning every step. The woman worked faster as the nun got closer, sloshing yellow curry over the rims of the bowls. Sister Marie stopped just a few feet from the woman.

"*Aai*," Sister Marie said in Marathi, "I'm leaving. You won't see me again."

The server sat down at a table and let her head fall to avoid the nun's gaze. Sister Marie took a small pouch from the belt on her habit, tugged open the drawstring, and tipped the bag's contents onto the table. Sister Marie separated out a bronze Ganesh amulet from the plastic beads of a rosary, and slid the good luck charm to the woman across the rough wooden table, then she walked away from the woman who had let fate adopt her daughter so many years ago.

SISTER MARIE GRACE TRIED TO turn her attention back to the instructions on counseling the sick and terminally ill, but found herself too anxious about the new assignment to concentrate. She looked out the windows. No plane sat the end of the gate, and the walkway bobbled side to side. In the distance, the trees bordering the airfield bowed to the wind. It had been raining when her plane skidded down the runway. Even now, the ground still had a wet shine, and the sky boiled with churning storm clouds.

The airport was as drab and boring as every other one she had been in, and while she could quantify the differences in architecture, the buildings all had the same expectant feel and sterile décor—rungless chairs, digital display monitors, tiny convenience shops, and gray; gray floors, gray walls, gray ceilings. Even the people were the same place to place. Among the travelers waiting for their trip to begin or continue, some were weary from too many hours on the move, some were fueled by the excitement of starting a new journey. Teenagers in worn shorts, with frayed hems and holes worn in the rear pockets, stared blankly while nodding their heads to the rhythm being fed to their ears by little white wires. Businessmen in suits sat hypnotized by the glowing screens of laptops, and honeymooners sunk into each other's eyes, oblivious to everyone and everything else around them.

THE WIND PUSHED TRASH DOWN the street. Little altars dedicated to Hindu deities were tucked into alcoves along the avenue, and the wind scattered the prayers of the devotees as the smoke from the sandalwood incense was blown away from the sight of the intended god.

Sister Marie had been waiting on a little wooden stool she had brought with her. There were children running through the streets, many she saw every day, for others it was the first time, but today she was waiting for one very specific child. A month ago, Sister Marie had seen the girl wearing the peacock blue *choli* and *lehenga* for the first time. She couldn't have been more than six. At first, Sister Marie thought it was just another one of the street children out looking for her friends, but as she watched, she realized the girl was avoiding everyone she passed. She walked very slowly along the wall, pausing to let others who hadn't noticed her step in front before she continued on around them. The little girl avoided eye contact with everyone, and walked with her right hand in a fist. Then she disappeared down an alley.

Sister Marie started watching for this quiet child. It took her three weeks to figure out the pattern: the girl came in the mornings every other day, and just before dusk on the alternates. Every third day she would come the way Sister Marie had seen her the first time. The other days she took different route; she would emerge from the alley, as if walking the route in reverse, or wouldn't be seen at all. It made for a complex puzzle that allowed the girl to seem familiar but unpredictable to those watching for wayward children. They were complex directions, but faithfully followed by the girl, which was exactly the kind of student the order tried to recruit.

As a member of the order, Sister Marie was expected to act in support of the orphanage's mission: To save the children of Mumbai. Unfortunately, as she was beginning to realize, her idea of salvation was not quite the same as those who came from other countries to assist the orphanage in its good work, and so far, she had found it difficult to find a parentless child that needed saving.

Sister Marie waited until the little girl wearing the peacock blue turned the corner and started walking down the road. The only embellishments on her clothes were stains dotting the fabric.

"I see you here every day," said Sister Marie Grace, crouching down and pointing to the little alcove bearing a crude representation of Kama, god of passion and desire, and his wife Rati, the goddess of love and longing.

"How old are you?" she asked in Marathi. The little girl looked at her bare feet and didn't respond. Sister Marie had asked a futile question. The girl didn't know the answer.

"Can I see what you bring them?" Sister Marie asked, pointing to the girl's fist. The girl didn't move at first. Then, keeping her eyes down, she lifted her hand, bending just slightly at the elbow. The rest of her remained as still as the statues on the altars. She uncurled her fingers. Inside her hand was a single flower petal. It was a simple offering, one that could easily be made by taking the petal from a tree, a garden, or a flower in a vase on a table without much thought for payment.

Sister Marie looked at the statue of the lovers, and knew where the girl lived. This was it. This was the first child she could save. The first child that Sister Marie could easily convince herself had no parents, even if it wasn't true. No one would come looking for her, the girl's mother probably wasn't allowed past the door of her building. But it didn't mean she wouldn't be missed, and it didn't mean the girl wouldn't cry herself to sleep in the dark.

"Come on," said Sister Marie, "I'll take you back home." The girl's skirt flapped in the wind and her tangled hair blew in her eyes as Sister Marie offered the child a hand. Just as she had returned hundreds of other children to their parents, Sister Marie Grace guided the girl back home to one of the brothels where her mother worked.

A WOMAN WITH THE SWOLLEN belly of a pregnancy in its fifth month ran down the hallway after a two-year-old girl, who was clearly excited by all the hustle and bustle of the airport terminal. The father followed at a distance, pushing a stroller piled with bags. The little girl's blonde curls bounced as she ran with the awkward steps of a toddler. She shrieked with delight. Her eyes shone, and a large open-mouthed smile absorbed her face in happiness.

Sister Marie watched wistfully as the mother played with her daughter, while the father settled them into a group of chairs a row over from where she was sitting. They seemed accustomed to travel. The mother wore jeans and hiking boots, and a long-sleeved blue T-shirt was stretched tightly across her midsection. A diaper bag on the back of the stroller had replaced the standard carry-on luggage. The father had a practiced sense of organization, and the terminal seemed as familiar as a neighborhood playground to the child.

WHEN ANILA BECAME SISTER MARIE Grace, she took the vows of chastity and poverty with the intent to leave behind her life of true poverty, just as she would leave behind the streets of Bombay. Only two things in life really sucked the soul out of a person and truly stripped away one's humanity: extreme poverty and extreme illness. On her own in Bombay, she would be subject to both. Anila had already lived through extreme poverty and didn't want to bear the hardship again. The order's idea of poverty was luxury to her—clean clothes, daily meals, a roof that didn't leak, and a mattress that wasn't made from dirty rags. What did chastity matter if she still had the joy of working with children? And the order said there were many unwanted children in Bombay.

With her admission into the order, she would be assisting in the good works by pulling these children off the street and giving them a home and a chance at a future in the orphanage. All run by different organizations, there were many such buildings in the city, mostly those operated by Christian missionaries or religious orders, which said they wanted to save the children. Hers was the Emiliani Home for the Orphaned and Abandoned. The number of children who actually fit either of those categories she never knew; most were deemed needy and taken to the orphanage without question as to the existence of parents. But then, few were ever claimed.

ENVY STARTED TO PRICK SISTER Marie Grace as the mother caught up with the little girl, then playfully chased her daughter in circles around a concrete column. The pregnant woman was the same age as Sister Marie. Her hair was cut to her shoulder, no doubt to keep little hands from pulling on it. The mother glowed with happiness, and the effort of keeping up with the toddler while carrying an unborn child was managed with a smile. Sister Marie Grace pulled her eyes away from the happy family, looked down at her little red book, and slid the prayer card out from its place. She thought back to the faces on the hospice pamphlet, old, weary, dying. She was being punished. The prayer card taunted her. Even the saint was surrounded by children tugging on his robe. She ran her thumb down the edge of the card, really wanting to pass it over the painted faces of the children, but not wanting to smudge the image. Sister Marie looked back up at the mother with the full knowledge she would never have the other woman's life. It was a fact she had not truly appreciated when she took her oaths.

The little girl giggled and shrieked, then shot out of her orbit around the column towards the nun. The toddler reached Sister Marie Grace before the mother could catch up. The little girl stopped at Sister Marie's legs and looked up expectantly, wide eyed. The child and the nun amazed each other. For all the years she spent with children, this one, in her little pink corduroys and white T-shirt, fascinated Sister Marie. Maybe it was the angelic curls dangling from her head, or maybe it had been the time sequestered in the monastery, whatever the reason, Sister Marie fell in love. She started to lift her hand to see if this child were real or just a figment of her imagination. The mother came over and pulled the girl from the nun's reach.

"I'm so sorry," the pregnant woman said, bending as best she could and taking her daughter's hands, "I hope she didn't bother you." Sister Marie smiled warmly, not the smile they taught at the convent that was supposed to convey contentment and peace, but a genuine smile fueled by the child's enthusiasm for life.

"No, it's quite all right," said Sister Marie. The mother smiled and nodded at the nun, and guided the young girl back to the outpost set up around the stroller.

Sister Marie didn't take her eyes off the child. The girl had a spark that she hadn't seen before, something enchanting. The mother had walked with the girl back to the stroller, and all along the way the girl was finding new things to stare at and reach for. When they reached the father, the mother positioned her daughter between her legs and the chairs. Soon the child squeezed away and started playing with the short tassel on the zipper of one of the bags.

She stood teetering at the end of the row where her parents were talking and checking their itinerary and tickets. She played with the zipper for a few moments before she grew bored and looked up. As Sister Marie watched, she realized it was the girl's curiosity, something that had been scolded at the orphanage, that captivated her. The little girl had a look of wonder that said everything was just as surprising and new as the thing before it. Life was an adventure, and the world was to be explored.

BY THE TIME THE POOR children of Bombay were old enough to walk, many had already taken on the look of resignation common to those in the lower castes who haunted life in the dust and sun of India. The streets of Bombay had always been crowded with the serious, the lost, the searching, the poor, the degenerate, and the hopeful. While opportunity was offered as a promise to all, poverty still begot poverty, ignorance begot ignorance, and the only equality was that opium addiction could ruin anyone.

Born a Dalit, Anila was one of the untouchables, easy prey for the missionaries and sex traffickers. The nuns got her first, pulling her off the street as she ran across Falkland Road on the way to gather water to scrub the floors clean of the latest customer's filth. The order told Anila she was an orphan, even though her mother was waiting at the opium house. When they said God would be her salvation, she thought they were talking about Krishna.

Anila stood shivering in the wind when she was stripped of her mud-caked dress and given a clean skirt and a metal cross. She could have left at any time, but her mother never came, and Anila, having seen the life her mother led, found little chance for a future in the smoky house placating drugged men on a street where she might disappear to far worse places. There were teachers at the orphanage. The first words she learned how to read were on the back of a prayer card with the picture of the orphan's patron, St. Jerome Emiliani, and English was taught through catechism lessons.

SISTER MARIE GRACE WATCHED AS the little girl played peek-a-boo with her father, using her mother's legs as a barrier. The mother stood with her hand on the small of her back, succumbing to the fatigue of carrying life inside her. The envy reemerged as a twinge in Sister Marie's chest as she watched the other woman. Finally, the mother gave in to her body's complaints and wandered away from her family towards the rest rooms, leaving the girl sitting on the floor at her father's feet. When the child discovered her mother's absence, she looked around frantically until she again found Sister Marie Grace.

The girl stared, then the radiant smile returned. The little girl pulled herself up using the seat of the chair next to her father who was reading a travel guide, then toddled to the nun step by step. When the girl reached Sister Marie, she held out a bag of Cheerios.

The PA announced the flight would be delayed. The high winds drove the heavy rains sideways, leaving diagonal slashes on the window that looked out on the planes, which shifted and shook visibly in the gusts. The father stood and, thinking his daughter was with her mother, went to the ticket counter to talk to a uniformed airline representative. When Sister Marie looked down at the little girl, she found the envy had spread. She was jealous of the girl's free spirit, youth, and innocence. She was jealous of the pregnant mother: already she had one perfect child, and she glowed with the joy of the second life she had created. Sister Marie Grace wondered what it would be like to have your destiny be your own, to be able to control the direction of your own life. Had she had any choice? If she had, she gave it up years ago to let her destiny be decided by others with the title of Mother.

THE WOMEN OF THE ORDER had been watching her for a long time. Anila ran barefoot down the same streets everyday, running the same errands for her mother and their landlord in an effort to stave off homelessness one day longer. They lived in the back room of an opium dealer tucked down a side street off Falkland Road where her mother waited on clients. The sex traders worked a few blocks away, and Anila's mother knew that any day she or her daughter could disappear into one of the cages lining Falkland Road, so she told Anila to run.

THE LITTLE GIRL WAS STILL staring up at Sister Marie, holding onto the hem of her habit with one hand. Sister Marie looked around for the mother and realized that, despite the crowds in the terminal, not a single person was truly aware of what was going on around them. Every single person was absorbed in his or her own interests and unaware of who belonged to whom. It was just like the crowds of Bombay, it was the same principle her order had used to find their students. It would be so easy to pick up the child and walk away with her just as she had done with children on the streets of India. They had all been her children, and she missed them dearly.

Sister Marie Grace pulled her rosary out of the leather bag and dangled the beads in front of the girl. The light danced on the facets of the plastic and captured the child's attention. She grabbed for the beads, and Sister Marie relinquished her grasp. The girl pulled on them and then shook them in her hand. Finally, she slipped the circlet of prayer beads over her head like a necklace. It sat slightly askew, the cross and medallion dangled near the girl's collarbone, while the bottom of the loop hung below her waist. The loop of the rosary looked out of proportion on her tiny body.

Sister Marie Grace looked around the terminal again, then stood, gathered her few belongings and offered the child her hand. Maybe the children chose the parents. Was that what the order had known? The girl took her hand without any hesitation. The nun took a few tentative steps to see what reaction she would get. The girl stepped with her, her free hand playing with the beads. No one else noticed. It would be so easy.

Sister Marie made it down the aisle and to the walkway when, from the corner of her vision, she saw the mother return. Sister Marie took a step back, placing a concrete column between them and the mother. In less than a hundred meters was a hallway leading to another terminal where they could blend into the crowds. She took a deep breath, then peeked around the column to see if the woman would notice them.

The nun turned just in time to watch as all the color ran out of the mother's face, taking with it the ability to move. First her hand came to life, griping her husband's arm forcefully, then her head swiveled back and forth, her eyes gleamed with fear and the first hint of tears as she swept the waiting area. It was a look Sister Marie often wondered about; she had always imagined the parents of missing children would react in such a way, but she had only seen the reunions.

Sister Marie Grace hesitated for a moment. She looked down the hallway, then back at the mother. The father had gone to the ticket counter and was talking to the airline representative. Sister Marie looked at the girl, who was already captivated by something else. This child would be missed. She stepped from behind the column, leading the girl away from her newest distraction, then waved her hand over her head to get the mother's attention. In an instant, the mother became reanimated and hysterical. She ran over to Sister Marie, bent over, scooped up her daughter, and walked away without a word to the nun or noticing the rosary her daughter wore.

AS A CHILD, ANILA HAD only received one gift, a bronze amulet of Ganesh, Lord of Good Fortune and Destroyer of Obstacles. It was a good luck charm her mother gave her when she turned a year old. Not that Anila remembered actually receiving the medal, but it hung on a red cord around her neck for as long as she could remember. When she was having a bad day—when the landlord beat her mother, demanding rent or harder work, when she had to hide under the bed so a patron in a heroin daze couldn't get to her—she would pull the medal out from under her *choli* and ask Ganesh to carry her away.

SISTER MARIE COUNTED THE MONEY—MONEY that she had saved from her monthly stipend over the two years she had been at the monastery and the bills the Mother Superior had given her to pay for meals and cab fares until she made it to the hospice where she was to be a care provider and spiritual counselor for elderly women whose only family were the other residents.

She was sure the order didn't want her any longer. Sister Marie Grace was not one they could save. Surely, they knew it and were sending her where it mattered least. She looked at the boarding pass that would deliver her to Boston, the final destination, and couldn't help but feel it would be *her* final destination. Along with the ticket was the newly obtained passport. The order had served her well, and she had served them well for more than a decade. Through it she escaped her fate in India. Now she wondered if it was time to escape the fate of the habit.

Her fingers spun the thick silver band she wore on her left ring finger which she had been given when she took the oath to the order. Sister Marie looked back at the mother and daughter, then back at her ticket. She was waiting for her connecting flight out of LaGuardia. New York City. It was the perfect place to start over. She would be able to find an Indian community full of people who had escaped their fates as well. The paper of the ticket felt thick between her fingers as the airline representatives called out rows. The mother took her little girl by the hand and walked to the gate where the father was waiting.

It was a risk. She only had enough money for a month in a city like New York. She realized there was a chance that the Indian community might not accept her. Maybe they would. She prayed to Ganesh that she wouldn't have to seek refuge in the Church when her money ran out. Maybe she could find a job as a teacher, maybe a nanny. Maybe she could have a child of her own, one with the same sparkle in her brown eyes that glistened in the blue eyes of the girl with the blonde curls. It was a risk, but life always was.

Sister Marie Grace walked over to the little girl. The mother was facing forward and didn't hear her approach, but the child turned to face the nun. The girl half hid behind her mother's leg with a playful smile and her fingers pulling on the rosary. Sister Marie pulled the prayer card out of her book and held it out to the little girl. The girl released her mother's leg, reached out and took the card, then Sister Marie stood and walked away, leaving her gate behind.

When she got outside, the wind whipped fiercely. People were rushing from their cabs and cars to snatch their luggage out of the vehicles and hurry inside the building to get away from the bite of the wind. No one seemed to have noticed the sun shining through a crack in the clouds. The sky behind was Bombay blue.

The wind tore the veil off her head and carried Sister Marie Grace away.

SHE HAD BEEN BORN DURING a monsoon, just before the rain started pouring down, when the wind whipped through the palms and tore the metal sheets from the roof of their shack. Her mother thought her daughter would be carried off in the gusts created by the storm and didn't dare name her until after the danger was past and the rains subsided. Anila she was called—Child of the Wind.

Kathryn Murphy

Tributary

KATHRYN MURPHY is a Vermonter by birth and a D.C. resident by choice. She holds an MFA from American University and a BFA from Emerson College. Her work has appeared in *Continental* magazine and the *Emerson Review*, among others.

O nce, the Riverfolk lived in waterways across the country. Their freckled skin was worn smooth from the sand. Their eyes were narrow slits, and their fingers were long and grasping. Wherever the water was quiet, they settled in houses you could see just under the surface. Once, their villages looked like doll-house versions of the ones nearby, and they shared the gifts of their waters with the human people above.

IT WAS ALWAYS ME AND Jasper who were supposed to do the washing down at the creek. Gram didn't let us do the clothes in the big river—the banks by our house were soft and sandy, and the water there left silt in pockets and hems. Plus, Gram said she didn't want anyone who came calling to see us at chores. I never understood that. When neighbors or the pastor saw a clean house and us in clean clothes, did they think that happened on its own? But Gram's word was final, no questions or back-talk allowed, so we hiked through the woods, hauling baskets of soap and dirty clothes to one of the streams that fed the river.

The creek we called ours was all rocks, hard on your knees but perfect for pounding dirt out of clothes. The river water was warm in the sun, but the creek water was icy cold. I had to rest every so often so I didn't lose the feeling in my fingers. I swear my knuckles turned blue by the time I was done. Jasper and I were supposed to take turns, but he got distracted too easily, and once he almost lost one of Gram's stockings downstream, so mostly I made him sit and watch for gators. Gram said it was nonsense, that they stayed away from our stretch of river, but Peter Wyatt from Sunday school swore he saw one in his backyard and I didn't want to get caught by surprise. It wasn't the bites that killed you, Peter told us. Gators would pull you down into the water with them, down deep into the muck, until you drowned. The thought of getting pulled under and then drifting down the river like Gram's lost stocking gave me the creeps.

The Riverfolk in the Delta would do favors for those families who brought them gifts. For a bit of string, they would find a ring that had slipped off someone's finger. For a thimble, they would trade a pile of shiny river rocks. They would even herd the bass onto hooks for a bunch of greens from the garden. It was a peaceful way of living for many years.

Fear of gators aside, the spot where the creek met the river was my favorite. If you waded out, the bottom was icy cold. Halfway up, though, it got warm, like you'd wet yourself. The swirls of water where the warm and cold met were like the tickling of minnows swimming past. We used to sneak back here with a cooler, me and Jasper and our other cousins, and take turns floating until we tipped. "Moses in a Coleman," our oldest cousin Jacob called it, and Gram would've whupped us as hard for the name as she would've for the game itself. Jasper wasn't good at playing in the cooler. He didn't understand that he had to sit still, and would always tip right away, as soon as he tried to stare over the edge. He always wanted to know what was at the bottom, deep under the water, where Gram used to tell us the Riverfolk lived. He wasn't scared like me. I guess it was because he didn't know how to be.

The other kids used to say Jasper was stupid, but I didn't think that was right. Gram told us that his brain just worked different than ours. He wasn't slow because he was dumb, he was just thinking other thoughts. She tried to treat us the same, but I got in trouble a whole lot more than Jasper did—even though I was a girl—since Gram said I knew better.

As time went on, the people's boats multiplied. The boats grew loud motors that churned up the sand and destroyed the Riverfolk towns. The Riverfolk were forced to move into deeper and deeper water, and as the waters they called home grew deeper and darker, so did their hearts.

The day it happened, we'd gone to the washing spot like always. It was a brutal hot day. For once I was looking forward to the cold creek water. My mind was mostly on the ice pops waiting for us back in Gram's freezer, and the plans I had for my afternoon. I was going to streak my hair with lemon juice and sit out with my pop, letting the sun give me layers of blonde as I watched the clouds crawl past. Jasper had been fidgety all morning, and Gram wanted us both out of the house.

"I swear," she said, "the heat puts ants in that boy's pants." She had me fetch her a fan and turn on the radio so she could hear the hymns, and then she sent us out.

I settled into my spot by the creek and told Jasper he was on gator watch. He had a big stick that I'd given him in a ceremony naming him Sir Jasper, Gator-Slayer of the Delta, and he was poking it into the shallows downstream, stirring up the muck. I pulled one of Gram's dresses out of the basket and sunk it into the water with both hands, watching bumps of air ripple it to the surface. The arms of the dress swayed like a beauty queen's wave. I scrubbed the hard chunk of soap into the fabric, and the skim of bubbles on the water surface moved quickly towards the river as I hummed to myself. I could hear Jasper splashing downstream and the birds in the trees overhead. For once, the hot air made the cold water bearable.

Eventually, the people forgot the Riverfolk. They forgot the tiny villages and the years of kindness and gratitude. In return, the Riverfolk grew angry. They raised the waters to flood the people's farms and helped fish avoid their hooks. They whispered their anger to the alligators floating by, convincing them to snap up pet dogs and cats. Most cruelly, the Riverfolk began to claim the children who strayed too far into the water.

I didn't notice Jasper was gone until I pulled a pair of his pants from the basket. I'd let the rhythm of the washing and the warmth of the sun pull me in, and my mind was drifting like the clouds. But as soon as I got hold of that rough canvas pant leg, I realized he'd been awful quiet behind me. I called for him first, putting the pants back in the basket, then jumped to my feet. I could see his gator stick drifting towards the river. I ran over to where it floated as fast as I could, stubbing my toe and scraping the side of my leg on a rock. I didn't see Jasper anywhere.

I turned to the woods—maybe he'd gone back to Gram?—but then turned back to the water. I knew Jasper too well. I waded out towards the river, where the water got deeper and the layers of warm and cold flowed together. There was a spot where the ground dropped off, and on instinct, that was where I headed.

Gram used to tell us tales about the Riverfolk. She said once there were whole towns down there, and that you could still find them in some of the creeks deep in the woods, where people hadn't had a chance to disturb them. The Riverfolk stories were Jasper's favorites. When I was younger, I wondered if maybe he'd come from there. If that was why he was different.

As I moved carefully towards the drop-off, I thought of the Riverfolk and their towns. I once cut my foot on a stone in the river, and Gram had studied the cut carefully as she cleaned and bandaged it. "Ah, you must've found a church steeple," she said, nodding. I pictured the Riverfolk in their pews, screaming and crying as a giant foot came down right in the middle of the sermon. I whispered an apology to the river that night before climbing into bed.

Jasper's face was turned towards the water's surface when I found him. His mouth was open a little, and his arms floated up, like he was trying to reach for the sky before he drowned. I tried to take him by the hand, but he was caught on something. A root, probably, but I got a sudden image of the Riverfolk trying to keep him, trying to take him back. I started crying, ugly and loud, and tugged his arm. "You can't have him!" I grunted, but I couldn't get him free.

I ran home through the woods without Jasper, without the laundry, weeds whipping at my legs. Gram was at the porch already and somehow pieced together the words I gasped out. Jasper. Trapped. Maybe—dead. *The Riverfolk.* Her face went pale and she hurried to the phone.

It took both Mr. Wyatt and Peter's older brother Josiah to pull Jasper free. Gram tucked a quilt around his body until the men from the funeral home could come. Peter had brought the laundry basket back, too, clothes half-washed and half-dry, the bar of soap lost somewhere in the water.

Gram didn't seem to notice me as she called the family together for mourning. I sat on the riverbank next to the clothes, then slowly pulled Jasper's pants from the basket, one leg wet where it fell into the water. I laid them flat and smoothed out the wrinkles. Then I pulled a shirt from the basket and did the same thing, making a Jasper doll on the sand. I sat next to his clothes and studied the water, waiting for a sign from the Riverfolk that they had him. I wondered what they would offer in exchange.

Lisa Nanni-Messegee

The Perfect Red

LISA NANNI-MESSEGEE is the Resident Director and Playwright of Acting for Young People Stages in Fairfax, Virginia. She's penned over fifteen productions (including *Just So, Mr. Kipling*, published by Eldridge Publishing) and four touring plays (*The Fisherman and His Wife.*) Along with her cowriter and husband, Todd, Lisa wrote the play *Carol vs. Christmas*, also published by Eldridge. They're produced screenwriters, having done rewrites for *Matchmaker Santa*, Hallmark Channel (2012), and are currently on contract for a romantic comedy for Larry Levinson Productions. They're also completing a young adult sci-fi novel. Lisa heads the theater program at Northern Virginia Community College, Sterling, Virginia.

C admium red mixed with a tiny dab of phthalo green makes a rather convincing color of blood on canvas. At least I always thought so until now. The blood I am seeing is thinner and has a more intense hue that would be difficult to capture in oil. A drop of blood tickles me as it slowly curls around my wrist and drips without a sound onto the marble floor. I look up at the 1960 Porsche. It's time to begin.

It's hard to believe I've been in this garage for three weeks. Garage isn't really an accurate word to describe this place. The two-story, rectangular space could probably house at least a dozen cars comfortably. The longer side of one wall is nothing but windows that overlook a stunning panorama of seascape. I feel cheated by these windows—they are soundproof, blocking out the rhythms of the tide and the screams of the seagulls.

There is so much history in this little hamlet of Amagansett. I imagine seeing Marilyn Monroe and Arthur Miller, hands clasped together, slowly walking the shoreline. I imagine Arthur would carry her sandals for her while she dug her toes into the cold sand. Her free hand would trap her platinum curls as the wind rushed in toward them, skimming off the ocean. I try to imagine having such neighbors but the image fades almost as quickly as it came. I spent most of my life living in an oppressive tenement in St. Louis with my mother and brother. Our house was never this quiet. There was always the sound of the trains and cars humming like an occupied beehive. That constant buzz would underscore the terrible fights my brother had with my mother. That was fifteen years ago, almost to the day—the day I finally broke free of my mother's talons, just like my brother had done before me.

To my right I can see the set of steps that lead to my modest bedroom loft with adjoining bathroom. There is nothing fancy about these quarters, which is in curious juxtaposition to the extravagance I see before me. Perhaps this is a clue to all visitors who stay here; you are welcome but only for a limited amount of time. Time seems to be important to the hostess who harbors me. A large moon-faced copper clock hangs directly above the door that leads to the outside world. The ticking of this clock is the only sound that breaks through the silence of this space.

My attention turns back to the floor of the garage. How many times have I marveled over this? There is row after row of hunter green marble inlays, etched with a gold flaked fleur-de-lis pattern as far as the eye can see. The marble confuses the eye, making it impossible to count every tile—and believe me, I've tried.

"Your breakfast, Madam." He spoke, loud enough to break apart my thoughts.

The young man must be no older than twenty with pale thin hands, very similar to my own. I am a woman who can easily fit into shadows. My brother told me that once. He also told me that I was as pale as the moonlight. I have long since given up the hope that the color of moonlight is beautiful.

Within moments the young man is gone and I am left alone with my breakfast. It consists of eggs benedict and fresh strawberries drizzled with a tangy orange balsamic glaze. This morning I also ordered a cappuccino to celebrate my final day. I say a quick prayer, hoping it doesn't cause me terrible stomach pain. I have always been a nervous person and my stomach constantly reminds me of this deficiency in my character. Despite the risk, the coffee is a welcomed treat on a day like today and this cup of cappuccino looks perfect. Atop the foam is a cinnamon colored image of a fleur-de-lis. I pick up the cup and the foam and cinnamon swirl together, transforming the image into something unrecognizable. I wonder how the food gets to me so quickly. I ordered it five minutes ago—or was it fifteen? It's so hard to tell in here, despite that beautiful clock. Everything about this place is a mystery. There is no kitchen in this garage, just a phone. The only function of this phone is to communicate with the main house. Dialing "three" connects me with the kitchen where I can order anything my heart desires. "Two" alerts the maids, who arrive within minutes to make my bed, clean my loft, and bring me fresh towels that smell like the salt air. "One" is the number I dare not dial. It's the direct line to the owner of this estate, Amelie Blanc.

Amelie Blanc. She's the reason I'm here. She's my savior and will be the key to my success as an artist. She picked me, out of hundreds—if not thousands—of eager applicants. And now that I am finally here, painting on commission, spending hours looking at the thing she holds most precious to her, I am determined to please her. I glance over at the painting on the easel. It's far from finished and I need to show my work by four o'clock this afternoon. I poke at my eggs, take a final sip of the cappuccino, and pat my mouth with the linen napkin. The fleur-de-lis embroidery brushes roughly against my lips.

A painting is like a lover. Not that I speak from experience—I've never even had a boyfriend. I have been kissed only once. He was a boy I knew in high school, and I had the biggest crush on him. Some years later we met again, thanks to my brother, who saw him on the street and invited him over for supper.

"Laura, this is your chance!" Mother exclaimed, clapping her hands together.

The next morning Mother took me to Pinkerton's Dress Shop to buy me a fancy dress for the occasion. I'd wanted the blue satin dress with the square buttons, but mother insisted that I be in white.

"It's the color of purity," Mother said, sporting the tone of a sage professor. "Just remember, Laura. No man wants a woman who's been taken out for more than a walk."

I think she thought the expression on my face was registering confusion. She sighed loudly and tried again.

"It would be like buying a carpet with a big stain on it. Who would want that?"

Her eyes were bugging out and her mouth was still open as she looked at me, hoping I had understood her metaphor.

"But Mother," I calmly replied, "I haven't even been taken out for a walk."

That remark didn't sit too well. Mother pursed her lips and gave me a steely glare. She took my arm and trotted me over to a rack of dresses. She pulled a white laced, high collared dress off the rack that was in my size.

"Now this is more like it," she said, and proceeded to take the dress to the lady at the counter.

Tom was to bring Jim O'Connor home with him, but he was already an hour behind schedule. Mother was furious and kept telling me the roast beef was going to dry up just like my chances were with Jim. To be honest, I was relieved they hadn't shown. My stomach was tied up in knots and I could barely catch my breath. Jim was a year older than me, but I knew everything about him. He was on the forensics team and in show choir. He also played basketball, being tall and angular at six foot three. We had one class together and I got to sit behind him. I loved watching the back of his head and memorized how his wavy brown hair would swirl around the cowlick at the base of his neck, creating the shape of an upside down question mark.

Just as we were about to give up on the whole night, Tom arrived with Jim. They'd already been to the local bar for a couple of beers before coming to the house. Mother gave Tom a threatening glance but Tom deflected, placing an arm around Mother and ushering her into the dining room. The table looked stunning. Mother had given me the task of polishing her wedding silver and it twinkled like little stars as the light from the candles reflected off of it. We had spared no expense for the supper. As delicious as it was, I could only take a few bites and then push the food around my plate, hoping Jim wouldn't notice. After the meal, my mother and brother quickly left the room and hid in the kitchen to give us some time alone. It was incredibly embarrassing and the words I wanted to say choked out of me, escaping as garble. Jim offered me a glass of red wine. It seemed like a nice gesture to get me to relax. He'd already had a few drinks and I could tell it had made him even more cheerful than usual. I accepted the wine but when I tried to swallow, my throat completely closed off and the red liquid came rushing out of my mouth, spilling onto my white dress.

"You look like a vampire, Laura!" Jim bellowed. "I love a woman who's not afraid to get a little dirty!"

He grabbed my shoulders and gave me a full, wet kiss on the mouth. He then walked into the kitchen where Tom and my mother were overhearing the entire conversation and asked for a wet towel for me. The rest of the evening went without incident but I was so horrified that I couldn't utter a single word. Tom drove Jim home with the promise to have him back for another supper very soon. A month later we received a wedding invitation in the mail. Jim was getting married and would love for all of us to join him on his special day. My mother took the news as hard as I did.

"Would it have killed you to say a word or two now and again?" Mother said to me with a long, deep scowl. "I don't know how you expect to get by in life being so silent and sullen. I'm your mother and I have to tell you, some days it's hard to love you."

I knew I disappointed her. She saw the potential in her daughter shriveling away. That potential was the glimmer of the star she gave me when I was born. That little star was the piece of her I took when I came out of her womb and entered the world. She'd given me a gift and she just couldn't stand to see it die. The day that invitation arrived in the mail was the day I started painting.

As I mix my paint on the palette I wonder if Jim's wife likes to get her hands dirty. I picture her in a picturesque garden, digging tulip bulbs on her knees with her bare hands. She pops up her pretty head and tucks a curly blonde lock behind her ear, effectively smearing her cheek with mud. She smiles and calls out his name. He calls her his "little vampire." He looks lovingly into her eyes and gives her a deep kiss. I recall the touch of his lips and his hands on my shoulders on that summer day. I can even smell the red wine. I touch my own hair which is mousy brown and hopelessly straight. My hands are dirty but not in a way that would attract a man. My nails are worn to the nub from my habitual nail biting. There's a smear of cadmium red creating a perfect line across the top of my hand. The distinctive, sharp smell of turpentine seeps from my pores. I am no one's bride. This painting is my lover and we will be parting ways at four o'clock.

I work my thirsty brush into the blended color I've smeared onto the palette. The paint escapes the brush, flying freely across the canvas. I used to be afraid of broad strokes, but now I like the feeling of moving the brush over a vast space of canvas. *I'm not that scared little girl anymore, Mother!* My brush strokes grow bigger and bolder. I think of the fame that will be sure to come when Amelie Blanc sees this portrait. I look up at my model.

Amelie told me this was a ruby red 1960 Porsche 356 Super 90 with a white leather interior. Upon first seeing the car, it reminded me of a very expensive, drivable candy cane. She said it was the first car she ever received as a gift from her first husband, the only man she truly loved.

"Robert would have wanted me to remarry. He only wanted me to be happy," she declared, "and now Rodney wants me to sell the car because he's jealous. Jealous of a car? Have you ever heard of such a thing?"

Rodney was Amelie's sixth husband. It crossed my mind to ask if it normally takes five tries to find happiness again. I decided to remain silent instead.

Amelia turned and faced me directly. "You're quiet but I can tell you're smart," she said, "if you play your cards right, you will be permanently placed in the gallery of your choice in New York City before the end of the year."

With that, she turned and walked with purpose toward the door. Her heels clicked lightly on the marble floor, keeping time with the ticking seconds of the moon-faced clock. In my three weeks in Amagansett, that was the only conversation I had with the woman who had given me the chance of a lifetime.

The background is finished and the car is framed in with color but something isn't settling with me. I look at the canvas and back at the car. I extend my left hand in front of me, squint my eye, and use my thumb as a measure. *No, no, no, this isn't right.* Is it a problem with the shadow? Maybe not dark enough? I dip my brush into the paint, trying to pull the shadow out and change the form of the wheel. I then reapply the highlight, just as I see it, bouncing off seascape windows, spilling onto the floor and bouncing up onto the wheel. The shadow is not the problem.

"This painting business is a fool's errand, Laura! You've got your eye on the wrong ball!" I can hear my mother's voice springing up in my head as if she were standing right next to me. I push her away by shaking my head side to side.

My eyes open and fix upon the canvas. It's not the shadow. It's the drawing. The drawing is incorrect. The wheel has to be moved a fraction of an inch down and slightly to the left. I am going to have to scrape down and draw again. I pick up the palette knife and start to scrape away the paint. Suddenly I am interrupted by the nameless young man with pale hands.

"Your lunch, Madam."

I turn and he has already reached the door to exit. I want to stop him and tell him I've just had breakfast and I'm not hungry. I look at the clock over the wall above the door. It's already two.

How can it be two o'clock? What happened to the day? I turn back to my painting. I must have moved too quickly because I suddenly become dizzy. It takes a moment for my eyes to readjust and I know that I need to stop and take a break.

The silver tray is polished to a brilliant sheen and I can see the highlights bouncing off of the dome that covers my food. I lift it to find a filet mignon wrapped in bacon, sautéed sugar snap peas, and a white whipped puree of some kind—potato or turnip—I can't tell which.

The steak knife is surprisingly sharp. It occurs to me that this silverware might be only used for guests. On the end of each piece of silverware—the steak knife included—is Amelie's signature fleur-de-lis.

I can only eat about half of the meal—not because it isn't delicious but because of the growing panic rising up from my stomach, moving into my chest. The last bite of steak doesn't go down. I have lost the ability to swallow, so I spit out the chewed meat into the linen napkin and bury it under the plate.

Recharged, I go back to the painting. I am determined to get this wheel rendered correctly. There is no room for error. I set about my task, focusing my attention on the front wheel of the driver's side. I align the wheel with the other forms, measuring negative space, rendering an ellipse.

"Tom gave you every opportunity to shine and you didn't say a word. You just spilled wine all over yourself like some…cave girl…and now I'm going to be saddled to a spinster for the rest of my life!"

Mother! Why is she in my head? She's not in my life anymore! I stole away in the middle of the night with just a suitcase and my oil paints, leaving her alone to fend for herself. Tom had left us both five years earlier. Now, after all this time, I am finally on the verge of success and her voice is slashing my concentration. *Think, Laura, think!* Focus on the wheel. The wheel? I look at the painting and a rush of fear washes over me. It's not just the wheel. It's the entire bottom of the car. A small cry escapes my lips as I begin to scrape down the paint on the lower half of the car.

I take a deep breath and fight back Mother's voice in my head. *Failure.* Draw again. Don't just look at the object—truly see the object. Rather than focus on one tiny piece of the car, I allow my eye to alight upon the entire scene for a moment. I want to see the car as an entire form in this space. It truly is a beautiful piece of craftsmanship—classic in its design, its color is arresting, and the tiny ripples in the white leather give the interior a soft but textured look. The white leather plays off of the honey colored wood paneling, making it clean and sleek. This car is the very symbol of perfection. Just like Amelie Blanc. Amelie Blanc, the voluptuous woman in her early fifties, married to a twenty-nine-year-old model who looks like a Greek god. Amelie Blanc, who will launch me into the big time by recommending me to all her friends and her gallery contacts in New York.

My eyes are now locked on the driver's side wheel. *You can do this.* I take a deep breath and on the exhale, I render the wheel. The ellipse is perfect. In one stroke of the brush I get the essence of the wheel, the form and the sense of its mass. I finish the wheel with a single dab of highlight, including a bit of the hunter green color that is bouncing off the marble onto the metal rim. The painting is starting to make sense again but then the throbbing starts. I feel it like a pulse in the middle of my back. Soon the pain is constant and unrelenting. It radiates from my back and shoots flaming arrows of pain toward the front of my body, just under my breasts.

I turn to look at the clock. It's three thirty. I notice that my lunch tray remains where I left it. What food has caused this? Was it the cappuccino? It doesn't matter now. There's nothing that can be done other than for me to keep working. One more wheel to go then blend the colors into a seamless finish.

"I wish I didn't have to say this, Laura, but some things just can't be ignored. Your brother Tom left us because of you! Some children are only born to disappoint."

Mother's voice is stronger, louder now. I toss down the brush and swat at my ear, trying to beat the sound out of my head. It only causes my ear to starting ringing.

"Do you want to know the truth about why your daddy left us? He saw how shy and plain you were. He knew he'd created a daughter who would end up failing in life. He couldn't bear to see it, so he left."

Stop it! I claw at my right ear, trying to get Mother to stop saying such hateful things at this moment when my life is about to change. My palette drops to the ground. Cadmium red, hunter green, and black commingle on the marble floor.

"Look what you've done, Mother!" I scream.

"What hurts me the most is to know the pain you caused Daddy was greater than his love for me." Mother's voice sounds hollow as it echoes in my head. Her words crash into me like a wave, tossing me over and over as I fight for my breath and my balance.

I catch a glimpse of my reflection on the marble floor. My eyes are wild with fear and my arms are wrapped tightly around my body. I cannot find the strength to stand up and face my canvas. The wave of nausea catches me by surprise. I have no choice but to heave bits of lunch all over the floor beneath my easel. My reflection in the marble floor becomes unrecognizable. I close my eyes but all I see is the red wine staining my white dress and then, darkness.

I open my eyes and try to get my bearings. I'm still on the marble floor and the paint mixed with my vomit is still wet. My mother's voice has quieted now, and all I hear is the ticking of the clock over the door. The clock! Amelie Blanc is coming to see me at four o'clock! It's three minutes until four! I have to clean up this mess before Amelie arrives. I have to fix the painting.

With Herculean effort I will myself to stand up. Careful not to step in the mess, I pick up my brush and blend the color of the lower half of the car into the upper half, sewing up the change with each stroke of the brush. I step away from the painting and take a look at the entire form of the car on canvas. It looks—beautiful. I don't think I have ever said that about my work until today.

There's a minute on the clock and no time to clean the vile puddle I've made, so I race to the door and pull up the welcome mat, placing it quickly over top of the smeared paint. I'll be able to clean it all up later but for now, it's best to hide the imperfection. I say a prayer, hoping the sharp smell of turpentine will mask the stench of vomit.

Within seconds, the door opens and an entourage enters the garage with Amelie Blanc leading the pack. I recognize Rodney, who is lingering behind the group.

Amelie approaches me and kisses both of my cheeks. "Laura, darling, I hope you don't mind, I brought some friends with me. Now let's see what you've been up to in my garage these last few weeks."

Amelie crosses in front of the painting, tilting her head slightly toward the right. I quickly step aside. I realize I have stopped breathing again and sneak in a quick inhale when I hear, "It's beautiful."

My exhale is long and deep. I try to keep my face from being too expressive but I want to burst at the seams.

Amelie continues, "But I have some issues. The main problem is that you didn't accurately capture the color. It's ruby red. The color needs to be more intense. It needs to be brighter and more…alive. You've created a dull red that doesn't work for me."

A man in a blue suit pipes in. "I agree Amelie. It tries, but it misses."

The whole group is now muttering and nodding their agreement. Rodney has stepped forward and is challenging my painting head on.

"I think it's a waste of good paint." Although he is looking for a reaction from Amelie, she doesn't give him the satisfaction. Instead Amelie has been looking at me.

"Laura, you're a good painter. Maybe not great, but good. It's just not—" She pauses and then offers me a sympathetic smile. "—what I was expecting."

Then a faceless voice in the crowd alerts the group that it's time for cocktails and they are off like a flock of birds flitting to the next amusement and leaving me alone with the painting.

Failure.

The word sears into me. My face grows hot and my eyes start to burn. The image of Jim enters my mind. I see him laughing with his blonde wife and playing ball with his little boy in their backyard. I watch them from behind a sturdy white picket fence, knowing that I will never be allowed to walk onto the path that leads to his door. I see my mother's face with its ever-present twinge of disappointment. She, too, closes her door and I know I will never be welcome again. And my brother Tom may have just as well been on the moon.

I'm holding something in my hand. It's the steak knife. *How did it get there?* I trace the fleur-de-lis pattern with my finger. I angle the knife toward the canvas and begin to scrape off the red paint from the car. The razor-sharp knife slices deep into the layers, revealing bits of gesso and canvas.

Once the car is scraped down, I take each tube of paint and carefully put them back in my paint box, leaving a single paint brush.

I pick up the steak knife and make a clean slice down the length of my left arm, starting at the bend of my forearm down to my wrist. I am immediately rewarded with a brilliant hue. The red is so bright it shoots from my arm like little stars. I take my paint brush and dip it into my blood until it fills the bristles with its deep, rich color. My strokes are broad, almost reckless. The blood mixes with the oil and I know I have captured the color that Amelie wants. I see the scared, delicate little girl in the tenement building, buried under her blankets, drowning out the sounds from the other room with her pillow. I imagine my mother's face twisting out of her disappointed scowl and transforming into a rigid smile. Her eyes crinkle and the smile relaxes and deepens. I put a single word into her mouth and it shoots out like flaming arrows bursting into the little space between my breasts, setting me on fire. I hear the word as I paint.

Perfection.

Allison Nichol

Balance

ALLISON NICHOL has been widely published in such journals as the *Pegasus Review*, the *Rockford Review*, *Common Lives/Lesbian Lives*, the *Evergreen Chronicles*, and *Folio* and the anthologies *Dykes With Baggage: A Lighter Look at Lesbians and Therapy* (Alyson Publications, 2000), *Family Celebrations* (Andrews McMeel, 1999), *Reclaiming the Heartland, Gay and Lesbian Voices from the Midwest* (University of Minnesota Press, 1996), and *A Loving Testimony: Remembering Loved Ones Lost to AIDS* (Crossing Press, 1995). Her first novel, *Contents Under Pressure*, was published by Intaglio Press in 2008. She is a life-long civil rights lawyer specializing in fighting discrimination and stigma faced by those with HIV/AIDS. She lives in Washington, D.C., with her wife of twenty years.

*B*rian says what really happened to the Virgin Mary is that, after Jesus, she had triplets next and moved to Mexico. He and his lover Jamie saw a documentary about it by no one particularly reliable. They are from Miami, there's a lot of sun there. We are two days into our trip to Boston, walking through Cambridge headed for Grolier's. Grey is leading us through the streets and he and Brian are fighting for position, wrestling over the correct ending to a much-told story about their college days here. Debutantes no more, the approach of forty has made the cataloguing of their history cause for light and loving argument. As I watch their words bob and weave, it is easy for me to imagine them as young as they are in the story they are telling, walking down this very street, skinnier, smoking, more reckless with their brilliance. Paul Monette said Cambridge during those years was the gay man's Paris of the '20s. You can feel it still, what remains of that warm bath of soft freedom. Young gay men exploring language by day, mapping each other by night. That was, like Paris in the '20s, before the War. A War that rages still, though the casualties ebb and flow with whatever treatments commerce will allow.

My straight friends all want to know how I will spend my free time, now that AIDS is over. They are reckless with their enthusiasm, dangerous with shallow certainty gained from skimming *USA Today*. I am hardened, harder to convince. I know the enemy is clever and glib. We ex-Catholics know all about limbo. I remember sitting in the third pew, the body of Christ stuck to the roof of my mouth, dry as a martini, while Father Michael explained how babies who died before being baptized did not go to heaven, rather they went to limbo. They went neither to heaven nor hell—an eternity of undetermined fate, an endless queue. This is when I first decided god was a complete idiot. I know now, of course, it's not god who is the idiot—just his advance people. So I forgive my friends their unauthorized enthusiasm; I know it is a product of being raised on the endless loop of *It's a Wonderful Life*. They don't know that ours is the eighteen-minute dance version with a heavy back beat. Clarence has not yet brought our George Baileys back from the brink.

As we dart across traffic, Grey takes my hand saying, "You're not listening, Ms. Holy Woman Tribe Child Thing Sister."

"Shut up. You know I hate that lesbian shit. Listening to what?"

"You are soooo behind sister. Let's see, we're in Boston…talking about my sordid past…hmmmm, who would we be talking about?"

"The father of darkness."

"You win the prize."

"Well, what about him? Did he buy a new coffin or something, are the '98 models out?"

"You can't talk about him like that, he's my former boyfriend," Grey says, doubling over in feigned hurt.

"Yeah right. What about him, what now?"

"He's written a new play, don't ya know."

"Well, based on the success of the first one, I think he should call this one 'Chapter 13' and cut out the middle man."

"Ohhh, you rule, Holy Tribe Child Woman Thing. You rule. Well, here it is," he says, stretching his arms their full length, "the store of stores."

Of course the woman behind the counter remembers him, even though he has not been here for more than five years. That is the infectious nature of Grey's energy; it leaves trace amounts everywhere. Grey had described Grolier's to me so many times over the years that my amazement caught me somewhat off guard. It was not a big place, though its eighteen-foot ceilings allowed it that grand Boston feel. I'd never seen a bookstore only for poetry.

We huddle together for a while near the front, silent. At first I let only my eyes gaze across the titles, then slowly reach my hand down and begin running my forefinger across the spines, lightly, as if touching a living thing. They are all here in this one place, all the poets I'd read and more. Voices that had changed my life. It feels holy, being surrounded by this much truth. My finger finds its place, coming to rest on Mark Doty's *Bethlehem in Broad Daylight*, long out of print but still finding breath here.

"Geez, I've been looking for this for like ever. Look," I say, thrusting the book over Grey's shoulder.

"I told you," he says.

"Here," I say, "be Dreamy Boy and pay for this for me, I want to look in the back before we go."

"That's me, Dreamy Boy. Don't dawdle sister, we are seriously hungry homos."

I walk to the back, neck craned full length, struggling to read the highest titles, momentarily frustrated by so many words out of reach. Do they ever tire, these words, from so much sweated order? Do they, late at night, thirsty for anarchy, slip quietly from between the covers, buzz and dive, leap shelf to shelf, turn answers back into questions, reconfigure riddles, tilt history in favor of more survivors, make furious ridiculous love till they lay giggling, exhausted, a puddle of consonants and vowels till morning?

"OK, Holy Woodswoman Crystal-Totin' Mama, I be the toady, here be the Doty, you be over forty, now feed me," Grey sidles up beside me and slips the book into my hand.

"You are a funny, funny man, Dreamy Boy, a funny, funny man. Where are Brian and Jamie?"

"Outside smoking, of course. Going now," he says, dragging me by the hand.

"OK," I say, "I guess we have to go even though I don't really want to—whine, whine. Even though I was having a moment."

"Moment, schmoment sister. We need food."

"I suppose the homosexual conspiracy has already decided where we are having dinner?" I add, as Grey pushes the door open and we step out onto the sidewalk.

"Yaka Ana."

"Yoko Ono? She opened a restaurant? I hope she cooks better than she sings."

"Don't start in on my Yoko now. Not Yoko Ono, Yaka Ana."

"And what might they serve there?"

"Sushi, please please please mom can we go there?"

"Let me just say this about that, yuck. What about Morrison's?"

"Oh, yeah, great, a steak place—perfect for my tender vegetarian sensibilities. You wound me, sister. What kind of lesbian are you anyway? I thought you people refused to eat dead animals. Isn't that against like the lesbian code or something? Aren't you all supposed to tend the land and what not?"

"Well, ya know, I would tend the land if it weren't for that pesky little rash I get if I live more than ten blocks from a Saks Fifth Avenue. OK, compromise, no dead animals, no unclear-whether-they-are-dead-or-not fish, let's do pasta."

Brian and Jamie nod agreement as soon as we assure them that Big Mama's had a smoking section and that Big Mama was really a big ole queen named Big Buddy. As Brian saw it, the whole point of coming for the Outwrite Gay and Lesbian Writers conference was to spend time with "family." As we wait for the light to change, Grey takes my hand, "Didn't I tell ya?"

"Yeah, what a great place. No wonder you loved living here so much. There is really something about Boston that is very you. Too bad we didn't know each other then, we could have gotten into some serious trouble."

"Like we haven't gotten into enough already?"

"No such thing as too much trouble."

We cut through Harvard Square, arms linked, walking slowly, falling farther and farther behind Brian and Jamie. It is a very mild night for February in Boston. One of the few benefits of El Niño. Grey's head is bowed, shoulders shielding the sides of his face. I am looking forward into the just-setting sun. Its colors through the barren maple branches run amber into purple into red. The colors of a wound. For a few moments we are silent. Although separate in our memories, we are flipping through the same dog-eared photo book, conjuring the same faces of lost friends, smiling at the same good parts. We are sloppy and awkward with our sorrow. I call the names softly to myself; the words of Audre Lorde hum in my head, "Respect the pain you bring back from your dreaming."

By the time we reach the other side of the square, we have grown impatient with our grief and dart through traffic with the full belief we can outrun it. We slump, winded, in front of the window of a small shop. Grey turns serious, begins quietly shouting, "I hate them you know. Hate them all."

"I know," I say in soft response, "so do I."

"All those complacent fucks who did nothing. I hate them all."

"I know," I repeat, "I know." I run my hand down the side of his face, smoothing his soft blond beard, answering the question reflected in his deep blue eyes, "No. We will never stop hating them."

Brian and Jamie walk back toward us looking both confused and a little annoyed. "What are you guys doing anyway? I thought we were eating?" Brian says.

"Sorry," I say, "We're just being pokey."

"Why don't you guys go ahead," Grey says. "We need to duck in here. I have to find something to bring back to Ronnie and I think this is the only chance I'll have."

"OK," Brian says. "But not forever. OK?"

As Grey opens the door for me, three small brass bells on the door ping in unison. The shop is very tiny and crammed floor to ceiling with every conceivable knickknack and notion. "Look at me," Grey smiles, holding a coffee creamer in the shape of a cow. "I've taken a notion. Get it?"

"You are a funny man," I roll my eyes. "Wow, look at that. I've never seen anything like that before," I say, pointing to the ceiling just above his head. As Grey lifts his head up, a broad smile spreads across his face.

"Now that really is cool. What is it? It's a cloud right? Oh, wow that's really great. But what is that sticking out of it?" he says, pointing to the Smurf blue rubbery face and hands sticking through the center of the soft circle of blue and white cotton.

"I don't know exactly. It's like an elf or an imp of some kind. It's total whimsy. I must have it. It'll look great in the loft space. Unless you're buying it?"

"Not unless they have a black one, sister."

"OK then," I say, "I'm buying, you're waiting and not breaking anything and then we are going to dinner."

We leave the store and step out onto the sidewalk, the cloud swinging between us.

"Hey. Come on, hey…"

"No."

"Come on, you know you want to, hey"

"Hey."

"You."

"You."

"Get off of my cloud. Hey."

"Hey."

"You."

"You. We are so lame."

"Are not," Grey laughs.

"Are to. Speaking of lame, how is Juanita?"

"Oh, I'm tired already," Grey fakes a yawn.

"Now, now, if I hadn't dated her I probably would never have met you. I think when last we left this story she was no longer a lesbian? Is that right? She seemed so much like a lesbian when I dated her."

"No, no, it's not that she's not a lesbian anymore. It's just that she doesn't like to be called a lesbian, doesn't want people to think of her as a lesbian."

"So what is that? Out of the closet and into the wash?"

"What are you asking me for anyway? I thought all you lesbian people stayed friends forever, just to keep the softball team together."

"No, we opted for that healthy hetero-based hatred of you ex thing. I'm a bad bad lesbian. Anyway I'm surprised we haven't seen her at the conference."

"Oh, my god, didn't I tell you that story?"

"No. Spill it. What story?"

"Ron and I were at Toys 'R' Us."

"Say that again please?"

"A Rosie O'Donnell doll for my niece."

"Oh, Rosie, yum yum."

"You are the only person I know who has erotic dreams about Rosie O'Donnell."

"No, I'm not. I'm just the only one who will admit to it."

"Anyway again, there she was, non-lesbian Juanita and her new non-lesbian girlfriend Holly."

"Holy?"

"Holly."

"Isn't that a potted plant?"

"Exactly. Anyway, we ran right into them. It was too very freaky, sister. After we all explained what we were doing there, which took a little time, Ron said, 'Oh, Grey's doing a panel at the conference in Boston in February, are you going?' Well, forget a pin sister you could have heard dust drop. And she says, get ready, 'Why would I go to a gay and lesbian writers conference?' And my sweet sweet evil Ronnie says, 'I don't know, maybe because you're a lesbian writer?' Honeey, them lesbians just turned on their heel and done be gone. Snap, snap, flick, flick. I just thought, you girls are just so old school homophobia, I can't be bothered."

"Despair can be so embarrassing. Geez, what was I thinking about, dating that much homophobia in a sweatshirt?"

"Steam."

"Oh, like you have such a flawless record, shall we talk about Butch Bob?"

"Hey, he was charming."

"Charming as a suicide. Where is this place anyway? We've been walking for like ever."

"A few more blocks. And at least our split was quiet. You and Juanita, you two put the break back in breakup. I still have the holes in my bathroom wall to prove it."

"Oh my god! Wasn't that awful? And on New Year's Eve. I still remember after it was over and she ran screaming out of your apartment and I was standing there looking in the bathroom mirror, my face cast in that dim yellow light, tears streaming down, and all I could think was, you know, other than my running mascara, I looked damn good for that argument."

Grey doubles over in laughter, grasping his chest. And I feel so lucky. For us to be here still, to be anywhere still. That the world's whim or grace had provided for us both a past and a present. I know how many others are wandering these same streets, memories thrown over their shoulders like warm handmade sweaters. Only that now. I see them, elegant in their grieving, retracing their steps, murmuring in shadow. A country of old men, eyes dark as this starless Boston sky, blinking back the loss of a generation. I let my eyes rest on Grey's upside-down face, that crooked smile. "Come on Dreamy Boy," I say, "at this rate we'll never get to dinner." As we pick up the cloud, it begins to slip from our fingers and we both rush forward, grasping for balance.

Maggie Nye

Devil's Dotter

MAGGIE NYE is a writer from Gaithersburg, Maryland, and a current MFA candidate at the University of Alabama. This is her first publication.

*O*ne day God was sat up on his sunshine rocking chair and the noise from all the prayers kept him from a nap so he plucked his left ear from his head and dropped it down to Earth to be rid of it saying, From now on, when you got a problem, don't come complaining to me, blame this man for your trouble and call him Devil, and sure thing when the ear landed on dusty ground, it sprang forth legs and arms and a head and the man was called Devil.

That's how Devil tells it, anyway. He's my daddy, always has been. Way back in the day, I had two sisters. They long gone now but when we was young and nesting together in Daddy's house, we was close as lips, teeth, and tongue. Me and the babies, Deux and Trois.

Daddy had a little farm in Spithip, Louisiana, that melted into a swampy bayou at the edges, where it stroked the hip of the River Prix. This was before that land north of Holborne got dredged. We farmed salty chickens and pigs, but we made most the money catching and trapping amongst the cypress knees. Muskrats, gar, and snapping turtles; we three sisters were his little huntresses, wading through the muck and pouncing like alligator babies. I loved wrestling the giant snapping turtles but I made such a racket sloshing round in the water and banging on their shells, I was always scaring away the mangrove creatures. As punishment, Daddy'd make me chase the snappers down once he'd chopped their heads off. They'd try and run headless, slipping in pools of their own blood and I was made to catch them and cradle them until they bled out and stopped twitching. It put me off snappers and gravy, but Deux ate my share. She was a tough little thing. Never saw anyone throw a fit far as she could.

Trois was more aerial. She had a long neck and she liked watching clouds. Of us three, she was fairest, lightest-eyed and I was jealous of her hair, fine and tame. I flung mud in it to make it ugly and once chopped off some locks while she was sleeping. I mashed them into my own dark hair and twirled myself around until Daddy found me and shook her hair from my head.

He said, "Dotter, you are my child same as she, but you're the oldest and you got the most of me. Means you got to stop pretending and prepare yourself to be tired. You know what tired means?"

"Course I do," I told him. "Means when your eyelids too heavy to hold up."

"Mmhmm. Pray that's what tired always be to you."

WHEN I WAS FOURTEEN, I went into town with Daddy to fetch new nets for the boat. There I laid eyes on the most beautiful boy painting the porch of a house so grand it looked like it might come tumbling down if I set foot in the doorway. The boy was shirtless and glowing in the sun. I could see his muscles moving under his skin, his body flecked in white paint. He had smart brown eyes and I wanted him. But I was old enough to know I couldn't have him. I was beautiful sure as he was, womanly and wild, but all us three sisters were marked as Devil's kin. Deux's cloven hooves she hid in shoes, Trois's swishy tail beneath her skirt; but me cover my mark? No chance. I stank of sulfur so bad folks took to keeping clothespins in their pockets for when they saw me coming. Daddy saw me looking and said, "Don't even think it, Dotter. No man but your daddy ever going to love you. Only heartache in dreaming otherwise." But I would not forget that beautiful boy.

Devil Daddy is a mean bastard but that wasn't always the way. He used to be nice when he first got formed into a man. Then all his neighbors wanted to unload their problems onto his back and give him blame. His fault the wife was cheating, his fault the man was beating, his fault fish was depleting. So he learned meanness quick as a whip and how to grow a leathery thick hide. And on top of that, Daddy couldn't have love from no woman. That was one of the curses got dropped to Earth with him.

Shame too cause Daddy loved women, he burned for them. Any time he laid eyes on some pretty thing, tendrils of smoke would be curling out from under his collar.

Daddy used to do really nice things for women he fancied. Like saving them from crocodiles or sucking the venom out their brother's rattler bites, but he couldn't touch no women except us. Soon as he did, they'd catch fire and burn up. Whenever Daddy acted the hero, these ladies was so pleased, they'd leap up to kiss him and for a second, I bet he was the happiest Devil alive, but in two seconds they was on fire and in ten seconds, they was dead. And everybody said, "Devil, stop acting what you're not. We don't want no favors from you."

Me and my sisters was each split from a piece of Daddy's black heart. That's another reason how come he's so mean. We each got a piece we grew out from and he only got a little heart left in his chest. By the time Trois got made, Daddy stopped doing nice things for pretty women. Matter of fact, he stopped doing nice things just about all together.

So it was no surprise that Trois was the first of us to begin straying. Soon as she had legs long enough, she'd walk the three miles to The Square just to see the ladies of fashion on Chambord Street. These were ladies she wanted to grow into and she always was tilted that way, away from Spithip. Trois had a way of walking looked like she was just going on fog. I wasn't the only one noticed it. She drew the attention of many gentlemen. Trois didn't never talk much, but she had a lot going in her head and one day, she came to figure the nearest thing keeping her from these finer people was us.

So she walked straight into a butcher shop with a stolen bottle of Daddy's liquor in one hand, sat plunk down on the counter and had the butcher lop her tail straight from her hind in exchange for the whiskey. When Daddy found out what she done he went roaring into town.

"Who cut the Devil out my little girl? Who took her tail?" Daddy found the butcher, took the tail back, and damn near wrang his whiskey out the butcher's skin. He came home with the tail in his fist and threw Trois over his shoulder, landing her on the kitchen table. Looking at him, you'd have thought it was his tail, ripped from his hind. His eyes was wild as a stuck beast and the pain set fire to his heart. For the daughter, now cut out of him, he felt it double.

He went into the mending basket and withdrew a large needle and floss then he made to start in on Trois, but she got up and gathered the hem of her dress in a fist, looking Daddy straight in the eyes.

"Don't you come no closer, Devil," she said. The voice that rose out her throat wasn't the singsong I remembered. It was solid as a woman's.

"Girl," said Daddy, "I got half a mind." But I knew Daddy would heed cause his words was tired. You could have knocked them over just blowing on them.

"Dotter," he growled at me, "put your sister back whole." He pushed the needle and thread into my hand.

Beneath Trois's dress was white silk panties. We used to laugh at the women who wore them silly silk curtains. As if we didn't know what they was trying to cover up. But looking at her now, I found myself drawn. She had learned coyness somewhere or maybe she was born with it. I was dying to see what was under them panties even though I knew damn well it would be legs, thighs, hind, and a dyke same as I had, but because she dressed it up, it was something different.

There was so much gone from how I remembered her. She changed in her dirty feet and fingernails for clean and refined manners. Even her legs looked replaced, like they never seen mud nor briars. Looked like she spent her whole life sitting in a marble bathtub. What she kept was the hardness we all had. Couldn't change that in for nothing.

"Go on Dotter," said Trois. She climbed back onto the table, belly down. Her voice was gentler with me but wearied and I felt her a woman and me a girl. It felt like me being punished.

I peeled her panties from her slow, unsticking the red-brown stained cloth from her skin. At the end of her spine was a hole like purple fruit without the stone. I tried setting her tail, but couldn't anchor the thing; it fell so limp. I fixed it with a shallow whipstitch, threading through the very top layer of skin. Still it drew small drops of blood, adorning her tail like scarlet beadwork, but it wouldn't do more than hang dead at the back of her thighs. I knew Trois would pick the thread out her skin when Daddy was asleep and I wanted her to do it.

Daddy kidded himself it was the same as before. He drank heavy that night and fell into slumber. Trois didn't want to live so low. Me, I got swamp mud in my veins. Couldn't get clean short of bleeding out. When Daddy finally woke, she was gone.

"She still of my bastard brood," he said. "She coming back."

But I stayed up all night. I watched her walk away, no swish of a tail under her dress and I knew she wasn't, not ever.

AFTER TROIS LEFT, DADDY GOT a whole lot meaner on account of he stopped sleeping. It was Devil Daddy's burden to hear out all the prayers God don't want to get dragged down by. Most people be praying when they need a thing. They sit down and clasp their hands and say Listen up Lord, we sure could use a little padding. God don't mind that. Just an itty bitty prayer come once in a while. But then there people who got so much need they can't stop from praying. They just got prayers coming out their pores. These the ones Devil Daddy had to hear every night while he was sleeping, when everybody else got to dream instead. But they got so loud they was keeping him awake all through the night, so he stop sleeping and started getting haunted by them prayers in his waking instead. Made him drink more. Daddy always did love he whiskey and now he wasn't never without it.

Meanwhile, Deux got it in her head to start going to church on the regular. She tried to keep it hidden from Daddy, maybe thinking he'd lost some of his sharpness but she wasn't too good at keeping things secret and Daddy sniffed her out.

"Something stinks," he said to Deux. "And don't you go trying to blame your sister neither."

Deux had a habit of trying to pawn off things she ought to take on herself.

"Daddy," she said, "I got no clue what you talking about."

"You come into my house reeking of incense and you got no clue what I'm talking about? Leave all them candles and make believe at the door."

But she kept going and not just on Sundays neither. Seemed like she was there all the time. She loved sitting confession like Daddy loved drinking whiskey. Neither one could get their fill and they both started sweating come too long without. Deux said every day she was making new sins but every day, the man behind the wall would give her the verses to lift them off her. And he had never known someone so eager to confess the kinds of wickedness Deux told him about.

That man started getting real curious. He'd put his eye up to the slots in the wood so he could see her and the more wicked things she talked, the more wicked things he pictured himself engaging her in until one day, he couldn't take no more. He went out from his holy side of that box and came to her on the side of the sinner, pressing himself close. Soon they was confessing their sins loud enough for heaven to hear and Deux got flooded with a holy ghost who lived in her belly now.

When she tried to sneak home so early one morning, Daddy was awake. He was sat in the door frame with one leg dangling down in the empty space below the house and the other leg on the stairs tapping his hoof, working himself up. He puffed on his pipe and the smoke went up above him and mixed into the dawn, making the light creamy. But when he seen Deux coming, he bit down sharp and chomped the pipe in half. All his tobacco fell to the stairs and then bounced down into the dark space under the house.

When she got closer, I saw her shoes was dripping blood and her fists was all balled up in pain but still she looked happy as could be.

"What have you done, girl?" he said, looking down to her feet.

"I finally got rid of all them sins I was born to," she said, "That means I got to have clean feet too. Can't have no hooves telling all the world I'm a sinful thing now that I got a holy ghost inside of me."

Daddy couldn't take his eyes off her bleeding feet.

"Ain't no such thing as a holy ghost," he said. "How come you don't want no part of me?" He dragged the outside of his hoof slowly over the floor watching it shave a curl of wood.

"You too holy for my house?" Daddy uncorked his bottle and drew a great swig. "I know what kind of man been touching your skin. Now you played me out too," he said and spat at her feet. "Just like your sister." He was changed into something hard and shadowy.

But Deux was possessed with the boldness of her new ghost and from her bosom, she pulled a long string of rosary beads. Daddy laughed at her.

"What you think you doing with that hoodoo?" he said, and made to grab the beads.

"Devil, be good," she hollered holding the poor hanged-up man to Daddy's face. "Let Jesus inside you." I thought for sure Daddy was about to give Deux the biggest thrashing of her life but instead, his body dropped slack. He opened his eyes real wide and made a show of groaning and quaking so terrible he fell to his knees.

"Now release all your evil," she said and Daddy foamed like a mad dog.

"The evil won't let go of me," he rasped.

"You got to fight it, Devil Daddy. The Lord want to help you. He want to float you up."

Daddy moaned and rolled around, kicking up splinters and dust.

"That's enough now," I said, tired of watching them get at each other.

"The evil going to flee him, Dotter," she said but there was a quiver in her voice said she was afraid.

I knew Daddy was duping her but he was so still I couldn't stop my mind churning. What if Deux's hoodoo was real? Daddy was the great boulder we'd been living beneath. He kept us sheltered and we wished every day for him not to crush us. And I was a little pebble wore away from his body.

"Daddy," whispered Deux, "I'm done now. You ain't got to be on the floor." She tucked the long strand beneath her blouse again but he wouldn't move and Deux started weeping. She got to her knees in front of Daddy and lifted his dirty palm from the floor.

"I'm sorry, Devil Daddy," she said. She used her kerchief to sop the tears from her face and cleaned his hand with the damp rag until the filth was gone from between all the lines and she laid her face in his palm.

Then I saw him turn his neck to look at Deux who was still weeping into his hand. He raised his eyes to me for a second and I was scared by what I seen in his face—that familiar wounded rage. Quick as a blink, he was up on his haunches. He tightened his grip on Deux's face and pulled her to her knees by her jaw. She whimpered and took in small gasps of air through her nose.

"You thought you'd just rattle your charms and curse your own daddy dead?" he said and his lips made an ugly crying smile.

"Please, Daddy," she said, "I thought I was doing you good."

He shook his head. "Get up," he said and she fumbled to her bleeding feet.

"Who you think is on your side, little girl," Daddy said. "You don't want me, then who you think is looking out?" Daddy stomped down on Deux's raw feet. She screamed so awfully, her voice cracked into a hundred pieces as she bled fresh.

"You ain't had nothing but the hooves on your feet," he said. "Now you truly got nothing." Quietly he said, "Go on, get out. You ain't none of mine." Deux looked so puppy dog sorry, standing there with her eyes full up of tears that I gave her the shoes off my feet. Then she was gone and it was just Daddy, some bloody shoes, and me, an orphan sister.

Devil Daddy turned his tongue on me too, when he came home from the sporting house liquored sick and strange. He stumbled through the door late one night while I was mending a pair of his trousers. He flung a painted doll my way but I'd gotten pretty quick at dodging anything came at me and it hit the floor. A piece of her porcelain hand shattered at the knuckle and made a small sound against the leg of the chair. She had a sad pretty face made me think of Trois. I laid her on the table and rolled her tiny broken fingers between mine.

"Snatched it out the fat fingers of a brat had too many toys to go missing one. And I thought to myself, Devil, you take it home and give your little girl something nice to play with."

"You can't go round snatching up whatever pleases you. And I don't play with dolls, Daddy, I ain't a child."

He lumbered himself over to where I stood and squinted in real close to my face. He looked me up and down then he busted up laughing, holding his gut. "You joking," he said. "Why else you still living off your daddy and stinking up his house when your two sisters all grown and moved away? I know you ain't a woman."

Devil Daddy looked the same age my whole life, but his face was changing in other ways—growing less familiar.

"Why you looking at me like that?" He angered quick. "Nobody begging you to stay. You fooling yourself thinking you doing me a favor." Then he seen the porcelain fingers I was holding. "Give me your hand," he said.

"What for?" I tried to pull away but he had my wrist clutched stiff.

"Teaching you what it means to be grateful. Breaking fingers for fingers, don't that seem fair?"

"Daddy, you wouldn't." I choked on the plea in my throat as he peeled my fingers backwards. The skin that fixed them to my hand went white while I faded away into the walls and the floor. I took a part of myself and hid it beneath the scraps of linen littering the far corner near the room we three sisters used to share. I hid my legs under the house where I used to stow the snappers I was too fond of to kill. My arms I hid in the wood of the table where we all used to gather, now covered with empty bottles and clothes for washing, my fingers in the only bottle still part full of grain liquor. My face with Trois's dried-up tail I knew Daddy still kept in his room, my hair I stuffed in Deux's old bloody shoes and whatever was left under Daddy's pillow. From my hiding places, I watched.

"No, I wouldn't," he said, easing his grip on my fingers as the blood tingled back into them. "That's the problem, ain't it? I'm too soft on you." Still he held fast to my wrist.

"Yes, Daddy," I said because I knew he was waiting on me to answer.

"I'm the one taking care of you, Dotter. Don't go getting that backwards." He picked the doll up from the table and shoved it into my chest so that my breath fled me. "Now go play out my sight," he said and let go of my wrist.

That night, I cleaned his pockets of his winnings and followed the Prix up river. I didn't much like going into town on account of my smell but the swamp heat in early fall is thick and lonely. There was a need akin to hunger growing inside me, and sometimes you got to see other people just to know they still there.

Along the river, the fishermen were plenty and they tipped their hats to me from the water. As I got closer to town, where I was one amongst many strange faces, I heard Daddy's name fouling everyone's lips. I seen a man with a sling on his arm walking up to the doctor's, talking with a friend saying Devil broke it in a one-sided fight. Two more men outside a gentleman's tavern, one a drunk and one a penny-beggar saying Devil drank me empty, Devil robbed me blind.

I took a room in town and started selling my stitch work at the market on North Gabriel. I had a little booth next to a priestess selling gris-gris and love potions. It was all feathers and sawdust but tourists had to walk by me to get to her and they often stopped to look at the dresses I sewn. I liked to watch the little girls putting their hands on the skirts and swinging them to and fro like silent bells of linen and lace. Sometimes their mothers asked me how much? Sometimes I forgot how to answer and when they touched the dresses, I wished they was touching me instead. But not even the smell of burnt sugar from the praline woman round the corner could cover up the smell of my skin and the women seldom bought from me. Now and then I'd see a woman pass that I thought my sisters might have grown into, but if they knew me too, they never showed it.

It wasn't long before Daddy's money was spent and all them passing people couldn't fill my lonesomeness. After the market closed one night, I walked north to Perdu instead of going home. On Highdigs Street, there was a bar called Tomber where I knew lost men to go wandering. I seen a man there trying to find his way in a glass of whiskey. His shoulders curved low so I knew he was a sad sinner. Daddy says all men carry their sin on their shoulders and that's how come old men always slouching, their sins too heavy to stand straight. I touched his hand and asked him if he was alone.

He said yes and looked at me like he found somebody he knew in my face.

"That how you want to be?"

He said no and I took him to my small bare room. The walls was white and on my bed, nothing but a thin white sheet and us atop it like a stain. We swung low and sweated out together. He held me so close we was nose to nose. He fed my hunger with sadness: I felt him full of it. Was nothing I had to learn but a thing I knew down to my gut, only to open my mouth and kiss it in. And didn't it feel like it was always there once it come in. That sweet sad taste of a man's lonesomeness.

"Oh God," he moaned and drove his grief so deep inside me.

"Hush now, baby," I said. "He ain't here."

The man's sorrow flooded me, and I clung to his slick back to press closer. I ground my hips into his, fusing bone to bone to keep from spilling a drop. Then I felt the sorrow pass through him, his body trembled, and his face faded to calm. I ate it up full and though I can no longer recall the man's name, his sorrow lives inside me.

On Highdigs Street, I knew many men possessed of the heaviness and I found love there in low-down places. I heard people preach about that ain't love, what you doing. I knew they wasn't thinking of me. They was thinking of someone lost and there's love in that. They would leave money out for me. I took it if I had need but I kept going back because my stomach was always churning for new grief and I knew I would find it cause there's no end to the sorrow of low people.

At the market, I'd go wandering from my stall when my feet hurt too bad to stand still. I was friendly with the fishmonger's woman and she watched my dresses and sent me to the cobbler's tent. Since Deux had my woman shoes, I'd been going all around in shoes too small for my feet and my toes was blistered.

On the South side of the market, along the water's edge, I found the cobbler sat up on a stool in the corner. He leaned his shoulders into the leather he was working. He was strong-bodied with none of that strong man threat and when he looked at me, his warm brown eyes was familiar, like I dreamed them every night and maybe I had, ever since I saw them looking out of the head of a beautiful boy painting a white house. But the rest of his face was awfully changed. His nose was sliced clean off and above his lips was only shiny white skin looked like the cracked top of a bread loaf. To keep from staring, I picked a shoe off its pedestal and fussed with it, turning it all around and squinting at it.

"Rap on it all you want," he said. "You can juggle it if you got the knack. Ain't falling apart. That there is a solid shoe."

"I don't believe it would suit me," I said. And it wouldn't have neither. It was some kind of rich-looking frilly thing. I felt myself flush and sat it back on the pedestal.

"No ma'am, I don't believe it would," he said, looking from the shoe to me. "That's a shoe for a different kind of woman."

"You better think before you speak next," I warned. I got temper thick in my blood.

"Calm down now," he said. "That's a shoe for a silly woman and you don't look like no silly woman." But then he looked down to my shoes and his eyes creased a smile. "Maybe you a silly woman after all. Why you walking round in sorry-heeled shoes like a little girl?"

"Why you walking round this earth with no nose on your face?" I said.

"Devil cut it off for his prize in a poker game," he said. "Didn't want no money, no favors, just my nose. Didn't know who I was dealing with. He looked just like a normal man, except with a tail and temper and the best hand I ever seen."

"What on earth he want your nose for?" I said, but I was pretty sure I knew what for.

"Don't know. I asked him Devil, wouldn't you rather have money or whiskey but he said no. So I asked him what you going to do with it? And he said question is what you going to do without it. Hurt so keen I couldn't see straight. But it's been months now and them nose holes healed right over. Truth be told, I hardly miss it. Only problem is now I can't smell a thing."

"Nothing at all?" I took a couple steps toward him, raising my arms, pretending to tuck away a curl of hair.

"Devil be damned," he said.

"Mhmm." Devil Daddy was a damned man but he done this for me.

"How about I make you a pair. Real smart and sturdy," he said. "My name's Walker."

"Dotter." He had a good handshake. "What you want for them?" I said. "Can't have my nose."

"Oh, you funny, huh?" he said. "I want to see you tomorrow."

"That's a steep price."

He pulled a penny from his pocket. "Flip for it. Heads and you meet me here at dusk."

"Suppose it comes down tails," I said.

"No point supposing against my own bet. I ain't worried. Always been a lucky man." I had to laugh for this man who lost his nose in a bet and still thought himself lucky. I knew which way I wanted that coin to fall and he knew it too.

"Better be some good shoes," I said, glancing the penny face up in his hand.

"Don't you worry about that."

WALKER AND ME WAS MARRIED behind St. Joan Cemetery. We held hands in the shade of a tall blackberry bush on a hill of fallen fruit. I was nineteen and he was twenty-two. We didn't have no rings and neither of us was much good at making speeches but I took off my girl shoes and he got to his knees and put the new shoes on my feet. They was a deep red leather with a sturdy heel like he promised.

In those early days, we didn't have much wildness in our lives. We built a place together just outside of town and worked out of our home, doing fix-ups for cheap. Reheeled shoes, sewed hems, mended holes, and in the evening, we put our feet up and rested together. The house we built was little more than planks and a roof. When it stormed the rain leaked through a crack in the ceiling, so we put a pot beneath the leak and had easy drinking water. We didn't have no fine things and I didn't mind, but it wore on Walker to have so little to give me, so he took to giving me promises instead. A wedding ring, if he ever found one deserved a place on my finger. Rich foods if he wasn't such a sorry cook. He would have promised me the man in the moon if he thought he wouldn't get outshined.

Walker was a good man and softer by miles than me. He believed luck was a thing made its way round to good men and since he was a good man, he thought something good was owed to him. When he got tired of waiting for it to come to him, he went searching it out instead. Can't say I blame him. Everybody got to believe in something.

One night, Walker was back late from errands in town. He came strutting into the house like he was something to behold and laid a tissue-wrapped package in front of me. I took my time sopping up the last bit of gravy from dinner.

"Ain't you curious," he said, still standing. I shook my head and chewed. I didn't want part in nothing that made a cobbler confuse himself for a king.

After wiping my hands clean, I tore away the paper. Inside was a satin gown, narrow at the waist and pale blue.

"I know that ain't for me," I said.

"Bought it for myself, but go figure it didn't fit right." He looked to me to let me know I ought to be laughing.

"Try it on," he said.

"Where'd you get money for it?"

"Earned it." He took a die from his pocket and showed it to me like it was a secret. "Told you I was lucky."

"Take it back," I said. "And give them men their money back too."

"You supposed to be happy," he said. "Can't you just enjoy a damn thing?" He slumped to his chair with his arms across his chest.

"You ain't on your own anymore," I told him. "It's not just you you're risking." He said he understood, but the dress never left our house. He hid it away on a high shelf in our closet and I pretended not to see it, pale and ghostlike, it gave me fright.

Not long after, things started to go missing just to turn up a day later looking brand new. The buttons on my blouses, a door knob here and there, the forks, then the knives, even the cut daisies on the table got their drinking glass switched for a crystal vase. Then bigger things: lampshades, curtains, bed sheets. Like the whole house was getting a polishing top to bottom.

And I went through so many years without seeing Daddy, there was days I forgot where I came from. Then one morning, he came knocking. Walker was a sound sleeper, but I heard the knock and got out of bed without stirring him. I hadn't seen Daddy in over a decade. Sometimes I'd walk by some poor man outside the sporting houses or getting hustled by a lawman and wonder who was under the brim of that hat. If I'm being true, I always had the notion I'd see him again. And when I opened the door to him, it was like I knew he was coming.

"Hello Devil," I said. "What's your business here?" He had not aged, still tall and lean as he ever was, only more used up.

"Morning, Dotter. Ain't you grown into something," he said, taking off his hat. "Can I come inside?"

"No Devil, we going to stay out here on the porch." I took my chair and he looked mad for a second but then it passed to tired and he took Walker's chair next to mine.

"How you been, girl?"

"I been mostly happy, Devil."

"You getting wrinkles round your eyes like you been stuck smiling," he said and touched his own face, rubbing the skin at his temples like he was trying to wrinkle it.

"How you been sleeping?" he said.

"Just fine, Devil. You sure got a lot of questions."

"Let me ask you something," he said. "What you dream about?"

"Listen to you going on about dreaming. Ain't none of your business."

"Come on, Dotter. You wouldn't have no dreams at all if it wasn't for me. I gone my whole life with no proper dreams and you going to deny me just one little one?" He was coiling his tail round his finger like some nervous little boy.

So, I told him something halfway dream and half made up.

"I have this one where me and Deux and Trois all playing in the swamp only it don't stink. Smells like peach jam instead, and Deux is trying to eat it all up. Trois is always a tiny thing in the dream, hardly any bigger than a snapping turtle and I've got her on my shoulders. She points downstream at a big gray cloud not far off and calls it daddy. The cloud rolls in fast and pours down on us. It's the only cloud in the sky, but the water rises so fast. We ain't scared though, because the water is warm and it smells like jam."

"Sounds like a good one," he said smiling faint and we both just sat there while the morning shook its chill but then I started to feel the air getting heavy with Devil's mood.

"I'm sick of all them sad man prayers. Ready to trade them over for real dreams." He looked at me like to see behind my eyes to where I kept all them dreams but I turned my face from him and fussed with the porch railing, sweeping away the dead mayflies. Still I could feel his eyes on me.

"Go on, Devil," I told him. "Say what you come to say."

He let his coiled-up tail slink down his finger and over his hand. "Where's that man of yours?"

"Sleeping, I expect."

"You ain't told him about me," he said, nodding. "Can't fault you none for that."

"You took his nose off."

"Just look, it done you both good," he said and I laughed even though I didn't want to.

"There's my girl," he said.

"I ain't your girl no more."

"That's right," he said. "You don't pay no mind to old Devil. You got yourself a pretty boy who can't sniff you out for what you really are and he's got a fat wallet and a lucky streak a mile wide." I had forgotten the way Devil could change so swift from man to beast. "Let me tell you something, girl. Unless you born with gold in your veins, luck don't come free and somebody got to pay for it. The more luck that man use up, the more he owe."

There was a time when I would have held my tongue but I had learned to be a beast too. "Devil," I said, "if you making threats, I will tear you from your shadow."

"Ain't making threats, Dotter, but a lot of men out there ain't honorable as me. Lot of men out there got jealous hearts and blood on their hands. You bear that in mind."

I played like I wasn't shaken. I got up and put my hands on the back of his chair. "It's time for you to go, Devil. Patience don't come free neither and you just used mine up."

Devil sighed and put his hat back atop his head. "I tried to do right by you. Your sisters too and maybe I did less right by them but no matter." He got up from the chair and it rocked easy between us. "It was good to see you, Dotter," he said. Then he walked off the way he came and I stood behind the chair watching him go because even after so long, little bubbles rose up in my lungs like I'm his young daughter still.

After supper that night, Walker took a small package from his jacket.

"I know what you want to say." He gave my hand a squeeze. "Tell me off and put up a fit, but just open it first." The box was light and wrapped in brown paper with a white silk ribbon.

"I don't care what it is," I told him. "I know where the money for it come from and I don't want no gifts bought on borrowed luck. How you going to throw dice against a man that cut the nose off your face?" I slapped the package down against the table. Truth was, Devil's visit had shaken me good. Walker swiped it up again quick and cradled it to his chest.

"You good at pretending none of it matters to you, but I seen your eyes go bright when you walk by a shop full of pretty things. I love you, Dotter, and I want to see your eyes bright all the time, give you the life you deserve to be living."

"It don't matter what I deserve. Ain't nobody keeping track, saying this man lived a good life. He deserves happiness, but this wicked man over here deserve none. You get what you get and you and me, we didn't get nothing for free. We got us and that's enough for me. Tell me that's enough for you too." Tears was growing under the skin of my eyes and I shut them hard to stop the tears falling.

Walker set the package down, shaking his head slowly. "You know it is."

"I don't want you gambling our lives no more. You got to promise me."

He put his hand to his heart. "On my life." He undid the bow and peeled the paper from the box. Under the lid was a gold band with flowers carved into it, all winding together and at the center of each flower was a small sapphire. "It was a wedding ring."

I lifted the ring out the box. It slid on my finger without no struggle. I twisted it round my finger with my thumb, watching as each of the dark blue jewels sparked the light.

"I'll wear it tonight," I told him. "But you got to take it back in the morning."

"I'll take it back tonight," he said. "Just you try and stop me."

I grabbed him by the belt and pulled him close. "You staying with me tonight."

We had some strong honey liquor in the pantry. We drank it and danced with no music at all. Walker swayed with one hand holding the bottle and the other on my hip. He poured some of the sweet syrup into my mouth and I undressed him while he kept dancing with his eyes closed. We drank and laughed and fell to the floor naked, him laying face down on my bare belly. Having no nose, he was flat against it and I felt his laughing in hot puffs that warmed me all the way through my gut.

Used to be, I was so tired, I'd fall asleep soon as the sheets was pulled past my toes. And I had let myself get taken by how good it was to go to bed with Walker just because I wanted him close. But I was double the fool he was because I knew better. I lied myself into the ruin and it came sure as the sun falls out the sky at night and woke me from sleeping.

It was well before dawn when the phone rang. I was alone in bed and my finger was bare. The man who talked to me, detective whoever said Walker's body was found on Highdigs Street. Didn't have much on him unusual, only a small empty box. Said it looked like a robbery. As he talked, I went away to the dream place and floated, face down on the peach jam swamp. I opened my eyes to the underwater and saw all of Spithip at the bottom, Walker and Deux and Trois and everybody waving up at me. I left just my ears and mouth at the phone. Enough to listen and say yes sir, no sir.

They brought his body to me and I buried him alone at first light. I laid myself down on the fresh dirt of his grave, sleeping with him one last time until the sun shone full. Then I dressed myself in a mourning coat of black and red and went to find the bastard.

I was hunting Devil Daddy and I wanted flesh. Wasn't never a hard man to find, though not too many folks, myself included, went seeking him out. I found him haunting the same houses he always did: the dim and musty dens of so little means, lawmen didn't even bother with them.

And there he was, slouched into a chair, his face angled at watching the door—looked like he'd just been waiting for me to come. He laid his cards on the table, face up.

All them other men, soon as they seen what stepped through the doorway, they started hooting and slapping their knees like they never seen nothing funnier.

"Ain't no place for a widow woman," said a sharp-dressed younger man next to Devil. A girl in a stained white slip came and draped herself over the man, her loose skin spilling out onto him like to show me what kind of a woman it was a place for.

"I got business here," I told the man and walked over to the table where he and Daddy was sitting. A fat man to Devil's left shook his head and said, "Not unless your business is putting down your dead man's money."

"Money or not," said the younger man, "black widows be poisoning all the luck. Go back home to your weeping."

"You ain't got to fear no poison," I told him. "My business is with this sorry Devil."

"Woman," he said, "bold and wise is opposites and you being extra bold. This man ain't someone to be trifled with."

Devil Daddy nodded to me. "Do your business, Dotter," he said.

So I smacked his jaw with the back of my hand. His pipe flew out his mouth and skipped along the floor. Daddy didn't move from his chair, just tongued his cheek like he had a toothache and looked back to me, so I hit him again, square in the temple with my fist and his hat fell from his head. He wrinkled up his eyes and drew his lips back, showing the pain in his teeth. I hit him in the gut this time and he doubled over but still, with his arms round himself, he looked to me, the whites of his eyes webbed in red. So I struck him again and then again and I did not let up. I let my arms fly and my fingernails tear like I was trying to get at what was inside of him. I didn't let myself think until my knuckles hurt too bad to take another swing. The other men was all watching and quiet, hidden in their tobacco smoke. Wasn't no one trying to stop me. Don't imagine they seen no one lay a hand on Devil before.

There was blood on my hands, mine and his, all the same muddy red. Devil Daddy was slumped over the table, his face raw and bleeding. He was holding himself up by his arms, which looked like another man's arms, no bruises or marks. He hadn't raised so much as a finger in defense of himself. He was breathing so hard it sounded like growling but he managed to raise his head one last time.

"Go on, baby girl, one more." He was laughing. "Go on and show me what dreaming really is." Like a good daughter, I obliged. Sometimes hurting someone else can make your hurt less.

"Now you all alone too," he said low, with his face still pressed against the table. "Goodbye Daddy," I said, kissed his hat and put it back on his head. My knuckles was throbbing and I'd done what I came to do.

"One more before you quit," he whispered when I was close so that only I could hear. "I still got so much to be sorry for." He was begging now. Hurting somebody only makes your hurt less for a little while, then it makes your hurt all the worse, so I turned from the table and left that place.

I SOLD THE POLISH OFF our house a little at a time. Some of them nice things were so out of fashion by the time I sold them, they didn't fetch more than the price of my supper. With Walker gone, a bare house was better. Nothing to remind me how, for a little while, I was really living. Cause there's a difference between living and just going on. I worked every day until my fingers was numb, which suited me fine—mending and fixing. I was a steady worker and at the end of the day, I took the garments to the tub with me and soaked them in a lavender bath to get out the smell of sulfur. When you ain't got nobody, it's real easy to slip by. Mend a couple holes, make a couple dollars, slip on by. And I found strange comfort in learning that no matter how far you slip, you can always be lonely.

One night, I woke in a cold sweat. My sheets was drenched too like I sweated out all the water in my belly. My head was full up of echoes and the dark of my room felt endless, like I fell off the edge of the world. I sat awake until morning burned away the darkness. But once all the sweat on my neck dried to salt and the sun was squinting in my eyes, I found I longed for dark again.

That was the first night of the prayers, passed down from Devil Daddy. They was familiar to me, like I knew them in pieces, but now they came full. Soon as my head was settled into sleeping, it was full up of praying. They was like if you put your ear to the heart of a thing and you heard, spelled out in heart beats, what the prayer was. Wasn't no human voice. Wasn't no Dear Lord, please. It was the cry of the blood in the heart.

If a prayer don't get heard, it bounces back to the man that prayed it and he feels his need doubled. There wasn't nothing else I could do for these prayers except hear them out, but that was enough. After so many years,

I began to go through my days waiting for sleep to come like that was my waking. I grew old and gray going on nothing but the echo of mournful hearts as the years passed me on the way out. Then it happened; I heard a prayer clear. The prayer said Pray the hurt go away pray she never be this alone pray someone going to hear me pray you let me stop falling. I felt the hurt of the prayer so deep inside of me, felt like it was me that was praying it, a life of sorrow. I knew this to be my daddy's prayer. Devil Daddy was put on the Earth to bear up burden but I am Devil too and it was time for me to bear up his.

So I put my old red shoes on my feet and started making my way from the ghost house of my old age to the ghost house of my growing up. And all that space in between full of low people, trying to find shelter from the life they found themselves stuck in. The sky was dark at the top but morning was rising up and I could smell the sweet brackish air drifting off Spithip like it had everyone's salty breath mixed up inside of it, all breathing together in one big sleep. I imagined casting a giant blanket over the whole town and it calmed my nerves.

They dredged the swamps some years ago and though the soft ground was paved hard, I thought I could smell sulfur rising up from cracks in the cement where crabgrass was growing in tufts. Less than a mile to Spithip and I'd taken care enough to avoid it for nearly sixty years. I hardly knew the way anymore. The streets was lined with rickety little houses and boarded-up windows. Seemed like everybody who couldn't make it in the city got pushed out to Spithip. Like it's the place people go to give up on trying.

I found Devil Daddy's house on feeling, a break from the line of sad row houses. It was pulled away from the street by a small yard and the grass was allowed to grow wild and tall. I climbed the steps of rot-softened wood and knocked at his door. He was slow to answer but after a minute, I heard shuffling and he opened the door a crack, the lock still slotted.

"Baby girl," he said, "look at how small you grown."

"You grown smaller too, Devil," I said. He opened the door fully and sat on the doorstep, so I joined at his feet. His back was stooped in threadbare linen pajamas and his skin formed to his ribs but his face was still unlined. It seemed unfair to me how he never could wear the tolls of his life on his face.

"I been having your old dreams," I said. He rubbed his hand over his forehead like he was trying to rub out the thought.

"You don't got to listen to them," he said. "Took me years to figure out there's a way you can block it out. Just don't let it get heard by your ears."

"That what you did?" I said.

"I'm sorry, Dotter. They wore me down so bad. How's a man supposed to live like that?"

"It's OK," I said. "You done what all Daddies meant to do. You passed down your blood and your troubles."

"Shouldn't have never been my troubles. Shouldn't be yours neither," he said.

"They everybody's troubles," I said. "They got to get heard."

"Why?" he said. "Why they got to be heard by you?"

"Because someone got to. Might as well be me." He took my hand and held it between his two rough ones, shifting them against mine, watching the thin skin on the backs of my hands wrinkle and stretch.

"You know what tired means, baby girl?"

"Yes, Daddy," I said.

"I reckon you do," he said. "There's a flood coming. I feel it in my bones."

"We seen floods before."

"Not like this one, baby girl."

"Then you, me, everybody low going to be adrift together," I told him and he squeezed my hand tighter. "Or else we all going to make a new life under water, everyone breathing easy."

"That how it's going to be?" said Daddy.

"Mhmm," I said.

"Then bring on the rain, my Dotter."

Daddy says he don't know his age anymore. Maybe he do, maybe he don't, but no matter, he don't want to know where he's going. He's done searching for the bottom. He says there's still so much farther to fall. But me, I feel myself at the very bottom where everything and everyone goes to rest. I am the place you lay your head without fear because you know you can't fall no farther.

Judith O'Neill
Pool Party

JUDITH O'NEILL, a former Peace Corps volunteer and now a retired teacher and technical writer, has published short stories in *Ellery Queen's* and *Alfred Hitchcock's* mystery magazines and in numerous short story anthologies. One of her stories was nominated for an Edgar Allan Poe Award by the Mystery Writers of America and published in *Best Mystery and Suspense Stories 1989*. More recently, her short story "William" received the third runner-up award in the F. Scott Fitzgerald Literary Awards Competition 2011. A poem, "Morning Commute," appeared in *OASIS Journal* 2011, and a short story, "Growing Up," won *OASIS Journal* 2012's second runner-up award in its annual Best Fiction Contest.

My father stands in front of me, blocking the glass doors to the deck. "Please forgive me," he says, "You must forgive me." I am carrying the huge bowl of potato salad that I have just spent an hour making out to the picnic table. Six kids are rocketing around the yard. It's crazy to dress them in their swimsuits, and then tell them they can't go in the pool until I'm out there.

They are anxious. Rain is threatening, and my head will hurt until it comes.

My husband, *not* the disciplining parent, stands at the grill on the patio. When we married, he had three and I had three.

"Pops," I say, trying to move past my father, "we've been over all this before."

"I need you to say it again," he replies.

"I forgive you, you know I forgive you."

His face floods with such joy that I stop beside him.

"Your brother and your sister have not," he says, joy fading.

He is right, and they are coming soon.

We have been estranged from our father. He chose to disappear when we were small. For many years we didn't know if he was alive. As it is, we remember a short-tempered drinker and how we had to walk on eggshells to keep from annoying him. He showed up last year, a changed man, no more drinking, penitent.

Dad looks good today. Always a handsome man, forty years of hard drinking have not entirely ravaged his face. He has a girlfriend, thank God. He will always have a girlfriend. She is not here today, double thank God. She has gone to visit her own children. She doesn't like to handle all of us together.

I know how she feels.

My brother Trace comes into the kitchen from the front of the house. Tall and broad shouldered, he nods slightly to his father, and stoops to give me a kiss on the cheek. His dark mustache and short beard tickle. He carries a pillowcase stuffed with mending to be done. His wife Mia, just behind him, doesn't sew.

Mia is a big girl, almost as tall as my brother's 6'1". She's a biker chick; her sleeveless white T-shirt says so. She redeems herself for the mending by bringing her seven-layer bean dip. Mia looks Latin—thick dark curls, big hazel eyes. She's not. She's Croatian/Italian, and thanks to two determined, long-lived grandmothers, she speaks both languages to some degree. Her name isn't really *Mia* either, it's Miriandaliese, but none of her little brothers could do better than *Mia*.

Of all of us, my brother, the very wildest, is the only one still in his first marriage. He and Mia met in junior high, and that was that. Jostling in behind them come their four children, the oldest not yet ten—three boys and the Little Princess. All are loaded down with bags of different kinds of chips, and all are in their swimsuits. My father is rushed by his descendants. Over their heads he says, "Mia!" as though he's waited all day just for her. She sets down the dip and gives him a hug. Mia likes my dad. Of course.

The youngsters head out with the chips and are met with squeals. Splashing is heard.

"I'll go out," Mia says, picking up the dip. I follow with the potato salad.

"They were in before I knew it," my husband Rick defends himself, "but I'm done, and I can watch them."

I let him off the hook. "We're ready," I say. As Rick sets down the platter of burgers and hot dogs, everything is on the table. Mia opens the chips, and Rick opens the cooler packed with ice and sodas. No alcohol here, in deference to my dad, and Trace, and baby sister Britt and their struggles with that demon. Usually, the kids get fed first, but no one will come out of the pool, so we each fill our own plate.

As we start, sister Britt arrives, current boyfriend in tow.

"High Maintenance is here," my brother announces. We turn our heads to see her burst forth onto the deck, tall and tanned, white shirt and shorts, long blonde hair catching the light. She almost shimmers. She calls down to us, "I put the ice cream in the freezer, four kinds." She waves to the kids in the pool, "Vanilla, mint chocolate chip, peppermint, and coffee." The swimmers respond with cries of approval.

"She looks so much like your mother," my father says in wonder.

Yes, she does. My brother and I have my dad's dark coloring—brown eyes, brown hair. Britt got Mom's bright hair and blue-green eyes. She moves and sounds like her, too. Sometimes, on the phone, just her voice makes me cry. Britt has had two husbands, but no children. Boyfriend Esteban has two little boys and even though they have been here before, they crowd nervously close to his legs. At four and five they are prepared for a water event. In matching swim trunks and yellow chest floats, they each drag a bright neon foam noodle.

Britt leads them to the steps at the shallow end where they are immediately taken over by my oldest, Lorra, and Rick's youngest, Amy. The two little boys know them and step off willingly into the water. Britt watches and smiles. "Great little mothers," she comments.

"Taught by the best," my brother says. I am unexpectedly touched by the compliment.

Britt strides to the opposite end of the table from my father, pulls up a lawn chair and sits down, leaving Esteban standing by himself. My brother sighs heavily, gets up, claps Esteban on the shoulder, and pulls up another lawn chair. "She had manners when she lived with us," he says. Esteban shrugs and laughs. Like Britt's two ex-husbands, he is extremely handsome. Britt is a Spanish teacher (and some French) at the high school. She spends most of the summer and many holidays in Latin America. Esteban has been around for a year or so. All we really know about him is that he teaches Spanish at the junior college, and he's from Mexico. She says she met him in a bar and that he's had five wives. This is to let us know she wants no more questions. She nods to my father and even favors him with a fleeting smile. I see his shoulders relax and he goes back to eating and conversing with a very polite Esteban.

My parents' idea of marriage was a mystery to all. My mother had worked in a big coat factory, and when he was around, and sober, Dad worked too, I think.

When Mom died, I was twenty, Trace was sixteen, and Britt twelve. None of us knew where Dad was.

With a lot of screaming and fighting, and a steady job at the coat factory (Mom had made good friends), I kept both Trace and Britt in school. Mia was already around and we were of like mind about Trace and his education. The long-legged, big-eyed girl who could swear in three languages was a huge help.

Britt, a scared, awkward little thing, did what we said, made perfect grades, and earned big scholarships. Every morning, I braided her golden hair, checked her clothes, and sent her off to school. There didn't seem to be enough hours in the day to know her better.

Nobody heard from Dad.

Now, he wants to be Father, Grandfather, Forgiven. We have begun to invite him and his girlfriend to family gatherings. He is pitifully grateful.

Happy kid noises come from the pool.

I look around the table and I am struck with terror at the strength of my love for each of them, even, for the moment, the elderly man with the older version of my brother's face. This peace cannot last, I know. But Kansas summers are hot and long. There will be time for more pool parties.

Thunder grumbles across the overcast sky, screaming erupts from the pool, hard pelts of rain send us running.

Bethanne Patrick

Make It Do or Do Without

BETHANNE PATRICK is the author of two books from National Geographic (*An Uncommon History of Common Things* and *An Uncommon History of Common Courtesy*) and is currently working on a new project with them. A publishing professional whose reviews have appeared in many places, Patrick has blogged for AOL, *Publisher Weekly*, BN.com, and others. She founded the social media meme FridayReads and tweets as @TheBookMaven. This is her first published work of fiction. Patrick lives and writes in McLean, Virginia.

She was still agonizing over what to wear at six thirty, and she needed to leave by six forty-five if she was going to be on time. Should she go for the "I'm attempting to fit in" look, the "Episcopal-lady-in-mufti" regalia, or the "I'm edgier than all of you, but I care enough to be presentable" outfit?

Her husband sat behind her on the bed. "That looks nice," he said, gesturing towards the black skirt and green T-shirt she'd tried next. "You look good. You'd better go."

She squinted at herself in the mirror. "I don't know. This is from Target. I don't think it's enough."

"Enough what?" He put down the remote—amazing. "You're just a guest, no one is going to be analyzing what you're wearing."

Oh, to be a man. She shrugged off the green shirt and rifled through her sweater drawer. All black would look too hard, too New Yorkahhhh, there. A old gray cashmere V-neck. No pearls, just earrings. Why was this so hard? Why was this making her stomach hurt?

The house was much as she'd imagined it. Large rooms, so well appointed that they seemed almost fated. She remembered a joke she'd read in *Reader's Digest* when she was a kid: A newcomer to Boston asks a matron where the matron bought her hat. The matron says indignantly,

"In Boston, we don't *buy* our hats. We *have* our hats." She'd asked her mother why that counted as a joke. Her mother made what she now knew to have been a derisive snort. "Some people think it's amusing when other people don't understand their little ways," said her mother, returning to her evening newspaper with a snap of the advice page.

Now she understood that some people wanted everything to stay the same, because it suited them. It suited them, and no one ever criticized what suited them, whether it was what they wore, what they served to guests, or where they went on vacation. When her family took their (rarer and rarer, as the years passed) trips together and they drove by rows of beautiful sea- and lakeside homes, her father would say "Ah, look, the stuck-ups have to put up with this rainy weather, too," then smile with grim satisfaction while steering towards their campground.

Her parents wanted everything to stay the same, too—the same for others as it was for them. Her church-school teacher always said, "Misery loves company" when she tried to cheer up a frowning student. It made sense that her parents were miserable, because she certainly was every minute of the nights they spent struggling with tent poles and then struggling not to touch tent walls lest the rain penetrate them.

No one in this house, she was pretty sure, had ever gone to a campground. If they went camping, it was in the wilderness, or with old friends from Europe ("Uncle Boogey will never get over being chased by that boar in the Schwarzwald"). A few wayward family members might have been sent to Outward Bound during their rebellious years and gotten really good at orienteering.

After the—waiter? Greeter? What did you call a hired staff person who answered the door?—took her coat, she wandered down the hallway towards the living room. The walls were covered, not with the kind of family photos she was used to, but with travel images varying from casual snaps (a smiling young woman in sunglasses silhouetted against a sail, toddlers in footed pajamas carrying fishing poles down the length of a dock) to professional-quality vistas of Venice, Phuket, St. Petersburg.

"Sarah, you're here!" She turned around to see Hillary walking quickly down the hallway towards her. "SO glad. Come in here with me!" Hillary took her companionably by the arm and guided her into what was clearly the formal living room where they'd be holding the meeting. "One sec." Hillary jackknifed her body backwards at the waist and waved someone or something furiously away, probably a dog. "Now, sit down, sit down! I hope you found the place all right?"

She wasn't sure of the proper response. Simply "Yes, fine!"? Or "I could hardly miss it!" She decided just to nod. She knew that she'd never driven such a long way to get to a private home before, and she also knew that she'd never visited a private home that was the approximate size of a hotel. She was intimidated, but she knew that if she showed the smallest sign of insecurity Hillary would be hurt. After all, they'd had long college conversations about class and privilege, and Hillary had always staunchly affirmed her "just one of the girls" status—watching the soaps every afternoon, making runs to the local supermarket for cheap diet soda, and wearing the same bookstore sweatpants with her parka as everyone else did.

Now, of course, they were grown-ups, and Hillary was dressed for both entertaining at home and attending a meeting, in cropped white chinos, a fitted shirt covered by a periwinkle blue cable cardigan, a needlepoint belt, and some sort of flat, slipper-like periwinkle blue shoes with tiny bows and piping in lemon yellow that stood out against the periwinkle of the rest. Hillary looked put together and rich, not at all like the kind of person who had to decide which Target T-shirt to wear each day.

The room they were in looked put together and rich, too, but not in the way she had expected. Since she had little experience in visiting rich people's houses, she'd assumed that they looked like the perfect, antiseptic rooms in her hometown's best furniture store. Everything would be new, and matching, and shiny. Hillary's living room—well, her family's living room—was anything but perfect, yet somehow everything belonged there. The wall at one end was floor-to-ceiling white bookshelves, crammed with all sorts of titles, some in piles, some in long sets, others placed haphazardly. At the other end was a large picture window that looked out over the lake, and an assortment of squashy chairs were gathered around a huge tufted bench that was piled with more books, magazines, trays bearing candles, and vases of garden flowers.

The bookcase area where she and Hillary sat consisted of two long couches (Hillary called them sofas), with lots of wooden chairs drawn up around for the League members. Between them was an enormous Oriental carpet, the most surprising mixture of gray, yellow, rust, and green—not at all the jewel tones of the few "Persian rugs" that she had seen at her great aunt's house or at college. This rug didn't look polished; if anything, it looked as if it were showing off its handmade quality. But it was astonishingly beautiful, intricate, and vibrant, all the same. She couldn't stop staring at it.

Hillary was talking to her, so she finally looked up. "What can I get for you?" said Hillary. "Coffee? A glass of wine? Tea?"

She badly wanted the wine, but the drive back was long and she didn't want to be sleepy. She accepted coffee and said she'd come along to the kitchen.

Hillary laughed, a sort of trill that bore little resemblance to her under-graduate guffaws. "Oh no no no no no, we're not letting you see where the sausage is made! I'll be right back. The others will start arriving any minute now. You stay comfy." Hillary trotted off on her silent loafers.

She took a hesitant seat on one of the sofas, felt the soft velvety fabric of the arm, then put her shoulder bag down next to her feet, off to the side and partially hidden. She had no idea what the other committee members would be carrying. Was this more of a social occasion, or would they get right down to business? Hillary had called her just a few weeks after she and Eric had settled into their married-students' housing, a grim two-bedroom apartment close to the university and light years away from Hillary's family home in a nearby suburb.

But Hillary didn't ask impolite questions about whether or not the hallways smelled (they did; so many of the other married students came from far-away places and cooked unfamiliar things), but got right to the point: "I'm so happy you're here now! I want you to come to our alumnae meetings, and I also hope you'll consider joining the admissions commit-tee." Hillary's voice lowered. "Mother still loves being on it, because of all her friends—but honestly, we need some younger grads, or the candidates are going to worry they're applying for a nursing home and not college!"

Of course she accepted. She was hundreds of miles from home and didn't know anyone in her program yet, didn't have any kindly relatives to telephone and visit. She'd signed up to volunteer at the local library, but even though she loved being there, had forgotten that it would be a quiet and solitary assignment. Every week the protective book jackets crackled beneath her fingers as she slid new picture books in place alphabetically by author, and every week as she did so she thought about her friends in New York and Chicago and San Francisco, taking a few minutes at the office to email or ping about evening and weekend plans.

Now she had some, even if this meeting wasn't the same as after-work martinis. At least Hillary had mentioned wine. That was a start. The few departmental get-togethers she'd attended centered around beer—most of her classmates were living on shoestring grants or credit card debt. After several years out of school and working, she was accustomed to wine, cocktails, and ordering as many courses as she liked at a restaurant.

Three older women, maybe in their forties, walked into the room, chattering animatedly. "…I told her, *next* year, we'll really do it up—maybe rent the villa near Parma again," said one, clad in a stylish tank top and denim skirt, a sweater loosely draped over her prominent collar bones. The two others nodded as they all chose seats and put their handbags down. Parma Villa said "Hello, I'm Padgett Ames. Hillary mentioned we'd have a new committee member tonight! Welcome!" The two others turned towards her, their eyes seemingly in synch with Padgett's gaze.

Damn it, she was blushing from nerves. "Thank you, I'm Hillary's classmate. Kristin. Kristin Bates."

Parma—no, *Padgett*, Padgett—said "How do you do, Kristin. This is Emily Stover"—she swiveled left, then right—"and Hallie Pendleton." Both Emily and Hallie leaned forward to shake her hand without getting up entirely from their chairs. She noticed that Emily was wearing the same kind of shoes as Hillary, except that Emily's were entirely navy blue. Hallie wore loafers with a brass bit beneath her well-worn jeans.

Hillary returned with two much-older women in tow, both of whom wore more formal trousers and shirts (what Kristin's mother would refer to as "slacks" and "blouses"). One of them had a silk scarf knotted around her throat, and the other wore a large silver pendant with a complicated monogram.

With all of the signs and symbols these women sported, she felt as if she were decoding tribal markings in her introductory anthro course. She'd known that these things mattered, at least to Hillary, who was constantly coming back to school from trips home with new outfits or "this year's cashmere sweater" after Christmas. Somehow it had never occurred to her that if expensive garments mattered so much to Hillary, that they must matter to other people, older people, as well. Her only experience with older people involved men who wore Dickies work pants on the weekends, with white T-shirts for informal occasions, and Dickies long-sleeved shirts on top if things were more somber. The women wore whatever style of "slacks" were most comfortable for the era, whether polyester boot cut or denim, with easy-care blouses and T-shirts. Very few of them had good jewelry beyond wedding bands and modest engagement rings; a few of the more successful couples had nice watches. Receiving a watch as a gift (for graduation, marriage, or retirement) was significant. Like cars, stereos, and TV sets, watches were meant to be cared for properly. They belonged to their owners. Hillary, on the other hand, wore a funny, oversized man's watch ("grandfather's") that slid around on her wrist and had dents and scratches from times she carelessly bashed it against things. "More character!" she'd say.

She shifted in her seat and tried to keep smiling politely, which she now knew meant just enough to show you were paying attention, but not so much that you looked dim witted. The much-older women, she learned, were Charlotte and Lillian, and Charlotte had just returned from Tuscany. She was instructing Padgett about all the things that could go wrong with villa rentals. "It wasn't always like this, mind you," said Charlotte. "When Hayes was stationed in Geneva, the children and I spent every summer at Lake Como and I never had to worry about being cheated. We could even afford a live-in cook and maid! Oh, thank you, Hillary sweetie," as "Hillary sweetie" handed Charlotte a glass of cold white wine. "The worst part was that the nanny couldn't cope with driving, so I had to take over any outing or errand that the maid forgot. Those roads!" She held up a hand that sparkled from a set of diamonds. "Hillary, the only woman I know who was ever brave enough to get behind the wheel *in Italia* was your mother…"

All of the women were now taking out folders, notepads, and pens, and Kristin assumed they were about to begin the meeting. But before anyone said anything brisk and official, another young woman stepped into the room, holding a child with each hand. "Hillary?" she said, an urgent uplift at the name's end. "Could I speak to you for just a moment?" As Hillary excused herself and hurried to the hallway, Padgett lifted her chin towards the door and said to Kristin "That's Whitney, Hillary's sister-in-law. Her daughters are sooooo cute." Padgett's cronies nodded along with her. "Well, now that we still have a minute before we start, may I freshen anyone's drink? Kristin?" Kristin, who had drained her sparkling water while waiting for the others to arrive, said she'd help, too.

Padgett ushered her into the very large, very white kitchen, the likes of which Kristin had only ever seen in the same magazines where she'd glimpsed the earlier living room (parlor?). Every surface and appliance gleamed, and there were no decorative trinkets like the novelty cookie jars and matching oven mitts her aunts and cousins favored. The only things on the counters were related to cooking: matching tins of spices in regimented rows, a magnetic strip covered in different sizes and types of knives next to the stove, and a floor-to-ceiling shelf of cookbooks that looked both well chosen and well used.

'So, you met Hillary at Wheeler?' said Padgett as she uncorked a bottle of wine. She didn't wait for Kristin to answer before saying, "What brings you here?"

Kristin refilled her glass and Hallie's ("She won't say anything, but she's pregnant") with the bottle of Perrier on the kitchen island. "My husband and I are in graduate school at the university. We just started this fall."

"Ooooh, exciting! Where do you live? In Drumkilbo Heights? Or downtown?"

Kristin said, "No, in married-student housing." If she'd been talking to one of her classmates, or even one of Eric's, she might have added "We couldn't afford anything else," but Padgett would see that. In fact, she'd be surprised if Padgett hadn't already guessed that.

When they returned to the living room, Hillary was sitting on the floor next to Kristin's temporary perch, her nieces in front of her. "Look, y'all," she said with a bit of forced gaiety, "Jane Carter and Emma Claire have joined us for a bit." She glanced at Charlotte and Lillian. "We're making them unofficial committee members tonight because their momma and daddy have a dinner to attend. Right, Emma Claire?" The towhead in question was about seven, her sister, four or five.

"Granny was s'posed to watch us, but she doesn't feel well," said Emma Claire. Hillary smoothed her niece's hair and said, "I'm just going to let those two paint their nails while we talk." She waved towards Charlotte to start and busied herself opening tiny bottles of varnish and placing them on the large stone hearth for the girls to use. Some of the colors had separated, and Hillary shook them hard with her periwinkle-cashmere'd arm. "I never do my nails anymore. I swear, some of these must be from our freshman year, Kristin!" Hillary laughed. "I just can't throw them out when they're half full. You know what Granny says, girls"—a smile for the children, who chimed in: "Use it up, wear it out, make it do, or do without!"

Kristin chuckled indulgently along with the others, but as Charlotte began the meeting proper, found herself remembering all the things she'd used up (the last bits of shampoo coaxed from bottles), worn out (underwear washed until it almost dissolved), made do with (yoga pants with bleach stains on the knee), and done without (lots of things, but definitely spring-break trips to beaches). She also remembered the Tiffany earrings that Hillary's father gave her one year for Christmas, and the pizza feasts for their seminar study group that Hillary could pay for although Kristin couldn't even have sprung for one pie without cleaning change out of pockets.

She wasn't exactly angry about the difference in income, at least not then she wasn't. She remembered staring at the pretty gold earrings in their unmistakable blue box and thinking not, "Why does she have those and I don't?" but instead realizing that she'd never seen anything from Tiffany's up close before. Hillary might as well have been a character in a fairy tale reaching out through a page, it felt that unreal and fabulous. There were people out there, Kristin thought, who actually live with the fine things I've read about. Up to that point, people like Hillary—and

Hillary's father—might as well have been fictional creations. She could not picture any one of her perpetually angry uncles taking time away from the horseshoe pit where they gathered at picnics to shop in any store, and their grim wives and daughters never went farther than the small local jeweler's to buy inexpensive charms or get their watches repaired.

When Kristin graduated from high school, with a National Merit scholarship, several academic awards, and a hefty grant paying most of her Wheeler tuition, her parents decided that she should help pick out her watch. It was the first time she'd actually been inside of a jewelry store, and while she knew that her mother and father were nervous about finding something she liked at a price they could afford, all she wanted to do was drift towards the back of the shop and look at the china, silver, and crystal displays.

She focused and picked out a plain watch on a brown band, one that she knew wouldn't stand out in any way, good or bad, and deliberately didn't look at the price. She told her parents she'd let them make the final decision between that one and a slightly different version, which bought her a few minutes browsing by the plates and bowls. Each china pattern was displayed on a little Lucite easel—dinner plate, bread plate, cup and saucer. Some of them, like the Wedgwood with the strawberries and the peach-trimmed Noritake, had little cards in front of them with careful handwritten legends saying "Chosen by Miss Natalie Giordano for her April wedding to Mr. Anthony Santoro" or "Selection of Miss Kathleen O'Callaghan and Mr. Brian Reardon."

Kristin never forgot those minutes. She recognized a few of the names on the cards. They weren't "stuck-ups" or rich people. They were people who lived in the same kinds of houses as her family did. They used Corelle ware dishes every day, too. But they also, it seemed, felt that they could ask for and then own things that were clearly lovely and precious. Her own mother's "wedding china" was so unappealing that the family didn't even take it out for holidays. It looked as if it had been purchased with Green Stamps. Why did the Giordanos down the street, whose children regularly flunked classes, feel comfortable announcing to the world that their daughter wanted Wedgwood china, when Kristin's parents still served soda in the free tumblers from Burger King but made sure she had a tutor for the SATs?

Lillian was saying something about how the admissions process worked. "The College mandates need-blind admissions," she said, underscoring something on an official document with her specially cushioned pen, above and below which her arthritic knuckles bulged. "That means we aren't supposed to ask the candidates anything about their household incomes, or if we do, that we are encouraged to leave such information ("ihn-foe-maaaayshun," in her soft Tidewater accent) out of our reports." She looked at Kristin, who instantly wondered if she were going to be quizzed on her own admissions interviews, of which there had been three: One with an alumna, one with an admissions officer, and one with the Music Department chair. She was slightly abashed to realize that Lillian was trying to make sure that she, the newest member, understood this principle.

"That makes sense," Kristin said. "The College is committed to diversity, right?"

Charlotte made a noise between a "hmmmph" and a throat clear, and Hallie snickered, but before Kristin could ask or figure out the issue, everyone heard a loud thud from somewhere else in the house. Hillary froze in the midst of painting Emma Claire's big toe, then said "Oh, dear. I hope Momma isn't feeling worse." She leaned towards Kristin and said quietly, "Just watch these two for five minutes. I promise I'll be back in a flash."

Kristin looked down uncertainly at the little girls. Except for some occasional babysitting for an undergraduate professor, she hadn't spent time with children in years. She and Eric talked about having their own every once in a while when the moon was full and they'd splurged on wine that came in a bottle and not a box, but thus far their "babies" were their dissertations.

Jane Carter held out her hand. "I'm next."

"NO JANE, Aunt Hillie was finishing my toenails!" screeched Emma Claire.

Kristin planned to ask them both to wait, then pack up all of the nail accoutrements and offer the girls juice boxes; she'd seen them in the enormous refrigerator next to a special rack that held half a dozen bottles of white wine. Just as she reached to tap Jane Carter's shoulder, Emma Claire shoved her sister backwards. Kristin caught a glimpse of "Ballet

Class" polish snake from beneath the younger one's skirt onto the multi-hued (but none of them pink) carpet just before Jane Carter fell back and the stain was hidden by her gingham tunic. As Kristin scanned the room, she saw that the other women were huddled over some pages spread out on the book-filled bench, none paying any attention to the young visitors. She decided to tell Hillary about it when she returned; nail polish wasn't something you could blot up with towels, like juice or sauce.

"Hel-LO Charlotte!" All Kristin could see as she heard the greeting was a suntanned and spotted hand clutching the doorsill, a hand with diamonds like Charlotte's, and bright melon-red polish on its nails.

Charlotte reached over and grasped Lillian's wrist; Kristin saw her give it a squeeze. "Jay! Are you feeling better?"

This must be Hillary's mother. Kristin had never met her, although she'd seen her at their graduation, sitting in a crowd at the special ceremony for English Department honors graduates. Her own parents had been beaming with pride and happiness, even if her father's chain-store suit and mother's well-pressed "best" dress weren't quite the same as the blue blazers, rep ties, and linens of her classmates' relatives. She remembered that Hillary's mother wore several shades of beige and had perfectly coiffed hair. She'd wanted to go up and introduce herself, to say how grateful she was for Mrs. Faulconer's allowing them to use the family house, but as she made her way towards them after the ceremony, Hillary saw her and hurried over.

"I was just going to go and thank your parents," said Kristin.

Hillary put her arm around Kristin's shoulders. "Oh they would love that, but they have to hurry over to the trustees' meeting. I was hoping you would let me meet your mother and father." And so Kristin found herself telling her parents about Hillary, about the week at the lake, about the generosity of the Faulconers. She could see her mother's eyes narrow, just slightly, could see her thinking "Oh, so this is one of those girls," as she said "That was nice of your family, Hillary. We'd like to thank your parents, too," and craned her neck as if she could already pick them out of the crowd.

Kristin dreaded having to explain about the trustees and how Hillary's mother was also an alumna of the college, so she quickly told her parents that she wanted to introduce them to her thesis advisor before he had to leave for the commencement procession. As she waited to see Hillary's mother in the doorway, she could still feel her cheeks burn slightly at the memory.

As Mrs. Faulconer entered the room (Kristin thought she would probably think of Hillary's mother as "Mrs. Faulconer" even when she, Kristin, was in late middle age), Kristin realized something was very wrong with her. She stumbled on the edge of the rug and caught herself on the high back of the chair in which Lillian sat. "Whooooo—oops!" she cried, shuffling her foot back into a low-heeled mule. She was wearing khaki trousers and a chambray shirt, both mussed from a lie-down.

Hillary walked quickly behind her, placing a hand on her mother's shoulder. "You need to go back to bed," she said, quietly.

"I most certainly do *not*," said Mrs. Faulconer. "I feel much better. Good to see you, ladies!" She walked slowly over to Kristin's sofa and sat down next to her. "Jane Carter, Emma Claire, Granny's fine now!"

As Hillary's mother spoke these words, Kristin smelled the whisky on her breath. Mrs. Faulconer wasn't "under the weather"; she was drunk. Kristin's parents hardly touched alcohol, but the horseshoe-playing uncles liked to keep a bottle or three of Jameson's on the picnic table near their case of Schlitz. She forced herself to smile in Mrs. Faulconer's general direction and as she did, saw Hillary's stricken face. Hillary wouldn't be surprised at the smell of her mother's breath; she'd smelled it before.

Kristin was thinking about how she might walk Mrs. Faulconer towards Hillary, and then towards the kitchen, when Mrs. Faulconer let out a loud cry. Kristin followed her gaze, even though she knew before seeing the large pink blot on the carpet what was wrong.

Mrs. Faulconer was screeching. "How did that stain get on my rug? Hillary, what happened?"

Hillary had no idea, and said so. Kristin looked at Mrs. Faulconer's face, apoplectic with outrage, eyes bugging out, lips twisted angrily, and nostrils flared. Those bugged-out eyes now shifted towards the two small girls, who were sitting extremely straight and still in their corner.

Kristin had seen that face before. Kristin had sat in that corner before. The clink of horseshoes, the click of a pull-tab can, the scratch of a wooden match—all of these sounds echoed in her head as she turned to

Mrs. Faulconer and said "I am so sorry. I spilled a bottle of the girls' nail polish during the meeting."

The eyes swiveled to her almost faster than the neck could turn. "Didn't you think to tell someone? To try and clean it up? My Tabriz is *ruined*!" The hot liquor fumes of her breath were closer now. Kristin winced, she hoped inwardly. "I really do apologize. I'll pay for a repair, or a new rug," knowing even as she said the words that she and Eric probably couldn't even take out a loan large enough for a down payment on the remarkable piece, let alone cover its full price.

But Mrs. Faulconer had taken her soused tears further into the room, towards Charlotte and Hallie and proper sympathy for her plight. Kristin was left with a pained-looking Hillary, whose cheeks were flushed and lower lip caught between her teeth.

"I'm sorry, Hills," she said.

Hillary glanced away, back towards the hallway. "Don't be. I doubt you had anything to do with it. Those girls never hear the word no." She turned back and looked down. "But Kristin, I can't promise she won't ask for money…" Hillary's voice trailed off, the unspoken knowledge of how difficult this would be for Kristin and Eric lost in a sigh.

"Hillary." Kristin waited until her friend looked directly at her. "It is *all right*. I should have spoken up about the stain as soon as it happened. I don't mind."

She looked at her watch. It was time to go.

SEVERAL WEEKS LATER HILLARY CALLED. "Hi, Kristin!"

She was about to speak when Hillary barreled on. "Good news, well, at least maybe a relief: We sent that rug out for cleaning and the stain is gone. Mother's forgotten all about how it happened, too."

She was relieved, but she also knew, from those last words, that Hillary probably wasn't. Probably never would be. There were things you could make do with—and there were things you couldn't do without.

"That's great, Hillary. I'm so glad the rug is all right again." She hesitated, but then decided to go ahead. "Please give your mother my best."

Valerie O. Patterson
Birdcage

VALERIE O. PATTERSON is the author of teen novel *The Other Side of Blue*, published by Clarion/Houghton Mifflin Harcourt (2009). Her latest book for young readers, *Operation Oleander*, was published by Clarion in March 2013. Her article, "Ten Myths about the Writing Life" was published in the November/December 2012 issue of the *Writer*. Valerie has an MFA in children's literature from Hollins University. She is a member of the Society of Children's Book Writers and Illustrators, the Children's Literature Association, and the Authors Guild. She lives in Virginia.

I touch the glass table, and the sensors blink ready. The computer says "good morning" and loads my messages. I don't even have to request them, though it recognizes my voice. It knows the shape of my fingers, the whorls on my skin, even the tiny bump on the middle finger of my right hand from where I used to practice the art of writing with graphite. Unlike me, Dad doesn't even have to speak to his machine. It simply knows the echo of his walk into the room, but I have a cheaper, older model. Not the latest thing at all. Which suits me fine.

Most mornings I'm pleasant to the computer and always say "good morning" and "thank you" even though I don't have to. For the assistant is a servant, and we have many of those. Still, the voice reminds me of my grandmother, the one who survived. Late at night, after my parents went to bed, she told stories of walking along high cliffs near the ocean, a place where she could have fallen if she had misstepped, and yet she talked of it with awe. As if risking one's life was something exciting, rather than foolish. Now we can sit in the Thematik chair right in the family room and surround ourselves with adventure from sky to the depths of the sea. No need to go in person. Not anymore. Even if you could.

"You have three messages. Shall we begin?"

I shake my head, and the computer goes silent. Merely a humming presence like the sound of insect wings I heard on Mother's audio guide to Natural Earth. She was researching a sound mix for an upcoming Wildlife Society gala. Mother is a great admirer of the anachronistic, she says. I just like the sounds, the richness, the unpredictability of birdcall, like the recording of a loon across an ancient lake.

Closing my eyes, I concentrate. When I open them I can predict what will appear. Scenes of pink iced cupcakes, which were once baked in paper liners. For a moment the room smells like warm butter and vanilla sugar.

In the past they allowed Teflon coating, which, when heated to cook with, reportedly poisoned pet finches—at a time when people could keep small birds in cages. Now the only birds that may be kept are Fabricates, which sing whenever you're in the room with them. When we go on vacation, we can reprogram them to wake up a few hours before we return. Teens no longer have pet sitting jobs to earn allowances.

Allowances are quaint. That's the word for anything old and outdated. Handheld mobile devices are quaint. Televisions are quaint. Even the word "quaint" is quaint.

The computer waits.

"Transmit," I say.

The first message is from my tutor. Mr. Euginides. Regardless of the subject, he's always my tutor. He doesn't really exist, other than he is a computer amalgamation, programmed by other people who all become Mr. Euginides. Because, Mother says, stability in learning is important. Routine and discipline and no distractions.

"Miri, today we will be learning about binding proteins." He doesn't make a joke about odors.

Again.

Models of binding proteins appear in front of me, their tangles a puzzle to sort. I have the most basic models down by now. I understand the power of carrier proteins called lipcalins. In the old days, musk and amber were natural derivatives, indispensable to perfumes. Not anymore. Mr. Euginides claims only a small sampling of real extracts even exists.

"I'll be back." I think about food, a snack, as I leave. That and a cup of something warm to drink. Mint tea like my grandmother used to make. Mint greets my nose in the hallway. But it's the wrong mint, not spearmint. It was spearmint she served? Fresh as spring and tender against my teeth?

Instead this is peppermint. It has a bite to it, sharp as metal edges. It's intermixed with the scent of cocoa, bittersweet.

I frown.

Instead of the kitchen, I stop by my parents' room even though they're not home. The décor is what my mother likes. Brightly colored rugs cover the floor. So real they have a woven texture. The walls glow like warm mud. Fabricates huddle in daubed nests and warble when I enter.

In the corner my mother keeps a small chest. It's real wood. Ancient and dotted with small drawers and ceramic pulls. The corner one requires a sharp tug before it loosens and slides out. Inside reside a few tokens that belonged to my grandmother. An ivory comb—unlawful except my mother has a certificate for it. And, then, my hands close on what I came for, a brass garden stake. From a time gardens used soil and sunlight. I run my fingers across the raised lettering. S P E A R M I N T.

I knew I was right.

I place the stake back in its drawer.

"Ariel?" I call for my sister. But no answer.

Ariel's door is closed but she never enables the lock. As soon as I step inside, I see her, dancing en pointe in the center of the floor. She's wearing a flimsy sparkly shift but in the walls all I see reflected—and all she will be able to see if she looks around her—is herself in pink gauze, a many-layered netted tutu. Her hair smoothed down over her head, ending in a ribboned braid at the back of her neck.

All around the room the walls have disappeared, and Ariel dances on a stage. For dozens of rows, stretching for hundreds of meters, sits an audience of admirers. If I look to the right I can even see backstage into an ancient theater, where red velvet curtains hang from the ceiling. Dust motes swirl in the air above her posed hands, graceful as a water sculpture. My presence doesn't even send a ripple into the scenery, that's how strongly my sister concentrates. I've never had her ability to focus. The moment someone enters my room or my consciousness, my scene dissolves like so much shattered dishware.

Ariel's to be a dancer. She used to like astronomy too. But there's no sign of the models of galaxies that used to project in her room. I run my finger along the wall. Before, the far sun's glow made me squint. Not even the hint of a shadow of the planetary systems remains.

When did Ariel give up astronomy?

When I step out of Ariel's room the draw of cocoa won't be ignored, and I accept the steaming cup from Cook in the kitchen. Even bittersweet cocoa with peppermint.

But I know it was spearmint my grandmother grew and brewed.

Back in my room, I return to the computer. I expect to see the covers of books—that's my mother's doing, her love of the anachronistic. The touch and feel of real books like they have in the Museum of Knowledge where she took me once a week this year until we had used up our allotted annual entrances. Cloth and paper and ink, that's what books are made of, and their scents make me dizzy.

Mother owned a book of Shakespeare poems, but she donated it to the Museum. "Something for generations in the future to see, to touch." Only the Museum doesn't let anyone touch it. The cracked leather binding isn't like the shells we use today, that animate in your hands. When crystals materialize in front of you and you can peel back the layers of a castle wall and see inside to how a castle really worked, down to the brick ovens with loaves of rounded bread baking during a raging battle, the smell of powder and bread and fear all mixed together.

No, the thought of old paper makes me sneeze and the Times New Roman script forces me to sit still and ponder the meaning. To imagine the sorrow of dust storms in the desert, without benefit of sound effects or olfactory cues.

"Miranda." When the computer uses my full name—and not Miri—it's being serious, the way my parents might be, or Mr. Euginides when I've gotten sloppy with my studies.

I think hard about words on pages of paper, and then I think about spearmint. But the assistant is stubborn. Swirls of sums splash on the screen instead, indicating I'm behind in math again. Even along the edges of the screen where the ads fill in for all the things I have wanted and didn't know I wanted, I see no book jackets. There are just ads for new mindware, the latest, the greatest. Requiring less energy—*it exceeds the government's standards for energy efficiency*—and less concentration. *Go further faster.*

On my computer tiny flashing ads focus on scents, labs, and clean rooms. They highlight employees, all female and gifted in the senses, testing products for accuracy, for sales appeal. Dad says my nose is better than twenty sensors. Last year I detected the fire in the sublevel when no one else did. Not even the security sensor sounded the alarm until we already were moving down the hall and into emergency chutes.

As a chemist I'll create new scents, or reinvent ones that have been lost. Scents like paper, ink. And spearmint.

The computer warbles. It knows my mind is not concentrating on proteins. It detects distraction.

"Go away," I tell the assistant without saying "please." The computer asks me more than twice if I'm sure I wish to disengage. I have two more messages.

I fold my arms, and my body tenses for a fight of wills. Finally, the computer seems to sigh, and the screen goes dark.

Around me, the whole house is quiet except for a low beating sound of wings from hundreds of small birds.

Eena Ruffini

Pregnant

EENA RUFFINI is a journalist and writer living in Adams Morgan. She writes fact, fiction, and the occasional socially mandated thank you card.

*I*t is a Wednesday afternoon, and Lilly is staring at an egg timer. God will forgive you for many things, Lilly's mother had once told her, but being a dirty pregnant whore is not one of them.

Make sure you are on the pill, she said.

Make sure you take precautions.

It seemed of little consequence that the very same dogma that forbade fucking before the sacrament of place cards and poorly plated chicken also prohibited the very prophylactics that her mother now endorsed. But avoiding hypocrisy was never high on her list of priorities.

For Mrs. Nelson Baker, née Larissa DeMauro, a pregnant unmarried daughter—no matter what her age, no matter in what age—was simply unacceptable.

God's forgiveness was easier achieved than the country club's.

She hadn't dressed for the drugstore. Instead, Lilly rolled topless out of stale, unwashed sheets, reached to the pillow beside her, and pulled David's ratty Dartmouth T-shirt over her black, boy-short panties. She snatched a plastic bag off the top of the BoConcept, espresso-stained, six-drawer dresser, where it had laid in state since the wake.

> Personal Effects: David A. Payton IV
> Cause of Death: Accidental/MVA

Popping open the seal, she took hold of a worn brown wallet. Inside, she knew David was smiling. Beneath the calfskin leather and the gold embossed letters, she knew David was seated in front of a benign blue backdrop, dressed in his usual white oxford, grinning from ear to ear. Lilly knew, but she didn't look.

The DMV had caused her enough pain in life.

It could not have her tears.

Keeping the billfold closed, she strategically slid a credit card out the top. The remaining objects looked up at her expectantly. A wallet in need of a pocket. Keys in need of a lock. A phone in need of a charge. A black flip notebook and his father's Montblanc pen.

"What is to become of us?" they asked from behind their flexible plastic shield.

Lilly refused to answer.

She was not, after all, prepared to entertain the inquiries of inanimate objects, no matter how persistently they petitioned. She resealed the bag and chucked the whole lot into the tangled abyss of overflowing laundry.

Two minutes and twenty-nine seconds remain on the clock.

Kicking her way through the mess, Lilly headed toward the hall. At the threshold to the bedroom, Kate Spade cups, bowls, plates, and chargers sat in neat piles, rapidly accruing mold.

Lilly wasn't really eating during the day anymore.

After midnight, when the apartment grew so quiet that even the constant traffic below couldn't drown out the silence, calories kept her company. Boxes of cereal with soy milk. Frozen appetizers pulled from the deep freeze. Apples with gooey jars of organic peanut butter. Blocks of imported cheese. An entire German chocolate cake.

The twelve place settings her mother insisted she purchase always seemed an unnecessary extravagance. They had few guests and even fewer friends. But with each clean dish pulled from the golden brown cedar cabinet, with each sparking utensil plucked from the handleless, self-closing drawers, Lilly found herself increasingly grateful. Volume was the only thing protecting her from paper plates.

The housekeeper had been banned from the building.

Lilly didn't do sympathy, and she most assuredly would not accept it in physical form when offered by a quasi-maternal figure reeking of goulash and bleach.

The woman tried to hug her and Lilly fired her on the spot.

But what was done was done, she told herself. No use crying over spilled milk, or the lack of well-trained professionals to clean up after it.

Guilt is not a flattering emotion.

In the significant open living space of their (now her) soft-loft luxury condo, the unwelcome material of a new day unraveled in three extra-wide bolts.

The floor-to-ceiling windows had been one of the apartment's biggest selling points. Now, Lilly wished they were cemented shut.

As the light draped across granite countertops and stainless appliances, lead crystal and Austrian chandeliers, Kensington leather sofas and flat-woven rugs, Lilly's focus fell on the dining set.

It had taken her months to choose those chairs.

She had researched. Hunted. Obsessed.

Those chairs, those black bentwood chairs with flax linen upholstered seats. Those six-hundred-and-ninety-nine-dollar-apiece, more colors available, no assembly required, delivery-included chairs would be the last set she and David would ever need to buy.

They had never been married, but they had been happy.

And they reveled in the glory of their chairs.

One minute, thirty-five seconds to go.

At Rite Aid, Lilly could feel the stares. Knee-high, hunter green rain-boots do not go well with underwear and eighty-degree sun.

A chubby elementary schooler pointed down the aisle and snickered. The glare she threw him included glass shards and hypodermic needles.

Procreation, she told herself, is highly overrated.

In fact, Lilly wondered how many of the shoppers in the family planning section had really *planned* to be there. She always assumed that most pregnancy tests were purchased by ruined teens from fundamentalist school districts in corn-growing square states. It never even occurred to her that some people welcome that little pink plus.

Not that plus or minus were the only options anymore.

As Lilly scanned the shelves, she marveled at the sheer magnitude of the array. Lines, signs, and LED. Floral, clinical, or minimalist design.

Mothers with babies and cartoons of cute-but-possibly-knocked-up girls on the go. Fast results. Scented strip. Easy grip.

It seemed a strange market in which to seek brand recognition.

Unwanted pregnancy, brought to you by Nabisco.

Personal ruination, new from Arm & Hammer.

They certainly weren't the type of logo you'd want to see embroidered on a hat or a company softball jersey.

The Elevated pH Panthers.

The Quick Response Raptors.

The Crimson Tide.

And the names. The names were the worst. Clearly chosen by boardrooms of men who thought these catchphrases would appeal to every iteration of whore.

"Answers." "Clear Blue Easy." "Choice."

What Lilly really wanted were "Easy Answers," or a "Clear Choice." Instead of "EPT" how about "OMG." "First Response" should be renamed "Last Resort."

She should have just killed a rabbit. It would have made less of a mess.

One minute and eighteen seconds left on the clock.

Lilly finishes wiping up the travertine floor of their (now her) en suite bathroom. She wraps the test tightly in toilet paper and sets it aside.

Lilly takes a long hard drink.

The vodka is stupid and a tad cliché, but Lilly doesn't care.

This baby, if there is one, is going to be screwed up anyway.

She watches as the dial winds down on her Williams-Sonoma Aluminum Kitchen Timer, $69.95, catalogue only, wipe clean with damp cloth.

It's been two weeks.

Blame it on poor nutrition. Blame it on stress. Anything but pregnancy. Pregnancy is impossible. Pregnancy is ridiculous. Pregnancy is dumb.

Surely by now all David's sperm are as dead as his rotting corpse.

Fifty-eight seconds to go.

Lilly briefly considers calling her mother.

But Mrs. Baker never liked David. Despite the fact that he was well-moneyed and handsome and successful. Despite the fact that he was kind, and thoughtful, David's significant assets were wiped out the moment he proposed moving in instead of marriage.

No need to be predictable, he told her. No need to rush.

Time, he said, was on their side. So were the interest rates.

So instead of a priest, they hired a Realtor. And instead of a chapel, they went to the bank. Dressed in their workday best, the two stood before the alter of Western Mutual Trust and lovingly recited their credit scores. The broker read aloud from the annals of mutual property law, after which the happy couple vowed loyalty, fidelity, and prompt monthly payments.

No one threw rice, but they did get to keep the pen.

Lilly thought her mother had gotten over it. She thought they had come to a pleasant, if rather persistent, detente. But when Mrs. Baker couldn't be bothered to pull herself off a St. Bart's beach to fly back for her daughter's nonhusband's funeral, Lilly realized that her highly mortgaged chickens had finally come home to roost.

Karma was a bitch. And so, it seemed, was her mother.

"Please. I don't know what I'm supposed to do," Lilly sobbed into her cell.

"That never stopped you before," her mother said, yelling a drink order at some unfortunate island underling.

And with that, the line went dead.

Thirty seconds to go.

Lilly always assumed that kids would happen eventually. Like paying bills, owning a sheath dress, or vomiting after high-carb meals, children are just something respectable women are expected to do.

That's why Prada makes maternity wear. That's why Louis Vuitton sells diaper bags. That's why BMW sells ergonomically advanced strollers.

Spawn are as much a status symbol as anything else.

More than anything else, that was the reason David had finally decided they should have them.

A few weeks before the accident, he informed her that it was time to start a family. He didn't have a ring. He didn't have a plan, but he knew what he wanted, and Lilly knew, as always, she would oblige.

"We'll get married within the year," he told her. "And if we get pregnant before then, so be it."

He then proceeded to throw out all her pills.

The buzzer sounds.

Lilly is so startled, she drops the test on the floor.

She takes a pregnant—though hopefully not—pause.

Maybe a child would be good for her, she thinks. It could be just the things she needs—giving purpose to her aimless, selfish life.

But raising a child isn't supposed to be about benefit for the adult.

When done correctly, child-rearing is an all-consuming, all-encompassing, soul-crushing endeavor. A marathon that only ends when you're dead.

Lilly is not an endurance athlete.

She gets overwhelmed babysitting her neighbor's mail.

Sure, she could go the other way. She could underpay a Guatemalan immigrant to rear her progeny. She could ship the thing off to boarding school the minute it hit third grade and never visit, even on holidays, and send the gardener to fill her reserved seat during graduations.

But not everyone followed her mother's pattern of parenting.

For Mrs. Nelson Baker, née Larissa DeMauro, the minute they cut the cord the kid was someone else's problem: The nurse, the nanny, the headmaster, the husband.

Lilly knows she could never treat a child like that.

Maybe she should just get rid of it.

Maybe she should just nip this thing in the bud.

But there was a problem. This is no accidental bud. It wasn't a drunken one-night stand. It was David. And if she is "with child," as bible-thumping, pro-life maniacs would say, then this is the only piece of him left. She couldn't end his life. She couldn't kill him twice. That just seems cruel.

Lilly reaches once more for the friend she's found in vodka.

She hopes the kick will give focus. Give courage. Help her choose.

Normally she wouldn't have to do this. Normally, someone would tell her what to do. That had always been one of David's most attractive qualities: he made the decisions for them both.

Unsure which bird is to blame for her nausea, the circling stork or Grey Goose, Lilly hangs her head between her knees.

Breathe. Just breathe, she tells herself.

Sunshine in, infanticidal tendencies out.

Lifting her arms ever so slowly, Lilly grabs the edges of the double-basin sink and pulls herself up. Staring down her disheveled double in the floating-mount mirror, Lilly reaches blindly for the test.

If she believed in anything, she would pray. If she trusted anyone, she would call. She tries to uncover the screen, but her hands refuse to move. Fear and uncertainty form a heavy paralytic.

Lilly grasps the wrapped-up test between her fingers. Her hands shake. There is sweat on her brow. She brings the stick to eye level.

"Come on," commands her mirror self.

But Lilly refuses to listen.

She will not, after all, succumb to the demands of a ranting, unwashed lunatic, no matter how insistent she becomes. Lilly plucks several moisture-enhanced tissues from the holder and crumples them around the stick. She then chucks the whole lot into the tangled abyss of the overflowing trash.

Lilly doesn't want to know.

She storms out of the bathroom, out of the apartment, and into the blissful ignorance of the world beyond.

Meanwhile, beneath the layers of Puffs Plus and two-ply Quilted Northern, the twenty-dollar digital display glows green with a single word.

Adrienne Benson Scherger

Juju

ADRIENNE BENSON SCHERGER spent much of her childhood in sub-Saharan Africa. Since then, she's worked to turn memories of that life into text. Her fiction and essays have appeared or are upcoming in the *Washington Post*, the *Huffington Post*, *Brain, Child*, and several anthologies. A native of Washington, D.C., she continues to live and work here. Her day job is collecting and preserving clients' life stories through her company, Open Book Personal Histories. In the leftover space she finds during the day, she writes and writes. Her work-in-progress is a novel in stories set in Kenya.

O n stormy days the sea rolled close enough to the garden wall for the waves to lick the mortar between the bricks, and for the salty spray to be felt from our balcony. But April 12, 1980, was a still, hot day. The beach was flat and white, and the waves were small. The centipedes in the garden curled up under the bird of paradise to nap, and when a neighbor's driver caught a mamba under a bush by the gate I saw him slam his machete down and laugh as the emerald creature writhed, headless, in the dirt. I was ten, and President Tolbert was shot in his sleep just before dawn and dismembered by his own army. When the static on the speakers cleared and the radio announced the *coup d'état* in shouts and chants, the army had already declared victory. *"In the cause of the people,"* the voices on the radio shouted from our kitchen, *"the revolution continues."* I was hidden up in the breadnut tree, cool between leaves that looked like hands, and watching ants trail along the branches when our neighbor's maid and Mohammad, our houseman, met to share a cigarette in the shade the tree threw below me. I heard them whisper the rumor to each other that Tolbert had been killed because he didn't have his juju stick, his protection, with him as he slept.

❧

LIBERIA SITS ON THE CURVE of West Africa's spine. It juts out where the Atlantic currents pick up speed and strength as they race away from the calmer shores of the southwest African nations of Angola and Namibia, and rush around the corners of Cameroon and make their way, curling and dangerous, all the way to America.

Pushing opposite to those ocean currents on a night flight from Washington, D.C., we'd moved from America to Monrovia, Liberia, the year before. Liberia was bright, flat sun that pushed down on everything below it, sun that burned in an instant, sun that made me light headed, and chilled me to the bone if I sat in it too long. Liberia was sweat that rolled down my back, tacked my shirt to my skin, filled up my ears, and dripped into my eyes. Liberia was tropical storms that would suddenly bunch up the sky in huge, black clouds to crumple what had been a flat hot day into a driving rain, which, just as suddenly, would stop. In the rainy season the storms came daily and the earth never dried out, but grew mossy and slick and smelled rotten. There was gray-green mold on all the books in the bookshelf, and bread left out lasted less than a day. Liberia was the constant taste of salty ocean air from the surf that roiled on the sand just on the other side of our garden wall, the incessant drone of the air conditioner, and the constant motion of living things: mold, centipedes, beetles, and plants that grew up thick and green and so fast I could almost see them moving, fed by the sun and rain. Liberia was mystery, too. It was black magic and juju and things that sounded like they could never be true, but which were. Things as true as a finger on a trigger. Things as true as blood.

ↄ

MY PARENTS ROTATED ACROSS AFRICA with my father's job. Two years here, three there, never staying long. Liberia, to them, was just another post. But my mother was an expert in the history of sacred African carvings, and when my father's job brought us to Liberia, she'd done a flurry of research and published a paper called, "Dan Tribal Initiations: Masks and Manhood in the Poro Society."

At dinner parties she'd fill our table with grown-ups drinking wine and eating expensive imported cheeses she kept hidden in the back of the fridge. I could crack my bedroom door open and hear her as she held court, regaling the guests with stories of the Leopard People and the masks they used to frighten other tribes, and the masks she wanted to see, and the ones she was desperate to buy.

The roving bands of folk art sellers who, for reasons we never knew, were called "the Charlies," were instantly my mother's favorite pastime. In her studies she'd seen examples of most of what they bought: carvings and masks, beads, and roughly hewn drums. The Charlies bought their goods cheaply from villages upcountry, packed them up in market bags, and went door to door, mostly to the homes of foreigners, spreading out the wares for profit. The Charlies were Africa. They brought the whole vast continent and all its dark secrets out of the jungles and right up to our back door. My mother never talked to me about her research, so the things in the Charlies's bags were new to me. They spread their newest acquisitions immediately at my mother's feet and then dug through their bags to find forgotten treasures. They allowed my mother to handle everything, and she took her time sorting through the carvings, the drums, the fertility dolls, the village jewelry, and her favorites, the masks that had been used by village witch doctors to cure ills or throw curses. If the Charlies were local, they would speak in singsong Liberian English, a Creole dialect that made English words incomprehensible. If they had made their way to our back steps from Guinea, or Senegal, or sometimes from Mali or Upper Volta, they would speak to my mother in smoky, palm-butter-infused French.

"I'm looking for a passport mask," my mother said one night, and the Charlies dug through their bags to draw out the small carvings, dark and delicate and as compact as shells. "What are they for?" I asked.

My mother laughed wryly. "Ugh! My paper is published; I should just dig up a copy for you." The Charlie sitting nearest me turned and said, "The juju can come to you wh'n you are sleeping." He was tall and had long hands. One held a cigarette that he drew on, tipping his head back to spout white smoke into the darkness above our heads. It hung there like a ghost. He continued, "If you can see the forest spirit, Gle, wh'n you are dreaming, you can tell the carver how that Gle was looking, and he will carve it for you like making a photo. Juju can come wh'n you sleeping. When you dream it can come." I looked at the masks my mother held; they were hardly bigger than her palm. One was a woman's face, topped with intricately carved braided hair; the other was a man's, with a pattern of tribal cuts fanned out across his wooden forehead. I wondered which she would buy.

"I have a sewing machine to trade for beads," my mother mentioned, and the Charlies dug deep into the bags at their feet and drew out parcels wrapped in soft paper or woody burlap and suddenly, draped across my mother's lap, lay strands of old fibrous raffia, strung with scores of trade beads with surfaces worn smooth and blurry. Mostly the Charlies ignored my eager hands, but one night one of them gave something to me as well, murmuring, "Small Missy, just take a look." He pressed a necklace made of smooth, brown seeds into my palm, then a carved wooden doll a girl my age would have carried, and dressed, and named. "It's nice, isn't it?" I ran my finger over the small wooden face, and felt the strands of fabric hair. "Oh," my mother said, hardly glancing up, "that's not even old. It's nothing but a village Barbie." She laughed at her joke.

My mother loved the classic blue trade beads that were made in Italy in the fifteenth century and brought to Africa on European ships. The beads were made by fusing together different colors of glass, and were striped, candylike. The Charlies mostly offered blue beads, but every so often one of the men dug deep into his bag and told my mother he had something special this time. He would unwrap a soft packet of carefully folded paper and bring out a few of the grass green ones. "Very rare," he'd say, "very expensive."

Village chiefs all across West Africa prized the trade beads, and strands of them accompanied the chief to his grave. As the chief's body dissolved back into the earth, as his clothes and bones and hair sifted into soil, the glass beads rose to the ground's dusty surface and were stumbled upon and scooped up. I thought of myself like those beads, carried to Africa from a home I could hardly remember, and lodged here for a time. The difference was the beads found a way to stay; they embedded themselves here, hibernated under the earth until they were born up again, African. I was plucked up by my nomadic parents and carried off again and again—native to nowhere.

၏

MY MOTHER WAS SHREWD, AND careful never to buy something from the Charlies that she didn't really want. She'd run her fingers along the edges of a mask, looking for fresh knife marks that would indicate the piece wasn't really old. She'd scrape her fingernail gently across the wood to see if dirt might loosen and prove a new carving had been purposely buried to age it. "Museum quality!" she'd announce when she found a piece she loved. Those nights when I sat next to her, watching her work, I felt invisible. Like the audience to the images on a movie screen: I could see her, but she was in another world from me. Apart. As exotic and distant as the carvings she held.

My mother went straight for the dark heart. She didn't turn away when the Charlies mentioned that one wooden figure had been placed under a dead body to help usher the man's spirit to a better place. It didn't faze her when they told her the mask she was holding had been steeped in the blood of a sacrificial goat, and that's what gave it its odd, dark patina. I was different from my mother in this way: I liked the new things better. The freshly carved pieces that seemed unfettered by a history of use, those were the ones that I would have chosen. I was afraid of the darkness.

၏

THERE WERE TALES OF UPCOUNTRY tribes that lived by the rules of black magic and curses. There were stories of how drummers could talk to each other over miles of air, through miles of thick forest, with the drums they pounded. There were the masked stilt walkers who danced in the streets and stopped passersby to ask for money. If you didn't give them what they were looking for, they would use their juju against you. In Liberia it was impossible not to believe these stories. It was impossible not to believe in magic. I felt the juju would hurt me. Once, a Liberian friend came over to play and when the stilt dancers came down the street where we were jumping rope, she squeezed my hand tightly in hers, pulling me with her as she ran. She leapt behind a parked car and hunkered down, her breath ragged and heavy from running, "Stan dah and don show me to dem!"

"What about me?" I shouted. I was panicked at how close the stilt walkers were. I could here the thumps of their worn wooden stilts on the road behind me, I could hear them calling out, and I could hear the intake of their breath and their clapping hands. "Don' fuss, n' mind ya!" my friend hissed, "they juju only works on us, Liberians, na on you." She crouched down lower and lower until she was almost under the wheel of the car. I stood there sweating and trying not to look up as the stilt walkers marched past me, clapping and singing and looking for people to get money from. They didn't see me at all.

∾

WHEN THE CHARLIES BROUGHT OUT the old masks, I tried to stop myself from looking at them. They terrified me. I hated to see my mother touching them, hated her turning them over and over in her hands. I thought the evil could leech into her skin, be absorbed right into her cells. "Mom, don't!" I'd beg when she reached out to take the old masks, but she would just tease me in French and the foreign Charlies would laugh. "Don't be silly!" she'd scold. Then she'd turn and finger the sticky wood, raise the face to her own and peer at me out of the carved empty eyes.

One night as I sat in the dark next to my mother, I heard her whistle low, through her teeth, and whisper, "Oh, that's a fantastic piece!" I looked at what she was reaching for and I shut my eyes tightly, but the mask couldn't be unseen. Two roughly carved eyeholes pierced a piece of dusky, gray wood. The nose was wide and straight, and the forehead had split slightly, so that a scar ran down the hard, angry-looking brow. The crack had been mended with bits of wire that gave the effect of crude stitches. Under the nose was the slash of a mouth; stiffly open as if the wooden face were trying to scream, and embedded in the mouth were six or seven yellowed, cracked teeth. *"C'est les vrai, vrai dents des gents, quoi,"* one of the Charlies murmured proudly. I noticed a local Charlie edging away from the wooden face, refusing to look in its direction. "It's a Dan mask," he whispered to me in a voice that made me shiver, "When the witch doctor must put on a curse." My mother didn't see him edging away from the mask. She didn't put it on and tease him with it, or tell him he shouldn't believe what he did.

I hated the mask. I hated my mother for buying it. I wondered how it was that she could look at the masks and the carvings the Charlies brought to her and say exactly when they were carved and by whom, and even why. She could spin stories of upcountry ceremonies that made her friends shiver at our dinner table with glee and revulsion. But when she looked at me, she didn't know what she saw. She hadn't studied me. She couldn't tell me who I was, or why, or where I belonged.

ↄ

THE CHARLIES STOPPED COMING IN the wake of the Tolbert murder and the coup. The army enforced a strict curfew—dusk to dawn, nobody was to be outside on penalty of death. From our balcony overlooking the beach, we watched soldiers in their camouflage pants and torn T-shirts sleeping in the sand. Even during the day, my mother wouldn't let me go down to the beach. "It's not that they want to hurt Americans," she assured me. "This is a local thing, it's not ours. But they're drunk, and armed, and not to be trusted." She wanted this to make me feel better, safer. She smiled when she said it, even held my hand. But it made me feel foreign to this place, an interloper—as odd and displaced as a broken bead on the forest floor.

ↄ

THE MORNING AFTER MY MOTHER bought the mask, my father dutifully installed a hook in the wall in the space between the bathroom and the guest room, and my mother stepped back to make sure it was centered and straight. At night, when I got up to use the bathroom, I edged past it with my eyes closed. During the day I ran past it as fast as I could. I didn't want the hollow eyes to follow me; I didn't want to see the broken teeth. At night I insisted on keeping the hallway light on while I drifted off to sleep. I thought about the mask constantly. I wondered if the teeth had been plucked from a dead person or, worse, if they'd been broken out of someone alive, someone whose mouth would have filled with blood and empty spaces.

ↄ

A WEEK AFTER THE COUP, thirteen ministers and cabinet members of the old ruling party were sentenced. The accusations were shouted on the radio, and the announcer's gleeful voice said, *"Justice will be served."* In the predawn darkness the next morning, the shouts of soldiers woke me up. I tiptoed to my bedroom window and peeked out. By the slashing light of flashlights the soldiers waved, I saw a line of men unloaded from the back of a truck. I saw them led, single file, over the gray sand by a sinewy-armed man who wore his mirrored sunglasses even though the sky was dark, and who waved a heavy-looking gun as he shouted at them to be quiet, to kneel where he pointed.

๛

THE SUN ROSE AND THE telephone rang and rang, waking my parents and sending my father to the floor next to his desk—away from the window—where he whispered into the telephone, compared notes with the U.S. Marines at the embassy, and tried to make contact with all the American members of his staff to ensure they were safe. Our neighbor, the consular officer, had left earlier that week for a conference in Abidjan, leaving his very pregnant wife at home, hysterical with fear. My mother slipped next door to help calm her down, and implored me, before she left, to stay in the windowless hallway. She didn't want me looking out at the beach, or sitting prone on the balcony. But the mask was in the hallway, too. The longer I sat in the dim light with my mother's mask staring down at me, the more frightened I got. The more I wished my mother had never bought it.

The men still knelt in the white sand that glistened like ice under the high, hot sun. The ocean had shifted from deep black to jade green. I didn't know when I snuck out here to escape the mask and the dim hallway that I would see the thirteen men still waiting, hunkered down and sweating in the sand.

I crept out past the prickly wicker chaise my mother loved and I slid to the floor next to the rustling leaves of the potted palm. I didn't know what I was watching. I just sat there, enjoying the feel of the sun on my face and the fresh air.

☙

THIRTEEN THICK TREE BRANCHES WERE whittled into posts and dragged onto the beach and set upright. The thirteen waiting men were made to peel off their shirts, and were tied with green plastic rope to the posts. I wasn't scared because it all seemed so calm. None of the men tried to escape, none of them screamed or begged for mercy. They simply stood, their hands tied behind them. They seemed tired, even bored. Sweat ran off the round, brown stomach of one, the glasses slid down the nose of another. I was shocked by the sudden snap of the bullets. They sounded distant to me, sliding high above the noise of the tide coming in. It was over so quickly. The bodies began slumping, one by one, crumpled in upon themselves in puddles of blood that spread out in the sand then were absorbed into it. I couldn't breathe, I couldn't move. I sat there in the sun, my heart shattering in my throat. My legs shook and my breath was short and ineffective. I felt the new sensation of fear physically. It forced its way inside me, it coursed thickly through my blood; I felt it curling around my bones like that writhing, headless snake.

☙

IT WAS MOHAMMAD, THE HOUSEMAN, who found me. Mohammad who put his arm around me and helped my shaking legs find their way back inside to that dim hall. Mohammad who brought me a blanket and a glass of water, and Mohammad who held my secret closely tucked away so that it never saw light. When my mother came back from the neighbor's house she found me curled like a snail on the floor, eyes shut tightly. I felt her crouching next to me. I heard her breathing as she tiptoed away. I wished that she'd sit next to me and stay, that she'd smooth back the sweaty hair from my cheeks.

That night, we ate a cold dinner of leftovers at our dining room table. My mother lit candles. Throughout the meal, fear coiled in my belly. I started at every loud sound; I avoided making too much noise. I put my silverware down carefully; I made sure my voice was low. I listened to my parents talking with one part of myself, and with the other part I listened to the silence beyond our walls, beyond our locked gate, beyond the sounds of surf on the beach, out to where the sun was sinking into the horizon in a puddle of disappearing light, and the dark was rolling in.

∽

IN THE FOLLOWING WEEKS THE government stabilized, the curfew lifted, and the Charlies returned. They came up the steps and waited. Mohammad whispered, as he always had, "Madam, they are here." I didn't join my mother on the landing anymore. I ignored the Charlies. I shut myself in my bedroom, pretending to do math worksheets, plugging my ears and remembering how to breathe when I thought I heard the sound of bullets whizzing through the air on the beach. Before I drifted off to sleep at night, I didn't think about the mask anymore. Instead I wondered about that girl who watched silently through the railings as those men in their droopy pants, with their glistening skin and bewildered eyes, were shot.

I didn't go to the beach anymore either. On clear Saturdays, my mother would try to tempt me with the suggestion of ocean swimming, picnics on the sand, kite flying. I never agreed. She didn't know what I knew: that the ocean had licked the blood from the shoreline and it swirled in the water now; there were bullets; there were beads of flesh rotting under the sand.

∽

THE YEAR I TURNED SIXTEEN my father retired and we flew away from Africa for good. We'd left Liberia long behind by then, and had rotated through other countries where I'd learned to push things away. When we returned to America, I knew how to smile when people told me I was lucky. I learned to laugh when people asked if I'd been afraid to live in Africa, if I'd been worried about getting malaria, or typhoid, or parasites. I had carved myself a brave face by then.

When our sea freight was unpacked in our new American house, the last things we found were the old boxes of art the Charlies had sold to my mother. Out spilled the dusky mud cloths, the collection of turtle-shaped passport masks, and the stout wooden carvings. They all looked so strange in the new, cool American light. The stone mantle dwarfed the

Baule pieces, and the passport masks—the dream juju—looked wan and impotent above the crisp, self-important wainscoting. The mask I'd once been afraid of looked like nothing more than old carved wood. Expectant and silent as a seed.

ↄ

BUT ONE NIGHT, NOT LONG after we'd returned, I dreamed I heard the Charlies talking. I could hear their low voices through the humid darkness as they came to sit at my feet, describing the things they brought, laying it all out for me. I could hear the ocean nearby, the surf cringing and spitting on the dark, bloodless sand. I saw plants that grew visibly thicker and more greener as I watched them, growing and climbing and curling like emerald snakes up over the stone walls of our garden and thickening into a forest I couldn't see through, a forest where beads of blue glass pushed constantly out of the dirt under my feet. And out there, somewhere out in the breathing darkness of that inky forest, the sound of the surf didn't mask the sound of guns, but instead gave way to the sound of drums, pounding and pounding away, calling out like a language, like a message, like a man staked in the sand with nothing but blood and spaces where his teeth should have been, hollow eyed, calling to me through the edges of my sleep, *You were here, You were here, You were here.*

Anne Sheldon

Garden Apartments of the Brave

ANNE SHELDON lives in Silver Spring, Maryland, with her black cat and four generations of books. Her work has appeared in *The Dark Horse, Poet Lore, Antietam Review*, and other small magazines. Her latest book, *The Bone Spindle*, from Aqueduct Press in 2011, celebrates the mythic women of the fiber arts: "Penelope…Arachne…the Fates…Anne Sheldon's heroines have lowered eyes and seditious smiles."

*M*argaret had been on her balcony, enjoying the unseasonably warm October weather with a glass of wine and an old rebound library book. Often she felt as if she had been put down in the world of modern traffic and loud music by some cosmic mistake. The world of Jeremiah Roland was as comfortable to her as an old shoe, though rather more hazardous.

> October 14. Redoubt number ten stands within twenty feet
> of the River York. Finally, to bring the matter of American
> Independence to Conclusion, it must be Stormed. The color
> of the Oak leaf here is not to be compared with that of old
> New England but it is Soothing to the Spirit. —*Diaries of a
> Connecticut Schoolmaster*, Jeremiah Roland, 1817, p. 49

Then she looked up from the yellowish page and saw a man with a gun—well, a musket, really, probably a harmless antique—but, dressed in the Continental uniform one saw so often on re-enactors here in Yorktown, he seemed to be casing her neighbors' apartments.

Though a librarian, she was accustomed to being mistaken, to finding that she had misread instructions or situations, or heard words that had not actually been spoken. But here was a man with a gun—she ought to do something. She didn't want to—she had a program to plan, on the Battle of Yorktown, for a roomful of Girl Scouts on the anniversary, and the nineteenth was only a few days away. The branch manager had directed her to discuss the siege, etc., without any mention of violence. Patriotism was a fine thing, of course, but nobody liked violence.

This seemed unreasonable. She wasn't likely to glorify bloodshed. She was a quiet soul who could hardly bear to watch professional sports on TV and, rather than step on a spider she found indoors, would catch it in a juice glass, clap a paperback over the top, and run out to the balcony to let it go.

So, in some ways, it had been a relief when Buck moved out, taking with him his wide-screen TV and racks of Super Bowl tapes. She missed his blue eyes and his laugh and the way he snuggled after sex, but she didn't miss the noise and the clutter and the smashing cars and bodies on the big screen, and she certainly had no wish to involve herself in any form of mayhem. But this man—in a blue frock coat and three-cornered hat—was pausing deliberately at each ground-floor window with a gun.

At Patriot Meadows, clusters of apartments surrounded a grassy courtyard—a sort of "village green" in which old one oak tree had been preserved—a point of pride with the developer, and a gesture to the Historical Society, which had objected to the apartments being built so close to Battlefield Park. The gunman stood now in front of a window from which the blue flicker and vague roar of some sporting event emanated. It being so warm, only a window screen stood between him and the room with the TV. Calmly, he drew the musket up into firing position and paused. His shoulder jerked backwards.

Margaret jumped up, knocking over her glass of wine. She ran back through the apartment to the hallway door and left it standing wide open as she careened down the stairs. What she remembered later, but didn't reflect on as her bare feet slapped against the cold slate stairs, was that she'd heard nothing.

When she pushed open the front door and ran out onto the lawn, he was gone. She stopped, wondering what she would have done if he had been there. Then she walked quickly over to the window through which he had shot the gun.

There was no hole in the screen.

There were no bodies on the floor.

There was no television.

She stood still, thoughtfully biting her thumb, as all her native uncertainty flooded back into her veins. She knew she had drunk less than one glass of wine. Feeling foolish, and wishing that Buck were there—he was never fazed by awkward situations—she tentatively knocked on the window frame.

A middle-aged man, his belly overhanging aquamarine running shorts, came out of another room. He held a huge bowl of popcorn in one hand and a just-opened beer, frothing a little, in the other. It must have happened during a commercial, she thought, or he'd have been in the room.

"Yeah?"

"Excuse me, but an armed man—a re-enactor of some kind, I guess— was just peering in at your window with a gun... I wonder if you're all right?"

He curled his lip with annoyed impatience, and she conceded silently to herself that no one had ever curled their lip at her when Buck shared her apartment.

"No, we're OK—oh my God, the TV! Where's the TV? Cheryl, call the cops! Somebody swiped the TV!"

"Well, actually," Margaret began, but she was talking to herself, for he had already run into the other room and now Cheryl was yelling. "Actually, my best guess is that he didn't steal it, he..." She looked. There was no shattered glass or plastic on the apple green shag carpet. How could he possibly have gotten in and out so quickly with such a large object? "...he, well, killed it... Or beamed it up. Or down."

She stood quietly on the lawn, still feeling foolish, while the frenzy continued inside. Too much frenzy, she thought, for a stolen TV. Even a murdered TV. As long as no one was hurt, she would just as soon go back to her wine and her book, but now they were dialing 911.

The officer, when he came, asked her to describe the suspect. She had been studying the cramped handwriting on his gritty little notepad. Would he be offended if she offered to sharpen his pencil? She looked up.

And there was her musketeer, leaning against the old oak. Unarmed now, but still in colonial dress, he gazed straight at her with a frank, pleasant smile. Perhaps forty-five, he was stocky but energetic looking, with a longish nose and large eyes. His dress, she noticed now, was not that of the famous men in the lithographs of the old book she was reading, nor that of the middle-class re-enactors she saw so often—the blue of his uniform was faded, the white facings were badly frayed, and there was a large dark stain on his waistcoat just below his collarbone, on the left.

A protective feeling made her reluctant to point him out, but she began to describe him, all the while staring at him, even gesturing in his direction. The policeman and the man and his wife followed her gestures, and looked where she was looking, but showed no sign they saw anyone or anything out of the ordinary. Conscious of the pleasant tang of wine still on her tongue, she worked out the different conclusions she could draw: either she was drunk, or she was crazy, or the couple and the policeman were blind; or the soldier in the tricorner hat was invisible—to everyone but herself.

> October 15. We took the Redoubt in a matter of minutes. We lost only 18 Continentals: 1 Sergeant, 16 rank and file, and, I grieve to put down, Captain Whitegrave, who has but lately been my own Schoolmaster. —*Ibid.*, p. 52

The next night, she sat again after dinner on the balcony, drinking a little wine and carefully turning the brittle pages of the old journal. She heard something in the bushes and looked up. He stood farther away this time but again he raised his musket toward the blue flicker of another living room, his shoulder jerked back, and the blue flicker went out.

She jumped up—and stood still.

She stood this way for several seconds, frowning with indecision. If Buck were here, she thought…but he wasn't. She quietly sat back down, took a sip of wine, and reopened the book.

About fifteen minutes later, there was a knock at the door. She opened it to the same policeman and a gnarled old lady in a fuchsia sweatsuit. From time to time, Margaret had seen her walking a little poodle. The fur of its face was always dark and clotted, like a man with yesterday's stew in his beard.

"Another TV's been stolen," said the officer, without raising his eyes from his pad.

"Right smack in the middle of *Desperate Housewives!*" the old woman snarled, peering around the policeman at Margaret's apartment. "One goddamn trip to the icebox, and, whammo! it's gone! What am I supposed to do for the rest of the night? Knit?"

Margaret conceded, silently, that it was impossible to imagine her knitting.

"Same thing happened last night," the cop reminded her, ignoring the senior citizen for the moment. "You said you saw an armed intruder."

"Yes."

"See anyone suspicious tonight?"

Well, he hadn't been suspicious.

"No. I'm sorry…I didn't."

"Aren't you going to search her apartment?" the old woman snapped.

"I don't have a search warrant, ma'am," he commented wearily.

"Please," she said pleasantly, "go right ahead." She would waive her Fourth Amendment rights until she really needed them.

Her neighbor badgered the policeman into every room and every closet. They both seemed to find the absence of any TV at all cause for suspicion, but the policeman left without fining or arresting her.

By then, it was dark outside. Margaret turned off the lights behind her in the living room and took the rest of her wine back out on the balcony. It was immediately what struck you, at night—the blue shimmer from nearly every window, distracting the eye from moon and stars.

Would all their TVs be stolen? If it was some kind of moral crusade, what about families that watched mostly public television? What about cable? Then she saw him again.

In the diffuse light of moon and stars and TVs, he looked more serious—the most serious person she had met or seen in months. But he was dead. He must be dead. Died at the storming of Redoubt Number Ten? Was that a captain's uniform he wore? Captain Whitegrave, who'd given up schoolteaching to fight for independence…and now come back on the anniversary, to shoot televisions?

He smiled his charming smile and bowed, sweeping off his tricorner hat. He might be dead, but he certainly had lovely manners.

He opened his mouth.

"Bread and circuses, miss," she heard in her mind, as if in answer to her unspoken question, and in a sort of antique Boston accent. "Bread and circuses…"

Well, a New England schoolmaster would know about Juvenal and his critique of the rotting Roman Empire. Rome had been a brave young republic once, too…

"Ah. Beer and football. Etcetera," she murmured. He nodded and smiled.

She was amazed how slowly each busy day passed that week, as she waited for evening and the rich quiet minutes sitting with his presence in the darkness.

That is, after the police had come and gone. Each night, up through Saturday, one more TV disappeared, and each night the unfortunate officer was a little more frustrated at his inability to solve the mystery of the disappearing TVs. But the neighbors seemed a bit more respectful of Margaret, and were now, occasionally, talking to each other in the evenings instead of sitting like statues in front of their private circuses. They were mad, for sure, to be the victims of theft, or whatever it was, but it wasn't unpleasant to be at the center of a mystery.

> October 19. Among us Continentals drawn up to receive the British Surrender, there was all manner of Raggle-Taggle Dress…but all of us are Conquerors and I believed our fallen comrades to be at Peace this day. —*Ibid.*, p. 61

Margaret's talk on Saturday went surprisingly well. She quoted Lafayette—

> In this business of storming redoubts with unloaded arms and fixed bayonets, the merit of the deed is in the soldiers who execute it—

—and one of the scouts asked through gleaming braces, "Why did they have to 'fix' the bayonets?"

Another twelve-year-old, with pierced ears and skinned knees, replied, "They were too poor! All their bayonets were broken! But they won anyway!"

Margaret explained that "fixing" a bayonet meant attaching it to the muzzle of the gun, thus making it a different kind of weapon, and went on to talk about what these men had given up—the quiet life of a schoolteacher, for instance—to fight for what they believed in. For the most part, she avoided a lengthy discussion of blood and gore.

She came home pleased and a little tired, but eager to do a bit of housecleaning—she filled a brown bag with the packages of Cheez Doodles and pork rinds that were still in her cupboard, and the few cans of Rolling Rock that were still in her fridge, and carried the bag out to her car. A quick trip to the grocery brought back several boxes of Celestial Seasonings, with their promises of enlightenment, and now they perched on the shelf above the little kitchen window as they used to do. She pulled a big carton of books out of the back hallway closet and returned her grandmother's leather-bound set of James Fenimore Cooper, in alphabetical order by title, to the table from which Buck's TV had routed it.

Margaret never saw Captain Whitegrave again, but each night he had appeared, after the first, she had refilled her wineglass and left it on the balcony when she went to bed. When she found the empty glass each morning, she felt as pleased as a child on Christmas morning, whose offering of milk and cookies has disappeared from its place on the hearth.

Note: "Recollections of a Connecticut Schoolmaster" is a fictional title, whose citations are based on material in *The Yorktown Campaign and the Surrender of Cornwallis, 1781*, by Henry P. Johnston, 1881, reprinted for the Bicentennial by Eastern Acorn Press.

Julie Shields

The Ice Storm Cometh, Stayeth, and Doesn't Leaveth

JULIE SHIELDS is the author of *How to Avoid the Mommy Trap: A Roadmap for Sharing Parenting and Making It Work* (Capital Books, 2003). Her essays and op-eds have appeared in the *Washington Post* and the *Baltimore Sun*. "The Ice Storm Cometh, Stayeth, and Doesn't Leaveth" is excerpted from "Team Mom," a women's fiction novel which won Politics & Prose's 2011 NaNo-WriMo contest. Julie Shields is currently working on a historical fiction novel about Georgia O'Keeffe and Alfred Stieglitz. A graduate of Johns Hopkins University and Duke Law School, Julie Shields lives in Northern Virginia.

6:22

I awoke to the sound of nothing.

Quiet, everywhere.

This was weird.

The weather report had predicted twelve to eighteen inches of snow overnight. I hadn't believed it. It was only early November. The forecasters were always getting excited about nothing. Washington, capital of the world, didn't know how to handle wintry weather. The girls had gone to bed wearing their pajamas inside out. They subscribed to the Virginia suburban legend which held that wearing pajamas inside out would lead to a snow day off from school.

Outside in our treed backyard, icicles and snow dangled in a field of bright, sparkling white. Beholding a true winter wonderland—which later became a horror movie reminiscent of *The Shining*, where I could not get out—I saw that for once the PJs trick had worked.

I turned on the TV in the family room so I could see what was going on. Did I really need a "meteorologist" to tell me that it had snowed, a lot?

6:28

As I popped down on my couch, Lucy descended on me, ready for play. She did her morning dance, tail wagging wildly. I bent down and patted her brown furry head.

"Good morning."

Lucy was always happy to see me, and never complained about the food or service. I wished we could all have her personality, me most of all.

Suddenly Maggie was at my side, ready for the day. I went into the kitchen, reached for the Starbucks Extra Bold French Roast, and measured ten heaping tablespoonfuls.

"Mommy, is there school?" asked Maggie.

"Doubt it," I said as I stroked her silky blonde hair. At ten, Maggie was tall and thin, with straight, cooperative hair. She had Tom's metabolism, lucky girl.

The television flashed a warning across a commercial for a twenty-in-one kitchen tool:

> Stay home. Thirteen to nineteen inches across the area. An inch of ice underneath the snow. Roads are impassable. Round two later this morning. Viewers are urged to stay home.

Finally, someone supported my career choice.

"Yay," Maggie. "Kate, KATE."

Maggie thundered upstairs, her lithe body and graceful feet stomping so hard on the floor that the recessed lighting shook. I poured coffee and then skim milk (cream was too fattening) into my favorite cheery yellow, blue, and red geometric-designed mug, given to me by Pam at my work going-away party. I took a huge sip. Energy coursed through my veins. I felt normal.

I decided to make buttermilk lemon poppy seed muffins. I put on Kate's apron, took out the potato peeler and started to grate the lemon zest.

"Mommy, NO," Maggie yelled from upstairs.

I ran up, two stairs at a time. "What, what?" I asked.

"You don't use a potato peeler. You need the zester."

"You scared me. I thought something was wrong."

"It is. You're losing the zest flavor. Mrs. Jackson says never to use a peeler for zesting."

My next-door neighbor, Deveraux, had just one daughter, Sasha, between Kate and Maggie's ages, and was a domestic goddess. Maggie loved Deveraux's cheery Stepford Wife demeanor, and her happy surrender to mini-van *Groundhog Day* life.

Maggie patted my arm. "C'mon, I'll show you."

Maggie and I worked together, bustling around the kitchen in our matching red and white floral aprons. She spooned poppy seed–inflected yellow batter into the muffin cups. Each time, she dropped batter on the edge of the muffin tin, counter, or floor. Still unfed and wanting her walk, Lucy lapped the batter from the floor. Clumps of flour dotted the black granite countertop.

My hair was streaked with lemon pulp. But we were warm and safe and baking muffins. Life was good. I looked out, comforted somehow by noticing that another inch of snow had accumulated in the rectangular shape sitting on top of our deck fence post.

That was stupid.

7:03

I tried to let Lucy out the back door to go down the back steps. She refused, the first time ever. The stairs were hidden by the snow. Kate came down in her ski pants, smelling of cherry lip gloss.

"Let's go, girls, we need to take Lucy out."

The girls put on all of their Under Armour, L.L. Bean winter wear, and cute light purple snow boots and hats. I donned my twenty-year-old nonwaterproof Timberland khaki green and brown leather hiking boots (snazzy in 1990) and an old pair of drawstring "warm-up pants." They didn't call them that anymore. Nobody in their right mind would have gone for a walk in over a foot of snow in those pants, whatever they called them now. Antiques, I guessed.

"What are those?" Kate asked, her mouth agape in horror. "I hope we don't see anyone I know. I'm glad The Gurlz live in a different neighborhood."

I was too. I didn't trust The Gurlz and wished Kate would find nicer, less popular friends. Oh, how I wished I had a middle school wallflower.

We opened the door and snow fell into the foyer. Outside, the wind had blown snow into uneven piles past our waists, well over Lucy's head. No matter. We were getting a start on the day!

7:15

My visions of a perfect snow day dashed.

I waddled down the driveway and fell into a sinkhole in our driveway, head first.

I looked up and saw Kate grimacing, trying not to laugh at her spread-eagled, face-down, snow-sprawled mama. I giggled. With permission, the girls howled, gales of our laughter piercing the eerie quiet. As I heaved my belly up and down to laugh, snow slithered between my sweatpants and my underwear.

The snow felt hot and cold and wet all at the same time.

Melting snow in your underwear is not a good feeling.

"Help me up," I said, holding my hands out from my kneeling position on the ground.

With difficulty, they hoisted me from the ground, each grabbing a hand and arm.

A muffled BOOM and a crackle sounded. A bright flash lit up the sky.

"Snow lightning!" Maggie said.

Six inches of fresh snow covered the street. Just about three-quarters of the road's width had been plowed. We walked in the middle of the road, the only people and dog out at that time. I was excited if imperfectly clad and cold and wet. Our cheeks were red, the air was sharp, and we were enjoying nature, a family out together.

7:20

When we rounded the corner, a hundred-year-old oak tree lay across the road, the only access out of our neighborhood. An icicle-encrusted black wire lay next to it. Neighbors were talking in a scrum a few yards from the tree.

"Let's go back," I said, grabbing Maggie as she started to head over to the exposed power line.

We trudged back to the house and slid down the driveway, unintentionally in my case, to the front porch. The brown leather and green canvas of my once-trendy Timberlands—hard now even for me to believe that they had once been trendy—was soaked, my toes frigid.

Maggie ran to the television. Nothing.

Kate ran to the computer. Nothing.

I ran to the wine rack.

All three new bottles of good red wine purchased the day before the storm were there. I breathed a sigh of relief. But would three be enough?

The girls and I looked at each other, pondering our next move.

"Mommy, let's go to the Ritz Carlton," Kate said.

That did sound good. But there was too much snow in our driveway for us to move ourselves even if that tree somehow disappeared.

BRRRRNNNH! BRRRRNNNH!

Next door, Deveraux was blowing snow into neat rows. She wore color- and pattern-coordinated light pink and green floral and plaid snow pants, gloves, hat, and boots.

"If we can borrow that, we are halfway to the Ritz Carlton. Be polite, girls," I said.

We trekked over to Deveraux's driveway. Big, blonde, fair skinned, church-y, tons of energy, drank no alcohol or caffeine, Deveraux was always working on some project around the house or in the kitchen. Making a bookshelf or running a school fun fair. That sort of thing.

We were very different.

I always liked to check with Deveraux to see what I should be doing, and get some help to start it, like asking the class valedictorian what we were supposed to do for homework and knowing that doing a quarter of what she told you would be just fine.

She turned the snow blower off. "Good morning! Enough snow for you?"

I forced a hopeful smile on my face. "There was enough snow for me at six. Now it's too much and I'm over it," I said.

"Can we put our muffins in your Easy-Bake Oven, Mrs. Jackson? It runs on batteries, Mommy," Maggie said.

Deveraux bent down and talked to Maggie. "Of course. I have some hot chocolate going. Go inside and Sasha will show you. Sit by the fireplace and get cozy with a quilt."

The girls ran, in slow motion and falling on the way, to get the muffins.

"Me too?" I asked Deveraux.

"Tom's away, isn't he?'

"Yes, Australia again. It's summer there," I said, wiping a hot snowflake from my chapped cheek.

Or was it a teardrop?

"I got up at four after the first snow and put some salt and ice melter down. It was all ice underneath. No car is getting out unless you did that."

"I didn't do that."

"That's OK, Kelly. It'll probably be several days before they get a plow in here. I'm going to stay ahead of the storm and keep shoveling with each snowfall. You have to." She shrugged.

I looked around, depressed by the beautiful snow all around us, and said, "It's too high. I thought I was up so early. I don't have anybody to shovel my driveway."

I felt like I was confessing to the principal that I had forgotten to study for the whole semester and was about to fail, or had failed, in one of those back-to-school nightmares which supposedly only afflicted the college educated.

"I know you don't. I got you on the waiting list for Woody. He's got a special ice chipper. Woody does my landscaping. Well, just the details I can't handle—"

"You're my favorite person in the world. Thank you," I gushed.

"But we're still looking at a day or two before we get power and heat back and they can plow. And then get the tree out. And then restore the power. You're welcome to come over and get warm around my fireplace at night. We'll have a giant sleepover."

Deveraux was never wrong.

A couple of days before I could get in the car and leave my beautiful house and beautiful children? Christ.

As I grappled with what a couple of days with no heat, power, television, hot shower, and hanging out chez Jackson, avec Lucy, would mean, I mentally searched every corner of my house for alcohol I liked in addition to those three bottles of red wine. Did we have any good painkillers left from when Tom had his wisdom teeth removed?

My cell phone rang.

"Cheers, mate." Tom's voice rang out heartily.

My body stiffened in an intense rage at hearing Tom's cheery "cheers," from my snow- and lemon-crusted hair down to my soaked frostbitten toes. "I was just thinking about my first drink of the day. Either that or a shot of morphine. Quick and painless."

"I heard about the snow. How are you making out?"

"There's no power, heat, or cable."

Recounting it all made me mad at Tom, as if he had caused this. My blood boiled. At least something was warm. "How's the weather?" I asked.

"Eighty-two. It's a little overcast. We're going on BJ's yacht today…"

I pressed "End Call." A wail escaped me.

"What's that?" Deveraux asked.

"We got cut off."

THE SNOW, ICE, AND WIND kept coming, and coming, and coming, for three days. By the fourth day, the joy and beauty of that magical morning from 6:22 to 7:24 seemed like it had occurred years ago.

Or had never happened.

Or had happened to a crazy person who didn't hate snow.

For the next week, we played the Game of Life Twists & Turns, Monopoly, charades, cards, and every other parlor game ever invented. Life had gone electronic since my day and added a tag line to its title: "A THOUSAND WAYS TO LIVE YOUR LIFE! YOU CHOOSE!"

As we womenfolk huddled in the cold over the Jacksons' golden oak game table, fleece blankets draped around us, I asked Kate to remind me of the point of the game.

"First, get your education. Then don't waste time doing anything but making money. At the end you can try to get Life Points and have a lot of kids and do stuff for charity. That's how you win," Kate said.

While the game's title said that there were a thousand ways to live life, the only way to win was to make money and be out for yourself. The game awarded 500 Life Points if you "party with your friends after your exams!" and only 400 Life Points for the following situation: "Your brother's having a tough time. Let him move in with you while he gets back on his feet."

What was Life teaching our kids?

The truth! Caregiving wasn't valued. Me-first-ism was the ticket.

Why wasn't I in Australia, or on my laptop, working on a report like Deveraux's husband, or saving children around the world like Lexi, my high school friend, instead of playing a game with my own children?

There were no points for staying home to raise a family and no bonus points for staying home with children in a mammoth snow storm and paying attention to them. There should have been. That or Valium taped to the box.

Use liberally, as needed. Or give to the dog so you don't have to worry about how she can get her exercise.

Maggie won every time. She liked money and had a knack in life and in Life and also in Monopoly for maximizing her income. She would go far.

During the last game, I decided not to venture into the Family & Friends area of the board. This, I realized, ten years and a few hundred games too late, was a trap. I was ruthless, confining my efforts to Earn It and Learn It. I piled on degree after degree and bonus after bonus. I pretended I was a 1950s male. Or my husband.

I lost.

"You can't forget about family and friends, Mommy. In real life they're the most important," Maggie said.

"You and Mrs. Jackson are here playing with us and keeping us warm and fed. We'd die without your care no matter how much money we had," Kate said.

Deveraux and I looked at each other and smiled, acknowledging something big, and lonely.

"Give me a hug, girls. Show me some love," I said.

For once even Kate embraced the embrace rather than suffering it. I sniffed their watermelon shampoo–scented hair, knowing I would not get too many more times to breathe them in. The still sweet-baby-smell of their skin would not remain for long. Kate's sweat had started to smell like, well, sweat.

In daylight hours, when we were not playing board games and learning the facts of money, I mean life, I holed up at our house with Lucy at my feet. I wore my long sepia brown North Face coat the girls found so unattractive and huddled under blankets. I sat on the couch (it at least had stayed to support me), reading next to the window in the pale light until the sun went down. I dispatched old favorites *Madame Bovary* and *Pride and Prejudice*, and made it halfway through *Anna Karenina*, because it was long, but not *War and Peace*, which was really long. Then I went to Deveraux's and helped with the communal meal—mostly setting and clearing the table—and ate too much. I returned to our house at night "to check" on things.

This was a euphemism for drinking all the wine.

During the day I dipped into the peach schnapps given to us a few years ago at Christmas by a German client of Tom's. That brought me back to freshman year of college. The warmth of the nostalgia or the liqueur almost warmed the tip of my splotchy red nose.

The girls made snow angels, a snow city, sledded down many hills, had snow ball fights and other, real fights, and played with their neighborhood friends all day. Even the kids got sick of hot chocolate by the fireplace.

Deveraux hated dogs and dog hair and dog smell and everything about dogs. The purpose and mission of her life—her calling, if you will—was to rid her world of dirt, hair, smell, and anything that was not sterile. She wanted to tame nature and conquer all mess. I, and anyone except for Lucy, would have preferred to eat off of her floor than our table any day.

She let Lucy camp out with all of us in her family room on a sleeping bag on the floor.

"At least it's not summer. That's when they really shed," she said each morning, using her battery-operated Dustbuster to suck up Lucy's golden hair from the formerly pristine white carpet.

Who had kids and bought a white rug?

With all the alcohol, homemade pizzas, cookies, brownies, and hot chocolate, and sitting around, my bathroom scale told me that I was gaining weight every day. Unfortunately, the scale was the only appliance in my house that was battery operated and had the proper batteries.

After five endless days filled with leisure and fun and camaraderie, and boredom, the tree was removed and the power lines restored. On the sixth day, we woke up at four thirty a.m. to the screaming burglar alarm at the Jacksons' house. The power had come on, as it always seemed to do, in the middle of the night.

"We're saved," chanted Sasha, Kate, and Maggie, dancing around with way too much energy for four thirty in the morning.

When we awoke again at the more civilized hour of six, we slogged and slid over to our house. The girls and I sat on the couch, rapt, as the blue light went on, signaling that the television was working again. We cheered. I have never been so happy to see anything as I was to see something other than a blank screen in my family room.

Community Access Channel? Score!

By the time Woody came the last time, both of our cars were buried in snow. They looked like two giant mounds of hardened, brownish-grayish snow, which is what they were.

"Hi, Woody," I said, rushing out of the house and greeting him at the bottom of our hill.

He said, "I brought the special ice pick and industrial snow blower and three guys. We're gonna get you out this time. Don't know that I have time for both cars though."

"Don't worry about that one," I said, pointing to Tom's. "Just do mine."

"Really?"

"Definitely. I'm good with that."

Woody and his crew spent a good four hours, and five hundred dollars of Tom's hard-earned money; at that point I wished I could have spent lots more. That night I left the girls with Deveraux and went out to meet Pam for dinner. I had never felt so carefree as I did when I drove precariously down our icy, hilly street to deliverance or death. After a white-knuckled ride that was surely injudicious, I arrived at our favorite Thai restaurant, and ran in, wearing my now completely trashed Timberlands.

Pam was already there, warm, dry, and in pristine, beautiful Uggs which had been untouched by snow. She lived around the corner in a high rise with a generator and underground parking and had not been snowed in during the storm. I gave her a huge hug.

"Are you OK? You didn't take the painkillers, did you? You look a little crazed," she said, worried.

"Just high on being out of the house," I said. "That was the longest year of my life."

"Sit down," Pam said, "I have to tell you the latest Internet dating fiasco."

"I want to know everything," I said, paying extra attention so I could be ready if I hit the singles scene.

I loved hearing about work in the Obama White House, how cutthroat people still were, and her dating stories, many of which were hilarious.

I settled in with my Thai iced tea, thrilled to be out and among exotic spices and different sauces.

"I didn't realize he was only four feet eight until he stood up at the end of the night," Pam said, laughing at the memory.

"I never towered over a date before," she said. "I finally understood why he said he wasn't the basketball type in his profile. He arrived early and he was sitting on a raised stool so I couldn't tell. I had this sinking feeling as he rose."

We laughed hard at that one. "No! Did you go out with him again?" I asked.

"I did. Once. Because of anyone, I should not discriminate against people for being vertically challenged. But he turned out to be a jerk."

She shrugged. I knew that "he's a jerk" shrug well. That's the way the stories always went.

TOM SENT SEVERAL FRANTIC TEXTS from the airport: *What type of Chanel perfume do u like? At duty free.* I opted not to respond, except to note that Australia was not known for its French perfume and that duty free was not an acceptable place to shop for a present from a faraway place. I was able to say this with just three letters and three punctuation marks: WTF???

Before Tom left, I had asked him to pick up beige Ugg slippers in a size seven, style number 8472, color 36—as it happened, just like the ones Pam had worn—some aboriginal art, or something interesting from Australia.

But apparently the yacht had not stopped anywhere where he could buy me anything actually from Australia.

When Tom finally came home from his business trip turned beach vacation when he couldn't get back to D.C., I was on the way out the door to play tennis. My friend Jennifer and I were going to eat lunch and go shopping afterwards. It was the first day for the girls back at school and my first day to move about again freely. I heard Tom's suitcase wheels scraping on the ice before I saw him. Tom didn't say anything when he rounded the driveway and witnessed the mound of brown-gray snow that was his car. Instead, he looked at me a second too long.

I almost felt ashamed for being so petty. Stepping out of the house, I said, "I wanted to make sure you got the snow experience. People are going to be talking about this storm for the rest of their lives."

"Don't I know it," he said, and walked inside the doorway, yanking his heavy bag over the wooden threshold. It got stuck. He pulled on it again as I walked to my car.

Notes to Self

- Move to apartment or townhouse?
- Go to gym twice a day for next year. Move to gym and save on housing costs?
- No pepperoni ever again (yuck)
- No cheese
- Swear off schnapps (this one's easy)
- Buy generator?
- Get battery-operated TV and battery-operated everything. And batteries!!!
- Move to Florida?
- Get Deveraux present
- Get Woody present. Apologize for hysterical voicemails and texts (hack into his phone and delete them???)
- Next time, make plane or hotel reservations when more than foot of snow predicted
- Do NOT wait until airports are closed and hotels booked and phone lines down.
- Explain to couples therapist how it feels to be left alone in storm of the century

Marija Stajic

Just a Boy

MARIJA STAJIC is a Serbian-American writer, journalist, and linguist and the author of three books of poetry. She has a BA in linguistics and literature from the University of Nis (Serbia), and an MA in international journalism from American University. She was accepted into the Jenny McKean Moore Fiction Workshop of George Washington University in spring 2012. She also studied playwriting at HB Studios in New York and short story writing at the Writer's Center, in Bethesda, Maryland. Her work has been published in the *New Yorker*, *VLP Magazine*, *Lunch Ticket*, *Epiphany Magazine*, *Writing Disorder*, *Orion Headless*, *Gloom Cupboard*, *Imitation Fruit*, *Inertia*, *Thick Jam*, *Circa*, *Yuan Yang*, and *Burning Word*.

The wind whipped my house and, with my head under a blanket and my nose tucked between my knees, I listened to its screams. I think my bed shook a bit. Or maybe my knees did. They still smelled of lavender soap, from the bath my grandma gave me that night, in the wooden tub I loved since my legs and arms were always hanging from it and I felt funny and like a spider. She asked: "Is it warm enough?" and I said yes, even though it wasn't, but I knew the war was going on outside of our house, and that we didn't have money. I took lukewarm baths for the same reason I ate cabbage, and potatoes, and parsley, and dark, hard bread we could have used as a weapon. My grandma never took baths. She just wet a long cloth and squeezed it hard and then wiped her underarms, and face, and legs. She never smiled anymore, not since both my parents left, first my father, three years, two months, and eight days ago, then my mother, a month ago.

My grandma yelled at my mother and even slapped her face before my mother swore at her and put her bag over her shoulder, slamming the door. "Where will your soul go?" my grandma asked, but I didn't hear what my mama answered. Then my grandma said: "I wish I gave birth to a stone," and that was the last time I saw my mother's big blue eyes. I thought maybe Mama was just angry with me and Grandma and she would come back, but when Grandma fell on our dirty mud floor and began crying into her apron, I knew she would not.

I heard guns somewhere up in the hills above Varazdin. I heard birds squawking loudly in the air. But I didn't think men were shooting at the birds.

"Nado, what are you doing under the blanket?" my grandma said, then sat next to me and pulled it off. Her eyes were blue too, like mine and Mama's, but not blue like a sky or a lake. They were as blue as the deepest part of an ocean.

"Nothing," I said.

"Don't be scared, child, it's just a storm," she said, and hugged me and my knees like a beach ball.

"Tell me a story, Nano! Please?"

"A story, huh? What kind of a story? I'm just a peasant woman, never learned how to read or write, what story could I tell you?"

"Something from when you were young," I said. "Some kind of tale. Tell me a tale, tell me a tale!"

"A tale, huh? I remember a tale, sweetheart, I heard it over fifty years ago and never forgot," she said and petted me on the head. I leaned onto my pillow even though the feathers pinched. My heart beat with excitement. My fingers and toes danced.

"A middle-aged man walked from his small farm to the village's only store. Walking toward him was a boy, no older than eight, with curly red hair and piercing green eyes. He wore a checkered red and yellow shirt, short brown pants, and dusty brown shoes, and he carried books under his right arm. The man smiled at the boy as they passed each other on the dirt road, when the boy suddenly stopped: 'You will die when you are fifty-three years old. You will fall from your roof. Your wife will be unhappy at first, but she will remarry within a year,' the boy said and walked away, leaving the man speechless and motionless."

"Oh, no," I said and pulled the blanket again over my nose and looked at my grandma's solemn face.

"It's a tale, Nado, just a tale I heard in my village when I was a little girl just like you. That's what you wanted, right? 'Cause if you don't like it, I have laundry to…"

"No, please, Nano, tell me, tell me," I begged.

"Where was I…the boy…the man, uh huh. So, the man was fifty-two years old, and his birthday was the following week. He indeed planned on working on his roof soon, since he felt a drop or two, lying in bed, last time it rained heavily. He stared at this little boy walking away, and thought that it would be silly to believe him. He's just a boy, how could he possibly know? He came home and told his wife what the boy had told him.

"'Well, don't fix the roof,' she said. 'Hire someone.'

"He thought that would be a waste of money, and if he were destined to die, he would die one way or another."

"A week later, he celebrated his birthday with his family and friends. His wife made him his favorite honey cake, with thick, heavy white filling, and brown walnut layers."

"The one you make for my birthday!" I yelled in joy, happy to be somehow a part of this tale.

"Yes, that very one. So, they drank the red wine he made himself, just like your grandfather used to do. But then it began raining, so his guests left to beat the storm, and he went to bed. Drops of rain woke him up before the sun rose. With the first sunlight, he put the ladder against the wall and climbed onto the roof, where he saw a couple of red bricks broken…"

There was a knock on the door. My grandma's face turned white, and that last light in her eyes somehow turned off.

"Get under the bed," she whispered. "And stay there until I say you can come out. I, and only I, you hear. And don't make a sound." I nodded and slid under the bed, holding onto its black iron legs, looking at the mattress above me, looking for spider webs.

I saw my grandma's wool slippers moving toward the door. "Who is it?" she asked in an altered, trembling voice. I didn't see her pick it up, but I knew she took the saber my grandfather had received as a gift for fighting in World War I just weeks before he died of stroke. And then a pair of military boots walked in, old, scrappy, and green, wool pants tucked into them. My grandfather's saber fell to the floor. My grandma propped her slippers onto her toes.

"Nado, Nado, come out!" she yelled.

Like a lizard, I slid from under the bed, brushing the webs and dust with my forehead.

There was a man standing in our hallway, his head and face grown in hair, dressed in a military uniform with shiny, colorful brooches, and at first I didn't recognize him. But then he smiled and pulled a doll out of his vest. His eyes sparkled green with tears.

"Nado, my precious!"

I ran, losing my slippers in the process, and hit him in the chest with my small body. He smelled of snow and pines as he kissed my head, cheeks, arms. My grandma cried.

"Tata, Tata!" I shouted with glee.

His uniform was cold and rough against my skin. But I didn't say anything, I didn't mind. I wrapped my legs and arms around him. The doll fell on the ground, but I didn't care.

He seemed like a giant to me, like a tall oak with thick, dark tresses falling all over my arms, his stubble tickling me as he kissed my cheeks incessantly, as if trying to suck them in or bite them off. My nose was stuffed up, my throat clenched.

"Thank God, thank God!" my grandma crossed herself. He lifted me up as if I were a feather and put me on his shoulders. I laughed. I liked it there. I felt like a bird, like I could fly. I wiped my face and I saw both my grandma and my father doing the same, Grandma with her apron, my father with his dirty sleeve.

"Where's Josipa?" he asked, looking around. My grandma looked at me. Her face turned red, then white, then red, then white, like a lollipop wheel. "Ivan," she said in an unfamiliar, rasping voice. "Forgive me, forgive me, for what my daughter did." Her voice quieted down as she began once again swallowing tears. Then it launched from her throat, desperate: "She left, Ivan, and I begged her not to. She said you were dead, otherwise you would have sent us word, it has been three years. She said she had to begin a new life and she couldn't do that with a little girl pulling her skirt. She met some Hungarian captain working for the Germans, God give her no happiness, and left with him. I begged her not to do it. I cursed her. I begged her again. But she's just like her father, stubborn, cold…he got her pregnant, Ivan!" Then my grandma turned into a storm all by herself, rain and thunders, until my father put his hand on her shoulder, gently. "Thank you for taking care of my daughter," he said. She took his blistered, massive hand into her little one, pale and wrinkly, and kissed it. He pulled it from underneath her lips, and gently put both of his hands on her face. "Thank you," he said.

THE NEXT MORNING, I WOKE up with a smile on my face. My new doll slept next to me, tucked into my bed as I was. The house was quiet.

"Tata?" I called. Silence. "Tata?" I called again.

My grandma appeared with her face red and swollen. "Where's Tata?" I asked, something scratchy in my throat. My grandma swallowed loudly. She petted me on the head like a dog or a cat. "He had to leave, honey, but he'll be back, he promised."

"When, Nano, when will he be back?"

"I don't know, he didn't know either because of this damn war, but he promised he would be back. "

I began crying and I couldn't stop, just couldn't stop, like when my grandma pumped the water pump in the yard, and the water kept gushing long after we needed any.

"Don't cry, my soul, if he said he would be back, then he will, God willing."

"But why, why did he have to leave me too?"

"He's a soldier; he had to go back to the war. He said he will try to…leave the war sooner since your mama left, he'll try to…cross from Croatia into Slovenia then into Italy, and then he'll see, he might send for us, God save him, but you have to be a bit patient, my sweetheart," she said, her palms wet as she touched my face. My grandma smelled of strawberries, even though there were none in the house or the garden. Then she continued talking but not to me anymore, to someone I couldn't see across the room. When I traced her gaze, I only saw a chipped, white wall, plaster pieces hanging from it as if it were cheese partly eaten my mice. Her voice was different too, somehow burdened and heavy: "People behave like beasts, Ivan said. Neighbors killing neighbors, Serbs and Croats turned against each other. He said he's afraid of committing a sin, he's afraid of those ungodly people, unjust war. He doesn't know when it will end, if it will end. He can't take it anymore, he can't wait…"

"But…he promised, right?" I said, and my grandma looked me in the eyes again.

"Yes, he said to tell you that he promised, and that you should take care of your new doll," she said, her eyes shining. "Now get up, get dressed, and we'll have some breakfast, some polenta. You like polenta with milk, don't you? Or do you prefer it with cheese and fried minced red peppers?" She kissed my forehead and began getting up from my bed by pushing herself up and making grunting noises. Her bones snapped. I pulled on her apron.

"Nano?"

"Yes, Nada."

"Could you finish your story first?"

"My story? Oh, yes. Yes. Remind me, where were we?" she asked.

"The man was on the roof fixing it," I said, hugging my new doll, "even though the boy told him that he will die, and his wife told him not to."

"Yes, that's right. As he came down the tall ladder, he lost his balance, fell, and died on the spot. His wife ran out of the house screaming and weeping. All the neighbors quickly gathered but there was nothing they could do. 'The boy, where's that red-headed boy? He did this!' the wife said."

"Through tears she told her neighbors what that boy had said to her husband just over a week ago, and one of the neighbors said:

"'He's the devil! Let's get him, before he kills someone else.'"

"The crowd gathered in front of the boy's house. He came out alone, no parents in sight, and began speaking to them, calmly: 'You, Nikola, will die when you're ninety, of old age. You, Zorana, will die at sixty-nine, of a heart attack. You, Milena, will die at fifty-eight, a tractor accident…'"

"He kept telling everyone's judgment day until the whole crowd quieted down, dropped their shovels and pitchforks, and left like zombies. The boy turned around and went back into the house. The end," she said, sighed deeply, and gently pinched my chin. There was something in her eyes I had never seen before, some kind of light, brightness.

"So, was that read-headed boy really the devil?" I asked, hugging my doll tightly into my chest.

My grandma scratched her head under her silky headscarf. Then she fixed her scarf. She looked at me and took a deep breath. "He was the devil for some, and an angel for others. But he was also just a boy, a boy with no parents," she said wiping her tears on her apron.

Suzanne Stroh

Quiet Enjoyment

SUZANNE STROH, an award-winning screenwriter in love with the Northern Virginia countryside, grew up in Michigan in a family of international brewers. After a bookish youth searching for the Homer or the Tolstoy of lesbian love, she decided to write it herself. *Tabou* is Stroh's debut work of fiction, a five-part novel cycle spanning one hundred years and four generations to bridge nine families on four continents. This story is taken from the fourth volume, "Aurore." Stroh is currently translating the French biography of Élisabeth de Gramont (1875–1954) and planning a new novel. Learn more at www.suzannestroh.com.

O n the morning of the trial, Patience Herrick awoke on Antigua with childlike anticipation.

True, she thought, cocking her head while examining her reflection in the bathroom mirror as she applied a subtle but breezy shade of lipstick, *I've lost every single legal maneuver thus far. A new low.* These embarrassing proceedings would now become a matter of public record. Photographers would be there at the courthouse. And reporters. *And Puppa's going to hear about the verdict even if I never tell him myself.* Worse, Patience was only a short hair away from losing her father's favorite fuck dock to the French champagne princess. Patience called her Horreur. *My nemesis.* That was the bad news.

The good news was encouraging. The magistrate had put her case first on the docket, so she wouldn't have to wait around all morning picking her nose and getting an allergy attack from Horreur's perfume.

She looked at the vase full of outrageously expensive lilies of the valley that her son, Max, had air delivered with irony. Lily of the valley was a Fillery scent. Horreur was the princess of Fillery. Patience closed her eyes and imagined Horreur handing these flowers chastely to her as a peace offering, in defeat, the way Patience had offered flowers to the princess at their last settlement meeting. Then she visualized trampling them. It was satisfying. Then something of Max's gentler spirit came in through the window with the early Christmas breeze and cloaked her like a mantle, and she thought she could hear him laughing.

Patience inspected her body for flab. She'd been to the gym every day for two months. For some reason she finally decided to take her Beverly Hills physician, Murray, up on that general physical exam of his. It had been a three-day pain-in-the-ass ordeal that startled one and all. She was in the best shape of her life. In triumph she carried the results around with her in her bag. For the first time in ten years she weighed less than a hundred and twenty pounds and she felt like a million bucks.

She hadn't forgotten to tan; her hair was soft and silky and fell down on her shoulders; she wore a timeless suit of white linen trimmed with navy that every official on this island had seen many times on various state occasions. And she'd never lost in court.

Patience slipped into the new pair of white-capped navy Chanel heels she'd bought just for today. She shut off the bathroom lights and headed through the garden for the car.

There they all were: the Herricks' loyal Caribbean staff. The gents had hats in hand; the ladies were wiping their hands on their aprons. Patience stopped, collecting her bag and her scarf and her slim briefcase, just the size for one or two juicy glam mags, from Emily, the best cook on Antigua. Someone came forward, shyly, and handed her a paper airplane. *A paper airplane?*

"Feel like settling?" Patience had written on a sheet of paper last night. She'd left it on Horreur's doorstep. Slowly, Patience unfolded the origami, realizing this was her reply.

"Not on your life," it read. *And she refolded my offer into the shape of the Concorde and returned it par avion!* *"Don't be late."*

"Where'd you find this?" Patience asked. Her driver, Jonas, pointed silently to the baobab just inside the ten-foot wall that marked the now-disputed property line. Patience put her hand on Jonas's shoulder. "Well I hope she has better aim at the judge." They laughed.

"Good luck this morning, Mrs. H.," said Emily, with her trademark boredom.

"Thank you, Emily. No worries, you lot," said Patience, playing along. *I know, I know: your part is to pretend you don't give a damn what happens to*

me, and my part is to pretend that I think you worship the ground I walk on.
"Hold on to your plastic explosives. Never lost in court," she said, following Jonas to the car.

ↂ

SEATED IN THE DARK COURTROOM with the giant mahogany ceiling fans whirring overhead, Patience and her bewigged English barrister were kept waiting nearly twenty minutes by the Frogs. Yet their motion to dismiss was ignored. The judge seemed very curious to meet the new princess. The day started getting unseasonably hot. Patience could hear the seats filling behind her.

Princess Marie Christine Aurore Faucigny-Lueur de Fillery finally floated in, wearing a lemony creation of silk and chiffon by Yves Saint Laurent. *By Saint Laurent personally*, Patience knew. It was the loveliest day suit ever seen on Antigua—and would have also won for loveliest single article of clothing had it not been for the pièce de résistance, Horreur's wide-brimmed floppy hat. The moment you saw the hat, you forgot about the suit. The hat was light straw sunshine with bits of the lemon and flecks of the white fabric woven into it somehow. The whole effect was dreamy and pure, like a culinary creation that only exists in the gleam of a chef's eye. The old, handsome colonial courtroom was now packed and buzzing behind Patience. She didn't dare turn around, and she couldn't bear to face her rival, so she doodled with her Montblanc pen and, of course, got ink all over her fingers.

The trial proceeded. Patience had met the judge recently at a dinner party and given him a good massaging. But Horreur took him firmly by the balls as soon as she took the stand. Suddenly he wouldn't allow a single objection by Patience's own lawyer. Aurore was allowed to lecture on State's interest in reclaiming the Herrick hillside and dock for the plantation of native species, never specified. She and the judge reveled in the romantic Latin names of possible plantations. In her notebook Patience wrote "Gimme a break! <u>Bitch is bluffing</u>," and showed it to her lawyer.

Trying to recover, Patience took the stand in an approach worthy of an Academy Award.

"Mrs. Herrick, are you comfortable?"

"Yes, quite. Thank you, sir," she said.

"May I ask, because you see that is what we must determine, why do you believe, Mrs. Herrick, that this dock belongs to you?"

"I don't believe it for one minute," she answered. Then she quickly added, "Your Honor."

"Mrs. Herrick," said the judge, "I would advise you not to make rash statements that could harm your own case."

"I do not own the dock, Your Honor," said Patience.

"You don't?"

"No. That is the point of my case. It is not my dock. And why I am being sued for it is, sir, beyond me."

"Well then, why do you say that the princess should not have it?"

"Objection! Your Honor," said Patience's own counsel. "Is the counter-claimant not to be queried solely by opposing counsel?"

"This woman and I are on good terms, sir. Mrs. Herrick, help me to determine the facts."

"Well then, I would say to you, sir, purely for your information, because I can't see how I myself have anything to do with this perplexing lawsuit—I would remind you that the princess wants to end my father's quiet enjoyment of his dock. My father who has undertaken a lifetime of service to this country while a resident here as three-time American ambassador to the Court of St. James's." *Take that for State's interest*, thought Patience.

"Why, yes, he certainly has." As the judge well knew, Ambassador Herrick had rebuilt nearly every school on the island, erected all the playgrounds, subsidized housing for the poor, and tried to dampen corruption on the island by financing free elections monitored by disinterested third parties. Plus he always paid for a round of golf.

Patience locked in her advantage. "And never until this moment has anyone ever suggested that his tiny little dinghy dock does not in fact belong to him. It seemed strange to me, Your Honor, that somebody would suggest such a thing now, especially..." Patience drifted off.

"Is your father ill, Mrs. Herrick?" asked the judge, worried.

"Well, he is eighty-three."

"My, my, my. Time flies," said the judge wistfully. Patience shot a glance at Aurore and saw her fidgeting. *Trying not to roll her eyes.*

"And then, Your Honor—"

"Please go on." His look at her counsel said *damned lucky to have such an organized and articulate client.*

"Well then there are the matters of *trespassing* and *frivolity*, which have greatly aggrieved me and my father's household."

The judge flipped uselessly through his papers. "You have been trespassing?" he bluffed.

"No, Your Honor. In the countersuit I point out that Mrs. Faucigny-Lueur, or Mrs. Scey-Brouillard, whichever one is in fact the claimant, or perhaps the two of them are in this together, in any case trespassed with malicious intent or malice aforethought or cruelty to indigenous species or something; I believe that was the legal language."

"Stipulated, Your Honor," said Patience's lawyer in support.

"She nearly cut down my baobab. Deposed royals with defunct titles and island properties should know better." Patience drew shrieks of laughter from the gallery.

The opposing lawyer said, "Your Honor, would the counterclaimant please refer to my client using the proper form of address?"

"Does he mean the name of that wine?" Patience mangled the word *Fillery.*

"Well thank you, Mrs. Herrick, that makes perfect sense to me. You may step down. Careful! There you go. Just there, where you were seated before, thank you. Excellent. Now. What say you, sir?" The judge now hit the ball back to Horreur's befuddled counsel. If Mrs. Herrick was still under oath, why was she now to be questioned at her lawyer's bench? The judge waived what he called a triviality and reminded Mrs. Herrick to go on telling the truth.

Patience saw Aurore kicking her lawyer under the table. He rose and inquired.

After this bizarre morning they recessed before the verdict. Neither woman left the courtroom. Both had snuck in something to drink. Patience could see, over her own copy of *Tatler*, that Horreur was pretending to read *Paris Match*.

⁊

AND THEN, STUNNED, PATIENCE SAT there, powerless, as the judge awarded the dock to Horreur. Disgusted, she turned to her opponent and contemplated murder by sharp pencil. "Let's go," she said quickly and quietly to her lawyer. "Don't speak to anyone. I'll meet you in the car."

Patience got up from her chair, a little shaky, took a deep breath, and left the courtroom. She sensed that old friends were all around her, but she met not a single pair of eyes on her way to the ladies' room. She walked in, shut the door behind her, leaned against it for a minute, then went straight to the sink. Above, another giant mahogany ceiling fan whirred, stirring the stale air. Patience ran the cold tap as high as it would go and put her wrists underneath. She took off her short linen jacket and stood there in a linen camisole, fighting for breath, splashing her face.

Which was probably why she didn't hear the door open and shut quietly behind her with two soft clicks.

Aurore waited a moment, watching. Then she strode slowly to the other basin. Making no noise, she undid the pins from her hair and took off her hat and placed it with her small Prada bag to her left, between her and Patience. She checked the perfect knot in her golden hair. She ran the cold water equally high. It was sweltering. She was perspiring. She took three fingertips and ran them under the water and undid the two top buttons at her breast and ran her fingers up from her breastbone. With her left hand she dabbed some water on the back of her neck. That is what Patience saw beside her in the mirror when she finally looked up.

Patience moved her right elbow, knocking the fragile hat to the floor, ground it with her heel, and sent it under the sink, where she hoped the rusty pipes would be dripping. Then she went back to washing her face.

Aurore instinctively put out her left hand to protect her handbag. Without appearing to see that gesture, Patience blindly swiped right, sending Aurore's bag and its contents all over the floor. As Aurore turned to see where everything was rolling, Patience cupped her left hand into a fist, took a handful of water, and threw it in Aurore's face. Dripping from the chin, Aurore registered no emotion as she filled both cupped hands from under the faucet and hurled the water right back at Patience. *Good aim.*

Patience was now wet through to the chest. Aurore attacked again and again. Patience threw her jacket. Aurore backed up, breaking a heel but deflecting the jacket onto the floor. Patience advanced, scattering Aurore's hairpins and splashing water from Aurore's sink onto her and all over, soaking the rest of the room. Water was now pooling on the floor and the sinks were going to overflow. When Aurore slipped then tripped on the broken heel and put out her arms, Patience grabbed them and steadied her but then shoved Aurore back against the wall.

At that moment Aurore was the sexiest woman Patience had ever seen in her life.

She lunged forward into an animal kiss, trying to bite.

Aurore was forced to defend. She tried to turn her head away. She succeeded just enough so that she could take in the scent behind Patience's ear. She had just enough room and time to nuzzle the sensitive place there.

Patience, with her mouth hungrily devouring Aurore's neck and jaw, felt the peaceful inquiry and froze. When she opened her eyes, she realized what a fragile, defenseless position Aurore was actually in. *I could break your neck with a sharp thrust of my palm.* Suddenly her heart just melted. She took her fingertips and placed them on Aurore's chin and turned her head back so they could be face to face. Their lips nearly met, yet at the same time, Patience took a tiny step back. No more than an inch or two, but it was enough to give the woman her freedom.

"I suppose you'll walk away now," said Patience, alarmed, ashamed, looking down, thinking she was talking only to herself.

"But I locked the door," said Aurore, running her hands slowly up Patience's side, tickling her slightly and making her shiver with cold on the hottest of days, to the point where Aurore's fingertips barely brushed the erect nipples beneath Patience's wet camisole. Then, because her blouse was open at roughly the same level (Aurore was an inch or two taller), Aurore rotated her wrists and undid two more of the buttons at her own breast. She watched carefully as Patience's eyes widened then went out of focus for an instant.

Patience undid another button herself and placed her hands inside Aurore's dress next to her skin, cupping her small, circular, obviously very sensitive breasts. She heard the plaintive begging sigh. Suddenly, for the first time, she could feel what Aurore was feeling. *Wanting me like I want you.* "I thought so," she murmured.

Undressing Aurore roughly, kissing her deeply and greedily and sensuously, Patience was making love in a whirling dance, flinging their shoes into the wall, groping for some place in front of the mirror, besides the sink, that would bear their weight. In the end Patience fell to her knees and pushed Aurore back against the stall. Lifting Aurore's tight little bottom up in both palms, Patience eased her slightly forward then down gently onto her very rigid tongue, rocking with her hands, trying to short circuit the woman's superior ability to think. And leave.

Then Patience felt Aurore pushing back, pushing it into her mouth. Aurore was quavering. Her hands were limp now on Patience's head. She no longer seemed able to stand up under her own power. She was moaning something incomprehensible in French. *I have you in the palm of my hand,* Patience was praying in a mantra, *and I'll never let you go.*

She withdrew her tongue slowly and slid farther beneath Aurore so she could brace her better and said "I love how you taste" to bring her back down to earth and "I love how you love sex" to bring them back together, and began slowly to lick and suck and nibble and murmur and penetrate Aurore with no more than the tips of her fingers as if she, Patience, had all day to screw in the ladies' loo of the Ministry of Justice on Antigua. Aurore came, softly and joyfully, in French. She pleaded with her hands for Patience to stand.

Aurore kissed Patience's eyes closed. Then turned her around to face away. As Aurore began to nibble her neck and run her hands all over Patience's slightly fuller breasts, Patience covered Aurore's hands lightly with her own and let her head fall back onto Aurore's shoulder. "I wish you had a thousand hands," Patience was thinking, unaware of the words escaping her lips.

"Then give me a thousand nights," whispered Aurore.

Patience thought they were the sexiest sounds that had ever glimmered over the sea in her ears. Her mouth was open as if she had turned skyward to drink the warm tropical rain falling from the leaves of the equatorial canopy. Water was overflowing the sink and flooding the room. Aurore began to swirl her hands lower and lower, murmuring and taking an eternity over the place below Patience's belly button but above her pubic bone until, finally, she stroked Patience between the legs with a firm, confident hand—with both hands—until she stiffened. Then came in hoarse cries and collapsed back into Aurore's arms.

When Patience regained a sense of her surroundings, Aurore was smiling, entwining their fingertips, kissing them and murmuring beneath them, "Jasmine. You smell like jasmine. The night flower. Not a morning person."

"I've never been beaten," said Patience.

"Now that I've got your full attention," said Aurore, pressing her pelvis against Patience's belly for comfort and running her hands through Patience's dark, shiny hair as if it were made of onyx baby corn silk.

"Yes," said Patience. "My full attention. *Domptée.*"

Aurore laughed. It was a saucy, loaded word that meant mastered, subdued, tamed. *As if*, the princess was thinking. "I wonder how long it will last?" *We French are so philosophical.*

Patience nodded. She turned off the faucets and reached down and picked up an article of sodden clothing. Her own. They began helping one another to dress while kissing and tickling and talking. Outside they could hear frustrated women complaining loudly when the door wouldn't open. Once she started grinning, Patience couldn't stop. "You never liked this island in the first place."

"*Non.* Detest the place."

"Your whole lawsuit was a sham."

"You're so easily distracted by a challenge. So predictable."

"You're very naughty."

"You're very darling."

"Well I can see how you're quite happy to spend my money, Horreur, to fulfill your brazen desires and satisfy your kinky lust."

"That is our little game, isn't it? Me forcing you to spend your money on something that makes you purely happy. Take me somewhere where you can have your way with me and call me Horreur at the top of your voice day and night. I want to hear the top of your voice. 'Cause if baby I'm the bottom."

"Horreur, no time for idle chitchat." Fully dressed now in dripping couture covered in grime, the two women appraised themselves in spattered mirrors and laughed. "This is the worst situation we've been in since you nearly cut down a baobab to get my attention." Aurore's fantastic hat was trashed. Patience felt a wave of grief. "We should give it a proper burial," she said. Patience binned Aurore's five-hundred-dollar shoes.

Outside the door there were photographers and journalists waiting for bitchy comments that would sell tabloids. *What the hell are we going to do? Plus we have lawyers to fire and a judgment to rip up.* "Look, I've got extra clothes in the car."

"You do? I don't even want to know why."

"Some of us exercise."

"Some of us don't need to."

"Because why? French women don't get fat?"

"In fact no. We do not. I'm to put on your sweaty clothes and face the press?"

"Well." They grinned. Patience dialed her driver as she stood on top of a toilet seat, unlatched the shoulder-width, foot-wide window, and peered out. *A five-and-a-half-foot drop.* "Jonas. Yeah, yeah. It's me. I'm still here. Quiet please. Listen to me. Please throw the lawyer out of our moving car. Go find the princess's car. Evict her lawyer in a similar manner. Tell them to keep the reporters busy for a minute. Say anything. Come around to the north alley with the stinking dead animal by the dumpster," she said into the phone while scanning the alley. "Get out of the car and come to the window. Both of you. We need both your help getting down from here."

Then Patience tried to motivate Aurore, who clearly had a fear of exposure. *But what's worse exposure: heights or paparazzi?* "Here, OK Horreur, follow me. Do as I do. Like this, mmm? Piece a cake. Just no trips to the emergency room. We're due on Mustique for lunch and if you fuck that up, I'll, I don't know, I'll sue your ass."

"For what?"

"Loss of quiet enjoyment," said Patience.

Mary Switalski

Where to Land

MARY SWITALSKI's work has appeared in *Dunes Review*, *Pinch Literary Journal*, *Copper Nickel*, *Obsession Lit Mag*, and elsewhere, and she has been honored with an Individual Artist Grant from the Maryland State Arts Council. She teaches composition at American University in Washington, D.C.

*M*y cap is missing. You think he took it? Was he loafing around here alone again yesterday?"

"Cap for what?" Judith Halloway asked her husband, Jefferson Barnes, as she laid his folded boxers and trouser socks on the bed beside his suitcases, squared their edges, smoothed the fabric, her ring finger winking like phosphorescence over the dark silk sea.

"The goddamned Nationals cap I wore when the firm got the suite last week. I want to take it with me. Go ask him."

"Your packing is manic. You've probably just buried it somewhere."

"Go ask him, Judy."

"This is ridiculous!"

"Ridiculous? I'll tell you what's ridiculous; ridiculous is a grown man living in my house for weeks, using my water and WiFi, a man who ostensibly cannot afford a hostel but can somehow afford to crawl the bars all night, and who examines every detail of my house with, with lust, Judy. Now my Nats cap is missing. What's next? Perhaps he'd like to steal a decent shirt from me, one with a collar, boost his chances of finding an apartment, maybe even a job."

"Hush, Jeff, he'll hear you."

"What if he does? I want you to ask him!"

"Anyone with his training would wait for the right position. Besides, he has a job. We just haven't needed him yet."

"Plugging in modems, Judy, rebooting a server for a bunch of used-up wives—this is not a job on which an educated thirty-year-old man should subsist," he groaned, furiously pulling up silver socks.

"I'm not used up, Jeff," she said, arms straight at her sides.

He changed his face, smiled with teeth, and said, "Not yet." When she turned away, he stood and encircled her, nuzzled her neck. "No, not yet, Judy, but I've got plans for you."

"It's not funny," she said, stepping out of his arms.

He pitched back onto his valet, arms folded, pantsless and petulant, bare legs jutting out from under gray silk shirttails. She had the urge to straddle one of his thick runner's thighs, to dig her nails into his hard chest and tell him to knock it off. "Of course you're not used up, darling," he continued as she laid his undergarments in his suitcase. "You're barely handled. It was an ugly thing to say. It's just that I've got this trip coming up and a man, a stranger, living in my house and just, please, ask him about the cap."

"Ask him! Ask him!" shrieked the hyacinth macaw stamping his talon on the dowel perch in the corner of Jeff and Judith's bedroom.

"Fine, Jeff, just please quiet down. You're upsetting Sarge," she said, handing Jefferson black slacks and a sport jacket fresh from the cleaners. He was only meeting with Marilyn tonight. "You don't need a tie, do you?" she asked him as he tucked and smoothed and considered his open collar.

"Never mind, Judy. I'll pick one out."

Judith descended the two short flights of stairs to where her houseguest, Andy Mack, was frying a hamburger in the cellar-level kitchen. It was a large kitchen with high windows through which leashed dogs and the knees of pedestrians could be seen. Its central stone-topped island had two barstools on one side, and on the other, a cabinet that housed one pot, one pan, and a blender, all of which had gone unused before Andy's arrival. The meals that Jefferson ate at home since he'd passed the bar could be counted on a hand, and it was too much trouble to cook for one, so Judith almost always ordered in, eating out of disposables while dreaming of the streamlined and manifold appliances of her future.

But since Andy had come, the kitchen and its three vessels got constant action. He'd wake up late, fry things, purée things. Come evening—and evenings were growing longer each day—he kept a carousel of meat and cocktails spinning around that stone-topped island. Tonight, he was boiling ears of sweet corn, grinding pepper onto mixed greens, unpeeling a stick of butter, checking the burger with his fingertips, dancing to rush-hour jazz on the radio.

"Hey, lady! It's happy hour. Margarita? I put a blenderful in your freezer."

"No thanks, Andy. Or in a minute. Listen, have you seen a red Nationals baseball cap lying around anywhere? Jefferson can't find his."

"Nope. When is he leaving? I'll want to thank him, you know, for his hospitality."

"The day after tomorrow."

"Should we all have dinner together tomorrow night? I'll cook for you both."

"Not going to happen," Jefferson said, padding down the stairs cinching his tie. "The firm is hosting a party at Old Ebbitt's for those of us working on the admissions case. Judy, I want you to come, and dress for it. Really dress for it."

"When will you be back?" she asked him.

"Can't say. I don't know what Marilyn needs—footwork on development contracts or something. But I owe her."

"For what?"

"You have to ask? For supporting my hire."

"Seven months ago," Judith mumbled.

"Don't get cute, dear," he whispered, kissed her cheek, and turned away, "and don't wait up." Then to Andy, "Could you cover that with a lid? You're getting grease all over the backboard."

Judith settled on a barstool and arranged Andy's place setting while he rattled through cabinets looking for a lid, finally finding one in the broiler drawer under the range. She squared the placemat with two edges of the counter, refolded the napkin, lay it on the placemat, linen edges squared, and set up the flatware, bottoms even, spacing balanced.

"You're missing a salad fork."

"I'm chilling it. I don't want to go pokin' my lettuce with a warm fork."

"Really?"

"No, not really, Jude; I'm teasing you. But listen girl, how are you doing?" he asked, leaning across the counter, taking her hands and rubbing them between his own, warming them. "Are you nervous about Jeff leaving?"

"Two months isn't that long. We've done it before. He's just so busy now anyway and well, you're here now. You'll find a job at a fancy restaurant and I'll visit you." He nodded. They listened to the sizzling burger as one might listen to rain, to soothe a silence.

"I'm going out after dinner. Why don't you come with me tonight? We'll see what kind of trouble we can get you into."

So she pictured following him out of the rowhouse door, into the blush light fading over the Potomac, and when the pink was gone the sky would be the color of the patina on all the brass statues at the FDR Memorial, and first stars would shine like Eleanor's touch-polished hands. Single men and women, after-gym clean, would debouch from their apartments in their pink shirts. She imagined the press of a bar crowd, amalgamated cologne, and everyone surrounded by a group. But not Andy, not yet. He was new. Anyone would think they were together, and ill matched.

"I've had a splitting headache all afternoon."

"Maybe some fresh air would help."

"Oh, I ran earlier today. Eight miles, plus the headache, so frankly, I'm just not up for it."

And before he could further cajole, Sarge came crashing down the stairs like a toy helicopter in a rubber room, careening off walls as he circled the kitchen. Andy thrust out his arm and whistled to get the bird's attention. Sarge was missing his left eye, so flight was a knock-around, counterclockwise affair. Judith's brother Jeremiah, a merchant seaman, had rescued the bird from some port thinking it'd be cute to be a sailor with a parrot, but merchant ships are no place for pets, particularly shrieking, half-blind birds whose flight is calamity. Years ago, Jeremiah had given Sarge to Judith, and she couldn't bear to clip his wings again. She never had any idea where Jeremiah was these days, or whether he was in trouble, so when Sarge cawed, "Keep it real! Keep it real!" as he sometimes did while watching the pigeons through the window with his one good eye, she would think of her brother, waving from a railing, pulling out of port. Sarge alit on Andy's outstretched arm.

"I'm sorry," Judith said, reaching across the island to stroke Sarge's breast feathers. "He never flies down here, so he didn't know where to land. He's taken to you, though. Maybe you remind him of my brother."

"Let me take him up to his perch. Then I'll make you a margarita, see if it whets your appetite. I made the sour mix myself from fresh citrus and cane syrup."

"I just can't go out tonight, Andy. Another time, I promise."

"Then have a drink with me here. I have something to celebrate," Andy said. He switched off the burner with his free hand and carried Sarge up to his window perch in the family room.

"See ya later! See ya later! Keep it real!" followed Andy back into the kitchen.

He assembled his burger and bit into it standing up. "I found a place today, a studio in Mt. Pleasant, small, but with a decent kitchen. I'll be out of your hair soon," he said, talking around a mouthful.

"Oh. OK. Congratulations."

"They need a couple days to clean it out," he said. "I know Jeff's leaving Thursday and you'll want to spend some quality time with him, so I'll try to make myself scarce," he winked.

"Suddenly we have an event to attend tomorrow night," she said, smoothing the placemat. "I'll take that drink now."

He snapped and retrieved the blender's pitcher from the freezer, pulled a bottle of tequila from the cabinet beneath the island where he'd been storing bottles of liquor during the fifteen days he'd been staying there. Jefferson only drank scotch, which he kept in a locked cabinet. Andy poured an unmeasured swoop of tequila into the pale slush in the blender, stirred, and poured a tumbler of margarita each for himself and Judith, chiding her for having neither proper margarita glasses nor rimming salts.

"What did you do with all the stuff you had back in Michigan?"

"Either gave it away or put it in storage. We're going to have work done, so we're waiting to pick out the furnishings, the tableware, the art."

"All your old paintings?"

"Storage. Jeff doesn't think landscapes belong in a rowhouse—a conflict of style, he says." They made fun of Jefferson's sense of decorum, and then they laughed about the rich old women at Judith's office where she'd contracted Andy to do technical work while he searched for the perfect restaurant in need of a sous-chef. It felt good to conspire. He finished his drink too quickly, she thought, then they both went upstairs, Andy to groom, and Judith, with half a margarita, to her bedroom and her journal.

SHE'D BEEN KEEPING JOURNALS FOR exactly half her life, the first entry of the first leatherbound book simply, "Judith Parker Halloway, age 14." She was not given a middle name by her parents; she'd chosen her own. Over the years, her journals had become physically smaller as she decided only to write down thoughts and plans she was awfully sure about. Increasingly, she wrote lists—wish lists, to do lists—believing that if one didn't keep it simple, life could easily become a collection of good intentions perpetually deferred, and useless sentimentality. Her current notebook had pages the size of recipe cards.

She sat in the wing chair that faced her blinded bedroom window and opened the book, flipping through it as if looking for clues, but to what mystery, she had no idea. Though she'd begun this journal over a year ago when she and Jefferson had just moved into the rowhouse on Capitol Hill, few pages were used. She had once been overjoyed with the change, the move, the rung ascended. She'd been glad to leave the Midwest, thrilled to make a home of her own with Jefferson. He had landed the internship and then the job with a top-tier law firm in the District. She flipped forward.

The previous September, Jefferson had gone back to Michigan to work on the admissions case. By October, Judith still hadn't gotten her period. Her first thought was, I can't tell him. He had the case and he was studying for the bar. She'd just begun her job with the Center for Philanthropic Development and she knew none of the four Potomac wives in her office well enough to confide in them. So she had to tell him. She'd cried when she said, over the phone, "I think I may be…"

Jefferson took a long breath, held it, released it. She'd written down what he said. He said: "It's appropriate." He said: "Let's not worry about it now; there will be time, later, to worry." The next day, she got her period.

And when that was over, she turned her attention to training for a triathlon. Since then, most journal entries simply tracked her running time and distance. She marked the day's mileage. And when she heard the front door slam for the second time that evening, she stood and pushed the blinds aside to watch Andy walk away into dusk, then got into bed where it darkened into agitated dreams.

IN THAT STILL-PINK LIGHT, ANDY hopped the four brick steps to the sidewalk and turned toward the Pennsylvania Avenue bars. He looked back once at the light in Judith's window. He took a slim cigarette case from the deep pocket of his Levis, pulled a joint from it, and lit up. Three men passed on the opposite sidewalk all wearing the same costume: baggy black slacks and blue button-down oxford, red tie, plastic ID tag. They make it easy, he thought, but then again, what do women ever see in me? He could think of nothing in particular, maybe just friendliness, or maybe he put himself in social situations where he looked unique in comparison to other men. Anyway, to overthink a thing is to jinx it, he supposed; if he identified his charm, he might wind up just putting it on. He pinched the cherry off the joint, put the roach back in his case, and turned the corner.

He sat at the bar in the Hawk 'n' Dove watching the Nats game on TV and staffers standing around with pints and martinis. He was sorry that Jude hadn't joined him; she was easy to talk with, no put-ons, no pressure. And he would have rather been at a gastropub, maybe just a bar with a good mixologist, but didn't feel he could afford that life yet, so he enjoyed the view. Hill garb, so dull on men, was delicious in its female version: button-downs tailored to the breasts and half open, black slacks with slit pockets hugging young, ideological asses, and creased down to the pumps. He tried some lines, got no response, and moved next door. Guys were playing pool. Girls were dancing around the Internet jukebox. He ordered a Corona and walked toward them, juicing the lime wedge, pushing it down the bottleneck. In no time, the empty bottle in his hand was resting against the lower back of a girl named Beth. Or Betsy.

JEFFERSON PAID THE DRIVER AND went inside where Sarge was still perched in the front window. He put his arm out for the bird and carried him upstairs into the bedroom where Judith was asleep with her eye-mask on. He turned on the light and put Sarge in his cage. He took off his shirt and smelled it: cigars, his own cologne. In the bathroom, he checked his face and neck for marks, and rubbing his hand over his stubble, he smelled Marilyn mixed with scotch. He closed his eyes, put his hands over his face and breathed her in, then turned on the shower and got in to scrub. After, wearing a towel, he stepped up to the full-length mirror in the bedroom. His eyes were red. He took a few jabs at the air, then stepped away from his reflection.

Jefferson climbed into bed and lightly shook Judith's shoulder. She woke and yawned, and he turned her body toward him and began kissing her. She lifted a corner of her eye-mask, squinting.

"You smell like alcohol," she said.

"I had two," he said, climbing over her, kissing her collarbones. He popped a snap on her pajama top, then another, and a third, and slid a finger down her breastbone. She was so warm, smooth, thin, familiar, and touching her squeezed his heart so that he felt a little sick and nigh-religiously grateful that he hadn't fucked Marilyn.

"Stop, Jeff. I'm sleeping." Judith didn't want him now; she wanted him tomorrow night, the night before he would leave her alone in the District for another two months. She wanted him tomorrow, and hard, so she could wake up on the morning of his departure and still feel it, and remember how much she'd been wanted.

"You can leave your mask on," he said, cupping a breast, kissing the nipple. She pushed him away.

"I'm asleep." So he left their bed and went into the den where he watched SportsCenter and fell asleep on the leather loveseat.

IN THE MORNING, JEFFERSON TIGHTENED his tie and said, "Ask What's-His-Name to actually look around his room for my Nats cap, which may have grown legs and walked in there. I searched this whole place when I got up early this morning, all except his room. Nothing."

Sarge said, "Ask him! Ask him!" bobbing up and down, restive in his cage. Jefferson opened the cage door, and the bird was free to move as he pleased.

Judith had never had a friendship last longer than a year, let alone a friendship with a man, so she didn't know how to explain or defend Andy

Mack, whom she felt had most likely not stolen her husband's baseball cap. She had moved around so much as a child that, by her teenage years, she'd stopped investing in friendships. Her father was an undertalented salesman, and easily bored. When his employers cut him loose, he'd move his wife, son, and daughter hundreds more miles in the family station wagon, beaming at a new city as if arrival itself was conquest. Sometimes the family didn't last a year.

Andy used to drop by Judith's desk at the university library several times a day; that was before he got his culinary arts certificate, when he was still working IT. Judith was a senior then, already married to her aspiring attorney. She'd taken the job at the reference desk because she liked having a purpose, but quietly so.

They were unlikely friends. Andy Mack had friends in punk and blue-grass bands, in fraternities, in software development, and in the Michigan Militia; he had friends in New York, in Aspen, in Seattle; he had friends with benefits. He fixed glitches. He threatened to quit daily. His restlessness and impracticality reminded Judith of her father and Jeremiah, but if she and Andy had anything in common, it was that neither of them fit in with the rest of the silverfish in the stacks; they were both biding time.

When Judith moved away, Andy enrolled in a culinary arts school. She was surprised that he'd kept in touch, that he included D.C. among the cities where he sought work, and that he asked if he could stay with her while he looked for a job and an apartment. She said yes without asking Jefferson. When she told Jefferson they'd be housing a guest, he'd said, "You have a friend?"

ANDY EMERGED FROM THE GUESTROOM around noon in mesh shorts, hair wild and eyes puffy. Judith was in the family room watching a Jackie Kennedy biopic on DVR. Jackie had just delivered a stillborn child while Jack was out to sea. She paused the program.

"Andy, Jefferson wanted me to ask if you could check your room for his…"

"Fucking hat. He already accosted me," Andy snapped. "Oh Jude, I'm sorry. I'm a dick. I saw him in the kitchen this morning. I got up to take a

leak and he asked me, for like the fifteenth time, about that baseball cap.
I swear to God, I've never even seen it."

"OK."

"Again, I'm sorry. Hey, why are you home?"

"Called in sick. I have to find something to wear for the party tonight."

"Try not to sound so excited. Remember, if you find yourself awash in a
bullshit sea, you can always call on me. I'll paddle on over and save you," he
said, and went back through the guestroom to shower.

JUDITH TRIED ON NINE DRESSES before she decided to wear a simple,
Empire waist gray with a charcoal wrap. The firm sent a Lincoln, which
deposited her on the curb before Old Ebbitt Grill at six o'clock sharp. She
entered and walked past the dark wood and green velvet booths to the
private room.

She could see him from where she stood between double doors, his head
bent toward some secret Marilyn was whispering behind her martini glass.
He smiled and touched Marilyn's bare, freckled arm; his other hand, with
the gold band, was wrapped around a rocks glass. Judith told herself it was
irrational to suspect anything other than professional esteem. Marilyn
looked her age; you could tell she'd been dying her chestnut flip. She was
soft, curvaceous, so many things that Judith was not. Jefferson couldn't
possibly be attracted to her, could he? She watched Jefferson's friend John
whisk Marilyn away. The only time Judith had ever seen Jefferson drunk
was the night, not long ago, when Marilyn had announced her engagement to John. Jefferson, too, watched the couple cross the room. His jaw
clenched; he rocked, heel to toe, then turned to the bar to take a refill of
Glenlivet. Judith stepped through the double doors and smiles were cast
her way like charity.

"There you are," Jefferson said. "Drink?"

"Let me have what you're having," she said, wrapping her shawl tighter.

"You'll hate it," he said.

"Give me one," she said. "I'll decide whether I like it."

Hours later, after crab soup and rockfish in cream sauce, champagne, and
port, the car drove them home. The moon flashed in Jefferson's silver belt

buckle. Judith threaded a hand between his shirt buttons and stroked the soft hairs on his belly. He watched the Smithsonian Castle, the staid Air and Space Museum, and the cantilevered American Indian Museum blur by his window, then, rising on its hillock, the resplendent white dome of the Capitol, at the sight of which he felt such a surge of affection for white marble and light that he bent down and kissed his wife deeply, driver be damned.

ON THE CARPETED FLOOR OF the guest bedroom, Andy lay naked on his stomach, a girl's ass in his hands, her heels gripping his back. He heard the front door slam; they were back early. The sound of footsteps resonated along the floor through Andy's flesh until they reached the guestroom door. He heard Jeff bitching, heard the door handle turn, and he thrust himself back to hold the door shut with his feet, never stopping with the girl who was gripping his head with her thighs, who shuddered and moaned, and who was all that mattered in that moment. Minutes later, he'd lie beside her laughing about the close call, about doors without locks in another man's house.

Upstairs, Jefferson ripped off his tie and coat and threw them on the closet floor. "I can't fucking believe it! I should go down there right now and throw them both out, and call the police. Do you think it's a whore?"

"Why would you even think that?" She stood clutching her wrap, watching Jefferson pace.

"He doesn't know anyone else in the city."

"He's never had any trouble meeting people." She started to undress.

"Meeting people? Do you find this acceptable?"

"No. I just don't see why it upsets you. Come to bed."

"I'm too angry to go to bed. I feel violated. I feel that my home, my generosity, has been defiled." He stomped around the bedroom, stripping and flinging his garments down.

Sarge, upset by the tension, circled the room screeching, "Ask him! Ask him! See ya later! See ya later!" First a lamp went down, then he got caught in a pull string and the blinds came down.

"Stop moving!" Judith yelled. They both stood still, facing each other from either side of the bed, she in her strapless bra and panties and he in his socks and silk boxers. Sarge finally alit on his dowel. Jefferson crossed to the bird and calmly extended an arm, walking him over to his cage for the night.

"I'm showering," he told her, and closed the bathroom door. She lay on the bed and stared at the ceiling. By the time he came to bed, she was asleep.

HE MUST HAVE AWAKENED EARLY, Judith thought, when she heard him padding around the bedroom the next morning and smelled his coffee and aftershave. When she heard him slam down his mug and run out of the room, she sat up and lifted her mask and looked at the clock—only 6:30 and already light. Sarge was out of his cage again. Judith went to the now-blindless window which was open to hot, damp air. She saw Andy kiss a girl in a red cap. The girl got into a cab and it drove away. She saw Jefferson bound down the four brick stairs, barefoot in his bathrobe and boxers. Sarge sprang from his perch, flew from the bedroom, and ricocheted down the stairwell. Judith ran after the bird who escaped from the open front door, ascending in a widening blue spiral between the oak trees.

"That was a fucking Terps hat! She's a graduate student at Maryland for Christ's sake!"

"I should be relieved she wasn't a prostitute."

"Fuck you. Hey, there goes your bird, asshole."

Jefferson lunged for him, but Andy dodged. They staggered into the street. Judith stood in the doorway looking from the men to Sarge, who had landed in a tree one house over.

"Rein it in, man," Andy said. "I don't want to fight you. Your neighbors are probably asleep."

"So now you're going to practice discretion?"

"Get over it! I couldn't exactly stop just because you came home."

"What kind of excuse is that?"

"Fuck your wife sometime and find out." Jefferson swung at him again, missed again, and spinning, saw Judith on the stairs. He straightened up, closed his robe, and stuck out an arm.

"Come on, Sarge," he called, whistling, watching Andy. Andy also stuck out his arm and began to call the bird. The two men walked in a circle in the street, each with his arm out, whistling to the hyacinth macaw in the oak tree. Sarge finally flew right back through the front door and to his window perch. The men, Jefferson first, walked silently past Judith and to their respective rooms.

Judith went to the kitchen and poured the last of the coffee for herself. Jefferson's car arrived and the chauffeur took his bags to the Lincoln. He came down into the kitchen, kissed his wife, and held her. Before he left, he opened a closet and grabbed a jacket. "Colder up there," he said, and "well, what do you know!" A curled red bill stuck out of the jacket pocket. He pulled it out and put on the Nats cap, winking. She listened for the door, and through the kitchen window, watched the car tires roll away.

Andy came down and said, "Jude, I'm so sorry for the drama. I never meant to abuse your generosity. I'm going down to the leasing office, see if I can start moving my stuff in today. Are we still pals?"

"Of course. You don't have to go. So who was she?"

"I met her at a bookstore bar. She was alone, house sitting for a professor in the neighborhood. She was different from the girls I've been meeting; casual, you know? And there was a full moon over Connecticut Avenue, color of a piña colada. We took a walk; a brass and drum band was playing south of Dupont and we danced. She told me the professor had strictly forbidden guests, so I asked her if she'd come home with me. I had no idea she'd say yes." They both smiled, and she lowered her eyes, stirring her coffee.

Later, Andy, too, said goodbye. He had an interview somewhere in the new Atlas District. And when Judith returned to her bedroom to prepare for her day, she picked up her journal. It fell open to lists: September triathlon; House-hunting: Maryland?; 10K for the Cure? Trip (after the case)? Development director position? Kids?

So many question marks. She turned past her latest training chart to a blank page. Slowly, deliberately, as if hand-addressing an invitation, she wrote: Happy Hour. She closed the book, tossed it onto the bed, and crossed to the window to watch Andy walk out her front door whistling some song she'd never heard before. She watched him disappear around the corner, heard Sarge, down below, echoing the song. She ran her fingers through the sweat on her chest, and brought them to her tongue. It was hot out there, and it would stay hot so long into autumn.

Sally Toner

Picking Blueberries

SALLY TONER is a high school English teacher and resident of the Washington, D.C., area for almost twenty years. Her work has been published in *Gargoyle Magazine*, and she is a two-time honoree in the F. Scott Fitzgerald Fiction Contest sponsored by the *Potomac Review*. She lives in Reston, Virginia, with her husband and two daughters.

*A*nnie had purchased a tick remover before she and Ella went camping—a medieval device that resembled a bright orange plastic corkscrew, except it dug into flesh instead of wine and scooped out the parasite before he knew what hit him.

Still, there was always Lyme disease. And Annie didn't want her daughter on antibiotics for fourteen days all for the sake of blueberry cobbler. She watched the little fingers plucking each bulb of blue and imagined the Rocky Mountain–fevered hitchhikers just waiting to leap from the tip of the pampas grass onto that perfect little elbow up to her hair that glowed in the afternoon sunlight.

Just waiting.

"Make sure they're dark blue, sweets," she said to the air behind her as the five-year-old grabbed her bounty a clump at a time. It surprised Annie that a group of six berries on the same branch could be, each one, a different color. Each was at a different stage of the ripeness spectrum, from tiny green to shriveled black. Didn't they all, on the same damn branch, get the same amount of sunlight? Rain? The same ratio of clay in the earth feeding their roots? So why were they all so different? Maybe it had to do with pollination. A bee scooted from one flower to the next, skipping some future strands of fruit in favor of others.

Annie put her right hand to her stomach as the baby kicked and looked back over at Ella. Surely these two berries would ripen at different rates.

There had been a lot of waiting—a test early on with numbers just a little low.

"Don't lose any sleep over this," her OB had said. "The alpha-fetoprotein test has more false positives than you could imagine. Just go ahead and get the amnio so we can be sure."

Annie's friends echoed his positivity, though they understood the sleepless nights were a matter of course. Annie already knew this truth from Ella, recalling the jaundice when she was born and the terrifying bilirubin lights and patches over her eyes. Then there was the Roseola-fed fever of 103 that made her stand over the baby's crib with a flashlight in the middle of the night, just staring.

"Jared. Look at her. Is she listless?"

"She's asleep."

"How the fuck do we know the difference?"

"I don't know. Maybe we should take her to the ER."

"You think?"

"You tell me."

Jared had been sanguine about the second test, as he was about everything. He often just stared at Annie with wide light gray eyes while she ranted and raved. Her frustration at her own loss of control and his calm only turned up the heat even more. Her fury tasted sour.

"Is this one dark enough, Mommy?" Ella held a blueberry up to the sunlight, and Annie saw the purple stains on her daughter's teeth.

"How many of those have you saved, and how many have you eaten, ladybug?" She sighed and fished a wipe out of her bag, removing the blue from Ella's cheeks. "They put spray on these, sweetie. It will make you sick." Ella let the berry thump inside the plastic container and looked down.

"But if I have a tummy ache, I won't be able to go to Ruthie's party."

Ruthie was a little girl at Ella's school she, and Annie, had been spending much more time with lately.

"I think it will be OK. We'll just have to wait and see, baby."

They plucked fruit in silence for a moment, and Annie thought about Ruthie. She'd met her mother at a support meeting soon after receiving the second test results she wasn't supposed to worry about.

Just an amnio—very routine—to rule out the false positive. Annie hadn't seen the needle. But Jared's almost invisible eyebrows went up the slightest when his eyes peered at her over the sheet. They told her to keep her own eyes on the ultrasound monitor, and she saw the tiny hand reach up and almost touch the bright glowing stick moving towards it on the screen.

"Be careful, little one."

Just an amnio. Very routine.

Except the results were not.

Annie had been curled up on the couch with Ella taking a nap while she watched *Beauty and the Beast* when the phone rang. She knew that they never wanted to give bad news over the phone. And this was the doctor, not the nurse. The nurse usually left a message when things were OK. Annie pressed him to tell her something before she came into the office.

"It's an extra twenty-first chromosome."

"Down's."

"I'm sorry. I do need you to come in so we can discuss options. And what to expect."

Those were few—options. She had felt this baby move. Seen the little finger almost pricked by that wretched needle—the glowing soothsayer.

Just an amnio.

Very routine.

Except when it wasn't.

"There are no easy lives," her mother had said over the phone as Annie managed to choke out the news that night.

Annie's mother had her children before the days of amniocentesis. Sometimes, knowledge was power. And sometimes, it only gave one more time to contemplate the uncontrollable. Skinned knees became flesh-eating viruses. A squirmy eight-year-old boy became a raging case of ADHD, in need of speed, of all things, to help him focus for the hours of high-stakes testing Annie's parents never had to worry about. When Annie hadn't made the basketball team in ninth grade, she'd been crushed. Her mother had shrugged her shoulders, told her female basketball players were lesbians anyway, and told her to set the table for dinner.

Annie knew her mother had watched her own little sister get run down by a delivery truck when she was thirteen. She had never talked about it. Just carried a card around in her wallet that Annie came across when she was a little girl.

When the Lord gives us rocky roads, He gives us tough feet.

"What's this, Momma?" Annie had asked.

"Something someone gave me once," she had said, snatching the card and stuffing it back into the slab of leather then back into her purse. "And who said you could go through my pocketbook, young lady?"

There are no easy lives.

"Mommy, how are these?" Ella was holding up more berries, and Annie was watching the clouds roll in.

"What do you want to get Ruthie for her birthday?" Annie absently held out the plastic bin and listened to the handful of berries drop in again. She imagined Ruthie's face—the extra large tongue, flat nose, wide-set eyes, and glasses. She tried to imagine her own features and Jared's on little Ruthie's open, trusting face. No matter how hard she tried, the image just wouldn't come.

Ruthie's mother, Susan, had been wonderful. She had two much older boys. And Susan had confessed that Ruthie had been an "oops." Maybe watching tween boys tear up her house had given Susan that blasted calm Annie so coveted. Ever since the ultrasound, Annie had looked everywhere for information, for comfort. She was a veritable encyclopedia on the syndrome—knew every statistic, every cognitive, emotional, physical possibility. Of course, that's all they were. Possibilities. Online there were sites dedicated to mainstreaming, sites dedicated to home schooling and self-contained education. Postings from parents and patients themselves ranging everywhere from a ten-year-old who couldn't walk or speak to an actual comedian with Down's mosaicism who toured the country with a show entitled *Dude, Where's My Chromosome?* The more she researched, the more confused Annie became. And the fuzzier this little face inside her appeared.

Susan had probably offered her the clearest vision of her future soon after they met when Annie had asked her, point blank.

"Tell me the truth. What's it really like having a child with Down's?"

Susan had thought for a minute, then offered a very specific answer to the vague question.

"It's like planning a trip to Disney World. Packing your suitcase, bathing suits, extra sunscreen, deciding how you'll split your time between the parks, which rides you'll go on, getting on the plane, all excited…Then ending up in Europe instead."

No better. No worse. Just different.

The problem was, Mickey Mouse ears didn't really blend on the Champs-Élysées.

Jared. He and Annie hadn't turned out as expected either. In the weeks following the amnio, those light gray eyes clouded over. He started spending more time at work. One night, Annie and Ella surprised him with pizza, a nice bordeaux, and several juice boxes. When they arrived, she saw his building was dark except for his office. Everyone else had gone home, and Jared was sitting with his back to them, alone, watching a DVD.

She and Ella stood there, watching him that night, as he stared at the screen and rubbed a balled-up piece of Scotch tape between his thumb and forefinger. He was completely oblivious to his surroundings—to them—and Annie lost her voice at that moment. The magic bubble had engulfed her and Ella, and she couldn't even speak his name.

Amazingly, Ella hadn't said a word either. So they turned around and left, taking their dinner home with them.

Pretty soon he wasn't staying at the office alone. One of the paralegals. So cliché on the one hand, but, in an odd way, Annie understood. Jared had never uprighted himself from Ella's birth. He was awkward in the role of father to begin with—sometimes even flinching when his own flesh and blood jumped up on the couch and tried to scoot her little body up against him.

It didn't shock Annie when he left. It seemed the natural progression. Though the quickness of it, that's what she couldn't get. There must have been something rotten germinating long before this mutant seed she carried inside her now.

Mutant seed. The cruelty of her own thoughts angered Annie even more.

"Mommy, my tummy hurts again." Ella was poking at her with a single tiny finger. Annie needed to trim her daughter's nails. She knelt down to see Ella's lips freshly covered in blue.

"Dammit, Ella, I told you not to eat these here. They have poison on them. Of course you're sick. Why won't you just LISTEN?"

Ella's eyes stared back at her—large and brown like Annie's own. They should have been frightened by the shouting. Annie rarely raised her voice to Ella. Instead, they were thoughtful, measured. Ella pursed her lips and glanced from shoulder to shoulder where Annie realized she had grabbed the child a little too tightly. She yanked her hands away as if they were burned and watched the red splotchy finger marks on Ella's pale skin. She knew they'd disappear. Not like the time when Ella was three and went through a pinching phase. One night, Annie had decided to pinch her daughter back. She had sworn it was to make a point. Granted, Ella had never done it again. But Annie knew, down in that dark place she never shared with anyone, that the three-year-old's pinches had hurt. For a split second, her reaction had been to hurt her back. Ella had forgotten about it by bedtime, but the mark stayed for about three days—a constant reminder of those split-second actions that made Annie hate herself.

Now, Ella just looked at her, crossing her arms in front of her chest and obscuring a little daisy sewn into pink cotton.

"Good mommies make good honeys," Ella said.

Honeys. Ella's term for babies, children, herself. Annie crumbled into a heap and began to cry. As she did, the raindrops started, making a splat sound against the plastic bottom of the berry container. When Annie looked up, she saw Ella still standing in front of her. Her arms were above her head, palms touching the sky. Ella's hair was a mass of red ringlets plastered to her cheeks, and her tongue was stuck out to catch the globs of water falling from the atmosphere.

Annie wiped her face with the rain. The sunscreen stopped stinging in the corners of her eyes, and she ran her fingers through her own hair, brushing it back behind her shoulders.

The baby kicked again, and Annie saw the lightening on the horizon.

"Come on. We need to get back to the car." She grabbed Ella's hand and dragged her through the clover. When she was in a hurry, Annie always saw the four-leaf clovers she had no time to pick. But on sunny days, when she and Ella had no playdates and wandered through the empty playground for hours, she'd look and look but never find one.

"But Mommy. We didn't get enough berries for cobbler." Ella held up her bucket, where the tiny bulbs of blue floated on rainwater, their stems pointing up to make them seem like miniature buoys on a clear lake.

"That's OK, love," Annie smiled. "We'll at least have enough for breakfast tomorrow."

Krista Waple

Loving Kerry

KRISTA WAPLE was born and raised in Northern Virginia. She attended college in Fredericksburg, Virginia, at the University of Mary Washington, and graduated in 2005 with a BA in English. She currently lives and works as a massage therapist in Falls Church, Virginia. Though in no way a prolific writer, she has a passion for the short story and hopes to create a collection of original works by the time she reaches her early thirties.

I

MY WIFE KERRY WAS SLUMPED on the floor with her skinny legs splayed apart, her swelling abdomen heaving with each hysterical breath.

"I want it out," she said.

"Shh, it's OK," I said to her, picking up the remote control from her limp fingers and pressing the power button to silence the blaring television.

She did a little convulsing movement, not at all involuntary, something in the way of a miniature temper tantrum. This was the best she could do given her present condition, otherwise she might have broken a few things in the house, sent the curtains into a pile on the floor and the rod spearing a hole into the carpet, or backhanded my parents' old wedding photo off the wall. At seven months' pregnant, the extra weight on Kerry's stomach disabled her most violent outbursts.

"I want it out of me *now*," she moaned, then started blubbering a bit, but without tears. Just whimpering while squinting her eyes into little agonizing half moons.

Kerry and her side of the family had continued to refer to our son as *it*, despite our having learned that our baby was going to be a boy. It was as if all of them, Kerry herself especially, didn't know if he was ever going to make it to being a full-blown human being.

Barb, Kerry's mom, had warned me about what this pregnancy might do to her daughter. Kerry had been on antipsychotic and antidepressant medications since she was fourteen years old, and had decided to stop taking all of them as soon as we found out she was pregnant. She had done some research on the Internet and declared to me six months ago that she would not give birth to a flipper baby, that she was off the meds starting that day. Ever since, her mental health has declined as my stress level has skyrocketed.

"And," Kerry said, taking in a deep breath and then letting it out in a whispery, maniacal giggle, "it's just too late." She let her head hang over her swollen breasts as the exhausted laughter fell out of her mouth and onto her stomach.

"You're doing a good job with our son in there," I said to her. "He's all curled up and happy inside of you right now."

I crouched down on the floor next to her and pulled her hair back into a messy ponytail. I fastened it with one of the rubber elastics I kept on my wrists at all times for the frequent occasions when she'd start working herself up like this. Her face would get so pink and sweaty, and I was afraid sometimes she'd overheat and pass out if I didn't clear all of that thick, heavy hair from where it would get plastered onto her cheeks.

"Let's go lie in bed and turn on the fan for a while," I said to her.

I got behind her to help her to her feet, but as I squatted down to hoist her up by her armpits, she elbowed me right in the dick and sent me queasy and stunned to the floor.

"Kerry," I groaned, "I know you're not feeling well, but you can't act like this."

I coughed deep coughs to get the vomiting feeling out of my stomach and throat, then turned onto my side to look at her for a moment. She stared off to the side of the television's blank screen. I rolled onto my back and stared at the ceiling.

"I'm sorry," she said.

We were on the floor together in silence before I felt the tips of the hair on my arms lift away from my skin a bit. In my peripheral vision, I could see that Kerry had shifted her gaze. She now had that familiar glazed-over look that told me she was slipping away from reality, and was directing it straight ahead at the apex of her stomach.

"Kerry?" I said. Sometimes hearing her name can bring her back, as long as she hasn't fallen in too deep. "Hey, *Kerry?*"

She balled her hand into a tight fist, wound back, and punched three violent blows into her stomach before I was on top of her, pushing her arms down to her sides and making sure not to put any weight on the baby as I straddled her and she writhed around on the floor.

"Kerry what the *fuck!*" I screamed.

"We shouldn't have done this!" she howled into my face, spit spraying from her dry lips. "It has to get out!"

I HAD TO PIN HER hands down with my knees for a few moments to get the belt loosened from my waist. I successfully restrained her this way on two other occasions when she had been trying to harm herself, but failed on one other horrifying night when she'd had a razor in her hand and cut herself free. This time I didn't even spare a moment to make sure she was comfortable, just rolled her onto her side and wrapped her wrists together too tightly with my belt. Her screams went straight to my stomach and nauseatingly echoed around inside it.

After securing her hands behind her back, I stood up and ran to the phone, then slammed it down and ran back to Kerry. An image of her rocking to her feet and doing a belly flop onto the floor had just entered my head, so I picked her up and carried her into the kitchen with me as she kept wailing that she was sorry but that we had made a mistake she had to fix. I set her in the heaviest of the mismatched chairs around our dining table, fastened my arms around her and it, and carried them both over to the drawer where I knew there was some duct tape. I sat on her lap as I flung the drawer open and chucked aside paperclips and scissors until I found the roll, then strapped her to the chair with layers upon layers of the duct tape until it was all gone.

I caught my breath and went back to the phone, which was not a wireless but rather an old hot pink monstrosity we'd picked up at the thrift store because it was too ridiculous not to own, and stretched the cord as far as it would go across the kitchen where Kerry was taped in the chair. I planted my ass back on Kerry's lap to keep her from knocking the chair over with her struggling, dialed her parents' number, and leaned forward with my head cocked to the side to keep the phone against my face.

BARB AND JIM WERE AT our door in only ten minutes. I hung my head down low when they walked into the kitchen and saw what I had done. By this point Kerry had exhausted herself and was just stuck in place with only her head rolling back and forth against the chair's headrest.

"Didn't want to take any chances," I mumbled.

Her parents worked to get the tape off while I put my elbows on the counter and pressed my palms into my forehead. I was dizzy but still clearheaded enough to think about getting Kerry a glass of water. I went through the cabinets to find Kerry's favorite thermos so she could drink through a straw, but then saw that it was lying in the sink, dirty. I turned on the water and washed it out, then filled it up for her and screwed on the cap. When I turned back around, I saw that Jim had untaped Kerry completely and held her limp body in his arms. He and Barb began walking to the door without waiting for me.

"We're bringing her to the hospital, right?" I asked them.

"We are, but you're staying here," Jim shouted over his shoulder. "You just get some sleep tonight, Justin. Understand?"

Barb turned around to give me this terrible, wide-eyed nod. *Do you see what's happening?* she said with her eyes. *What did I tell you?*

They were gone with Kerry before I could even give her the water. I took the lid off the thermos, poured all of the water over my head, then lay down on the floor to allow myself to cry.

JIM CALLED ME FROM THE emergency room to tell me that everything was fine, and that they covered for Kerry, telling the hospital staff that she had tripped and fallen forward up the stairs. She didn't give it away in front of the doctor, Jim told me, because she just came across as being delirious from freaking out about the safety of "the fetus."

"Thanks for the help, Jim," I said into the phone, "but I really wanted to be there with Kerry."

"Justin," he said, "I think you two really need a break from each other right now. Barb and I have talked it over, and we've decided Kerry's going to stay with us for the rest of the pregnancy."

"What? No, please—"

"It's really not up for discussion, Justin."

"Wait though! Can I make a suggestion? Please?"

Jim sighed into the phone. "What's your suggestion?"

"I do want your help—that's why I called you guys. And I'm so grateful that you and Barb came right over and took care of this—though I really wish you hadn't left me at the house—but anyway, here's what I really think would be best: When I'm at work, I worry about Kerry and the baby like crazy, and obviously there's some danger of—of this sort of thing—happening again. I mean, she hasn't been herself for a while—"

"Which is exactly what Barb and I predicted would happen."

"I know, I know. You guys were right. It's been extremely hard for her."

"Kerry can't be off her meds."

"I know. I think she should get back on them. All of that stuff she read on the Internet—there's just such a small risk for birth defects. I think her irrational behavior puts him in much more danger than taking her pills would. I mean, are we on the same page here?"

Jim let out a sarcastic chuckle. "Justin, you know as well as Barb and I do that if Kerry sets her mind to do something, she's going to do it her way regardless of what anyone else tells her. What do you want to do, tape her to a chair and pinch her nose, then force the pills down her throat?"

The duct tape. It was a low blow.

"Jim, about that—"

"It's OK. Honestly, Barb and I have done worse before when she's had her—her whatever you want to call them. Her fits, I guess."

I know, I wanted to tell him. *She's told me all about what you two have done.* I knew they didn't understand her like I did.

"Jim, please don't take her away from me," I begged. "Please don't take them away from me. I fucked up tonight—I didn't know what to do—but I've done a lot of reading on her disorder and we've done group sessions and I really think I know how to help her."

He sighed again. "Barb and I would really feel better if she stayed with us until this is all over and she decides to go back on her meds again."

"That's great! That's what I was about to say earlier!" I said with some hope. "I think, since Barb is home during the day, Kerry should stay over there while I'm at work, and then I can pick her up on my way home. Then she won't have to be alone during the day."

"No, we've already made arrangements. Marlena is going to move in for the next few weeks to help Barb watch Kerry."

"The *maid*? She doesn't speak English, Jim! Who's going to talk to her when she needs someone?"

I heard the phone being knocked around, and then Barb's voice replaced Jim's.

"Justin, this is not up for discussion," she said. "Everything has already been decided, and what you need to do right now is just get a good night's rest. You may call the house tomorrow, but do not call tonight. Go to bed."

II

IT'S BEEN OVER TWO WEEKS now since Kerry moved back in with her parents. I go to work and then come home to our empty house, call Kerry, then pace and sleep. I visited Kerry three times in the first week, but on the third visit Barb told me I had to stay away because Kerry started crying. Barb said seeing me was making it harder for Kerry, but I know Kerry is getting worse at her parents' house. Her voice is completely unrecognizable lately. She sounds distant and vacant, and she keeps fixating on things that only make sense to me because I know her, and I understand the metaphors and the nightmares. I have all of the details of her life to draw upon when deciphering what at first seems unintelligible. At her most lucid, when she's not communicating through abstractions, she just repeats the same creepy things over and over again, often impervious to any of the things I say to try to soothe her.

She says she can smell the baby's skin, that she can smell the texture of it. She says the smell feels like the soft, velvety flesh of a peeled banana. Other than that, she will not talk about our son without dissociating and heavily cloaking her statements. Whenever I bring him up she gets on the defensive, descending into a variety of rants on seemingly tangential subjects, and I have to sift through the madness to find the point.

She talks a lot about some imagined estuary where a giant river of oil dumps straight into the sea.

"And the ecosystem thrives off of the oil," she says, "and the concentration has to be half and half, and it keeps catching fire and killing all of the birds who swoop in for food."

"It'll be OK through the next few weeks, though," I tell her," as long as no one tries to cut off the estuary. Right?"

"I don't know, I don't know," she says. "It's just, there's a whole ecosystem at work here."

"But help is on the way, you know. It can all go back to normal soon once the oil river's treated. Or, just treat the oil river now," I say, hoping she'll understand what I'm trying to tell her—that she should get back on her meds.

"Lots of long-term damage to prevent. Dead birds putrefying in the ocean. But it has to be half and half," she says.

There's also the Rocks and Blankets speech.

"You wrap a rock in a thick fur blanket and you throw it through a window and the glass smashes but the rock stays intact, but if the fur falls out and it's just the hide, the rock cracks in half when it hits the window, so what do you do? What do you do?"

"I think you just wait until the fur grows back before you try to smash any windows," I tell her.

"Nope. Impossible. Dead skin can't regenerate fur. It just gets worn down hair by hair every second until there's no layer of protection. So what do you do?"

"Do you know?" I ask.

"Yeah, you act fast before it all falls out."

I know that she is the balding hide, that she thinks our baby isn't protected inside of her.

"No," I say. "You keep it safe from the elements. In a warm bed, maybe. And you don't move it around too much. Avoid friction."

"You may be right," she says to my relief. "It could work, possibly."

"Try that, OK?"

"I'll try."

And then there's The Face.

"It'll start coming through the wall in my old bedroom, and then I move to another room and it starts pushing through the walls in there too, and if I go outside sometimes, from the woods, it gets all the way out to the neck and then screams at me until I go back in."

"Is it always the same face?" I ask.

"Different contortions of the features," she says.

"But on the same face?"

"Mm."

"Yes?"

"I think I know who it is," she says.

"I think I do, too."

I think The Face is our baby, and that she thinks he's crying to get out of her, but she also knows that she can't just take him out to save him.

"I don't want to talk anymore," she says.

SOMETIMES I LIKE TO SPRAWL on the floor and listen to music in an effort to relax, but usually the songs make me yearn even more for the life Kerry and I used to have, and painfully so. I listen to Elliott Smith a lot because, unlike many of the other artists I usually like, his songs don't exude the sort of energy or nonchalance that alienates me these days. His songs hit me like a punch to the stomach, but at least I can relate to them. At least I can feel something.

I remember the day Kerry and I lay on the floor of our first apartment together, head to head with our legs stretched out in opposite directions, staring at the ceiling as we listened to "Between the Bars." We were both crying, and our tears slid away from the corners of our eyes, then seeped together where our cheeks were touching, making a cool wet spot between our faces. I asked her why she was crying—Elliott Smith hadn't yet killed himself. She said she was crying because the song was so perfect and beautiful that it made her stomach ache with that good, loving ache you only get when something is that perfect and beautiful. She asked me why

I was crying, and I said for the same reason she was, which was true. More specifically, though, I was crying because I realized at that moment that the song could have been written from me to her—a song about loving someone so self-destructive so much. Until listening to that album, which I'd had for years, that night on the floor with Kerry, I'd only been a sort of admiring tourist to that kind of pain.

Even in hindsight, even after two years of marriage, I can say now that I did indeed know then the sort of chaos I was going to have to live through if I decided to love Kerry. I was ready to take all of the bad with the good, was willing to spend the rest of my life with her through all of her attempts to hurt herself if it meant I could also be right beside her when she was thriving—when she would make me collapse with laughter, when she would spontaneously break into song and dance, when she was brought to tears by a song's sad beauty and perfection.

But what do you do when you love someone who can at times be very self-destructive, once that person's self encompasses the self of your unborn son?

III

A MONTH HAS PASSED, AND I finally decide to call my friend Nate. I tell him everything.

"That's fucked up, Justin," he says. "I think that's the most fucked-up real-life story I've ever heard. In my entire life."

This is why I've avoided calling Nate. I love him, and I've wanted to reach out to him so many times during the past few weeks, but I know he won't hesitate to tell me what he thinks of the situation. I have a feeling he'll judge Kerry's actions harshly.

"You have to divorce her, man," he says.

"What?" I say. "No, that's not the answer."

"You need to leave her and get full custody of the baby—which shouldn't be too hard to do, given that there's documentation of her stays in psych wards that probably stretches a few pages long—and then you need to get on with your life. You make enough money that you could take off for a while to take care of the baby or hire someone to watch him while you're at work."

"I'm not leaving her, Nate."

"Hey, I really liked Kerry, even though I knew she was a little fucked up. This is just too much, Justin."

"I have to forgive her," I tell him.

"No you don't. This is too disturbing."

"But she's sick right now. She's not a bad person, she's just not well."

"Yeah, I don't know about that, Justin."

"What? She hasn't taken her medication in eight months because there's a tiny chance it could harm the baby, and that's what led to all of this. Don't you understand?" I say. "She got to this point because she made a selfless, dangerous sacrifice and now she's so fucked up because she's trying so hard to make sure he comes out healthy and normal."

"I want to say something that I know is going to upset you," Nate says carefully. "Someone who has to take pills to not do terrible things is a terrible person at heart."

I say nothing.

"She tried to punch a baby out of her stomach," he says.

"She's been going though psychosis, Nate! And she didn't do it to hurt him. We've been talking, and she thinks her body is poisoning the baby, that he needs to get out of her as soon as possible so she doesn't infuse him with the horrors she's experiencing. She didn't want to miscarry—she was confused and just wanted him out of her, where she thought he would be safer."

"What's going to happen when he *is* out in the world?" Nate asks. "What if she gets some crazy ideas then, too?"

"She'll be stabilized on her medications," I say. "I know she'll be OK once this is all over. It's just one more month."

"I just don't think she can take care of him," he says. "Not after hearing about this. She's just a ticking time bomb until her next episode. You've told me she gets violent."

Again I say nothing. I hear the call waiting signal on the phone during my silence.

"Nate, I have to go. I think that may be Barb and Jim on the other line."

"All right, Justin. I love you, man."

"I love you too, Nate. I'll talk to you again soon."

I switch over to the other line and am surprised to hear Kerry's voice.

"Justin," she says.

"Kerry?"

She hasn't called me the entire time she's been at her parents' house. Every time we've spoken, I've called her.

"I don't know what's real anymore," she says. She sounds worn and debilitated, her voice slurry and resigned, but she doesn't sound manic right now. She sounds less like a stranger.

"I know. I know, baby," I tell her. "I'm sorry you feel so terrible."

"I wish I could figure out a plan."

"You don't have to plan anything, Kerry. The baby is going to be just fine in your body until it's time for him to come out, OK?"

"I wish I could explain why I did it," she says, finally initiating this talk of her own accord.

"You don't have to explain anything," I tell her. "I understand."

"It was faulty reasoning. It was crazy. I feel terrible about it."

"It's OK," I say. "Everything is going to be OK."

Kerry laughs weakly. "You're a real good sport, Justin. You deserve better. You deserve a nice, normal girl."

"You are exactly who I want, Kerry, no matter what."

"Oh, honey," she says, "you are the sweet, twirling axis in my spinning world of shit, and I'm going to try to make my way toward the center."

"Do it. No more tilt-a-whirl."

"Makes me want to barf."

"Me too," I say, "watching you."

"I'm really sorry," she says.

"Don't be sorry. Just get better when you can."

"I want to get out of here, Justin," she says. "Will you come pick me up?"

I am both elated and scared. "Of course!" I say. "What about Barb and Jim?"

"They're asleep. Marlena's watching her shows in the basement."

"I'll leave right now."

"I miss you," she says. "I've missed you so much."

"Kerry, you don't even know how much I've been loving and worrying over you from here. I can't wait to see you. You really want me to come and get you right now?"

"Right now," she says.

IV

ON THE DRIVE TO PICK her up, I recall the time five years ago when Kerry rushed me off to the hospital after she accidentally caused me to have an asthma attack from laughing so hard. It was the first time I'd heard her Nico impression, and it was dead-on. She puffed up her flat stomach and tucked her chin into her slender neck to make her voice deep, and perfectly mispronounced the lyrics of "These Days." She sang the entire song, her voice cracking every now and then as she stifled a laugh, and I was doubled over on the floor waving for her to stop. She didn't realize until she was done and I was struggling to breathe that something was wrong. I gasped out that I was having an asthma attack, and that there was an inhaler in the medicine cabinet, one that I'd held onto since I was about fifteen even though it had expired. It didn't help, so she frantically called 911 and was told an ambulance was on the way. When they didn't show up within two minutes after she hung up the phone, she draped one of my arms over her shoulders, then wrapped one of hers around my ribs, and supported most of my clumsy weight on her tiny frame down six flights of stairs to my car. She drove me to the emergency room, even though she still hadn't earned her driver's license. She cried the whole way, thinking I was going to die.

Tonight I feel the same sort of urgency I imagine Kerry felt then. When I pull up to her parents' house, I find myself trembling slightly and don't completely understand why. I park the car and get out, but I don't know what to do next. I step quietly over the lawn and look up into Kerry's old bedroom where the lights are on. I stand waiting, and soon I hear the squeak of the basement door opening behind the house, then Kerry's soft footsteps over the grass.

I don't see her until she emerges from a tree's shadow and into the moonlight. We just look at each other, silently, the way we do when we know we don't have to speak to understand what the other is thinking and feeling.

When she reaches me, I wrap my arms around her, leaning over to keep from pressing against the baby, and she rests her head under my neck as she moves her hands over my chest. I step back and place my hands on her stomach. This is what I hope it feels like when you die—timeless, placid, and still, with the things you missed now so close to you that you can't imagine there could ever come a time you will have to miss them again.

I lift Kerry up into my arms and, suddenly overcome with giddiness, I whisk her off to the car with ease, her body like a weightless bubble. We're giggling and full of adrenaline, both of us breathing as if we've just made it to the top of a mountain and are looking out over everything. I place her in the backseat, because the airbags are dangerous to the baby, and kiss her long and deeply on her beautiful mouth. She grabs me and yanks me in closer with such force that I have to hold the handlebar over the window to keep from toppling onto her. She loosens her grip and I get her strapped in, giving her one more kiss on the forehead before I duck out of the backseat.

When I get behind the wheel, I look in the rearview mirror at Kerry's reflection and see that her eyes are already on mine.

"Ready?" I ask her, and turn the key in the ignition.

"Yes," she says. "Let's go home."

I'm grinning as I pull out from the curb and begin driving to our house. I look at her again in the mirror, and she's still watching me, smiling with her lips touching.

"I think everything's going to be OK," she says to me. "I think everything can be wonderful."

I nod my head at her reflection. "Yeah," I say. "I think so, too. I know it."

She looks out the window, her expression peaceful. I begin to calm down, too. I feel the excitement turn into something different, something that feels like hope but also like falling. I let it pass through me, I feel it all, and I put my eyes back on the road.

RICHARD PEABODY is the founder and current editor of *Gargoyle Magazine* and editor (or coeditor) of twenty-two anthologies including *Mondo Barbie*, *Conversations with Gore Vidal*, and *A Different Beat: Writings by Women of the Beat Generation*. The author of a novella, three short story collections, and seven poetry books, he is also a native Washingtonian. He won the Beyond the Margins "Above & Beyond Award" for 2013.

Cover artist SHEEP JONES studied art at the University of Maine in Portland. She works in oil and wax and has exhibited her paintings in several solo and group shows and galleries in the United States and Europe. In 2003, she was chosen as Artist of the Year at the Torpedo Factory. Her work is in art collections at the University of Maryland University College, Dominion Virginia Power Co., and law offices in Maryland and Virginia. Galleries that represent her include the Torpedo Factory (Alexandria), Steven Scott Gallery (Baltimore), Plan b (WDC), Glave Kocen Gallery (Richmond), High Street Gallery (Belfast, Maine), and Susan Maasch Gallery (Portland Maine). She splits her time between the Washington, D.C., area and Belfast, Maine.